WHERE THE STARS REMEMBER US

Cabrera

Where the Stars Remember Us

ISBN 13: 979-8-9986964-0-4

Cabrera

DEDICATION

To Tracy and Stacey, thank you for being the family I always needed.

To my readers, I hope this book and these characters give you a reason to stay.

They did for me.

I love you.

Cabrera

PROLOGUE

I was running, feet were hitting the pavement one after the other. The cold Seoul air cut into my cheeks as if razors were trying to make me bleed more than my already broken heart. I clenched the letter in my hand, its paper deteriorating with moisture. The heavy rain hitting the top of my head was my only reminder that what was happening was real. *He was gone.* He left me with nothing but that damn letter. Did he plan this? Was it all a lie? Did he even love me? I turned the corner; I was only ten steps away from our home. I run closer and closer until... there's nothing.

The home that was once beautifully colored and decorated was now stained black. The FOR SALE sign on the front lawn, bright red and annoying, was the only thing that reminded me that he even existed. No car, no dog, no him. Trembling, I approached the front door and reached for the handle. The door didn't budge. I pushed with all my might and yet it didn't budge. Not one creak. Not one groan. Nothing. I looked for the spare key that was hidden underneath the bushes. I clawed at the dirt, getting it on my pants and underneath my fingernails. I found relief when I felt the tiny, jagged teeth of the metal. I faced the door again, inserted the key, and turned the handle once more.

The door opened.

I looked everywhere for him. There was nothing in the house anymore. The dog bed, the TV we picked out, even the color on the walls that I spent so much time painting—it was all blank, white, as if we never existed. Walking upstairs, I found the door of our bedroom cracked open. I felt my knees give out. I cradled my head between my hands and wept. I cried and cried until my eyes were bloodshot and heavy from exhaustion. I cried because I knew.

Cabrera

This was it.

This was real.

This was the end.

He left me in the ruins of the life we had planned to have together and I didn't even know why.

I don't know how long it was until Haeran found me. I felt her hands before I heard her voice.

"Yunseo-ah! Yunseo-ah! Do you want to die? What are you doing here," she said as she shook me. "Get up, idiot! Get up!"

I didn't move. I didn't have the strength to. He was my strength.

And now he's gone.

CHAPTER ONE

Yunseo hated how small his apartment was. The faucet was constantly leaking and his clothes never fully dried in the machine. Yunseo thought about putting them outside on a line but after a heavy thunderstorm ruined one of his most expensive shirts, he decided he couldn't afford the weather ruining anymore of his things. Yunseo had very few possessions of importance left. He looked over at his clock lazily and found that he had only twenty minutes left to get to work. He promptly dried himself off and ran over to his closet. Today was special. A day that marked the beginning of a fresh start. Today was his first day of working in Incheon International Airport. One of the best and most competitive places to get hired as a pilot. As he finished buttoning up his uniform, his phone rang.

"Hello?"

"Hey! Yunseo-ah! Are you crazy? I've been trying to get a hold of you all day!"

He rolled his eyes as he closed the door to the apartment and punched his code into the keypad.

"Noona, it's five a.m. How could you have been calling all day when the day has just started?"

"Oh, so now you have enough brain power to talk back to me but not enough to answer your phone?"

Yunseo didn't respond as he walked into the elevator and descended to the car basement. He didn't have time for Haeran's tantrums today. He needed to get to the airport in the next ten minutes or he'd be fired. After not hearing him respond for several minutes, Haeran sighed dramatically as she cleared her throat.

"Yunseo," she began as he earnestly looked for his car.

"Doctor Im called. She said you haven't been to your appointments in two weeks," her voice hardened as she continued. "You have to see her this week or I'll drive you there myself."

He stopped his search and looked down. Yunseo had meant to tell her. Meant to tell her how he had found other ways to cope with his... bursts. That he didn't need the pills anymore. He just never could find the right time to do so.

"Noona," he said as he started walking again, "I meant to call. I didn't mean to hide this from you. It's just that—I...um..."

"What, Yunseo? You what?"

"I found another way to cope."

He was met with silence. In that silence, two things happened. He found his car and quickly climbed inside, throwing his suitcase into the back seat. The second was Haeran's disappointment.

"You've said this before. That you have found a non-medicated solution to your problems. But you and I both know they never work. If I don't hear that you went to your appointment this week, I'm coming down to Seoul and dragging you to Dr. Im's office myself. In handcuffs if I must! Do I make myself clear?"

"Yes, Noona. Crystal."

He sighed as he harshly pressed his forehead onto the steering wheel, wishing that this conversation would end.

"Yunseo?"

"Hmm"

"I love you," Haeran whispered, feeling guilty for scolding her brother and wishing that he could see that she only wanted him to be healthy and stable.

He waited a moment or two before responding.

"I know. I love you, too."

After she hung up, a gut-wrenching feeling echoed throughout his entire body as he looked down at his watch.

Shibal.

He's late!

✦ . ⁺ . ✦ . ⁺ . ✦

The employee entrance was on the other side of the airport's main entrance, which is incredibly inconvenient when you are running late and every single ahjussi and ahjumma decided it was time to fly on every single plane at six in the morning. Yunseo rushed to the entrance and quickly scanned his photo ID. As the door opened, he was quickly met with an irritated woman. She was four foot ten with a tight bun and a clipboard. She seemed to be in her late fifties or early sixties. His ears were pounding with so much adrenaline that he had missed whatever she had said.

"I'm sorry, what?"

"Not only are you late, but you're also deaf, too?"

"No, madam! You see I was just late and then there was traffic and—"

"Mr. Jeong, as you know we have a policy here. You are to be here at six a.m., which means you should be here ten to twenty minutes before the hour of five has finished."

Fuming, the woman looked him up and down, disgusted with the mere presence of the young man.

"I suggest that in the future you make it a habit of being on time unless you want to lose a job you haven't even started."

He tried to swallow. His throat, suddenly tight with tension, was in desperate need of water. He said nothing back and bowed apologetically, fearing that words would only worsen the situation. The woman sighed as she gestured for him to follow her.

"You have been assigned to be one of the primary pilots to the family of Chairman Park Kwangsoo of the NSCo. You will be flying to Bangkok and back within the day. You are not to look nor speak to them. Do I make myself clear?"

"Yes, Sunbaenim."

"Good. You might not be as incompetent as I thought."

Yunseo swallowed back a remark as she walked them through the airport. The airport was beautifully decorated and beyond any of his expectations. The structures were pristine and lit up eloquently. Millions of stores lined the walls, and seas of people from all walks of life drowned them all. A delicious mixture of languages greeted Yunseo's ears as he struggled to keep up with...with... He didn't even know this woman's name.

"Excuse me? I don't know your name, ma'am," he said as she directed them to a door that he assumed led to the tarmac.

She ignored him as she opened the door and guided him through the chaos of the tarmac. She took him to a plane that he could only guess cost at least 123 billion won. It was a Gulfstream G650ER with a gold stripe going across the entire plane. The plane was so clean that the reflection from the sun hitting it blinded him as they approached. Waiting on each side of the plane were six bodyguards armed with guns. Yunseo, feeling extremely nervous as he neared the steps of the plane, darted his eyes from the bodyguards to the ground, hoping to camouflage into the chaos. When nearing the stairs of the plane, the woman grabbed his arm before he could climb them.

"Mr. Jeong, remember what we spoke about. No looking, no talking, nothing. Understood?"

"Yes, Sunbaenim."

"Excellent."

Yunseo nodded his head as he began to climb in the jet.

"Myunghwa."

Turning, he looked at the woman with confusion.

"What?"

"My name. It's Kim Myunghwa."

She left without giving him another look.

What the fuck is my morning, Yunseo thought as he entered the plane.

Once inside the plane, he was welcomed by two lovely-looking flight attendants. Bowing, they all exchanged pleasantries. Their names were Ahn Soyeon and Seo Soae. Both twenty-three and polar opposites. Both were shorter than Yunseo and beautiful. Soae had long blonde hair, pale skin, and a thin frame, yet the first thing he had noticed was a single dark beauty mark under her left eye. Soyeon wore her long black hair in layered curls, had beautiful caramel skin, and the most curvaceous body Yunseo had ever seen. Her uniform, freshly pressed and stainless, only highlighted her wide hips and pump rear. It was striking just how different the women were, as if these women were yin and yang personified. Both shared stories of their time in high school and complained about how tiny their apartment was, which made him laugh at how similar their situations were. Once they found out Yunseo was twenty-six, they instantly started addressing him with honorifics. Yunseo laughed at their forgetfulness. He wondered if they forgot honorifics often.

He climbed into the cockpit only to find that the co-pilot seat was empty. He placed his suitcase in the corner and asked Soae to come over.

"Soae, do you know where the co-pilot might be?"

"No, so far you are the only pilot that has been on this plane today."

"Oh."

"But they better hurry. We leave in an hour."

Yunseo hummed a reply as Soae returned to Soyeon. He took out his materials: charts, headphones, pens, and, most importantly, his journal. He looked around to see if Soae or Soyeon were near before opening his beloved journal. He flipped through its pages, recounting every memory written inside. Memories that haunted his dreams and flooded his eyes with water. Pages stained with tears and black ink were never in short supply. Big black Xs had been crossed over the most vulnerable parts of himself he could no longer stomach to think about, let alone read. Some were drawn so thickly that some pages were consumed by the black ink entirely. He was in the midst of flipping to another page when he heard the curtain of the cockpit pull open. He quickly hid the journal in his bag before turning his head to greet the intruder.

"Good morning," a man said as he entered the cockpit.

He was wearing sunglasses and a crisper version of Yunseo's crinkled uniform. The sunglasses he was wearing were not of the cheap kind. They were the kind that you could only get if you were from a wealthy family. He seemed to be around Yunseo's age. He had a strong build, handsome face, and seemed to be six foot in height.

"My name is Lee Subin. I will be your co-pilot for today."

"Good morning, sir," Yunseo said as he stood up to bow.

Subin shook his head as he motioned Yunseo to sit back down.

"Please, there is no need for that. What year were you born?"

"1997."

"Ah," Subin said cheerfully as he placed his suitcase down and turned towards Yunseo, taking off his sunglasses. "We're the same age! Let's speak comfortably with each other."

Yunseo chuckled at Subin's forwardness and replied with a simple "Okay," while turning his head to look at the runway in front of them. The runway was pale gray and scuffed with black wheel marks from planes taking off. It was kind of funny, how a beautiful appearance can still have ugly pieces of itself scattered in its backyard. It feels almost familiar, to believe something's appearance without checking its background.

"Excuse me, Oppa," said Soyeon as she opened the curtain. "The passengers are boarding now."

"Okay. Thank you, Soyeon-ah."

"Mm."

He turned to look back at Subin who was looking at him with a smirk.

"They're pretty, aren't they?"

"Don't be a pervert."

"What! Me? No. Never," he said as he nudged Yunseo and prepared to speak into the intercom.

He could already tell that Subin would be like a friend. Painfully annoying, but enjoyable, nonetheless.

They took off after being told by Soyeon that everyone was settled. It was smooth, and the weather seemed to be on their side, but Yunseo wondered for how long. Flying planes meant being okay with the unexpected and unreliable, two things he struggled with.

The skies were clear once they settled above Korea's polluted air. Yunseo had almost forgotten how clear the sky could be and would only be reminded when he flew. He remembered asking his mother why the skies were so beige, mucky, and dead looking to which she only responded in her usual condescending tone.

"Obviously, it's because of the planes and people, Yunseo. How could you not know this? You're already five years old," she huffed out.

Yunseo knew she called him a daft child under her breath, but he liked omitting that from his memory. He knew she saw him as an idiot, why add salt to his wounds?

Yunseo's eyes kept darting from the clouds to the instrument panel and controls, too busy to see Subin's hand stealthy making its way to the autopilot button and turning it on.

He began to panic when the plane was unresponsive to his turns and turned to Subin, frantic for help, believing somehow, he had ruined the plane.

Imagine how deeply irked he was when he was met with Subin's crooked smile and mirth-filled eyes.

Yunseo's breath could not be quicker.

"Please tell me you did not switch on the autopilot while I was in the middle of flying."

Subin's smile became brighter.

"Yup," he pronounced every syllable in the simple word as if he were a child feeling victorious about doing a naughty thing.

"Why the fuck would you do that! What if we had crashed, huh! What if I lost control and killed all of us!"

"I'm pretty sure that's the autopilot's job to prevent."

He could not believe this man. The man in front of him was smiling smugly while he was trying to control his racing heartbeat. Out of all the co-pilots he has had, he has never met one so reckless.

"You cursed."

"What?"

"You cursed at me."

"Yeah, so what? You wanted me to speak to you comfortably, how's that for comfortable?"

Subin nodded as he reached into his bag and pulled out a pack of ramen, breaking it in half and splitting it with Yunseo.

Yunseo stared, tilting his head.

"What is this?"

"A peace offering for a joke not well landed," Subin said as he leaned closer, invading Yunseo's personal space. "Just take it. I don't want someone I want to be friends with's impression of me being that I am a jackass."

Yunseo stared at the broken pack of noodles before snatching the flavor packet and pouring most of it onto his share.

"I get most of the flavor as punishment."

Laughing, Subin surrendered the packet to Yunseo as he sat back and snacked on his portion. Subin hadn't thought the joke was that terrible, but he felt bad that Yunseo was so angry. He only wanted to turn on the autopilot so that he could get to know Yunseo better.

The tension cooled and Subin was the first to speak.

"Are you still mad?"

Yunseo swallowed the last bit of the noodles.

"Maybe."

Subin let a lazy smile come over his face as he leaned forward his chair and placed his bland noodles on the floor.

"I don't want you to be mad at me for the rest of the flight. I turned on the autopilot early because I wanted to talk to you."

Yunseo eyed him closely. He didn't trust those who were overly enthusiastic about getting to know him. Not anymore.

"Why? What do you want?"

Subin jerked his head, taken aback at the sudden accusation.

"Want? I don't want anything. Just want to talk... about... you know, stuff? Hell, who knows, maybe we'll be best friends at the end of the conversion."

Yunseo let out something that was a cross between a huff and a laugh.

"Yeah, I don't think so."

Subin pouted at this.

"Why? I'm a good guy! I made one mistake!"

Yunseo looked at him up and down before returning to the view before him.

"We don't have enough time."

"We literally have six hours."

"I guess you better start talking."

✦ ⁺ ･✦ ⁺ ･✦

Subin was a talker. He went on and on about things that had very little importance or nothing to do at all with one another. And while they bonded over many things like music and art, Yunseo stayed quiet for the most part. He wasn't a big talker. He found it easier to listen than speak. If it hadn't been for the city below coming into view, he would have thought he was going to be trapped in the clouds with an endless chatterbox for the rest of his life.

When Yunseo flew planes in the Korean Air Force, the runways weren't remotely as bad as these were. The bumps from the Suvarnabhumi Airport's runway were probably the worst he had ever experienced. Despite this, the airport from above was arguably more beautiful than Incheon Airport. Even the country had an air of warmth that didn't seem to come from the constant tropical heat the country was known for. Yunseo would be lying if he didn't say he had a desire to explore the city himself. Subin and Yunseo stationed the plane to where they were guided and opened the latch.

"I'm sweating balls. I can't wait to get out of here and back to the cold fresh air of Korea."

"Yes, the cold and very polluted air of Korea."

"Hey! Are you forfeiting your partisanship?"

"No," Yunseo said as he took off his hat and reached for his phone, pulling up the weather report.

Eighty-three degrees and counting. He flipped the phone to show Subin.

"Just stating that Bangkok wins when it comes to South Korea in terms of weather."

Subin playfully gave Yunseo the middle finger. The two had gotten quite comfortable with each other during their six hours of flying. Yunseo was about to give the same gesture when a man opened the cockpit's curtain and informed them that the family would like a word with them. Yunseo recognized him as one of the bodyguards from before. He quickly grabbed his things and stepped out of the plane. The sun greeted their eyes before they could adjust from the dark lightning within the plane. Yunseo cursed himself as he covered his eyes with his hand for not packing his sunglasses once he saw Subin reach for his own that hung around his neck. Yunseo rolled his eyes at him as he tried to focus on the sight before him. There stood two women in bright green and yellow sundresses under a black umbrella.

Behind them were two black SUVs with the same bodyguards from when they first boarded the flight. Yunseo felt a hand wrap itself around his arm as he began to walk toward the women. It was Soae, her right arm linked with Soyeon by the elbows. Yunseo was about to say to let go, in case the women in front of them thought they were being improper, but then Yunseo saw her face. She looked worried and even a little scared. Soyeon mirrored her expression as well. Yunseo quickly understood that being surrounded by strange men with guns in a foreign country could raise some concerns in their minds. Yunseo gave her hand a tight squeeze as he guided her and Soyeon toward the two women under the umbrella.

When the four were in front of the women, details of who they were started to appear. The woman in bright green looked to be in her early forties and five foot six in height. Her skin was a lovely natural tan color that stood out against the emerald and gold adorning her wrist and fingers. Lips painted a rosy color and hair auburn. She was truly beautiful. The woman to her left was shorter than she was, most likely the same height as Soae and Soyeon. Her dress was the same as the woman in green and her hair was as well. Unlike the older woman, the woman in yellow seemed younger, early twenties and her skin was a bit darker than the former. Both had matching custom Dolce and Gabbana purses, a detail his creative director sister would appreciate he noticed. No matter how much he tried, he would never be able to forget the brand names and authenticity tells that she had burned into his mind.

Greeting them with a smile, the older woman returned the crew's bow with one of her own and took off her sunglasses.

"Good afternoon, everyone. My name is Park Ahin, and this is my daughter, Minseo," the woman in green said as she playfully bumped her daughter with her shoulder. "She is shy, but quite talkative after a few drinks."

"Mother," Minseo shouted as she quickly placed her sunglasses back on to hide the growing redness that began to spread across her cheeks. Seeing this exchange must have relaxed Soae because Yunseo felt the grip on his arm weaken.

Mrs. Park looked back at us, laughing with a twinkle in her eyes.

"I can only assume that you may be confused as to why I have asked you all to meet us here. Well, truth be told, I am as well. The plan was to meet my son on the platform and fly back to Korea. It should have taken no more than one to two hours, but I was just informed that something has come up for my son and we will have to stay here until tomorrow morning. We have already spoken to Incheon Airport, and they have agreed to the extension of your services. You will be paid double for the inconvenience and will be staying in one of my son's all-inclusive hotels. Hopefully, that is not a problem, is it?"

They had all exchanged looks before shaking their heads in unison. With a smile, Mrs. Park turned to call over one of her many bodyguards, informing them to tell her son they were on their way. As the bodyguard walked away, she suggested that the group quickly made their way to the SUV to her left. Yunseo and Subin went first as Soae switched from hanging onto Yunseo to grasping the arm of Soyeon as one of the bodyguards opened the black van's door for all of the group to climb into. The poshness of the car stopped Yunseo from automatically climbing in. The interior screamed expensive, and he was almost too afraid to soil it with his non-extravagant clothing.

Yunseo was brought back to the present when Subin cleared his throat and glanced at the guard. Seeing the impatient face of the guard, he felt embarrassed for being so dazzled by what was, to the guard, a simple vehicle. He hung his head low as he climbed in, Soae and Soyeon following closely behind him. They sat in the two seats in the front while Subin and Yunseo took the two seats in the back. When they had all climbed in and the guards finished packing their suitcases in the trunk, they began to drive away from the plane, towards a large metal gate. *It looks like a prison gate*, Yunseo thought as the car passed through and made its way onto the road.

The car was quickly filled with Soae and Soyeon speaking rather loudly of all the things they could do before they flew back and Subin trying to find a way to get into the girls' night out. Yunseo smirked at Subin and decided that he was going to spend the rest of the ride listening to music blaring from the speakers and, occasionally, making fun of Subin for failing to catch the hints Soae and Soyeon were throwing at him.

The ride to the hotel wasn't too long. Being a pilot, nothing is too long anymore for Yunseo. It took about an hour to arrive at the tall and luxurious hotel, which resembled a mini skyscraper. Unfortunately, Yunseo's salary did not allow him to afford such lavish accommodations.

As the guards opened the hotel's doors, the four were led through the lobby towards the front desk. Waiting for them were Mrs. Park and her daughter, Minseo, who appeared to belong to the hotel. The opulent decor, affluent guests, and the luxurious conversations that filled the air were a stark contrast to Yunseo and his friends, who looked out of place.

Serpentine green marble flooring and ceilings high enough to put heaven to shame, with a large strip of paneled windows that allowed the beaming, hot light of Thailand to stroll in. The very lobby was the size of an opera house and on each side of the group was something new to gawk at. On Yunseo's right was an array of tiny dining tables, with candles and fabric he was sure was worth more than anything he would ever own. Behind the chairs and expensive décor was a large bar with wide dark brown sliding French doors leading to what seemed to be the hotel's patio. Yunseo couldn't get a close look at what exactly was out there, but he assumed it was nothing short of glorious.

On Soae's left was a horizontal wall-length mirror that showed their outliner uniforms against the array of Italian leathers, linens, silks, and cottons of the people walking among them, speaking about things far behind their financial comprehension.

And, at every corner, every nook and cranny, was a plant. Be it as large as a bird from paradise or as small as a peperomia, there was always a spy of Mother Nature lurking about.

The hotel was as if nature herself laid claim to the hotel and everyone else lived around her, obeying, and bending around large leaves and stems. A stark contrast to the way Korean hotels looked. Cold and made of steel. No warmth or love was put into it unlike this shrine of green, wealth, and love.

"Well now that we are all here, I have taken the liberty of securing your rooms. Here are your room keys," Mrs. Park said.

"Excuse me, madam," said Soyeon as she raised her hand as if she was still in high school.

Mrs. Park smiled brightly at Soyeon as she was handing her the key and nodded her head for her to continue.

"I was wondering if we were allowed to leave the hotel?"

Mrs. Park chuckled and looked at her daughter before looking back at the group.

"Yes, of course. But only if you take my daughter with you," she said as she looked at Minseo and handed Soyeon a piece of paper. "I'm afraid she doesn't get out much."

"Mother," Minseo grunted embarrassingly as she turned

around, room key in hand, and dragged her mother by the arm to the elevators, bodyguards hot on their heels.

The others rushed after their superiors and were relieved to find her bodyguards waiting for them.

"Come on in, I must show you to your rooms," Mrs. Park hummed as the rest made their way to stand behind her.

"Oh Sajangnim, you don't need to—," Yunseo began but he was silenced when Minseo turned and shook her head.

"Don't even try, she will fight you tooth and nail," Minseo said as she landed her head on her mother's shoulder. "Omma has always insisted on being a good host."

"But," Subin interrupted, "we're not guests? We work for you."

Subin stilled as Mrs. Park turned and squirted her eyes at him.

"That doesn't make you any less important, Mr... What is your name?"

Subin bowed his head nervously.

"Lee Subin, Sajangnim."

Mrs. Park guided his head up and spoke in a soft voice only a mother could have.

"I understand that at this moment, you all work for me and my family, but when you are with me, you are to be treated equally," she said as she fixed Subin's tie and turned back to look at the gold-colored doors. "I hate when those with money treat others poorly as if we are better. We are lucky, nothing more."

Soyeon caught the chests of the bodyguards swell with pride as Minseo patted her mother's back as if to say, *That's my mom!*

Yunseo felt himself relaxing at the refreshing attitude of their employer. He had been so used to being inferior to the rich, he had forgotten it was just a status, not a personality.

The doors opened and the inhabitants of the elevator were welcomed to a sea of varying shades of greens and golden detailing. Mrs. Park flowed down the hallway, like a dancer making their rounds across the dance floor, leading the crew to their respective doors.

"Here," Mrs. Park said as she stood in the middle of the hallway, pointing to her right. "This the boys' room, and this one," she said as she pointed to her left, "is the girls' room, have fun now."

Their eyes followed the wealthy woman and her daughter as the bodyguards silently stared at them, like an unspoken threat, before following their boss down the hall.

"I'm in love," said Subin, fanning himself dramatically.

"Keep it in your pants," Yunseo said as he waved goodbye to Soae and Soyeon.

Upon entering the room, Subin was the first one to call dibs on taking the first shower in "the rich people's bathroom," as he put it. The room was beautiful in every sense. For the amount of money people spend to stay here, Yunseo supposed it would be. It mirrored the hotel in every way. Silky green sheets covered the beds, and the crystal water bottles lining the desks next to their beds illuminated their walls like their own personal stained-glass window. The frame that entrapped their beds had Mother-Nature's children carved into them; leaves and flowers of which names Yunseo was unaware of.

He surveyed the room and chose the bed closest to the balcony. The view was breathtaking. Their hotel room was on the 50th floor. *The 50th*. Yunseo was grateful that he wasn't afraid of heights because he would have been royalty screwed. Bangkok winked at him as the sun shined on the buildings in front of him as a huge body of water laid before him. It was filled with boats carrying passengers and goods alike, but Yunseo was too distracted when his eyes caught the sight of a huge Ferris wheel off to the right. It was all vase and breathtaking, but Yunseo had a sneaking suspicion that at night, Bangkok was an entirely different world.

Turning away from the city, he shrugged off his bookbag and placed his belongings on the desk in front of his bed. Exhaustion taking hold of him, he stripped down to his undershirt and briefs and decided to wait for Subin to finish showering before taking one of his own. However, sleep had cast its spell on him, and he was out before Subin could even close the faucet.

CHAPTER TWO

It was nighttime when Yunseo awakened. He looked around the room for Subin only to find a sticky note attached to his backpack. Yunseo walked over and plucked the note.

Went out with Soae and Soyeon! Wish me lick! Oh, I mean luck!

Yunseo huffed out a laugh while drinking from the crystal water bottle from earlier, knowing damn well the girls were giving Subin hell for intruding. Yunseo thought it best to take a shower and explore the hotel for a bit. Only having a white button-down shirt and blue slacks, he decided to wear them and rushed to get out the door.

He hadn't noticed that the elevator was beautiful enough to be its own room. It had intricate carvings of leaves and lotuses of varying sizes ingrained into the wood and glass panels fogged to give the passengers privacy, but enough clarity to see the passing floors. Such a beautiful piece of work that held so much charm in its simplicity. The elevator opened and Yunseo was greeted with chatter and laughter, a completely different sight than what he was first greeted with. Crowds of young teenagers roamed in and out of the lobby seemingly having the time of their lives. It made Yunseo regret sleeping in and missing the opportunity to bother Soae and Soyeon with Subin.

After several minutes of asking fellow guests for directions, Yunseo was able to find the pool bar. The bar was in a hut with wooden bar stools, tables and chairs scattered throughout the patio. He didn't even really know why he was even there; he wasn't a drinker and usually got drunk after one drink. But having seen the doors of the patio earlier and now having seen the décor in detail, he felt like it would be a waste. After all, what else better does he have to do in an expensive hotel where everything is all-inclusive.

Yunseo quickly moved towards an open seat after spotting a group of women out of the corner of his eye. He quickly waved down the bartender and ordered a mojito with a glass of water. The bartender was cute. Tan skin and the loveliest smile Yunseo had seen in a long time. Yunseo had decided to chat with him, but only after drinking a generous amount of the alcoholic beverage that now sat half full.

It took a while to get his attention again, considering how the group of women had flocked toward him like bees to honey. He had tried to shout for the bartender, but the leader of the group, an older woman wearing way too much makeup, slammed her hand down next to Yunseo, startling him.

"Hey, Annop! Get me and the girls a round of cosmopolitans."

Yunseo watched as the man's shoulders slumped, and his cute face grew tired. Yunseo may have not understood Thai, but he could understand an annoying customer any day. It reminded him of his days in the bookstore he used to work at back in college. Placing back a clean glass, Anoop threw a white towel over his shoulder and faced the group of aging women.

"Mrs. Rattanakosin, I would be happy to get you and your beautiful friends some drinks. Will it be with an open tab like last time or closed?"

The woman placed her forearms on the bar table, taking most of the space and squishing the slightly buzzed Yunseo. She placed her index finger on her temple and tapped as if she was thinking. She was not.

"Open tab, Annop," the older woman said as she leaned forward and held a black card between her fingers. Her breasts were pushed up by the table and Yunseo saw Annop's eye twitch in annoyance. "And keep it open, dearie. Hopefully, then, you could finally join us, and we," she said as she jerked her head backward, "could have some real fun."

Anoop breathed deeply as he plucked the card from Mrs. Rattanakosin's fingers.

"Your husband might have a problem with that."

24

"*I* don't see him. Do you?"

"No, Mrs. Rattanakosin."

"Then there is no reason for you to give me unsolicited advice, is there?"

"Yes, Mrs. Rattanakosin."

"Good. Be fast with the drinks, you've soured my mood a bit."

Annop only nodded as the group of women laughed and settled onto a table near the pool. The pool was vast and had beautiful clear water with a light blue tinge to it. Its barrier was made of glass and gave the illusion that the person was swimming midair. Everything was serene and those outside spoke in hushed voices. Yunseo was sad to see such a peaceful area be destroyed by the women's shouts and the sound of chairs being dragged across the floor.

"Sorry about that. Mrs.Rattanakosin can be quite the character."

Yunseo turned back towards the bartender as he wiped the card and began to squeeze fresh lime into a tall metal tin.

"You speak Korean!"

Annop laughed at Yunseo and poured in the lime, cranberry, vodka, and ice. He slammed the metal top onto his tin and began to shake it vigorously.

"It's required. I needed to learn it for the customers."

"But, why Korean?"

"Because of the owner."

Yunseo tilted his head in confusion before he realized why he was staying here in the first place.

"Right."

Annop finished shaking and poured a beautifully colored liquid into a martini glass. Yunseo had only seconds to admire it before Annop had started on another. Then another. And another. Six minutes and seven martini glasses later, Annop, who preferred to be called Kai, had given the drinks to a waiter and began to teach Yunseo how to make his mojito which now replaced his once empty glass. Yunseo was still surprised with his perfect Korean and willingness to speak with him. He couldn't take his eyes off Kai's hands and how skillfully they moved. Yunseo blushed when he looked up and saw Kai staring at him with knowing eyes.

Kai leaned and whispered into Yunseo's ear—the latter began to feel shy.

"You shouldn't stare like that, love. Someone will catch you and I will be punished."

Yunseo stared at the side of his neck and briefly considered kissing Kai when he saw him pull away, smirking. Yunseo's drink was definitely hitting him now, and Kai noticed the faint red blush that was creeping up onto his ears. Seeing his bashfulness, Kai's flirty comments descended without shame.

"You know, you're cute when you blush. Makes me want to make you blush some more."

Yunseo knew his ears were wearing red and wished it would stop. Yunseo reached up to cover his ears, but Kai slowly shook his head.

"Don't do that. It'll make me want to mess with you more."

Yunseo dropped his hands and lowered his head, groaning into his elbows.

He heard Kai chuckle above him as he listened to another customer talk to him. It was interesting to hear Kai go from Korean to Thai. Two completely different languages in every sense yet he made them flow flawlessly. Yunseo didn't look up until he felt a tap on his arm.

"So shy one," Kai said as he started to mix an old fashioned, a taste that still haunted Yunseo from his freshman year of high school. How stupid he was to steal that drink from his unconscious father. "Is this your first time here? I have never seen you before."

Yunseo flashed a drunken smile.

"Yes, this is my first time."

"How come?"

"How come," Yunseo said, astonished that he even had to ask. "Look at me! I don't belong here."

Kai tilted his head.

"Here?"

Yunseo felt the cooling blush heat up again.

"You know, a place for rich people. People who belong in places with cute bartenders and fancy bars. A place where people like me can only dream of going to."

Kai smiled at Yunseo's confession as he poured the old fashioned into its glass and handed it to its rightful owner.

"Cute bartender, huh? You wouldn't be talking about me, right?"

When Yunseo didn't respond, Kai took that as a signal to drop the flirty façade.

"Why are you here then?"

Yunseo's eyebrows quirked up.

"In this hotel? One of my boss's children—"

"No," Kai laughed. "Why are you here, in this bar, admitting to the cute bartender about how low you see yourself?"

Yunseo was stumped by the question. He allowed himself to lie back into his seat and carefully rimmed his glass. *Why am I here?* Why didn't he just stay inside his room, where he could spackle the broken parts of himself back together?

Kai watched him as he searched for his answer, but he knew. After years of bartending, he could pick up a heartbroken soul out of a room of rich, horny, pompous customers that came in here every day. Customers like Mrs. Rattanakosin. Yunseo wasn't here for sex. He was here for a distraction. A person to talk to with whom he had no connection or promise of ever seeing again.

"What was his name?"

Yunseo sprung up surprised, not expecting such a question.

"Who's name?"

"The guy that you're still hung up on."

"How do you know it's a guy?"

Kai stared at Yunseo, his expression practically shouting, *"Are you kidding me?"*

Yunseo blew out a laugh as he downed the rest of his drink.

"His name was Kim Taesung."

"That's funny."

Yunseo looked up from his empty glass.

"What is?"

"It's just the guy who owns this hotel, his name is Taesung as well."

Yunseo understood where Kai was going and laughed harder than Kai had.

"Yeah, no. My Taesung was not rich enough to buy a hotel.

Let alone in Thailand."

Kai nodded as he reached for a glass left on the table and began to clean it. He was waiting. A skill Kai had honed during his time here.

"He was my first."

"First what?"

Yunseo reached for his glass of water and took comfort in the way the glass bit into his palms, rooting him in place.

"Everything."

Kai grimaced at Yunseo's answer and reached down for a shot glass. He placed the glass in front of Yunseo and filled it with Don Q. He knew he shouldn't have this customer mixing his liquors, but he felt like Yunseo might need it more than he needed to follow the rules. Plus, his manager called in sick, and he was the only bartender there.

"You know, those have the funniest way of haunting you."

Yunseo eyed the shot in front of him. He weighed the pros and cons of taking the shot. Pro: he would be drinking free alcohol. Con: he would fall into the pool, drowning.

Kai watched in amusement as Yunseo stared at the glass.

"Don't worry, it's good and cheap rum. I keep it here for people like us."

"Us?"

"People who can't afford to have an open tab."

Yunseo hummed as his hand inched closer to the glass.

"I'm a lightweight."

Kai smiled. He lifted the glass and downed it. He replaced the glass with a fresh one and filled it up once more.

"You see. It's not too bad. You'll be fine," Kai said as he took Yunseo's hand and pressed it into his palm. "Just do it."

Wearily, Yunseo crashed the shot against his lips and threw his head back. He winced at the sweet taste and slammed the glass back onto the table.

"Woah!"

"That's what I'm talking about!"

They laughed and were shushed by a jealous Mrs. Rattanakosin. She looked at Yunseo longer than Kai before turning back to her friend, presumably gossiping about the two. Some time had passed, and Yunseo's happy buzz had turned to one of sadness and memories. Once Kai had come back from making the older women's cosmopolitans, he continued their conversation.

"It's been five years and I'm still not strong enough to leave it all behind."

"Strength," Kai whispered. "This had nothing to do with strength. You were hurt."

Kai shuddered.

"That type of soul-slicing, bone-shattering event never leaves the fibers of your being. Not really."

Yunseo sipped his water as he realized he may not be the only one with a blood-sucking leech attached to his heart.

"That bad, huh?"

Kai had laughed hard enough that Mrs. Rattanakosin and her friends turned their heads in unison, curious to see what joke they might have missed.

"You have no idea."

Yunseo all but challenged that statement with a raise of his glass and a slight smile.

"Try me."

Kai smirked as he brought Yunseo's old shot glass against Yunseo's water, cheering for his impending victory. With a lick of his lips, he told his story.

"A few years ago, I met Narre, beautiful and daring. Reckless! She was temperamental and volatile, yet she loved so hard that it made you think that even the sun itself paled in comparison to her heat. She was fire personified."

"What happened?"

Kai cast his eyes down as he eased himself onto the railing behind him. The lined bottles shook slightly under his added pressure.

"She burned me alive."

Though he knew this was a metaphor, Yunseo couldn't stop himself from searching Kai's body. He looked for scars or burns, but was only welcomed by smooth skin. Kai's chuckle caught his attention.

"Not literally, um…"

"Yunseo."

Kai flashed a grateful grin before continuing.

"She exhausted me with every fight we had and would ignite me at night for her own personal selfish use. After a while of me declining to give in to her desire, she went looking for another." Kai looked back up. "My brother."

Yunseo's eyes widened.

Nodding, Kai slammed back his shot of Don Q and grunted deeply before reaching for the bottle again.

"She was furious when I confronted her. She threw things and threatened me to no end. I left the next day for Bangkok. I got this job soon after and everything felt okay again. Safe." The pouring stopped. "She showed up everywhere soon after. I had to get a restraining order when I found the door of my apartment open and her lipstick mark on everything I owned."

Sighing, Kai straightened up his body.

"I couldn't sleep for a while after. Now I try not to think about it anymore. She was my first."

There was no doubt that Kai had won the miserable pity party he and Yunseo created. Kai was hesitant at first, he had always been the one people told their darkest secrets too, not the other way around. But, seeing Yunseo's challenging stare, he knew he had to win. And so, he did. Another gift his ex-girlfriend had given him after they had departed.

"Jesus," exclaimed Yunseo. "Who knew having a stalker wasn't all that it was cracked up to be?"

Kai chuckled as he wiped the corner of his mouth with his sleeve, still tasting the sweet rum.

"Yeah, well, that's my life. She threw me away just to cage me in my own filth."

Yunseo couldn't help but look at him with eyes filled with silent understanding. Although he was trying to lighten up the mood, he understood how hard it must have been to share something so tragic and heart-shattering with a stranger.

Kai's eyes darkened when he looked back up to see Yunseo pushing his glass of water towards him.

"That was for you."

"And now it's for you," Yunseo replied.

Kai snarled at the iced water in front of him.

"Don't pity me."

Yunseo recoiled at Kai's tone. It was cold and empty. It reminded him of someone he knew. Shoving the water deeper into Kai's hands, Yunseo bowed his head as he rose and took several steps back.

"I didn't mean to anger you."

Kai said nothing as he gulped Yunseo's water, silently feeling terrible for his outburst.

Yunseo kept his head down and his tears in. He was not a stranger to male anger. Being a man himself, he was often quite hot-headed. Something he probably got from his father. His father had quite a temper. Yunseo could still feel his father's words bewitch their way through his skin and into his soul, crawling around and burrowing themselves inside. At times when Yunseo would look into the mirror, he could see the words from his journal levitate onto the reflective surface: worthless, thing, waste of space, mistake. These were the less severe ones, but his father's favorite was, "You are nothing and will be nothing without us!" That sentence will forever be singed into his mind and sting with every thought that passed it by.

Yunseo felt it arise. The sweating palms, the labored breaths, the numbness in his thighs. He knew the attack was coming and he needed to get out of the bar, one way or another. Yunseo attempted to get up but failed, falling on his ass.

"Yunseo!"

Kai said as he rushed forward, but Yunseo backed away, afraid to let Kai touch him. Crawling backward on his hands and feet, he spun around and ran away. He could hear the faint yelling of Kai's voice, but he couldn't afford to have someone see him in his failed state. He believed he had control of it. That he had overcame the shadows that lurked in his mind. He believed he conquered his father. So why, after all these years, was he back? Even in death, the man hated his son more than he wanted peace.

He couldn't see straight. Fleetingly, he looked at the faces of those he ambushed and saw his old friend, disgust. His family was disgusted with him. Hated him enough to chase him down and beat him to his bare bones. He knew he shouldn't be running. That he should get a grip and be a man. Why was he troubling the high class with his humiliating, revolting trauma? He ran faster wanting to escape from his mind, from his reality. But he couldn't. He couldn't stop the memories from coiling their way around his mind and forcing him to adopt their truth. That he was worthless and a waste of space. That all the verbal and emotional abuse that he endured was deserved. He served no purpose and was only a theft of opportunities that another deserved. That another was worthy of.

As the elevator came into Yunseo's line of sight, he closed his eyes and pushed his legs to go faster. He just needed to get there and find a place he could hide from them. From the words and memories his mind seemed keen on taunting him with. He ran and ran until he bumped into something hard and fell to the floor with a yelp.

He was splattered onto the cold floor, body aching from impact. He opened his eyes and blinked slowly as he looked up, locking eyes with a group of finely dressed teenagers that had come out of the elevator. The group consisted of two white girls and three white boys, all looking wealthy beyond compare. They were all shocked and grossed out by Yunseo's disarray. One of the boys wearing a yellow linen shirt and Italian leather shoes pulled Yunseo by the front of his shirt and sneered closely to his face.

"You fucking chink! How dare you run into me! Do you know who I am! Do you know how much my family is worth!"

Yunseo clawed at the English-speaking boy, not understanding him. He wanted to yell and cry out, but all he could manage to do was pull at the young man's wrists. Yunseo wasn't strong enough to fight back. He wasn't even strong enough to fight his own mind.

"Aw look, Allen. You have the foreigner scared. Maybe you should let him go," one of the girls said as she played with her unnaturally blonde hair.

"Fuck that," the young boy said. "I wanna know how this thing got in here. Security!"

Though Yunseo couldn't understand what had been said, he felt like he was going to urinate himself once he saw four strong, intimidating, and sharply dressed men walk towards him. He felt his eyes sting with tears, and he tried ripping himself out of the teen's grip. He had almost succeeded when he saw the boy's fingers begin to slip but his excitement was short-lived when one of the other boys trapped his forearms in an iron grip.

"Where do you think you're going?"

Yunseo let out a cry when the boy dug his nails into his flesh. *Damn them.* If he had better control of himself and had not ran into these teenagers, he wouldn't be in this situation. Yunseo looked back to see if the four men were still coming, but instead he was greeted by the sight of a man in a plain shirt and faded jeans.

He craned his neck more to get a closer look. The man was handsome. He had to be six foot one with a strong physique. He looked about the same age as Mrs. Park, yet youthful in the face and aura.

The man had closed in on the group and simply slid his hands into his pocket, seemingly unbothered by the scene before him.

"Put him down, Mr. Baldwin. My boss can't have you making a mess in his lobby."

The blonde boy growled at the older man, annoyed that security had ignored his call.

"Who the fuck are you? Do you know who I am?"

The man rolled his eyes.

"I said your name, didn't I? My boss never told me you were deaf," the man laughed as he rocked on his heels. "Now, let the man go or I'll have to call my boss and have him explain to your father why you have a bloody nose."

The yellow-shirted boy only laughed and tightened his grip on Yunseo's collar.

"And who is your boss?"

"The owner of the hotel your father is currently trying to book a catering deal with. Let. The. Man. Go. The next time I ask, your yellow shirt will have a pop of color to it."

The boy reluctantly released the front of Yunseo's shirt and snarled when his body hit the ground. The boy walked up to the man and his group could only watch in horror at what happened next.

The boy launched forward and tried to mash his fist against the man's face, but was confused when the man had disappeared. Turning around he was welcomed by the callused fist of the brown-haired man paired with an uppercut. In the blink of an eye, the entitled teenager was down on the floor holding a bleeding broken nose. His friends rushed forward to his side as he moaned in pain.

"How dare you! I will be telling my father about this!"

The man laughed and raked a hand through his soft hair.

"Yeah, you go do that, Malfoy."

The moans of the boy were still heard as he and his group guided him out the door of the hotel. It would have been funny to Yunseo if he wasn't sitting on the floor looking at the back of the man who had just saved him in terror. He turned around and held his hand out.

"My name is Choi Minseok," the man said in Korean as he pulled Yunseo up from the ground. "I'll be accompanying you on your flight back to South Korea tomorrow."

Yunseo couldn't take any more of this. He could only stare at the man and gripped his arms flush against his body.

"Please," he said brokenly, his voice a mere whisper. "Just take me to the elevator."

Minseok bowed his head and placed a warm hand on Yunseo's back, guiding him into the elevator. Minseok pressed the button and when it appeared and Yunseo rushed in, he wanted to offer his company to Yunseo, only to be silenced by Yunseo's fist smashing the close button.

Yunseo faced away from the golden doors and slid down the opaque window, pulling his legs to his chest and slumping over his bent legs, hoping it would be enough to hide and muffle his escaping cries. Upon returning to his room, he discovered it in disarray with clothes strewn about. Following the trail, he found Subin asleep in his boxers with a strong smell of alcohol in the air. Yunseo predicted a hangover for his friend.

He quietly walked around and climbed into bed, too tired to undress. He spent the night listening to Subin's drunken snores and his own muffled sobs, recounting the events of the night.

Where the Stars Remember Us

CHAPTER THREE

The next morning happened as Yunseo predicted. Subin's groans filled the room as he got out of bed and rushed toward the hotel's trash bin. Yunseo's phone filled the once quiet room with the sultry song of DPR Ian's *Seraph*. He didn't want to get up from the bed, but wanting it to stop, he answered and was greeted by Soae's anxious voice on the other end.

"Oppa! Oppa, please, please, please tell me you're up and ready to go! The bodyguards knocked on our door and said we should have been ready by eight. It's eight twenty-five," Soae yelled as the moans of Soyeon could be heard in the background.

Cursing, he looked back at his phone to check the time. He quickly called out to Subin while reassuring her.

"Soae, breathe. I understand you're nervous, but Mrs. Park seems to be a very kind and understanding woman. I'm sure she will forgive this offence."

"I don't know about that, Yunseo."

He paused, feeling unsettled that she used his name.

"What did you do?"

"Well," Soae started nervously, pacing about the room and digging her heels into the hotel's carpet. "Remember, when... hmm... Mrs. Park asked us to take her daughter out?"

"Yeah?"

"Well, we did."

"Okay?"

"And it sort of. Well, it kind of ended in her taking body shots with us."

"You took our employer's daughter to do body shots on strangers!"

36

"To be fair, the shots we did were on each other, and we only drank from each other."

Feeling like he was losing his mind, Yunseo counted to five before resuming the conversion.

"Soae, did Subin do a shot off of her?"

The question was met with silence, revealing the answer.

"Did they," Yunseo looked up to the ceiling, not ready for the answer his question was seeking. "Did they do anything else other than body shots together?"

Soae gasped out loud into the phone, "Oppa! Of course not! What type of person do you think I am!"

"Considering I'm talking to the person who let the daughter of our employer do body shots off our sexually-innuendo-addicted co-pilot, can you blame me for asking such a question?"

She nodded her head sideways and breathed a quick "Fair" after hearing his reasoning.

Yunseo sighed, taking a seat at the foot of the hotel bed.

"Listen, whatever the consequences are, we will get through this together, okay? But right now, is not the time to wallow in self-pity. If you really don't want to get fired, get in the shower."

"You're right. I'll see you in ten minutes."

"Okay, bye."

"Wait!"

Soae giggled as she pulled the phone closer, anticipating his reply, "Did you do anything exciting last night?"

Yunseo grimaced at the memory of the night before and willed his mind to ease its assault.

"I didn't do body shots if that's what you are asking?"

"Would you have been willing to do them last night?"

Yunseo smiled at her question.

"No."

"So does that mean you would've been too scared to do them," Soyeon yelled as she lifted herself out of bed and into the shower.

The phone call ended with Soae laughing.

After ending the call, Yunseo felt content, even a bit gleeful. Without wasting any time, he gathered all his belongings in haste to take a shower while Subin gradually regained consciousness and took hold of his endless vomiting. The shower, with its expensive porcelain and gold fixtures, was a little too lavish for his taste. He wondered if that was truly his opinion or his Appa's. He stiffened at his mind's mentioning of his father. All the memories of last night started to rush back into his mind. The alcohol, the teenagers, the panic attack, Kai. Kai was the memory that made Yunseo crouch down and hug his knees. He couldn't believe he allowed someone to speak to him in such a way; the way his father used to speak to him. He lost control. By the mere mirroring tone, he lost control of his mind and spiraled so deeply that he ran away from the bartender. Yunseo felt bile fill his mouth. He swallowed it back down, afraid of dirtying the expensive bathroom with more than his presence.

His father had a disdain for expensive things. Most likely due to not being able to afford any of it. Omma was the breadwinner and that brought great shame to his Appa. Maybe it was his bruised masculinity. Or perhaps it was his inability to keep Yunseo's mother from coming home late at night smelling like cologne that caused him to abuse his son.

Though he had experienced beatings, he had no scars on his body. Unlike others, Yunseo's scars lived in his mind. The countless remarks of how miserable he was, how he was nothing without his parents, and that no one would love him forever lived in his mind. Yunseo willed his mind not to run down the tunnel of overthinking he had created since the age of ten. Today was not the day and he certainly didn't have the time either, not after yesterday. Turning off the faucet, he put on lotion and got ready to meet Soae and Soyeon.

After ten minutes, Soae had her arm locked in with Yunseo's. Soyeon sported a small smirk every time Subin mumbled about how much his head was hurting and how he didn't want to be out in the Thai heat. Bodyguards met the group at the entrance of the hotel and guided them to the same vehicles they had driven to the hotel the day before. The group quickly climbed inside and had a peaceful car ride with the occasional mumbling of Subin and the whispers of Soae and Soyeon. The weather was hot, but not sizzling. It was more comforting, and the breeze felt like a gentle caress on Yunseo's face. Windows down and eyes closed, it was peaceful, which was a stark contrast to the mayhem waiting for the group on the runway.

The entire road was filled with cars, bodyguards, and more suits than they had arrived with. The group grabbed their luggage and walked down to greet Mrs. Park and Minseo. They had both bowed and, unsurprisingly, the group held their bow as Soae was the first one to speak.

"Good morning, Mrs. Park. I speak for all of us in saying that we are all deeply sorry for being late and not arriving before you."

Mrs. Park glanced over at the young woman while an amused smile crept onto her lips and up to her eyes.

"It's fine, darling. My own son is late, again, to the flight, so all is forgiven."

The group lifted their heads and quickly nodded their thank-yous to Mrs. Park before excusing themselves to prepare for the flight. It wasn't five minutes later before Soyeon called Subin and Yunseo to come outside and greet Mrs. Park's son.

Yunseo had a hard time finding his footing with the Thai sun piercing its rays into his eyes. He began to pull his hat over his eyes when he heard a motorcycle's engine in front of him.

There were four motorcycles parked in front of them with a red and black Harley Davidson as their leader. The bikes were a sight to behold. One was completely matte black, rivaling the night's sky. If the motorcycle wasn't an indication of the leader's position, his stature was. Six-foot-two, tan skin, muscular, and very attractive. That was only what Yunseo could see since the mysterious man still had on his helmet. The other bikers got off their bikes and greeted Mrs. and Ms. Park with a bow before going back to the man in the helmet and taking turns smacking his head. Yunseo found it bizarre, but a little funny.

"M&Ms, enough! We're already late and this isn't a good impression to leave on the airplane workers," Mrs. Park yelled as she walked hand in hand with Minseo passed Yunseo and his friends and into the aircraft.

The first biker to greet the crew was a muscular man with black-rimmed glasses and golden rings on his fingers. He looked as if being a bodyguard was just a day job and his real job was being an underground fighter. His name was Kang Moonbin. The second to greet them was, surprisingly, a very fit and good-looking woman with cherry red hair and a tall stature. Her ponytail was long with bangs perfectly cut and styled in place. Her name was Suzuki Mikasa. After bowing, the crew waited as the third biker made his way towards them, taking off the bandana that wrapped around the lower half of his face. Yunseo's eyes widened as he recognized the man's soft brown hair and handsome face. He lowered into a bow and spoke loudly.

"Choi Minseok, thank you for last night."

Minseok laughed at the display of gratitude and pulled Yunseo upright. Once closer, Yunseo started to make out the sudden features of the man's face. His skin was smooth and sun-kissed with a beautiful golden tan and two moles on the lower right side of his face, just below his lips. The man's eyes were mono-lidded and sharp. As if with one look, he could steal your breath and hold it captive forever.

"Don't be like that. We work for the same people," Minseok said as he brushed off invisible tint and straightened Yunseo's tie. "Just don't crash the plane. I don't think I can save you from that."

Yunseo nodded his head sheepishly as Minseok introduced himself to the others. He watched as Subin threw him an intrigued look and saw a faint blush come over the women.

"Don't worry," Moonbin said as he whispered closely against Yunseo's ear. Yunseo had to root himself in place to avoid jumping thirty feet into the air. "That rich kid had it coming. I'm just sorry I couldn't get a hit in myself."

Yunseo turned towards Moonbin and shyly flashed a smile.

In front of him, he watched as the bikers conversed confidently while they held helmets. Yunseo knew, without a question in his mind, that all three were intimating, fearless, and unquestionably attractive, which made Yunseo think; *how handsome is their leader if they look this good-looking already?*

They patiently waited for the mysterious man to finish giving instructions to the bodyguards who were now handling the bikes. The bikers remarked about how close the girl with red hair was to winning their race.

Finally, the man began to approach the four very hot and slightly melted crew members and bowed in apology to them. After shaking a blushing Soae and Soyeon's hand, he took off his helmet.

"Good morning, everyone. My name is Park Taesung and I'm looking forward to flying with you all today."

✦ ⁺ ✦ ⁺ ✦

Yunseo couldn't feel his legs. He could feel his chest caving in and his breath quickening. The last thing he needed to see was Kim Taesung. The man was the reason why he had to take numerous pills, attend therapy sessions, and deal with his overbearing sister. Taesung's departure was the reason for the endless chain of failed dates and countless nights of tears and torment. After five years, the scar left by Taesung's departure felt like it was opening again. His presence, a mixture of salt and lemon.

"Kim Taesung?"

Taesung turned his head and looked stunned at the fact that Yunseo used his old name.

"It's Park now."

"You two know each other," asked the biker with the black-rimmed glasses.

"Yeah, back in college before I transferred to Thailand," Taesung replied. "It's been a while hasn't it, Yunseo?"

Five years

Five years

Five fucking years

Yunseo couldn't find the words to describe his disdain for the man in front of him and he did not want to make a scene in front of the others. He simply bowed before returning to the cockpit. He had a million questions on his mind and couldn't find the answer to any of them. Everyone's tells were different. Labored breaths, faintness, trembling knees. Yunseo's were his hands, trembling with every movement he took and shaking every bottle he picked up. He downed his meds before Subin walked in, trying his best not to choke on the expired pills. Subin said nothing as his frantic co-pilot swiftly closed his suitcase and turned to face him.

"Mr. Park said to let him know if we are having any trouble?"

Subin sighed as he dropped his hungover body onto his seat.

"He also said that it was good to see an old friend."

Old friend

Yunseo grimaced at the words, but said nothing in return. The things they did. The secrets they shared. The places they touched. *Old friends.* He crossed his arms while waiting for Soae to give the go sign. The only thing that he could think about was the fact that Taesung did get one thing right; they were old and old means in the past. So why is he here now? Why did he have a new name? Where did all this money come from? And, most importantly, why did he have a new family? He thought about writing this down, but soon Soae gave the pilots the go sign and the jet came to life.

The two men flew the plane smoothly into the air, and after a few good feet in, it was now Yunseo who turned on the auto-pilot. Subin acknowledged this but said nothing. Yunseo turned, picked up a small portion of his things, and walked to the bathroom. He caught glimpses of his friends and passengers as he walked into it. As he closed the door, he heard a familiar laughter that made his stomach churn and throat constrict. Throwing his personal belongings into the sink, he turned to empty the contents of his stomach into the toilet bowl.

When was the last time I have eaten? Was it yesterday? The day before? Why am I so overcomed?

The vomiting was endless, and when it finally released Yunseo from its grip, he fell backwards and braced his back against the door of the small compartment. There was a ringing in his ears now that wouldn't stop its assault. He raised his hand and rummaged through the sink, looking for his earbuds. His fingers went in circles before feeling the smooth corners of his device and brought it down with urgency. He flipped the top open, jammed the two nickel-sized buds into his ears and swiped his phone open. Soon the ringing transformed into the instrumental sounds of Lynn Ahrens and Stephen Flaherty's *Once Upon a December*. Though, yes, it was from an animated child film, it brought back memories of Yunseo when he was happy. Of when he needed comfort.

This was the song he played the most when Taesung had first left him. It transported him to when he was locked in his room, shirt dirtied with stains and wet with tears. He had been going through cycles of binging, purging, and starving. His room stunk and the blinds to his windows were glued shut; the sun was too precious to look upon his misery. He lived in Haeran's spare room as he could not return to the place that once felt like home.

Yunseo was lost. He didn't want to be here. He didn't want to open his eyes anymore and not be welcomed by the spiked cologne of Taesung, or the messages that filled his phone before he could open his eyes.

What's the point of being alive? I should just go into the bathroom and end it all. I don't deserve to be loved. I don't deserve to be cherished or promised a life of joy and adoration. Why did I think he would be different?

There were many times he had taken those thoughts seriously. As intrusive as they were, they made sense to him. When he walked into the kitchen, the knives that sat neatly beside the rice cooker looked more and more tempting as the countless pills that sat on top of his bathroom sink were like a siren call to his pain. *Come to me,* they said. *Eat me and I will give you a dream that will never end.*

Yunseo would reach for those bottles, the treasures inside ratting as his inability to keep his hands still made them sing. He would pour them into his hands and count how many there were.

Thirty-four.

Thirty-four saviors.

Thirty-four promises.

Thirty-four dreams.

He would bounce the tantalizing number in his hand before pouring them back into the bottle and reaching for his phone. He stared at the constant messages from his sister and her begging for him to wait. Wait for the pain to pass. Wait to feel alive again. Wait for her to get there and smother him with kisses and hair strokes. His guilt made him throw up again and no matter how hard he tried to bite down, the body always won, and every time he wiped his mouth and climbed into the white covers of his bed, his headphones were there to welcome him; his song giving him another excuse to stay alive a little while longer.

When he fell asleep to it, he replayed the day of Taesung's departure. His body would recoil at the memory of the piercing rain, the unruly wind, and his sharp intakes of breath as he ran to their shared apartment. He could still feel the peppered kisses of Taesung as he said goodbye to him as he went over to Haeran's for their bi-weekly sleepover. He laughed as Lino bit at the bottom of his trousers and petted the top of his white curly hair. Taesung whispered upon his cheeks that he would see him later. That he couldn't believe it had been a year since they had met and been together. He boasted about how he had the best evening planned out and that he would see Yunseo the next day.

That day never came.

Yunseo had awakened that day to a pounding on Haeran's apartment door and a bouquet of black dahlia with a note attached to it. He had picked it up and read the note. The sound of glass shattering and squeaking sneakers was all that Haeran could hear before she saw her brother running down the hallway, screaming for him to stop and tell her what happened.

Clutching the note in his hand, he entered the once-shared apartment and digested the bareness of it all. He paced around and soon found himself on the floor, kneeling before the bed he had once shared and birthed the beginning of his new life. Yunseo did not hear Haeran come into the room or register her touch. His sight soon turned black and all he could remember was the feeling of the cold tiled floor of his once beloved dream.

Yunseo was brought back to the present when he heard knocking on the bathroom door. He cursed under his breath when he realized that the song had repeated itself for what must have been its tenth time. He half-haphazardly pulled himself up and splashed his face with water, trying to wash any fragments of the past that were plastered upon the creases of his flesh away. Once done, he jammed all of his belongings into his bag and opened the door, only to be greeted by Minseo.

"Ms. Park," Yunseo said, shocked. "I apologize. Have I taken up too much time in the bathroom?"

"Not at all," Minseo said as she watched a drop of water fall from Yunseo's face onto the plane's black carpet. "I was just worried. I saw you go into the bathroom around ten minutes ago and was worried about you. I thought I should come and check on you."

Yunseo nodded and gave her a short bow of appreciation.

"I feel regrettable to have made you worried about me and promise not to do it again. Now, if you excuse me," Yunseo said as he moved around her and turned towards the cockpit.

"Wait," Minseo exclaimed as she grabbed onto Yunseo, startling him, and making him drop his things onto the floor.

The chattering of the passengers stopped, and Yunseo felt a particular pair of eyes on him. Yunseo hastily bent down and grasped at his things. Minseo bent down as well and grabbed hold of Yunseo's earbud case and phone.

"I'm so sorry, Yunseo," Minseo said as they stood, passing him his devices. "I didn't mean for that to happen. I only wanted to know if you were alright."

Yunseo looked at her confused, "Of course I am. Why do you inquire?"

Minseo came closer to him and whispered in his ear.

"May I speak informally?"

Yunseo was surprised by this request and their proximity, but nodded all the same.

"I know a pair of red tear-stained eyes when I see them," she said as she pulled away. "I've had my fair share."

Yunseo reddened with shame and searched in his mind for a believable excuse yet was interrupted by the touch of Minseo's hand on his.

"It's fine. You don't have to tell me. Just say you'll be okay."

Knowing he couldn't trust his voice, he only nodded. Which seemed good enough to Minseo because she patted his hand and gave him a smile to which he returned.

"That's good. I must return to my mother. She'll be asking me what happened here."

She must have seen the panic in Yunseo's face because she began to shake her head.

"Don't worry, I won't tell her. It'll be one of our first secrets."

Yunseo was puzzled by what Minseo meant by this, but he bowed all the same and retired to the cockpit. He placed his items back into his large bag and groaned deeply as he pulled his pilot hat over his eyes.

Subin looked over at his friends and chewed on his lips, not knowing if he should ask what was the commotion that had happened moments ago. He briefly heard the conversion and wanted nothing more than to comfort his new friend, he just didn't know how. New friends were complicated in that way. So, he did the best next thing he could do.

"How about you sleep, and I'll take care of this flight. If we blow an engine or one of our wings gets clipped, I'll wake you."

"Subin, you don't—"

Subin reached over and pulled the hat harder over his eyes.

"Come on man, let me do this for you. Think of this as an 'I'm sorry that I went out and did body shots off our boss's kid' present."

Yunseo chuckled as he interlaced his hands together and placed them behind his head.

"You're going to have to do a lot better than that, my friend."

Subin's heart warmed at Yunseo calling him his friend and punched him in the arm to which Yunseo returned the gesture. He fell asleep soon after.

◆ ⁺ . ◆ . ⁺ . ◆

Yunseo awakened with a gasp as he felt the clashing of the plane's wheels onto the Incheon Airport's runway, effectively knocking his hat off his head. He looked around frantically before settling his eyes upon a laughing Subin, whose face changed in color from a pale white to one of bright coral.

"Did I disturb you," he chuckled.

Yunseo shot daggers into Subin's head as he calmed his beating heart and grabbed his phone. It was four in the afternoon and the sun was beginning to settle its last rays upon the peaks of South Korea's numerous skyscrapers and apartment buildings. Based on the shivering of the men helping guide the plane into a safe spot, the humid weather of Thailand was behind him, and the cold clammy hands of his motherland were aching to get themselves on his face and pinken the tops of his ears.

"Why didn't you wake me?"

"I only said that I would wake you if we were in peril."

Subin lifted his right hand and gestured to the darkening view of Korea.

"As you can see, we have made it safe."

"Asshole."

"Nice one," Subin laughed.

Yunseo punched Subin once again, before turning his head and letting a smile creep onto his face.

This is what it must feel like to have a brother.

With the plane parked, Subin and Yunseo collected their belongings and got up to greet the passengers as they left the plane. Soyeon had already pushed open the door and Soae waited at the bottom of the steps with a professional smile plastered on her face. Yunseo went to do the same until he caught Minseo's eyes. She was the first to walk towards the trio, putting her hand out and grabbing onto Subin's firm and calloused hands. She blushed slightly as she thanked him for an eventful trip, to which he responded with a sly smile and a quick wink of the eyes.

"Mr. Jeong," Minseo said, "thank you for our safe landing and pleasant flying. I look forward to flying with you again."

Yunseo grabbed her hand and was in the middle of bowing when he registered her word.

"Again?"

Minseo smiled and made her way to the others and down the stairs. Mrs. Park followed her daughter's departure, giving the crew a tight squeeze around the shoulders and a kiss upon their cheeks. She left them warm and content. Mikasa, Moonbin, and Minseok were the noisiest of the bunch and as they passed the crew with firm clasps on their shoulders and a lingering hand upon Soyeon's hand that Yunseo was sure he was the only one to have perceived, Yunseo was met with the eyes of Taesung.

Time slowed. The air stilled and his blood congealed. He watched as Taesung neared them, and before he could make it three feet from them, Yunseo dashed out of the plane, down its stairs, and ran past the group without much of a goodbye. He knew he had bumped into someone, but he didn't care. He needed to get away. He needed his comforting bed and the safety it provided. He needed to disappear and try again tomorrow. He needed to forget Taesung even existed.

As the clouds gathered above him, and tiny drops from the sky began to dampen the dry cement, Yunseo pushed himself harder to get into his car and coaxed it to awaken. Once alive, he reversed his car and drove out of the airport solely to be stopped by the traffic that cluttered the road home. The tiny thrumming of the rain only heightened Yunseo's desperation and aided in the remembering of his past. But it didn't remind him of his song or the smells of his stained shirt. Not of his sister's perfume or the sound of rattling pills. Reminded him of the words that tainted the note he had clenched in his fist five years ago. The words swarming around his brain and strangling it like a viper. Yunseo's subconscious traced the letters with its fingers as his mind sat in chains, helpless to stop the display of torture.

I'm leaving. Don't look for me.

And while Yunseo pulled out of the parking lot, Mikasa rubbed her shoulder, curious eyes watching as the dark blue car sped off.

"What's wrong with him," she asked.

Minseo had opened her umbrella, now standing under a big shadow of yellow.

"Maybe, he's just tried."

Moonbin walked towards the men unloading his bike from the aircraft, letting the rain shower him.

"You don't run like that when you're tired," Moonbin called out. "You run like that when you've seen a ghost."

"Perhaps he did," Minseok suggested, nudging Taesung gently. Taesung's gaze met Minseok's, conveying an expression that sent a sharp pang through Minseok's entire being. It was a look of agony, of anguish, and something else. Something Minseok couldn't figure out.

"He'll be fine," Subin cut in, not wanting the attention to be on Yunseo. "He actually told me he needed to get home and feed his dog."

Taesung turned at this, shock evident in his every feature.

"He got a new dog?"

Subin furrowed his brows.

"He had one before?"

48

Taesung shook his head as he approached the men unloading the last of the motorcycles. Impatient to wait, he nudged past them and swiftly freed his bike from its restraints. Mounting it quickly, he hesitated momentarily, considering whether to reveal the truth to the onlookers before him. He pondered confessing his desire to chase after Yunseo and his role in Yunseo's panicked departure. However, he opted instead for a simple farewell, wishing everyone a good day, and promising his friends he'd catch up with them later. With a swift departure, he left behind a cloud of smoke in his wake.

Moonbin glanced at Minseok with curiosity before hopping onto his bike and speeding away. Meanwhile, Mrs. Park, already seated in one of the SUVs, called for Minseo to join her before the impending rain worsened. Waving goodbye, she settled into the vehicle, resting her head on her mother's shoulder, enjoying the comfort of the radio and the warmth from the car's heater against her skin. *What a day*, she thought to herself. *What a day.*

Minseok grimaced at his family, then turned toward the crew, his smile strained, and arms crossed.

"I guess that's my cue to leave. Thank you all for your hospitality and professionalism. Get home safe," he said, bowing and dashing to get out of the rain.

Subin bid farewell to the three remaining women with waves, but surprisingly, he also kissed his co-workers' cheeks goodbye, leaving them taken aback by his unexpected display of affection.

"Pervert," Soyeon remarked, grinning as she looped her arm with Soae's as she attempted to usher them into the airport.

"Wait," Mikasa shouted, shielding her eyes with her hand. "Can I talk to you for a second?"

"Me," both women questioned simultaneously, prompting Mikasa to give a lopsided smile.

"No," she clarified. "The blonde one. Soae."

Soyeon frowned as she turned to Soae, noticing her companion's wide-eyed expression, seemingly mesmerized by something in the rain. Soae glanced at her friend before rushing back over to the woman with red hair.

"Yes," she asked, intrigued by what this stranger had to say to her. Mikasa pulled Soae closer, shielding her from the rain with her body. Though only a few inches taller, Mikasa's protective stance, with Soae's hands grasping her forearms and Mikasa's hand covering Soae's eyes, left Soae unable to focus on anything else.

"Can I have your KakaoTalk," Mikasa asked.

Soae tilted her head, puzzled by the sudden request.

"Why?"

Mikasa lifted Soae's chin, gazing into her eyes.

"Because I'd like to talk to you outside of work. Maybe even go out for dinner and a movie," she suggested, her lips glistening with raindrops, momentarily distracting Soae. "Unless that's not something you're interested in doing? With me?"

As their cab drove them home through the rain, Soae found herself lost in that moment. Despite feeling cold and exhausted, she couldn't shake the warmth on her cheeks or the rapid beating of her heart as she replayed her answer.

"Yes. I would very much like to go see a movie with you," she finally confessed, her voice barely audible over the sound of the rain.

CHAPTER FOUR

The room felt small. Yunseo found himself sitting in a well-lit room with his three other co-workers and Myunghwa. Yunseo believed this was the last day of his employment, and why wouldn't it be? After he took off without a word to his employers or co-workers and drove like he was auditioning for *Fast and Furious*, he wouldn't fault them if they did fire him. His keypad almost cracked with how hard he was pressing his password into it. The rest of the day was a blur and by the next morning, he was fifteen minutes late with Soyeon and Soae rushing him, saying that they had been called in for a meeting with Myunghwa. Subin clamped a hand on his shoulder telling him to send a prayer to God that they don't get fired. Not that that would help. Yunseo wasn't one much up for faith.

"Good morning, everyone. Please take a seat," Myunghwa commanded as she took the seat in front of the four.

Intimidation. Nice.

"Except you, Mr. Jeong. I wouldn't want you to get scared of me and run out like a child without a bow."

Yunseo stilled, his head hung low, wishing that the world would split open and swallow him whole. Nothing but the worms and wet soil of the Earth to keep him company instead of a makeup-stained Myunghwa, the cranky old lady from when he first arrived.

"Now, other than the rudeness of your fellow colleagues towards this airport's most influential donors, I would like to report that the Park family had a pleasant experience."

The four looked at each other smiling at the news of completing a job well done and at the prospects of keeping their jobs. Yunseo's smile turned into a faint one, remembering who the four had picked up.

Yunseo couldn't sleep during the night. Even with his journal's presence beside him, a reminder of his growth, Taesung still lurked at the center of his mind. Hauntingly, Taesung still looked the way he did in his mind: tall, confident, and dangerous. His mind persecuted him with recounts of the words that they used to whisper to each other's ears when no one was listening and then to the weeknights when Taesung had to leave for work, leaving Yunseo with nothing but a kiss on the forehead and sweatshirts containing his cologne.

While Soae and Soyeon dreamed of men with muscular arms and motorcycles, Yunseo laid suffering in his empty bed, wishing to find mercy in the darkness of his mind.

Myunghwa clearing her throat was what brought Yunseo's absent mind and the others' chatter to an end.

"That being said, you all did such a good job that the Park family has called and asked us to have you all contracted to be their private jet crew for the next year."

The four halted at this news, not expecting such an announcement. Everything happened in slow motion. Soae and Soyeon shouted with glee while a concerned Subin looked upon Yunseo, waiting for something. Subin could tell that there was something more between Taesung and Yunseo based on his co-pilot's reaction to his arrival. He just didn't know what.

"The job comes with a fifteen percent pay raise and all-inclusive rooms at any hotels they stay in. You will be on call at any time they need you and they will be your priority for the length of time you are contracted to them. Now, you will beg—"

"No."

Myunghwa narrowed her eyes.

"No?"

Yunseo tightened his hold on his hands as he straightened his back, looking down at Myunghwa with a dejected yet firm look.

"I did not come here to serve others privately. I came to fly planes, not jets. I'm sorry, but I cannot accept this request."

Myunghwa stood up from her chair and collected her things.

"You think you have a choice, Mr. Jeong? You have embarrassed not only your colleagues, but this airport and all that it stands for. The airport has already agreed to their request and have set up a meeting for tomorrow for you all to discuss any further concerns. If you do not show up tomorrow, you and your friends will be fired. You will never work at another airport ever again and I will personally call every airport in South Korea to explain how impotent, spineless, and ill-bred you and your friends are."

He heard the breath being sucked out of Soae's lungs as she twisted her wrists together. Soyeon stopped her once she saw her friend's wrists turn a slightly bright red. Soyeon looked to Subin, asking for help in calming her down. Subin took the silent hint and reached to hold Soae's hand, drawing soothing circles into her skin. Soae's breath soon calmed into a steady rhythm, and she shot a quick look of gratitude in his way. A slight nod was all Yunseo could see before returning his attention to the authoritative woman in front of him.

"Therefore," Myunghwa said cheerfully as she flashed Yunseo a mocking smile. "If you do not want to be the reason for your friends losing their jobs and becoming unemployed, you will go to the meeting and beg them for forgiveness."

Myunghwa turned to leave, but before the door closed, she called out to Subin, "I will be emailing all the information to Mr. Lee seeing that Mr. Jeong is emotionally incapable of being a man."

She slammed the door, leaving a dejected Yunseo to face three unsettled faces.

Eerie quietness filled the room. No one uttered a word until Soae slowly got up and hugged Yunseo before leaving. Soyeon soon followed behind her, kissing his cheek as she passed by. The only ones left in the room were Subin and himself. Subin had his face turned from him as he settled next to him, feeling a bit frightened of his friend's response. Subin turned to look at him and it was as if his eyes were begging a question that he knew he could not ask.

Why?

Realizing that Yunseo was not going to explain his sudden outbursts as of late, Subin stood from his chair with a groan and patted his partner on the head.

"I will send the information to you when I receive it."

Left alone in the back room, Yunseo all but wished that he had the backbone to tell his friends the truth. He buried his head underneath his arms and stayed well after the motion-detecting lights had turned off. The darkness soon came to comfort the water dripping from his face.

He had had enough. The incessant tears and whimpers were becoming unbearable. He thought he had finally found a way to deal with his past through journaling, meditating, taking walks in the park. But despite all his efforts, he was still failing. It was frustrating and disappointing. He was still struggling with his emotions. He believed that the military had beaten it out of him.

He remembered the day he had received his letter, calling him to his duty, which every Korean man had to fulfill. When he first received it, he requested his university to send back a degree-seeking form so that he could attend college and then serve when he was twenty-four. He thought the loophole was a gift. He knew of no classmate who was excited about serving their mandatory military service. Many bad-mouthed it and contemplated injuring themselves just to evade it. Yunseo considered the idea quite pitiful.

When his school asked him if he wanted them to send the form again, he opted out, saying he wanted to get it over with. Those six weeks were the most rigorous weeks of his life. The moment he got off the bus and his feet hit the Yongsan Garrison soil, he was yelled at for being slow, screamed at for walking too far ahead of his instructors, and humiliated for not knowing what he was getting himself into. The men were gathered at the center of the parking lot, trainees looking longingly at the buses pulling out of the lot, realization dawning on them that this would be their life for the next few years.

The group had over thirty men in it, all of varying ages and sizes, yet somehow, they had all scored one to three out of seven on their mental and physical exams. Yunseo was starting to wish he had scored a four so he could be a public service worker instead of active duty. He was in the fifth line, sixth row back when he saw a short and stubby man with the same shaved head as himself be scolded for chewing gum. The instructor made him spit it out as others around them watched him jump up and down at the number of chews he had done to his gum; he stopped after number forty and placed his hands on his knees as the instructor laughed and moved on to his next victim.

"Hey," Yunseo whispered. "Are you okay?"

The stubby man looked at him, breath still coming out in fast puffs, clouding the air before him.

"I would be better if I had never chewed that gum," the man said, straightening himself up and forcing his body into the straight and stiff stance their instructor had shown the groups minutes ago.

"My name is Park Gohyun. Yours," the man asked, holding his breath as his tormentor passed him by.

"Jeong Yunseo. Nice to meet you."

The following days were diabolical. Waking up at the crack of dawn, learning that everything Yunseo had done before—eating, cleaning, talking, and so on—was all wrong. Learning how to shoot a rifle, throw hand grenades, and so much more. Reprimands were the new hello and all the other trainees were following commands to absolute perfection. Yunseo found the spare five minutes he had every now and then a blessing and would often find drool on his sleeve soon after. Having no voice was not new to Yunseo but he watched as Gohyun struggled with not being heard. In their shared bunks, he could hear the fellow trainee crying softly into his pillow, the rest of the room oblivious to what was transpiring around them.

When washing his comrades' boots, he wondered if any of them shared Gohyun's struggles. At times, he would hear the others gossiping about how it was ridiculous to have them have no contact with the rest of the world. No one wanted to be here, sacrificing a year and ten months of their youth in preparation for a war none of them asked for. Yunseo felt the isolation of it all to be a bit much. None of them were *actually* trying to be soldiers. Yes, they were learning how to maneuver in difficult terrain and basic combat skills but so had the rest of the male population of South Korea, and yet no one he had ever met had the skills to be great. Until Gohyun.

It was the day of 화생방 훈련, the chemical, biological, and radiological training day they had kept telling his unit about. Gohyun had been particularly excited that day, which confused Yunseo greatly.

"Why are you so happy," said Yunseo, his hands preoccupied with trying to fit the used gas mask over his face. Gohyun fell into step with Yunseo, abandoning his previous fast pace.

"It's CBR day. It's the day I've been waiting for."

"Why?"

Gohyun groaned, his eyes looking at the front of their unit, making sure their instructor didn't catch them speaking out of turn.

"My family back home are military dogs. Each one stayed after their enlistment was over and don't think I can do the same," he said as his hands grabbed onto his belly, jiggling it up and down. "I understand why they think this, but I will prove them wrong. If I pass this test, then I would have done it. If I pass, I win."

Yunseo's heart softened as his eyes looked at the chamber's door. The chamber had been a singular storage room in the middle of the woods. The instructor yelled at everyone to get ready and before they knew it, they were inside.

The room was filled with white smoke, its swirls hypnotizing its invaders. The masked instructor yelled for them to kneel and remove their masks, something Gohyun was the first to do. The room was soon filled with depictions of agony. Men had tears streaming down their faces and had them mixed with the excessive saliva dripping out of their mouths. Some spat and spat, desperately trying to rid their bodies of the fumes, but all their efforts proved futile. The gas stole any breath you had managed to find and attacked any exposed skin you had. Yunseo's skin felt like it was being poked and prodded by thousands of needles, injecting their invisible poison into his flesh.

He couldn't see. He reached for his partners next to him and succeeded in grabbing hold of one while the other shoved him off. Wiping his eyes repeatedly, he looked at his partner and saw Gohyun. Gohyun was wet and flushed from the gas and his own bodily fluids, his face contorted in absolute torture. Yet, his hands… His hands clung to Yunseo like a silent promise, vowing never to let go, to never leave him behind.

The lesson lasted another five minutes: men started running towards the door, pleading and begging to be let out, yet the instructor on the other side pounded back, yelling for them to stop being "pussies". Once the door opened, Gohyun led Yunseo out of there, pushing and shoving those who tried to push them back from the door. Leading them a little ways out of the crowded area, Gohyun dropped them onto the ground, rolling onto his back and throwing an arm over his face. His skin hurt like hell, his lungs were fighting for any breath that could push past his lips, however he felt glad. He had won. His eyes crinkled under his arm and tears slid their way down the outer corners of his eyes, swollen lips forming into a weak smile.

The next six weeks, Gohyun had excelled, letting Yunseo tag along with him. Yunseo never heard anything else from Gohyun about his family or where he was being moved to after their training was done and they had been organized into their respective battalions. He never heard from him again, but he liked to think that Gohyun was out there, fighting as a respected and important member of the Republic of Korea Armed Forces.

Upon arriving at Seoul Air Base, Yunseo discovered that true freedom awaited in the skies. Soaring over South Korea and the DMR border itself filled him with a sense of control and exhilaration, unlike anything he had experienced before. For the first time in months, he felt as if he had wings to fly. Serving for twenty-two months posed no challenge for him, as he knew the moment he got back, he would be enrolling into Korea Aerospace University. Without a shadow of a doubt, he was going to be the best pilot he could be.

Being a pilot was better than being an office worker. Being a pilot meant being out and open, feeling freedom in a way most people would never experience in their life. For the first time, he wasn't afraid of the unexpected. He couldn't have been happier when he graduated early due to his Air Force training and received the acceptance letter from Incheon Airport stating that he had gotten the job and now—now he thought it best to take a sick day and go back to his apartment. The perfect place to fall apart without prying eyes to come and ask questions he himself was not ready to answer.

He planned to hide underneath the covers of his bed and disappear. He knew his room would be in disarray, but he didn't care. He wanted peace. He wanted familiarity. The good kind. Not the kind that reminded you why you felt so worthless to begin with. While driving down a road and seeing a bento box vendor, he decided to make a quick stop at the convenience store before returning home, knowing he had yet to go grocery shopping.

Upon walking in, he was overwhelmed with choices: ramen, bento boxes, sweet potatoes, fish cakes, kimbap, candy, chips, drinks, etc. He wanted it all. He decided to get a bottle of soju, ramen, onigiri, sausage, mochi, and red bean paste bread, since today was a special day. He placed his basket on the counter and let his eyes wander to avoid staring awkwardly at the cashier in front of him. His eyes caught sight of his favorite ice cream ever. Strawberry Melona! Excusing himself, he grabbed six bars before bashfully handing them to the cashier. Once he paid, he ran out, climbed into the car, and raced home just to avoid the treat from melting. As he raced past cars and towards his building, he chuckled at how ridiculous he was acting to avoid ice cream from melting. Again.

The building was tall, pale gray, twenty-four floors; he hated it. He paid close to one thousand two hundred dollars for a studio apartment that constantly had problems and was a pain in his neck. Probably was his biggest problem until recently. *Very recently*. He lived on the fifteenth floor and was grateful for one thing: the view. The balcony was the first thing the sun would hit when it was setting. Yunseo could remember the countless times that that view saved him from his mind. Engulfed in overthinking, one look at the sky or moon would quiet all his pestering thoughts. It was probably the only reason he stayed in this horrible place.

While punching the code into the keypad, he thought about buying a dog, but he quickly shot that idea down when remembering the last dog he had; Lino, a Maltese with the sweetest smile and the droopiest eyes. It was quite the combination. Yunseo still remembered the happy moments it brought to him. He remembered a smiling Taesung lifting the dog in the air. Yunseo had been looking at them from the living room, thinking how he could have been so lucky to find the perfect family after all the suffering his own had caused him. Yunseo wondered if it was at all real.

Not wanting to think, he thrust the bowl of cheap ramen under the leaky faucet and pressed the hot water sign. After carefully not getting burned, he set it aside and heated his sausage before his cell rang. Dreading to answer the call after seeing the name, he was left with no choice, knowing the individual would pay him a visit if he did not answer.

"Hello," Yunseo said, wincing, waiting patiently for his sister's apprehensive tone of voice.

"I won't ask why you haven't returned my calls. I just want to know if you have called Dr. Im to make sure your appointment is still on for tomorrow in the morning?"

His sigh was enough for Haeran to know that he didn't call his psychiatrist.

She groaned, wanting nothing more than to punch Yunseo in the face.

"I will not be here forever, you know. One day I will be gone, and you will be on your own."

"Great. Nothing different than before," he hissed as he placed the now hot sausage next to the steaming cup of noodles and tuna onigiri.

Haeran was silent for a moment before responding.

"What is that supposed to mean?"

"It means I'm tired of you on my ass, Noona. It means that I am a grown man, and I can make choices all on my own."

"Oh, like how you took care of yourself after Taesung left," she screamed as she stood up from her deck, body tense with adrenaline. "You sent yourself into such a depression that you've never been the same since. You know, sometimes I wonder if my brother died that day."

"Maybe I did," he declared. "Maybe I wish I had."

"Yunseo," she gasped.

"What," he screamed. "You know what I say is not a lie. You left me, Haeran. You ran away like a thief in the night and damned me to live with our parents while you were free. Did you think of me? While you laughed, fucked, and chanted into the night with your happiness, did you ever think of the insults and beatings that Omma and Appa gave to me that were meant for you? Did you even care at all!"

"Yunseo, please! You must know—"

Yunseo cut her off, rage pouring out of his heart and onto his tongue.

"You didn't give a fuck about me! All you cared about was yourself and now you wanna play house? Seriously? I needed you and you weren't there. You weren't fucking there!"

Haeran's choking sobs and gasping breaths were Yunseo's only answer. He couldn't bear to hear how broken she was; the sounds only reflected the cracks he had inside.

"Goodnight, Haeran."

"Yunseo, wai—"

He looked up to the sky as he hung up on her, not wanting to argue with the one person who still loved him. Not after saying the one thing that he knew hurt her to her core. After eating his food and calling his doctor's office, he laid on top of his bed feeling too tired to pull the covers down and over his body. He stared at the ceiling for what felt like ages and soon found himself falling asleep when he heard the chime of his phone. He cracked his drowsy eyes to look at the screen and could only make out a few words.

"Meeting, 10 a.m., dress nice."

Yunseo shot out of bed, cursing that his appointment with Dr. Im was at nine a.m., but rapidly calmed down, remembering it was a telehealth appointment.

He found himself standing in front of his closet looking for a "presentable" outfit but settled for a white T-shirt and jeans that his sister gifted him for his birthday two years ago. Hoping that this outfit would deter the Park family from signing with him on the contract, he cheekily set the outfit aside for tomorrow. He wouldn't risk his friends, but he never said he wouldn't risk himself. He set an alarm for tomorrow and decided it was best to shower and prepare for sleep.

As he was putting on clothes on his dam skin, he saw his journal sitting there, patiently waiting to be opened again. Yunseo approached the journal with great caution and opened it, staring at the pen inside. He sat hunched over his weathered journal, his hand shaking as he picked up the pen and pushed it down on the white paper, soaking it in black fluid. He began to dip and lift his pen across the pages, pouring out thoughts he dared not say out loud.

His brow furrowed in concentration, his eyes darting back and forth as he captured every detail of the past few days, the ink flowing freely from his pen as if guided by some unseen force. Each stroke was deliberate, each word carefully chosen, as he chronicled the events that had unfolded, the emotions that had stirred within him. As time went on, the sound of his tears hitting the pages and the scribbling of his pen marked the deepening crackling of his heart.

As he finished, he heard a knock on his door. Not understanding who would want to visit him at such short notice, he wiped his eyes and opened his door. He was greeted with the sight of a pastry bag from his favorite bakery and the smell of rose tteokbokki. He slumped onto the door frame as Haeran lowered the bags and offered him one of her sad smiles; the ones that dip at the corners no matter how hard she tried to keep them up. The siblings were in an intense moment, eyes locked together and neither trying to move closer. Her eyes held tight onto tears that were threatening to spill over at any wrong movement her brother could make.

"Truce," she said. The quivering hope in her voice was as evident as the tears in her eyes.

Yunseo held his posture and stared at her. He noted her clothes first before looking at her briefcase that she clutched in her left hand. It was red and marked with what he assumed was Sharpie and tailor's chalk. Her long garnet-colored nails added to her contrast with her white skin. Her clothes were of olive-green cotton and hung heavily off her frame alongside her white trench coat and baby blue scarf. His eyes traveled up to the hair that clung like a rope around the delicate blue fabric. He noted that she had finally cut her burnt coffee hair into the long-textured wolf cut she had contemplated for as long as he could remember.

She looks like a dog that was punished to drown outside.

Yunseo smirked inwardly at his mind's comment before looking back at his sister's face and seeing that the dam in her eyes had broken.

"Please," she cried.

He rolled his eyes as he dragged his sister into his tight embrace, understanding that this was a gesture of peace and that she wanted nothing more than to be on good terms with him. He wanted that too. After all, she was all he had.

"I'm sorry! I'm so, so sorry. I'm an awful sister. Awful," she repeated into his chest as she clung onto his pajama top.

He all but cradled her. It was then that he realized that she *was* soaking wet; she must have driven over and gotten caught in unexpected rain. He moved them from his front door to the kitchen.

"Shh, it's alright. I forgive you."

"I shouldn't have left you. I just didn't know what to do! I wish I had done differently. Please, forgive me. I—"

Yunseo held her tighter.

"Stop. Let me get you some clean clothes and you can spend the night here. Let's just calm down, okay?"

Haeran wiped her nose repeatedly as she mumbled an "Okay" to her brother. Squeezing her against him one last time, he ran to his bedroom and retrieved a pair of pajamas Haeran had left the last time she was here.

He handed the clothes to her as he guided her into the bathroom. He removed her drenched trench coat and scarf before closing the door behind him. He quickly threw them into the washer and took out the food Haeran brought. He also took out the soju he had bought earlier as well as two shot glasses. He smiled when he heard the sound of his hairdryer, concluding that Haeran found it best to wash her hair as well.

Only after he had set the table did Haeran come out of the shower, freshly clean and absent of any wet streaks that glittered her face moments ago. She ran over to him and squeezed him before sitting down to enjoy the meal. The two ate dinner in silence as they saw glimpses of remorse from one another, still feeling guilty about what had transpired. As she cleaned the table after insisting, Yunseo retreated to his room to secure a little surprise.

"Hey," he said as he leaned on his door frame and pulled out two of her favorite face masks and a newly bought KakaoTalk Ryan hairband, "Let's go watch *Goblin*."

She rubbed her hands together before running over to grab the gifts, yelling out, "I'm rewinding every time Lee Dongwook is on the screen," as she headed towards the couch.

"Like always," he mumbled as he went into the kitchen to grab the baked goods she brought and ice cream.

"What did you say!"

"Nothing!"

CHAPTER FIVE

"Why have you been avoiding me, Mr. Jeong?"

"Mr. Jeong? Wow! You must be pretty mad at me."

Dr. Im released an annoyed sigh as she settled into her chair.

"I'm not angry with you, Yunseo. I am disappointed that you did not call me and schedule this appointment yourself. We have not spoken with each other for almost two months. How are you functioning without the Klonopin?"

Yunseo turned down the volume on his phone, knowing that the response he was going to give would severely unsettle her.

"I have been rationing expired pills until I desperately needed them."

"How would you like me to respond to that, Yunseo?"

"Um," Yunseo hummed. "What do you mean exactly?"

"What I mean, Yunseo, is that my client of two years has just told me that he has been rationing his medication in order to avoid facing his doctor and speaking face-to-face about the problems he is having. You do understand that this could kill you, correct? Your diagnosis is not something to fool around with. I didn't diagnose you with G.A.D for you to ration 0.25mgs of Klonopin. I diagnosed you to help understand yourself."

Yunseo rolled his eyes as he turned his car into the street that led to an area of South Korea that you couldn't get into unless you were in the public eye. Seocho District. As long as you were well-known and had lots of money, Seocho was your playground. Yunseo had never really been to this part of South Korea. He had stayed in Incheon his whole life until he had to move to Seoul for

Yonsei and then to the Gyeonggi Province for Korea Aerospace University. He still remembered when Haeran left for Seoul.

♦ ⁺ ♦ ⁺ ♦

The night Haeran had left was dark, cold, and lonely. When he had awakened in the morning and heard the screams of his mother and sister, he knew. He knew that something had snapped in her. He could see it on her face as they entered the bus and disappeared into the school. He tried to speak to Haeran when they got back on the bus to go home, yet she wouldn't respond; a permanent blank canvas was his only answer. Once they arrived home, she ran and locked herself inside her room, ignoring a sleeping Appa on the couch in front of the TV and the blaring sound of guns ringing out of its speakers. It was midnight when Omma got home and broke in the door of Haeran's bedroom, smacking her clear across the face. Yunseo would never forget how bright her blood shined on their dark ebony floors.

It was a noise from the kitchen that lured him out of his bedroom. His sister was on her knees, shoveling cans of food and processed meat into her bag. Her face was already forming a bruise and her lip had a tiny bandage that spanned across her bottom lip. He didn't dare to speak, nor did he dare to stop her, because the moment their eyes met and the same broken sob broke out of them, he knew; this was the last time he was going to see her. Neither moved and when she tried to step forward, he backed away, his back flushed against the wall, hands balling up at his sides. Haeran's shoulders slumped, and tears fell onto the polished floor. With one last look over her shoulder, she quietly opened the door and sneaked away. Haeran was eighteen years old.

His parents were like wild animals when they discovered she had escaped. They tried to pry the information out of Yunseo. He screeched and cried that he did not know, however that did not stop the blows that came from his father and kicking from his mother. After some time, his parents stopped asking, the beatings stopped hurting, and when people asked about Haeran, they would say that she was off to boarding school for troubled children. It wasn't until a year later that Yunseo walked into Haeran's room and discovered a creaking floorboard. He pried it open with a flat head and found a phone number on the back of a fortune cookie slip. He still remembered Haeran's soft voice when he called, her words flowing like wet silk.

"I knew you would find it!"

It had been three years since he had last seen his sister, and for three years, he sneaked off during his lunch breaks and spoke to her. For twenty minutes they were together again, fighting against the world as a duo. No one noticed that he disappeared during those breaks; he had no friends. For a while, he began eating in the bathrooms until his sister forbade it. Instead, he would just sit there and cry into his sleeves, trying to muffle the whimpers from his classmates. He didn't need the upperclassmen to have another reason to stay away from him. Yunseo felt pathetic. Everyone around him had friends, no matter how fake or terrible they may have been, and here was Yunseo, sitting on a dirty toilet, trying to make no noise, hiding from others. The only comfort he had was his sister's voice. He still felt angry at her for leaving him behind, but relieved she still cared enough to answer his calls. For a long time, he was of two minds about his opinion of his older sister. He still was.

When he was accepted to Yonsei University his parents began threatening him not to leave. Disgust was etched into his parents' faces when he announced he was going to the school, and the sting of his backside only confirmed the loss of control his parents were experiencing. After graduation, when his parents were drinking on his behalf, he snuck out and boarded a bus to Seoul. To his sister. To liberation.

It was the best thing he could have ever done. He called her when he arrived in Seoul and cried in her arms as she guided him into her car and held him until the sun came up the following day.

◆ . ⁺ . ◆ . ⁺ . ◆

"I understand Dr. Im, but are we sure I have generalized anxiety? I mean, maybe I'm just a normal person that overthinks too much," he began.

He passed dozens of tall, luxurious buildings. Giant and proud. They were saying, "Look at me! Bask in my glory." Yet, all Yunseo wanted was to hide. He didn't want to be driving down these streets, he didn't want to see Taesung and be hired as his private pilot, and he sure didn't want his psychiatrist to go digging through his mind and make him feel smaller and more pathetic than he already was feeling.

"Please tell me you're joking."

"Well…"

"The person talking to me can't be the same person who has had panic attacks extending ten minutes and constantly worries about being normal though his doctor, me, has reassured him time and time again that he is. Please tell me you're not the same person."

Yunseo groaned and hardened his eyes, unable to find a clever way to talk himself out of this.

"I believed I discovered a way to control the attacks. I thought I had finally had it covered," he admitted.

"And did you?"

He leaned his head against the wheel, "No."

Breathing heavily, Dr. Im allowed her concern for her client to creep into her voice, understanding that regardless of everything Yunseo did wrong, he was still hurt and needed her help.

"Yunseo, when was the last time you had a panic attack?"

"I had one two days ago. It happened at work and was caused by an outside trigger."

"What was the outside trigger?"

He felt his hands clam up. He glimpsed at his GPS and briefly closed his eyes shut. He was getting closer to Taesung's home. Five minutes away. Five minutes away from *him*.

"It was my ex," Yunseo said.

"Taesung?"

Yunseo nodded even though she could not see him.

"He's back."

Dr. Im straightened up in her chair and continued to take notes.

"How did this exactly happen, Yunseo? How did he trigger you into a panic attack?"

Four minutes away, the phone announced.

His eyes began to water.

"It's too painful."

"I understand, but in order to get better, you must tell me the events that happened."

Taking a sharp, painful breath, he parked his car a block from his destination and enveloped one hand into the other.

"I," he stopped, clearing his throat and biting the corner of his lips. He didn't want to do this. Why was he the one broken if it was the other person's fault. Why must he repent and patch together pieces of himself that another tore apart? *Fuck*, he said to himself, *I hate this shit.*

"Please, Yunseo. Let me do my job. Let me help you."

He knew his face was drenched in tears, but he didn't bother to wipe them away.

Why wipe what continues to be broken after the fact.

"Three days ago, I was ordered to fly a group of influential donors from here to Thailand and back. Unfortunately, we were delayed and had to stay in a five-star hotel owned by one of the family members."

"Did anything happen in this hotel?"

The bartender's face entered the forth front of his mind and his heart, for a moment, seized to beat.

"Everything happened," he continued. "I met a bartender at the hotel's pool bar and talked about my past with him. About my insecurity being around rich people and how I didn't deserve to be in such a nice place—"

"Why did you think that? Why were you telling this stranger your deepest feelings?"

"I don't know," Yunseo yelled. "Call it loneliness or attraction, I just did. I told him about my insecurities and about Taesung. He recognized the name but, thankfully, he didn't realize the person I was talking about was the same one who was the owner of the establishment he worked in. We talked, drank, and everything went well until... until..."

Dr. Im stilled her pencil and listened closely to Yunseo's shallow breathing.

"Until," she said softly.

"Until he sounded like my Appa," Yunseo said as more, burning tears slid down his face and puddled in his whitening hands.

Dr. Im waited for him to continue.

"He shouted at me in a tone I've only ever known my father to use. And I ran. Okay, Dr. Im? I ran like I did when I tried to escape my father's beatings, and then I bumped into a group of entitled Caucasian teenagers calling me things I couldn't understand. I couldn't speak. I couldn't even move as they grabbed me and dug their claws into me. I just stood there like a child until I was saved by one of the family's bodyguards."

Yunseo allowed a smile to sneak its way onto his face as he wiped a tear off his nose, "He broke one of their noses."

"Oh," Dr. Im said.

"Yeah," he said. "The bodyguards informed me that the kid was known to stir up trouble, I was only there to witness the punishment."

"Mr. Jeong, I'm sorry that that happened to you, but how does Taesung fit into all this?"

"He's the son of the family I was employed by. *He* was the reason why we were there and *he* was the reason we had to stay another day. The fucking bastard couldn't even bother to board his own fucking flight."

Dr. Im's eyes bulged out of her eyes as she took apart and examined the pieces of the picture Yunseo was painting for her.

"What else?"

"I couldn't handle it," Yunseo whimpered. "I locked myself in the bathroom after putting the auto-pilot on and freaked out into exhaustion. I slept the rest of the flight, and when I had awakened, I feebly dashed away from him when we landed."

The only sounds that filled the car were the sniffles and heavy breathing of Yunseo alongside with the scribbles of Dr. Im on the other line. Yunseo darted his eyes at the clock and registered that he was now, effectively, eleven minutes late to the meeting of his and his friends' lifetime. Straightening up, he sucked in a breath to announce his departure when Dr. Im interrupted his impending exit.

"Yunseo, I think this is for the best."

He stared into his phone, thinking this woman was insane to suggest such a thing.

"Oh, how so," he responded bitterly as he cleaned himself up, not wanting anyone to see his red eyes and tears.

"You have been avoiding dealing with the trauma that Taesung has caused."

"That's not true. I have spoken about my... issues."

"Mr. Jeong, be honest. You call your trauma 'issues'. Issues are like your leaking faucet or forgetting to turn off the stove. Reuniting with your ex-boyfriend who left you five years ago without an explanation is not an issue, it's an opportunity. An opportunity to heal and get some answers that you couldn't before. Seize it, Yunseo."

"I'll try," he whispered.

Breathing heavily, Dr. Im closed her notepad and scheduled his next appointment.

"I will see you in a week."

"Wait, not two? Like before?"

"That was before you reunited with Taesung and rationed your medication. I'm scheduling an appointment with you every week and I will be expecting to hear from you every single time."

"Seriously?"

"You want to be reprimanded by your sister again?"

He grimaced at the memory of yesterday. He couldn't handle another fight with his sister. Especially with her practically licking the screen every time Lee Dongwook came on. He was pretty sure he wasn't going to be able to hear the next day.

"Fair."

"I will see you again at the same place, same time. I will be sending you 0.25mg of Klonopin to the pharmacy listed in the system and you should be able to pick it up on Monday."

"Okay."

"Seize the opportunity, Yunseo."

"Mhm," he replied weakly, hanging up.

He sighed as his anxiety melted a little bit as he started his car and drove up the street. As he neared the front of two large mahogany gates, two bodyguards came from its side and caged Yunseo's car in place. Both put their hands on the weapon that poked out from their belt and motioned Yunseo to lower his driver's side window.

"Good morning, Mrs. Park is expecting me."

The guard stood looking at Yunseo unfazed. The man must have not heard him.

"Um, sir? I said I—"

"I.D."

Startled by the guard's rough tone, Yunseo took out his I.D. and handed it to the man. He was acutely aware of the bodyguard's partner looking into his windows. The guard with the I.D. pressed a finger into his ear and began to talk to someone on the other line.

"Excuse me, Sajangnim? There is a man saying that you are expecting him."

"What is the man's name?"

"Jeong Yunseo."

"Ah, yes! Please let him in."

The bodyguard handed back his I.D. as the large wooden gates swung open and welcomed Yunseo into the long driveway of a beautiful two story house. The house was surrounded with trees changing into autumn colors, perfectly manicured green grass, a driveway that rivaled the landing strips of the Qamdo Bamda Airport, and mammoth sized statues lining the driveway.

The statues, ten feet tall in height, were carved of white marble and looked as if they were draped in fabric. Limbs and faces poked out of the fabric and the sight made the pit in Yunseo's stomach clutch. They looked like they were screaming. Yunseo drove slowly down the road, trying to capture the details of every statue he passed by. At first glance, you would have thought that they were of Greek origin, yet the kkotsin shoes and gat hat of a male statue and the chima skirt and dtgoreum ribbon of a female statue annihilated that possibility. As he got closer, the more overwhelming it all became. Rounding another gigantic fountain that was embedded in the front of the house, he beheld the mansion that was covered in vines, flowers, and twigs. It was sublime and looked as if it came out of a storybook, except for the six bodyguards that lined up the steps of the home.

Yunseo was thinking about driving away when he saw Ahin come out of the front doors, waving enthusiastically at him, smiling like a little girl seeing her father. He swallowed his nerves and exited his car, forcing a laugh as he walked over and bowed to her, demanding his face to keep his false smile.

"Good morning, Sunbaenim. I apologize for being late for our meeting."

"Oh, hush. Come inside already. The others are here," she said as she slipped an arm into Yunseo's and dragged him inside.

As he passed the bodyguards, he saw them smile at their boss's extroverted nature.

Inside, the house was just as stunning as the outside. The house was covered in shades of light blues, neutrals, dark wood, silver, and gold. Unlike the entrance to the manor, the inside felt like a home. There, on the walls Yunseo was only able to get glimpses of as Ahin pulled him like luggage throughout the house, were frames family photos of all holidays and ages. Along the same walls, were perfectly lined and filled bookshelves that gave the illusion that the books were floating. She tried to absorb everything as quickly as he could, and when Ahin stopped long enough to open the double French doors to the backyard, Yunseo narrowly avoided smashing his nose into a glass panel. As she dragged him onto the landscape, he turned his head and realized that the home was made up of vast windows that let in massive amounts of light. The high ceilings deserved some credit too.

The yard was simple and unnaturally green, yet it paled in comparison to the most magnificent greenhouse planted in the middle of the open space. The word 'greenhouse' grotesquely undermined the colosseum before him. It was an extension of the castle that was falling back behind them, its connection evident in the symphony of silver and gold accents that was across its expansive structure, shimmering like precious jewels under the embrace of the sun. The panoramic view was encapsulated by large windows that stood like guardians, offering a glimpse into the verdant sanctuary within. Its arched window-paneled door groaned as Ahin jerked it open and dashed inside.

Distracted by its beauty, Yunseo failed to realize Ahin had stopped moving, crashing into her, and falling onto the ground. Ahin brought her hands to her mouth, trying desperately to hide her laughter, but failed miserably. She stretched out a hand and offered it to him. He laughed as well as he pulled himself up. Hearing more than one laugh fall from Ahin's lips, Yunseo realized that they were not alone. In front of them sat Soae, Soyeon, and Subin, all still laughing at what just transpired. He felt his cheeks blush with embarrassment.

"Jesus, Yunseo! Did you really have to crash into the woman like that? You've caused our jobs now," Subin said as he leaned forward on the rustic farm table provided by the lavish greenhouse. "You're already late."

"Oh, stop it, Subin. I'm sure that Yunseo has a perfectly good explanation for why he is late," Soae remarked, her voice still vibrating with her laughter from moments ago.

Seeing everyone waiting for his response, including Ahin, he tried to come up with the best excuse he could.

"Traffic," he shrugged dramatically.

Subin and Soyeon narrowed their eyes as Soae and Ahin accepted his response without question.

"Go sit down, Mr. Jeong. I will review what I have already stated to your friends," Ahin said as she closed the door to the greenhouse and settled into her chair, facing the group perfectly.

"Yes ma'am," he muttered as he rounded the table and sat next to Soae, pleased that Subin was as far away from him as possible.

No more teasing for now.

"Now, I understand from your superior that this has caught some of you by surprise, but please understand that I have been looking for a group of intellectual and kind individuals to come and work for my family. I have had experiences where the people we have employed have tipped off news outlets or NSCo.'s competitors, and it has all been a very heavy burden to bear. The trip to Thailand had been a test, one which you all passed," Ahin finished with a smile. She had been thinking about this meeting since she first woke up, eager to employ those who seemed skilled enough to do their jobs properly without risking the safety of her children and relaxed enough to embrace her family's personalities.

On the night that they stayed in Taesung's hotel, her daughter came stumbling into their hotel room, holding her hair as she ran into the bathroom. Ahin threw her daughter into the shower with cold water hoping it would shock her awake. To her disappointment, she found Minseo sitting on the floor of the shower complaining about how she was so tired and didn't feel like standing. Ahin was able to put Minseo into bed and planned to call and complain to the airport about how their employees took her daughter drinking.

"I know that look, Omma. Don't do it," Minseo slurred as she turned towards her mother, who was sitting on her bed.

"What 'look'? Don't do what," Ahin asked, confused at her daughter's sudden drunken statement.

"That look when you're about to call someone's supervisor. I'm fine. They took care of me."

"But you're drunk! They should have known—"

"Didn't you tell them to take me out and have some fun?"

Ahin snapped her mouth shut, realizing that she indeed had said that, and they had indeed had fun.

"Omma, it was the most fun I have ever had. They treated me like a friend. An equal. Not like *his* daughter," Minseo spat as she whipped her head to the other side of the pillow. "Promise me that we'll keep them. Please! Please! Plea—"

"Stop it, Minseo! Stop chanting! You are going to throw up again!"

"Not until you promise me."

Minseo hiccupped as she began to lift herself from the bed and jump up and down.

"Alright! Alright! I'll hire the Incheon workers," Ahin shouted as she tucked her drunk child back into bed.

"You're the," she hiccupped, "best Omma ever," Minseo murmured as she let her eyes fall close and let sleep take over.

Ahin shook her head as she let her face fall into her hands. Her shoulders shook as laughter soon took over and she found herself grateful that her daughter had gone out and had young fun. After everything they had been through, that was all that she wanted for her. Gone was her anger in her chest, replaced with fondness and gratitude for the Incheon workers. Ahin had decided to call the airport about her decision after she landed in South Korea.

Ahin smiled at the memory as she looked back up to the four Incheon workers and began to speak again.

"As you know, we are willing to offer a fifteen percent pay raise, all-inclusive rooms at any hotels we stay in, and paid days off. Notices will be needed in advance, of course. All we ask in return is hospitality, availability, flexibility, and compassion. You will receive our numbers in case of emergency as well as when and where we will need to go in the future. The plane we rode on to Thailand is the family's so that will be the plane you will be using for the next year. The only ones who will be using your services will be myself, my daughter, and my son, Taesung."

Yunseo felt a pang in his heart when he heard Taesung's name, not wanting to be reminded of Taesung's inclusion in this otherwise fantastic opportunity.

"Now, after hearing all the benefits and demands of the job. What is your decision? Please be prompt, we need to fly to Tokyo on Monday."

There was silence as the four looked at each other and, of course, Soae had been the first to speak up.

"If we say yes, does that mean we can have a tour of your beautiful home?"

Laughter erupted, but was short lived.

"If you think the house is beautiful now, it's even better in the spring," a dark and soothing voice said as the door of the greenhouse opened. "It's as if the entire house comes alive again. Especially with the smell of mangos Omma uses to make *bingsu*."

There stood Park Taesung in all his glory, wearing a beige ribbed knit top with white trousers and dark brown alligator dress shoes. All things Yunseo knew he shouldn't have taken note of. He looked expensive and new, as if he had lived the high life his entire existence, even though Yunseo knew the truth. He remembered that only five years ago this man was giving him tips on how to make his money last throughout the month and how to create a bank account for the first time. He remembered the stories Taesung told him when they were in his kitchen late at night, him sitting on the counter and Taesung leaning against the fridge, trying to scrape out what was left of his mint chocolate ice cream while reciting the memories of his Omma trying to make ends meet. His *real* Omma. It felt like a dream. A dream that has now become a continuous nightmare.

Yunseo drew his hands together underneath the table, trying to get their shaking under control. He couldn't afford anyone seeing him like this. Especially Taesung.

"As for the tour," he said as he threw an arm around Mrs. Park, smiling endearingly at her. "I would be more than happy to give you a tour. That is, if you all have already agreed to being our pilots and flight attendants. Have you?"

Silence descended as Yunseo's friends nervously turned towards him and encouraged him to give his answer. Subin, Soyeon, and Soae would all respect his decision, but it would come at the price of an explanation. He knew that. He bent his head down and with all the energy he could muster, lifted his head and stared into Taesung's eyes.

"We'd be honored, Mrs. Park."

✦ ⁺ ✦ ⁺ ✦

"And this is the kitchen, where the only mice we have are these three," said Mrs. Park pointed at Taesung's friends as she walked everyone into the massive kitchen. It complimented the rest of the house perfectly, just with more warmth, as if it were the beating heart of the home.

Taesung's friends were crowded around a white marble island that was hard to miss. They were dressed in casual attire and hovering around... cookies?

Moonbin had been in the middle of devouring a cookie when he was outed as a rat. He roughly swallowed the baked good before chasing it down with some milk.

"Oh please, Mrs. Park. If we weren't here, who else would eat your delicious cookies?"

"Maybe my daughter?"

"And, let that brat have all this deliciousness to herself? I don't think so."

The crew gasped at this, never imagining a person to say such a thing about Ahin's daughter in her very own home.

Ahin was quiet for a moment before developing a seriously evil plan. She reached into her back pocket and pulled out her phone, quickly typing a message to a certain someone.

"I'm telling Minseo you called her a brat."

Moonbin's face was now pale white.

"You wouldn't."

The sound of Mrs. Park's phone was his only answer as everyone heard the opening of a door and the running footsteps of Park Minseo.

"Oppa," Minseo screamed as she reached the kitchen and ran towards Moonbin.

He cursed as he stuffed one more cookie into his mouth and made his way around Mikasa and Minseok, both laughing at the scene transpiring before them. Minseo chased Moonbin out the kitchen and into the front yard. She believed she held the upper hand until Moonbin suddenly turned around and picked her up bridal style, spinning them to his heart's content. While hitting Moonbin in the chest, she screamed for him to let her go. His roaring laughter was her only answer.

Everyone watching either laughing outwardly or in secret, including the bodyguards stationed at the front door trying desperately to hide their chuckles and snickers.

"Wait, Omma," Taesung interrupted as he turned to his mother. "I thought no one was allowed to yell in your house? You chewed me out the last time Mikasa and I were arm wrestling."

"I want a rematch, idiot," Mikasa said as she neared closer to him.

"Yeah, whatever."

He laughed as he rested his arm on her head.

"You'll lose. Again."

She shrugged his arm off and punched him in the stomach. "We'll see."

Turning from the window, Mrs. Park looked at her son with an indescribable and mischievous joy gleaming in her eyes.

"Just wait, my dearest son. Just wait."

Suddenly, water erupted from shiny silver sprinklers like a volcano, completely soaking the two spinning in the front yard.

"And, that's what you get for yelling in my house," howled Mrs. Park as she ran out the front door and scolded them from the steps.

They paid her no mind as they were too busy falling onto the ground, muddy and wet. Both couldn't stop laughing at how ridiculous they looked.

"Taesung, remind me never to get on your mother's bad side," Minseok said fondly as he pushed the rest of the cookies toward Yunseo and his friends, while Taesung poured them glasses of milk. He handed everyone the glasses but lingered a little longer when handing Yunseo his glass. He remembered the times their skinship would leave them both tingling and gasping. Sometimes breathless, too. But, that was for an entirely different reason. Taesung slowly let Yunseo's hand go when he saw the panic in his eyes, not wanting to make Yunseo more uncomfortable than he could already see.

Seeing this exchange, Minseok spoke up.

"So, what are you guys doing here?"

"We were just hired to be the family's aircraft crew," Soyeon said as she wiped a crumb off the corner of her mouth.

Shit, she thought, *how the hell is it so buttery and light at the same time?*

Don't moan.

Keep it together, girl.

"You don't say," Mikasa said as she handed a napkin to Soyeon and Soae, noting how cute she looked today. "Why don't we celebrate? It's not often we get attractive people around here."

"But, you're attractive," squeaked Soae, slowly sipping on her milk.

"Not as attractive as you, Soae" Mikasa said as she leaned over, stealing the cookie closest to Soae.

Soae said nothing as she blushed and hid behind Soyeon. Soyeon took note of this and smiled sheepishly into her cup, earning her a pinch from Soae.

"Yes," Moonbin said as he dragged himself back to the counter, throwing his jacket on the massive marble island. "That is exactly what I need, baby."

"We're not going for you, Moonbin," Taesung said as he peeled the soaking wet jacket off his mother's island and threw it in the sink. "Still, it will be fun all the same, right guys? What do you say? BBQ?"

The crew couldn't have said "Yes" fast enough, which left a brooding Yunseo with no choice but to go.

Where the Stars Remember Us

CHAPTER SIX

"Taesung," Ahin said as she guided Minseo back into the crowded house, keeping her muddy daughter at arm's length. "Could you take us to Shinsegae in Gangnam?"

Taesung looked up from the towel he was using to dry his hands and walked over to Ahin. Standing before her, he took in his soaking sister and his bright and smiling stepmother. He glanced at the subtle crow's feet forming at the edges of her eyes and the twinkle in them that had been strained for more than a year now. Sometimes he wondered to himself what had made her so happy for a woman married to his father.

At times it scared him how singular his father's tastes were in women. The way Ahin swayed her hips and laughed with mirth reminded him of when his Omma wasn't bedridden and yelled for him to come inside to eat dinner. That was a lifetime ago.

"Must it be right now? I thought we were going to show the new hires around the house?"

Ahin cast a look over the kitchen and smiled.

"Let the M&Ms do it. I need a new dress for an event I am going to. It can't wait, my dear."

Taesung pressed his lips into a fine line and looked back in the same direction. He wished he was a painter so that he could immortalize the scene before him. His friends bickering and teasing one another as the others oversaw it and hid their smiles behind their clear cups of milk. And then there was Yunseo.

Taesung stretched his hands before laying them flat against his trousers. His eyes outlined the shirt Yunseo had worn and the occasional flicker of his wrists.

He's nervous, he declared to himself.

Because of you, you fucking idiot, his mind echoed back.

Taesung let out an exasperated breath before feeling his heart hollow. He pinched the bridge of his nose as he sealed his eyes. *What am I doing,* he thought. He didn't know how to speak to Yunseo nor how to capture his attention. Every time he would try and reach for those rich colored irises, the smaller man would turn away, gluing his eyes at anything else that was not Taesung's likeness. Taesung felt the same icy-hot feeling he did when he first surveyed the profiles of the pilots the Incheon Airport selected for the family's flight. His nerves danced their cold fingers across Taesung's once-warm insides, leaving behind a brittle, crystalline landscape in their wake.

He thought himself prepared to face his ex-lover, but he was sadly mistaken when he recounted the swiftness Yunseo had entered the plane's bathroom and imprisoned himself inside. He was moments away from knocking on that door when his sister excused herself and did so herself. The view of Yunseo coming out with reddened eyes and skin dripping was enough to bring him to his knees. His legs twitched as he saw Yunseo drop his things. He ushered the contents of his drink into his mouth when his sister lowered herself back to her seat. When asked what happened by their mother, she only remarked that Yunseo needed to refresh himself. Minseok eyed Taesung as he reached over and refilled his glass with golden liquor. He said nothing while his friend supported a scowl and pursed lips for the rest of the flight.

Releasing the bridge of his nose, he turned to his mother. "Someone has to stay here and monitor everything."

Ahin laughed and scooted over to her son, placing her damp hand on his shoulder, "Don't you trust our bodyguards?"

"Don't you," Taesung smirked.

Ahin raised herself on her toes and looked back over where her waning cookies sat.

"Point taken."

"I'll stay," Minseo blurted out. She had been so quiet during their interaction that they had momentarily forgotten her.

Taesung raised his eyebrows, surprised she would give up a chance to grab her favorite whip cream filled waffles.

"Are you sure, Sweettooth?"

Minseo laughed at her brother and gestured to her being.

"Oppa, look at me. I'm soaking wet. I'd rather stay here and take a shower."

"But, your waffles—"

Shaking her hands, she stopped him from continuing, "Just bring me two of them, okay?"

He smiled and placed his hands on top.

"Extra Nutella and strawberries?"

"With toasted marshmallows on top," she grinned.

He nodded his head as he brought hers forward and placed a kiss on it. He wished her good luck as their mother took his hand and led him out of the house.

Minseo smiled after them and reentered the kitchen. Everyone looked over at her and snickered at her sullied clothes and hair.

"You," she said as she pointed at Moonbin, "and I need to shower. We are tracking in mud and Omma probably would have hosed us down if she hadn't asked Taesung to take her to Shinsegae."

Moonbin furrowed his eyebrows, "You gave up Waffle Shop Croffle?"

"You see," she said as she placed her hands on her hips, tilting them to the side. "When you say shit like that, it's hard for me to take you seriously."

Moonbin laughed and looked at the audience before them, "So you want me to get naked here or…"

Soyeon had choked on the last bit of cookie that had gone down her throat. Her eyes darted side to side as she chased it down with the rest of her milk. She could feel heat blossom on her cheeks as Soae and Yunseo rolled their eyes and the rest giggled. Mikasa pulled a sour face. Minseo clicked her tongue as she reached into the sink and threw the sopping wet jacket at its owner.

"Go to Tae's bathroom and I will go to my own," Minseo walked towards the stairs and stopped at the doorless frame of the kitchen. "Omma promised to give them a tour of the house, so could you please give the house tour until I'm clean?"

Minseok and Mikasa looked at each other, smirking that now they were the babysitters.

"Just go shower," Minseok said as he began to clear the crumbly mess that was on the countertop.

Satisfied, Minseo left and Moonbin soon followed after her since Mikasa had to peel him away from grabbing one more sweet. Moonbin grumbled all the way until he reached Taesung's door. Turning the handle, he walked in and made his way to the bathroom, already searching for a spare towel. The cabinets creaked after a while of not being opened and he found an old washed-out blue towel sitting in the corner of one. Grabbing it, he turned and peeled off his soiled clothes, dropping them in a heap beside the old toilet. The water sang its lullaby and calmed his aching body as he lathered himself in saffron and orange blossom-scented soap.

The water traced the contours and ridges of his sculpted body, curling around his cock. He groaned deeply as he massaged the back of his neck, letting his fingers travel to his trapezius muscle, gripping the sore muscle and letting his head fall.

I went too hard yesterday. I feel like I could stay here forever.

He allowed himself to think about taking a day off from the gym while the mudded water turned clear, and the wrath of the water cooled into a neutral state. His hair was the last thing he washed before shutting off the water. He rubbed away any droplets he could find and went looking for some clothes to wear. Raiding Taesung's closet, he found only a black tank and a pair of gray sweats that could fit his enlarged body. Taesung was by no means small in any way, his strength at times rivaling Moonbin's own, but Moonbin was always the bigger one. He could still remember the names that the boys in his hometown used to call him. Fatso, Lardass. Jumbo... His personal favorite was Fat Jjanggu. When the boys ripped his bento box out of his bookbag and found it covered in Jjanggu stickers, he was forever called Fat Jjanggu. Moonbin still couldn't see the cartoon the same way.

Rubbing his hair with the towel one last time, he grabbed the puddle of discarded clothes, slapped on his glasses, and headed towards the door. He felt something course through him as he opened the door and came face to face with a distressed-looking woman. Her face looked erratic and her posture troubling. She seemed lost and maybe a little intimidated by the glistening man before her. After a few moments, he recognized her as one of flight attendants and quickly stepped through the doorway, closing the door, scanning the hallway for anything that might have frightened her so.

"Is everything okay," inquired Moonbin.

The woman blinked her eyes repeatedly. She seemed in a daze and her hands tugged at the ends of her long blackened braid. She was scanning the man before her and felt her lungs burn, begging for her to inhale. Her eyes traced a small little droplet making its way down the man's face and watched it disappear into the corner of his mouth. She was too distracted to notice Moonbin had switched the dirt encrusted jacket from his right hand into the other and was now gripping her upper arm, his burning touch breaching her puzzled mind and forcing a reply from her throat.

"I'm lost," she said. "I lost Soae when Minseok guided us to one of the painting rooms and I don't know where the others are. I was supposed to follow Minseok and... and," she blushed as she nibbled at her bottom lip. "And now I'm lost."

Moonbin stared at her. He knew he should guide her to the others. Knew that he should call Minseok and have her regroup with her friend, but the way she swayed on her feet and bit her lip anxiously, made him want her for himself.

"What's your name again?"

"Soyeon," she said, her voice wavering. "Ahn Soyeon."

Moonbin smiled and removed his hand from her arm, grabbing onto his jacket again.

"Soyeon," he tested the name on his tongue, liking the way his tongue had to graze the back of his teeth just to say it. "Nice to officially meet you Soyeon, I'm Kang Moonbin. I'm the hot one in the group."

"I know," said Soyeon.

Moonbin raised his eyebrows as he soaked in her response. He smiled deepened as he saw her eyes widened and her mouth slacked.

"Oh—no, that's not what I meant! I... huh..."

Moonbin shook his head as a deep chuckle rumbled from his chest. Soyeon felt her heart swoon at the rich noise and knew she wanted to hear it again.

What is wrong with me? I just met the man and now I wanna jump his bones? God, I need to masturbate more.

Moonbin stared at her a bit more before starting down the hallway. Startled, Soyeon followed him and kept a close distance.

"Where are you going?"

"I wanna show you something," Moonbin said, descending down the mousy colored stairs. Soyeon said nothing as she held her breasts down, trying to keep up with the meaty man as she sent a prayer to the universe, hoping that the man before her wasn't a serial killer.

His pace exhausted her. Soyeon wasn't particularly a short woman, but the man's tall stature and long legs, equal to his strength, were something else entirely. He walked past the once noisy kitchen, down another massive, delicately colored hallway that was detailed in the same shades of green, white, and metallic colors as the rest of the house then turned, a large matted black door greeting Soyeon's gaze. The door, seven feet in height and its handle, engraved with swirls and white hot in color, made Soyeon understand what the entrance of hell looked like. As she watched Moonbin switch the weight of his clothes in his hands and reach for the handle, Soyeon reached out and grabbed his wrist.

He turned his head, slow and analyzing like a snake, and laid his eyes on where her hand was. His eyes traced the veins on top and the swirls of white on her long pink nails. Moonbin took particular interest in the shape of them. Elongated and eye-catching, yet calm in colors and rounded at the tip. He wondered if they burned when they were dragged across the skin.

"Um—Moonbin," she said.

Moonbin quietly groaned as his name fell from her lips. The pronunciation leaves her mouth partly open, giving him a glimpse of her tongue.

"Soyeon," he said thickly.

"Am I safe with you?"

Moonbin's caged heart tugged at its restraints and if he wasn't holding such ruined clothes, he would have wrapped her in his arms, crushing her against him until she felt the worry melt away. He could only offer her his hand around hers, bringing it to his lips.

"I never mean harm to those who mean no harm to me," he whispered. "Especially those as beautiful as you."

Soyeon felt a strange grip on her heart as Moonbin held his lips hovering over her fingers. She stared at the faint smile of his mouth, distracted by how lush and plum his lips were, shaped like an archer's bow and thicker at the bottom, and gasped as he nibbled one of her fingers with the edge of his teeth. When she looked back up, she noticed that he held her stare and his eyes were gleaming with a danger only the books she read at night knew.

"Say you believe me," he said, his voice darker than before.

Soyeon dropped her hand from his hold and lowered her head, giving him the smallest of nods.

Moonbin smiled while grabbing ahold of the handle that belonged to a large matted black door and gave it a mighty push. The door let out a horrifying groan as it opened up to a beautifully lit garage with tall, satin finished walls and three luxurious cars, with three familiar looking bikes lined up in front of them, waiting to be mounted again.

The cars were parked side by side one another and had overhead lights beaming down on them, demanding Soyeon's attention. As Moonbin threw his clothes on to the side of the bike neared to the right, Soyeon neared the three vehicles with great caution, as if they were great beasts slumbering, waiting to strike those who dare to wake them. Soyeon registered the cars one by one in her memory. The one to her left was a glossy forest green color with pearly white rims and a wood grain interior. As she touched the pearl handle of one of the doors, she slid her eyes to look upon the one beside it. The next one had been a pale two-toned yellow trunk with silver features and black rims with the insides white. Soyeon traced the letters F,O,R,D with her index finger as she practiced the word on her tongue. The surface of the car had been polished to perfection and had it not been for a speck of light that caught her eye, she would have been entranced by its flawlessness forever.

Wish I was this captivating.

She was still wrestling with the thought when she stood in front of the very last car. Dark mauve with the same polished detailing as her brothers, but she was different. Unlike the others, she had been topless. A convertible with four person seating with the darkest blue leather detailing Soyeon had ever seen. She rounded the car and leaned closer to it, tracing every dip and curve with her eyes; the dashboard looked as if Tag Heuer had designed it themselves. The power the blue color had with the purplish-gray made her feel like this vehicle had to belong to one of the women of the family. It was sexy. Sophisticated. Desirable. All the things she wanted to be.

Absent-mindedly, she reached out to touch the matching leather wheel when Moonbin's voice ripped her away.

"That is a 1954 Mercedes with a 300SL body," he said as he strode over to her. "It had been imported from America and detailed here. In fact," he said, opening his arms wide, "They all were."

Soyeon tries not to get distracted by the muscles constricting in the man's arms and walks back over to the pale green car.

"What's this one?"

Moonbin placed his hand firmly onto the vehicle, almost possessively.

"This beauty is a 1971 Ford F-250 Camper."

"And the last one."

"Continental Bentley."

"They're all so beautiful."

"Well, they better be. They were a pain in the ass to fix up and paint. I didn't sleep for weeks."

Soyeon whirled her eyes back to Moonbin.

"You did this?"

Moonbin smirked, padding the hood of the yellow car as he walked backward, still facing the opened mouth woman.

"Don't look so surprised, darling. I'm not just a pretty face."

Soyeon couldn't help as a smile made its way to her mouth and turned her face to look at the vehicles again. She couldn't help but wonder how they sounded. What noises they would make with her hands all over them. Pushing and pulling for them to go faster. And when she looked up, seeing that Moonbin was watching her, hands deep in his sweatpants, she wondered if she was still referring to the cars.

"Would you like a ride?"

"Are we allowed?"

Moonbin smiled and turned his head as he walked back to his black bike and grabbed his blue flamed helmet. He still remembered the day he had painted the neon flames onto it. It had been the same day Mikasa had finally earned enough money to by her very own bike after growing sick of the boys having all the fun. It had been the day he painted her bike with flames of its own, hot pink in color and wicked to the eye. It had been the first gift he had given her. The one he would proudly smile upon every time she took the lead in one of their usual races. *Better to be beaten by something I made than something I didn't*, he always thought.

He turned and held out the blue helmet.

"I wasn't talking about the cars."

Soyeon felt the gesture lick its way down to the infernal heat between her legs. She turned, leaning against the car, needing to feel something steady beneath her, her knees buckling. She felt her breath come out in small puffs and, after screaming at herself to pull it together, she faced him again and clasped her hands together.

"Maybe another time. Right now, I just want to find Soae."

Moonbin's smile faltered a bit and nodded, placing his helmet on top of his seat again. He bent down and quickly shoved the sullied clothes from before into the bag he kept under his seat. After dropping the bag next to the bike, he moved back to where Soyeon was and held out his arm.

"Ready, m'lady?"

She released a small laugh as she wrapped her hands around his bicep and gasped audibly at the hardness of it. Her hands couldn't even fit themselves around it. The veins beneath her fingers felt like steel and she could have sworn that she felt him flex.

Looking up, she saw something swirl in his eyes. His eyes searched hers for a moment, lost in their color.

"When are you free?"

"What?"

Moonbin leaned closer, his nose brushing against the shell of her ear.

"I said, when are you free? I need to show you how to ride at some point and I prefer it to be soon," he said, his voice causing her skin to prickle.

Soyeon didn't dare to move. One missed step and it—whatever this was—would be over and for some reason, she didn't want it to be.

"Tomorrow," she breathed, her breath fanning the space between them. Moonbin had to shut his eyes and clench his jaw to avoid leaning even closer to her sweet breath. He wondered if she tasted sweet as well.

"Then I'll come get you in the morning."

"Okay."

"Perfect," he grinned as he walked them towards the black door again. Soyeon ignored the tightening of her stomach when he placed his hand on her lower back, leading her through the door first. While Soyeon thought of ways to distract herself from her lustful imagination, Soae was upstairs, currently consumed by the painting before her.

The room they occupied was filled with paintings of different sizes, one more beautiful than the last, and while there were certainly more floral and theatrical paintings and sculptures around her, she had made a beeline to one of the biggest in the room.

The painting was massive, taking up most of the giant wall in front of her. The canvas was strained with dull red, white, and shallow ranges of black. The red was used in a range of incomplete circles, the shapes resembling upside-down cities, while the white served as the surface where the black was splattered, dotted, and blotched. It made Soae lean in closer, wanting to delve into the painting that filled her with "whys" and "hows."

"What did you say this was called again, Mr. Choi?"

Minseok, who was leaning against the wall a little further behind her, smiled at her formal use of his name and walked over, thumps in his belt loops.

"Suicide d'un Magnolia. Painted in 2017 by Jung Yeonmin."

"And how much did it sell for?"

"₩4,200,512."

Soae hummed and pulled herself back from the painting, turning Minseok.

"I would have thought it would have been more. It certainly looks like it's worth more."

Minseok nodded as he walked around her and looked at the painting next to them. It was painted pure black with a single swirl of white in the middle. It looked like a falling angel.

"In the world of art, some artists believe it should be unattainable. That it should be put into museums for those to only look but never touch or have the price tag so high, they could never own it. Then, there are artists like Jung Yeonmin, who paint with a passion so beyond comprehension that you are almost certain that she does it for the love of it, leaving money only a by-product of her love. In a world of auctioneers, there are still those who price their work fairly, even if who they are selling it to are the Parks."

Minseok lightly touched the white image with his fingers as he breathed it in. Soae watched him as he did this and felt her heart melt.

"How did you get into art?"

His eyes stayed on the painting.

"What do you mean?"

"You speak with so much passion about art, I just assume you have a love for it."

He dropped his hand and shifted his gaze to her, leaving his expression open.

"When I served in the 707, lots of my comrades were in to," he stopped, making sure he was picking the correct terms to use in front of a lady, "less than appropriate content. They often spent their spare time talking about the women in the videos they watched or their very own girlfriends. I was single and had no interest. So I turned to books. I read about war, love, loss, but art had it all. It brought me peace and sharpened my mind and so for that reason, I believe I never stopped learning and loving it."

Soae pictured the man in front of her suited up in top-to-bottom camo, guns of varying lengths in his trained hands. She tried to imagine him hunting the enemy and pulling the trigger if needed to, yet watching him…having seen him speak so passionately about art…witnessing the gentleness the pads of his fingers traced the falling white swirl. She couldn't even imagine him hurting a fly.

She walked over to him and stared at the painting.

"I can't picture you as a soldier."

Minseok smiled, "Because I'm old?"

Soae shook her head softly, turning to look at him.

"Because you're gentle."

Minseok's eyes blinked a few times before he smiled at her. He was touched that a complete stranger could see such a characteristic in him. One that opposed everything he had done and everything he was still doing.

"Ms. Seo, during the time that we have been talking, have you noticed that one other person has not joined our chat?"

Soae looked at him puzzled before whirling around, scanning the room covered in paintings for Soyeon. Panic made its way into her body, chest rising rapidly up and down and her eyes wide, when Minseok gently touched her elbow, causing her to look back at him.

"She'll be fine. The others and I are the only ones allowed to be in the home. If she is lost, then Mikasa and Moonbin would have found her by now."

Soae tried to calm down, but Minseok could still feel the tremors in her arm. He gently grabbed her shoulders and turned her to face him.

"If it makes you feel better, I will take you to the library. It is the place where the others and I always find ourselves when we feel lost or need space. If the others have found her, then that's where they would have brought her."

Soae eyebrows knitted together and while she still felt uneasy, she whispered a small, "Okay," to him as he moved her to the door of the room making them descend down the stairs. Minseok kept his gaze where their elbows interlocked and while noting the small dots of dirt that glittered the once clean step, he recalled something he had read once in a book.

Art outlives its human masters.

Yunseo shared this thought as he flipped through the first edition of Charlotte Brontë's *Jane Eyre*. The book had been large in size and skillfully styled in full tree calf with elaborately gilt-decorated spines, raised bands, as well as red and green Moroccan spine labels. When he had first opened the novel, he noted how aged it was, brown at its corners. The paper felt very thin and the lines were so close together, Yunseo was surprised that they hadn't merged. It was overwhelming and impressive to hold such an old and important book. He looked back up and scanned the shelves once more. The shelves, olive green wood that was smooth to the touch, reached from one end of the room to the other. It seemed to be a study but was as large as a living room. The furniture was two long and cushioned velvety blue couches in the middle of the room and an equally large clear coffee table decorated with coasters and, what Yunseo assumes, priceless flowers. The lilies brought light to the dark decor and highlighted the contrast between the two.

Mikasa and Subin had stepped out and were currently in the kitchen, retrieving glasses of water. Yunseo was asked to go with them, but after the day he had, all he wanted was some alone time.

Yunseo turned and moved around the ladder attached to one of the higher shelves, making his way over to a globe of the Earth. He placed his hand on it and turned it gently, eyes dancing across the Atlantic and Indian Oceans, over the mountains of Japan and landed on a red pin on Thailand. It was painted in an array of greens and highlights of gold and the label of the country was carefully written in calligraphy.

"That was a gift for my 20th birthday."

Startled, Yunseo jumped and dropped the book. The echo had rung out throughout the room and the books rattled as his hand grabbed onto one of the bookshelves behind him, avoiding falling himself. He quickly turned to see the intruder. It was, surprisingly, Minseo. Dressed in a seafoam green sweater with white leggings, she covered her mouth with her hands as her shoulders shook. Her nude nails were a stark contrast to the brightening of her face and the sight of her messy bun wiggling side to side made Yunseo laugh just as hard. Soon the library was filled with their loud laughter and the confused faces of six people.

"The hell was that," Soyeon said as she walked further into the room, leaving Moonbin's body cold in the absence of her warmth. For mere moments, Moonbin's feet followed after her before he could register the action.

"Oh—oh, it was nothing. I just scared Yunseo shitless."

"Language," Minseok hissed as he released Soae and plucked a glass of water from Mikasa's hand, to which she glared at him as he sat on one of the couches.

"Oh, don't show your age, Minseok. It's unattractive," said Minseo as she gathered herself and walked over to pick up the forgotten book from the floor. She dusted it off before handing it out to Yunseo.

"Make sure to sign it out before you leave."

Yunseo rolled his eyes and smiled.

"I feel bad for dropping such an old book."

"Don't worry. That's one of my mother's favorite books and she has dropped it several times so it's resilient."

Yunseo started to relax when Minseo continued.

"Now, if you dropped my *Pride and Prejudice* novel, I would have to throw you outside and turn on the sprinklers."

The room erupted into a symphony of laughter, as Yunseo stood there, visibly scared of the possibility of being drowned like his sister had the day before. When the noise died down, Subin held out a glass of water to Yunseo, to which he gladly took, gulping it down fiercely.

"So," Subin said, familiarity creeping around the edge of the singular word. "Will you be joining us for dinner tonight?"

Minseo tilted her head, her eyes landing on Minseok for an explanation.

"We," he said, lifting his hand and waved it around, "are going to BBQ tonight. Although, we don't know where yet."

Minseo felt a slight bump in her throat as she took in the number of people that would be coming with them. She has never been good with socializing, not after Sungmin's funeral.

"Don't worry, Sweettooth," Moonbin said. "We aren't going to a club afterward. Just family going out for dinner."

"Family," Yunseo said, puzzled at the sudden declaration.

"When you work for Taesung and his family," Minseok offered. "You are automatically family. So, for now, you're family."

"And," Mikasa chimed, tired of being silent. "If you ever need anything, you come to us for anything."

"We don't even have your numbers," Soyeon said.

"I can rectify that," Moonbin said.

Walking over, he held out his phone to her and waited for her to grab it. When she did, he noted the smooth chill that erupted in her body, caused by the metal covering of his phone. He guided her to his KakaoTalk and together, they managed to create a group chat consisting of all the members' numbers, excluding Minseo and Taesung.

"Employees deserve privacy too," Moonbin said. "I can't believe I had forgotten to take your number before. I won't forget something that important again."

Moonbin pulled the icy phone out of her warm hands. Her mind reeling on how close he had been to her. Again.

Mikasa made eye contact with him as he settled himself back into his spot. Their eyes spoke a language no one else could understand. Eyes widening and tightening when wanting to convey the exact words they couldn't voice out loud. Mikasa threw a glance at Soyeon and twitched her left eye, as if to say, *"Are you flirty with her?"*

Moonbin bit his lip, his brow arched as he responded with a resolute "Yes." Mikasa stifled a silent chuckle. Moonbin then turned to Soae and posed the same question.

"Maybe," Mikasa's expression said. *"Maybe."*

Yunseo was brought back from the display before him by Minseo grabbing onto his arm.

"Yes, Ms. Park."

Minseo's smile was bright and if Yunseo had a chance in another lifetime, he knew he would fall in love with her.

"Follow me."

Minseo led Yunseo to a connecting room while the others engaged in meaningless discussion. The room they entered was like the room before except instead of books there were windows with throne-like chairs before them. The large windows held no curtains and were as bare as can be. Settling herself on one of the plush chairs, she patted the one next to her. Yunseo sat in the chair and Minseo soon reached out and grabbed the old novel from his hands, placing her hand on the cover and lifting her head, eyes closed and expression peaceful. Yunseo looked upon it with a mixture of awe and jealousy. He couldn't remember the last time he had been so relaxed.

"We call this the Sun Room," she said, her eyes still closed. "Taesung and I would come here and watch our mother tend to the weeds and plant the freshest flowers money could buy. When she wasn't in the garden, we would just sit here on the cloudiest of days and watch as the rain rolled off the greenhouse like our own waterfall."

Yunseo marveled over the way she spoke Taesung's name so lovingly. It reminded him of when he once did the same.

"Just the two of you? What of your father?"

The words had slipped out of his mouth before he could stop them.

"Ms. Park, I—"

Minseo's fingers slipped slightly and her eyes reemerged, a sadness lingering in them.

"He does not come here. This residence belonged to my mother's family and he doesn't like sharing land with others."

Yunseo sat in peace as he watched Minseo open the ancient book, fingers tip lightly grazing the middle of the pages.

"Yunseo," she said. "Could you call me Minseo? I detest being so formal with you. I want us to be friends during your time here."

"What would your family think?"

Minseo smiled sweetly, her fingernail scraping the faded lettering.

"Do you hate the idea so much?"

"No—"

"Then you have nothing to worry about."

Yunseo was suddenly tired. Minseo teasing and wittiness reminded him of a certain man's and that only added to his exhaustion. He turned his head onto the serenity before them and gawked at the rose-colored jewel at the top of the greenhouse as it cast a tinted pink light onto the very room he was in. His hands were drowned in light and highlighted every wrinkle and fainted cut he had ever had. He turned to Minseo and swallowed. She bathed—no—commanded the light to shine on her. The soft hair at her nape curled forward and the freshness on her skin only made her look that much more unattainable.

"Yunseo, what is your favorite part of a book?"

The question caught him off guard. He rubbed his knuckles together as he beckoned an answer forth.

"The ending, I suppose," he offered. "Knowing that a story is over and that you can move on to the next without wondering if the characters ever relapsed."

Minseo weighted his answer in her mind as she closed the novel, handing it back to Yunseo's unsuspecting hands.

"Mine is the binding," she smiled. "The threading of the pages and the glue of the spine; brings me peace. Knowing that it was sewn to last a lifetime, regardless of its owner's obstacles. That it will be together no matter the tragedy," she shook her head. "Books are better than us in that way."

Soon the clock struck twelve-thirty, and the crew bid the M&Ms and Minseo goodbye. As Yunseo drove down the highway with his new companion sitting quietly on his lap, he stroked its spine, committing its ribs and scars to memory.

CHAPTER SEVEN

Everyone met in Seoul for dinner. Soyeon and Soae decided it was best for all of them to arrive together, suggesting it gave off a more united front. What they didn't account for was how different they all looked. Soyeon had worn a skin-tight black shirt with light colored jeans and a pair of white sneakers. She left her hair in the long black braid from before and added in silver jewelry for a bit of a more put together look. Soae wore a simple crop T-shirt with a long black skirt. She sported a low bun and golden jewelry that adorned her fingers, neck, and ears. Subin wore a dark orange sweater with an old pair of jeans. His sweater reminded Yunseo of an orange that only existed when the sun was setting, more red than yellow. Yunseo looked around the cab before looking down at his own outfit. A boring olive-green sweater on top of a black undershirt with black jeans. He didn't want to be there, let alone bring attention to himself, but he couldn't help wishing that he wore something a bit more exciting.

As the crew's exited their cab, they were greeted by the sight of four motorcycles coming down the street. They watched as Minseok lead the rest of the group into a large, empty parking spot.

"Hey guys," Mikasa said as she rushed over joyfully, helmet in hand.

"Hope we didn't let you guys wait too long. Someone wanted to race," she yelled over her shoulder, giving a pointed look to Moonbin. Moonbin threw her an eye roll while he turned off his bike and undid his gloves. He walked over and pulled Mikasa tight to his body, the breeze lovingly caressing his face.

"You're just mad that you lost."

"To Minseok, not you," she sneered as she pushed Moonbin off of her and walked towards Soae. "Hey sweetheart, doing well?"

Soae blushed and toyed with her hair as she responded, looking through her lashes.

"I'm fine, thank you. How are you?"

Mikasa smirked, picking up on the bashful behavior.

"I'm perfect, sweetheart. Absolutely perfect."

Mikasa leaned over to Soae's ear, brushing her golden earring with her nose. *Good, she looked so, so good.* Mikasa wanted to bite down and suck on her earlobe, imagining the sounds Soae might make. She often thought about those sounds at night, imagining her hands wrapped around the back of her thighs, holding them apart, with Soae begging her to stop out of ecstasy. Mikasa wondered how many orgasms she could coax out of the smaller woman, how she would react to her fingers moving in and out of her, curling at that special spot that sent her over the edge.

Mikasa hadn't called nor texted Soae since their flight two days ago. She had been busy with training, unable to find the time to reach out to the blonde woman. Mikasa was on the verge of calling Soae when Taesung briefed her that Soae and her friends had been hired to fly the family for the next year. She wanted to congratulate her, but Mikasa *knew.* She knew the moment that Soae picked up the phone and greeted Mikasa with that smooth and velvety voice of hers, Mikasa would be begging to see her, yearning to see what lay underneath that damn flight attendant uniform. It would have ended with neither of them sleeping for the rest of the night.

Oh, but how worth it, it would have been.

"I apologize for not texting you or calling you, Soae," Mikasa said, breathing heavily. "To make amends, I intend to spend the entire night getting to know you better. Then, when you're back home and relaxed, I'll call and pose the same questions all over again."

Soae felt light-headed by Mikasa's intoxicating perfume and reached out in front of her, grabbing onto the front of Mikasa's hoodie. She had never been so enraptured by a woman before. *Sure,* she thought, *I've liked girls and wanted to know what it was like to be with one.* Yet Soae never got the chance to explore that side of her. However, now, in front of Mikasa, she could think of nothing else than the promise that left Mikasa's soft lips.

"Why would you ask me the questions again? Wouldn't you have your answers?"

Soae could hear the grin in Mikasa's voice as she leaned even closer, her arm snaking around her waist, black chipped nails toying with the hem of Soae's skirt.

"To hear your voice, and when you tire of answering the same questions, I'll make up a billion more, just to keep you talking."

Mikasa heard Soae's breath hitch and felt the grip on her hoodie tighten. She chuckled quietly and placed a gentle kiss on Soae's temple, letting the scent of hairspray and roses wash over her.

Soyeon was going to intervene, wanting to know what the two were talking about until she made eye contact with the Moonbin's black frames. He was openly staring at her, hands in pockets with a lollipop in his mouth. *Did he always have that lollipop in his mouth?* Soyeon dropped her eyes down at the sweet trapped between the man's teeth.

He pulled the lollipop out of his mouth, swirling his tongue on the tip of it. Soyeon couldn't peel her eyes off the treat, mesmerized by the way this man was shamelessly displaying his skills in public. *Skills?* Was she really that sex-deprived that she believed this man was licking his sweet in a way to attract attention? Shaking her head in hopes of casting out such ridiculous notions, she looked back up, only to find that he had been watching her the entire time. He winked at her, secretly hinting that he knew what he was doing. How it was affecting her. Clearing her throat, she looked down at her shoes before looking back up, finding Moonbin now wearing a full blown smile. He nodded his head towards her and walked over, taking hold of her hand.

"Soyeon," he purred. "You look absolutely stunning."

Soyeon's eyes were glued to where his lips were, skin burning.

"You look handsome as well," she said, her words coming out higher pitched than she intended.

Moonbin smirked at her voice as he toyed with her hand, his other coming up to pull down on his glasses ever so slightly

"I aim to please."

Soyeon groaned quietly in her mind as Moonbin's smirk seared itself deep into her mind and began to pray that someone would save her from this man and the thoughts he conjured up in her mind.

"Anyone hungry," Minseok said as he walked over towards them, Taesung only a few steps behind.

Thank you, Jesus! I knew you loved me.

Minseok's white turtleneck and brown trench coat had been a stark contrast to what he had worn earlier that day. He usually chose to wear more casual clothing when working but tended to dress up more when going out. Unlike Mikasa, who had decided to wear a simple dark red hoodie and black jeans and Moonbin with his white T-shirt and black leather jacket. Though Taesung was always well dressed, Minseok was caught off guard when he met up with Taesung earlier that night. Taesung, someone who he had known to wear a simple dress shirt and jeans whenever they went out, opted for a tight, short sleeved turtleneck and a pair of his fancied white trousers. Looked like he was going to a fancy dinner then some hole in the wall for some *samgyupsal gui* and soju.

"Starving," Subin replied, rubbing his hands together in excitement. He had been excited all day at the prospect of meat and soju on someone else's dime. Subin looked around for Minseo, seeing how nervous she was to hear about their plans when they mentioned it to her as they left her home. "No Minseo?"

Mikasa shook her head as she moved back from Soae's hair and kissed her hands before stepping a few paces back, thinking it best to not rush their developing situation. She looked at Subin and thrusted her hands into her hoodie, Seoul's air growing colder by the second. No matter how long she had been in South Korea, she could never get used to its unforgiving weather. Don't get her wrong, Japan was very cold, especially in the rural areas, but South Korea was a whole different beast. One that she was sure she could never tame.

"No," she said. "She was happy when the waffles Taesung got her and decided to stay home with Mrs. Park."

Taesung smiled at the memory of Minseo's cream covered face and directed his attention back onto the group. The two quartets looked impossible different from one another, but together they fix like puzzle pieces long lost to one another. His eyes found Yunseo and the breath in his lungs was stolen by the sight. He wore a soft olive-green sweater with a black shirt underneath it and had jeans of the same color, sculpting every outline of his lean legs. His hair, *god his hair*, was tousled and softly blowing in the wind. Taesung shifted his feet and swore at the growing pain forming between his legs.

I'm not going to last any longer like this.

"Let's go, everyone. The reservation is in five minutes and the place is just down the street," Taesung announced as he met everyone's eyes and settled on Yunseo, taking in his appearance.

He allowed himself a few seconds of staring before waving to everyone to follow him down the street. Following him, everyone was overjoyed with the promise of a good time while Yunseo was slowly recognizing his surroundings. They were in Itaewon and were heading towards a very, very familiar building. The horror didn't set in until the words 아줌마의 바베큐 came into view. Auntie's Barbeque was a restaurant Taesung had introduced to Yunseo when he had first told him he had never visited Itaewon. Taesung was shocked and promised to show him a good time. Auntie's Barbeque had been their first date. And, their second. And, their third. It was their place. Their very *special* place. So special, he hadn't been back here in five years.

"Hello, Auntie? I have a surprise for you," yelled Taesung as he entered and walked toward the back of the restaurant.

Yunseo tried to make a run for it but was stopped when Soyeon hurried him inside so she could close the door. Feeling like there was no way out, he rushed inside and hid behind Subin once he saw a familiar pair of bunny slippers come his way.

"Aigoo, is that Park Yunseo that I see there? Come over here and hug Big Momma," exclaimed a short Asian woman wearing a visor and an apron with the words, "GIVE MOMMA SOME SUGAR," on it. Her hair was permed, eyes aged with joy and laughter, and wore flowery pants to top it all off. Yunseo couldn't stop his body from moving forward as she approached him.

He buried his head into her neck when she wrapped her arms around him, petting his head the way she did when he was younger.

"It has been forever since you've visited me! I have missed seeing you two every Friday! What happened," Big Momma begged as she stopped to hug Yunseo, keeping him at arm's length, trying to get a good look at the boy who always tried her crazy food ideas.

"Oh! Um… school got to me, Big Momma. I just couldn't find the time anymore," Yunseo lied as he nervously shifted weight from one foot to another.

"Oh, that's terrible, but why did Taesung just dis—"

"Alright, Big Momma. I'll tell you everything another day, but right now my friends and I are very, very hungry," Taesung interrupted, guiding Big Momma to one of the largest tables in the restaurant.

Her laughter was full of merit as she patted Taesung's hands on her shoulders and spun around to squeeze his cheeks.

"Oh, fine, but I expect a full explanation after. Now introduce me to everyone."

"These," Taesung cut in, leading Big Momma to the front of the M&Ms, each one bowing, "are my friends: Minseok, Mikasa, and Moonbin."

"Mikasa," Big Momma questioned, her hands making their way to her waist, as if she were to scold the red head. "Isn't that a Japanese name?"

Internally, Mikasa rolled her eyes as she exchanged a knowing look with Taesung, who tried to reassure her as subtly as possible that it wasn't what she thought it was.

Sighing, Mikasa bowed again and, making direct eye contact, spoke.

"Yes, ma'am, it is. I am from Shibuya City. I moved here three years ago after meeting Taesung when he was on a business trip. South Korea has been my home ever since."

The crew held their breath as Big Momma squinted her eyes and hummed, while the others braced themselves for one of two outcomes: 1) Big Momma berating Mikasa for perceived sins still contaminating South Korea for centuries, or 2) Big Momma on the ground with her arm twisted behind her back before anyone could blink. Moonbin looked at Minseok, signaling him to ready himself for whatever might happen next.

But instead, Big Momma raised her hand and, to Mikasa's surprise, pulled her into a tight hug, squeezing the daylights out of her.

"Oh, how wonderful! My son just came back from his honeymoon visiting Osaka. What a wonderful coincidence."

Soae watched as Mikasa's shoulders relaxed and she hugged the woman back, a smile now replacing the downturned corners of her lips. Moonbin and Minseok smirked at each other, relieved that options one and two had been avoided. Big Momma released Mikasa and greeted the rest of the group, squeezing everyone's cheeks and remarking on how beautiful and handsome they all were, cracking jokes that she herself used to be quite the looker.

"I don't know, Big Momma," Subin said, leaning closer to the woman as she led the group through the tables and towards the back. "You look pretty attractive right now. I can't imagine it getting any better."

Big Momma laughed and swatted at his arm as he winked at her flushing cheeks.

"Such a flirt," Big Momma said.

The table before them was long and square, with a copper-colored grill in the middle and a ventilator on top. Yunseo settled himself further towards the end of the table as the others bid Big Momma farewell, Subin and Taesung each planting a kiss on her waiting cheeks. She soon spotted Yunseo and hurried over to him, leaving a sloppy, mother-like kiss on his cheek.

"Oh, how I've missed you, my dear," she said as she stroked his cheek, leaving him aching with guilt for not visiting her. By the time everyone settled into their seats, they were still laughing and talking about how cute Big Momma was.

"What a cute ahjumma," Subin joked as he sat next to Moonbin.

"Oh! Don't let her hear you say that. I have a feeling meat won't be the only thing we will be peeling off the grill tonight," Moonbin added as he bummed Subin's shoulder playfully.

"Yeah, you may be right," laughed Soyeon as she settled herself onto Soae's right side and Mikasa settled herself on Soae's left, not wanting to miss an opportunity to be closer to the blonde haired woman.

Taesung had picked a chair diagonally across from Yunseo. Yunseo acted like he didn't notice this, pretending to be too engaged with the conversation beside him to even notice the man's presence.

"I'm thinking of samgyeopsal, yangnyeom galbi, chadolbaegi, and soju," announced Minseok as he saw the server approached the table with a large tray of side dishes.

"Can we also get some mul naengmyeon, bibim maengmyeom, and rice please," added Mikasa, pouring herself some water from a jug placed at the end of the table.

Minseok nodded his head and finished the order by adding some beer for Moonbin and Taesung, knowing they'd give him hell for not ordering it.

As the food began to slowly come out, the table quieted into small talk, though Yunseo didn't participate much in the conversation. He was all too aware of a certain pair of dark brown eyes on him. Yunseo grabbed onto the cold beer bottle that was pushed into his hand and downed about half of it before coming back for air. Minutes passed and as the beer infused with his body and manipulated his brain chemistry, he found the courage to look up at those eyes.

Big mistake.

Yunseo felt his body pinned to his seat as his gaze locked with Taesung's. Taesung was bigger and taller, appearing to have gained thirty pounds of muscle since they last met. His eyes, nose, and lips appeared sharper than before, and his hair was styled differently, no longer the platinum blonde from years past. Despite these changes, Taesung's eyes remained the same; Yunseo recalled how they made him feel safe and grounded every time he looked into them. Now, he wished they had changed too.

Yunseo had only allowed himself to hear Taesung's voice, never truly looking at him. Not in Thailand or at Mrs. Park's house. He allowed his eyes to trail down from his face to his arms. The once pale skin was now tanned and had more protruding veins then before. There was a bright red line that curved around the back of both of his biceps, but Yunseo couldn't get a good look at it from where he sat. Curiosity was starting to nudge at Yunseo when Taesung turned his head to take a drink from his beer. He saw that there was a red tattoo behind his ear. He just couldn't make it out. Before he could lean in and try to, he was pulled in by Mikasa and handed a shot of soju.

"Geonbae," cheered the entire group as Soae and Soyeon giggled and Moonbin and Minseok high-fived each other.

"Man! Two fucking months without soju. Feels good," Moonbin rejoiced as he refilled his glass.

"I hear you," Minseok agreed.

"Why haven't you guys drunk soju in the past two months," questioned Soyeon as she played with the rim of her beer bottle.

Moonbin stared at her index finger for a few seconds before answering.

"Trainer's orders. The bastard has had us on a special diet. It's been killing us."

"Us?"

"Minseok, Mikasa, and myself. We all have to train and workout together every day. Taesung joins from time to time."

"So, you're breaking orders," Soyeon remarked as she picked up her metal chopsticks and placed strips of marinated beef onto the hot grill.

Moonbin tilted his head.

"Yeah, I guess you can say that."

"Won't you get in trouble?"

Moonbin smirked and leaned in her direction.

"Trouble is something I'm very, very familiar with. What about you?"

Soyeon raised her eyebrows.

"What about me?"

"Are you a good girl who follows the rules? Or, are you someone who likes the thrill of breaking them?"

Soyeon felt her face heat up as she reached for her beer. She had never expected to be asked such a question, especially in public! If they were private like before, then maybe she would feel differently. If they were back in that garage with him still holding out his helmet to her, maybe then she wouldn't question why she was feeling two heartbeats in her body.

"Oh! Soyeon was a total troublemaker back in college. She almost got into a fight with a girl who believed her boyfriend was cheating on her with me," Soae remarked as she took another shot of soju.

"Why would she think that," Mikasa inquired, smiling at Soae's loose tongue.

"Because she was a lowlife with nothing better to do than bother Soae with her insecurities," Soyeon hissed as she polished off her beer and waved down the server for another one. Moonbin watched her with amusement and made a mental note to set an alarm on his phone to ensure he would be early for their date tomorrow. He couldn't risk fucking it up. He needed to see more of this side. He didn't know why, but he needed, wanted, *craved* to see more of it. More of *her*.

"Taesung," Subin said after stuffing a piece of beef into his mouth. "What's the story between you and Yunseo. How did you two meet?"

Yunseo felt his stomach drop. He worried this would happen. He looked over at Taesung, seeing one of the corners of his mouth quirk upward into a sly grin. Yunseo knew that grin and wished he was the one currently downing shots with Mikasa instead of Soae.

"We met in a bookstore," Taesung replied as he took another shot of soju, downing it with some beer. "Isn't that right, Yunseo?"

Yunseo felt the alcohol rumble inside his stomach. His grip grew taut around his beer bottle, a detail Taesung didn't miss. Yunseo ran his tongue along the inside of his mouth before drawing in a deep breath.

"Yes! I used to work at a bookstore and he walked in needing help with a purchase."

Subin looked back and forth between the two before narrowing his eyes.

"Is that it?"

"What," Yunseo choked.

"You guys obviously were closer than that."

Taesung chuckled as he made eye contact with Subin.

"Oh, we were. We spent almost everyday together. We were best friends, really."

Stop talking, you fucking monster. Stop pulling our memories from the well I threw them in.

"Wow! Really," Subin exclaimed, his eyes darting back and forth between the two individuals. "Yunseo never mentioned anything."

Taesung glanced at Yunseo, ignorant of the fact that the smaller man's knees were growing weak as if he were about to collapse from his chair. Yunseo clutched his beer bottle tightly to his chest, his knuckles burning bright. His sleeves covered his hands, giving him a vulnerable, childlike appearance. He seemed small and timid. Taesung's hands twitched, longing to reach out and hold him. A lump formed in his throat, which he cleared in an attempt to regain his composure.

"I'm sure he didn't. It was a long time ago. I'm surprised he remembers me. I thought I would never see him again when I left for Thailand," Taesung said.

Subin wanted to delve into what had happened for him to make such a statement, but their server returned with a large, heavy-looking plate. The aroma of bread and beans filled the air as she cleared away some empty plates and set the tray down on the table, directly in front of Yunseo.

Yunseo stared at the horror in front of him.

Bungeoppang.

The fish-shaped treat was the first thing Taesung had brought for Yunseo upon his return to the bookstore. He was leaner, his platinum blonde hair tucked under a black Nike hoodie, topped with a black leather jacket adorned with various colorful patches. His outfit was otherwise simple: faded jeans and a pair of blue Converse sneakers. However, his hands concealed something behind his back, prompting Yunseo to raise an eyebrow as Taesung approached the counter. While Yunseo packaged his novel, he felt Taesung looking at him. Trying to divert attention from himself, he inquired about Taesung's thoughts on the book he had first purchased.

"How did you like the *Third Grave Dead Head?*"

"Loved it," Taesung whispered in a low, rough tone.

"What was your favorite part," Yunseo said, his fingers deftly wrapping the novel.

"Reyes," Taesung replied, his voice carrying a hint of mischief.

"Really," Yunseo's eyebrows shot up as he passed the book back to Taesung.

"He was quite something," Taesung remarked, his fingers lingering on top of Yunseo's hand for a moment longer than necessary. "Especially in that scene where he pinned the main character against the sink in her bathroom."

Startled by the sparks erupting from their touch, Yunseo quickly pulled his hand away.

"That scene caught your attention?"

Taesung nodded, a sly smile playing on his lips.

"That's not the only thing I found captivating."

Yunseo felt a hot flush creep its way over his body, his hands growing clammy and his heart racing. Taesung's smile only intensified the pounding of his heart.

"I even brought you something," Taesung said, placing a brown paper bag into Yunseo's hands.

"Bungeoppang! I love them! How did you know," Yunseo exclaimed as he retrieved the treat from the bag.

"Lucky guess," Taesung winked as he sauntered towards the exit of the store. "See you later, Little Star."

Yunseo always appreciated the nickname, finding it endearing that Taesung had coined it from the stars drawn on his name tag. It had always served as a conversation starter, but Taesung had been the first to give him a nickname—one that he had always used with affection.

Five years later, Yunseo found himself battling to suppress the bile rising in his throat. He had believed he was adept at concealing his reaction until he glanced up and encountered Taesung's concerned gaze. He lost his mind soon after.

CHAPTER EIGHT

Afraid of causing a scene, Yunseo dashed to the nearest bathroom, his heart pounding against his ribs. He needed to escape Taesung's smothering. Relief washed over him as he found an empty sanctuary, a large, welcoming stall beckoning to him. With trembling hands, he pushed the door shut behind him, the click echoing in the silence.

Barely able to contain the rising tide of nausea, Yunseo dropped to his knees in front of the toilet bowl. Tears streamed down his face as he emptied his stomach, the acidic taste of bile burning his throat. Gripping the sides of the seat, he clung to the porcelain like a lifeline, finding solace in the physicality of his discomfort. Despite the disgusting nature of the situation, Yunseo found it preferable to the harsh reality awaiting him outside.

A noise behind him snapped him out of his reverie, but he dismissed it as the stall door banging against its frame. After what felt like an eternity, he rose unsteadily to his feet, the aftermath of his ordeal lingering in the air like a heavy fog. With a deep breath, he flushed the toilet and made his way to the sink.

Turning on the faucet, he let the cool water cascade over his hands, washing away the remnants of his ordeal. Methodically, he scrubbed his mouth and face, each motion a deliberate act of cleansing. He rubbed his eyes vigorously, as if the memory of Taesung would fall out from his eyes and down the drain.

"If you rub any harder, an eyeball may fall out."

Startled, Yunseo looked up to see Taesung leaning against the wall, a smirk playing on his lips. The sight of him sent a shiver down Yunseo's spine, a reminder of the tangled web of emotions he had long tried to bury.

"Why the fuck are you here right now," Yunseo demanded, his voice tinged with bitterness.

Taesung's eyebrows shot up in mock surprise.

"Well," he grunted as he leaned forward a bit. "I guess that was a warmer welcome than I was expecting," he finished with a grin.

Yunseo turned around at this, a little too quickly, sending his hands scattering behind him for a good grip on the sink; the sink was the only thing keeping him grounded in this otherwise unthinkable situation. Yunseo clenched his jaw, the muscle in his cheek ticking.

"Are you kidding," Yunseo breathed, straightening himself up. "I'm lucky enough to not be having a panic attack right now."

Taesung tilted his head to the side as he exhaled a tight breath.

"But, you are."

"What?"

"Your hands," he began, stepping forward, hands slipping out of his pockets. "You've been trembling since the minute you laid eyes on me."

Yunseo looked down and, to his surprise, he was shaking. It angered him that Taesung still remembered this. Remembered such intimate details of himself.

"How did you know that?"

Taesung scanned the ceiling before replying.

"I remember when I had to hold you whenever you recounted arguments with your parents." Taesung looked at him remorsefully. "I counted the minutes it took for your body to stop trembling."

Yunseo saw red.

"Had? When you *had* to hold me?"

He had said the wrong thing. He just didn't know how to talk to Yunseo. Not after all this time.

"What are you doing here, anyway," Taesung said as he leaned back on the wall. "I doubt that sister of yours would allow you to be out drinking so late."

"Don't speak about her!"

110

Taesung's hands up in surrender, not wanting to anger Yunseo anymore than he had.

"I'm a grown man and I can do whatever the fuck I want," Yunseo said as he pushed off from the sink. "I've been out before and have drank with many men."

Yunseo decided to leave out the part that most of those outings had been friends and some were women. He wanted to see how angry Taesung would get. He remembered that Taesung could be quite jealous when it came to him.

The muscle residing inside of Taesung's cheek twitched, his teeth grinding on one another. He hadn't expected Yunseo to wait for him after everything, but to hear this, and seeing him for the first time in years, was almost too much.

"Did they fuck well?"

"Fuck you," Yunseo roared and lunged himself toward Taesung, his fingers curling into fists as he grabbed for the older man's collar. His chest heaved with pent-up fury, every muscle coiled with tension as he sought to unleash the torrent of emotions swirling within him.

"You used to," Taesung's voice was a low, taunting drawl as he effortlessly flipped them over, reversing their positions with a fluidity that left Yunseo reeling. The sudden power shift sent a jolt of adrenaline coursing through Yunseo's veins, his hands grasping desperately at Taesung's arms for support as he found himself caged between the wall and the imposing figure before him.

Taesung's breath was hot against his ear, his voice a seductive whisper that sent shivers down Yunseo's spine.

"I can still remember the noises you would make," he murmured, his lips tantalizingly close as he relished in the memory of their past encounters. "Some nights, I can still feel your nails digging deep into my back."

"You son of a bit—," the sentence hung in the air as Yunseo shift and lowered himself onto Taesung's knee. He looked and saw that it was just below his bulge. Taesung followed his eyes and noticed the same. He tried carefully to remove his leg, but it bummed against Yunseo again, ripping out a noise from his throat—a shameful, embarrassing, and damning sound that echoed in the small space. Taesung's eyes danced between Yunseo's lips and eyes, waiting for him to stop him, but with such hunger and intensity, Yunseo didn't want to.

Shit. I might fuck him right here, Taesung thought. *If he allowed me to, I would have him bent over the sink. I'd do anything to feel those hands on me again.*

Taesung slowly, ever so slowly, moved his knee back into place and brought it up and down, relishing in the way Yunseo trembled beneath him. He smiled as Yunseo bit into his hand, the sensation sending a shiver through Yunseo's body, and brought his other hand against Taesung's chest. Taesung waited, anticipation building as he waited for Yunseo to push him away.

Don't let him see his effect on you, he said to himself. *You can—*

Taesung applied more pressure.

"*Shibal,*" Yunseo blurted, his hands slamming onto Taesung's chest, fingers digging into the fabric as he clamped down around his knee. Tremors wracked his body as he approached his climax, biting desperately into his lip, the taste of metal coating his tongue. "I'm gonna come!"

Taesung grabbed onto Yunseo's hips and pressed him down harder onto his knee, his body ablaze with desire. In that moment, the restroom faded into obscurity as his focus narrowed solely on Yunseo. He yearned to bring him pleasure, to make him come undone in his grasp, yet as he glanced up from Yunseo's trembling legs and saw the desperation in his eyes, the effort to stifle any sounds of their illicit encounter. Taesung released him, pushing himself against the opposite wall, locking eyes with Yunseo, his gaze filled with shame and regret.

"I didn't come here for that," Taesung said, his lungs fighting for air. "I didn't want it to happen this way."

Yunseo braced himself on his knees, his gaze falling to the tiled floor. He fought to suppress the rising tide of frustration threatening to consume him, clenching his teeth in a desperate bid to stifle any screams that threatened to escape.

"Yunseo," Taesung said, reaching out to touch his shoulder. Yunseo recoiled, keeping his hands firmly planted on his knees.

"Don't fucking touch me," Yunseo spat, staring up at Taesung with a hatred he had never witnessed before. "I hate you."

Where the Stars Remember Us

Taesung's heart seemed to stop beating, his breath catching in his throat as Yunseo's words wrapped around his throat. After what they had just done, to hear Yunseo say such a thing—it felt like a dagger to his chest. With a heavy heart, Taesung pushed off from the wall and strode towards the door, leaving Yunseo dazed and disoriented in his wake. The bathroom felt so empty, the air thick with the weight of their unresolved emotions as Yunseo struggled to make sense of what had just transpired.

For several agonizing minutes, Yunseo remained rooted to the spot, his mind a whirlwind of conflicting emotions. His breath came in shallow gasps, each inhale a struggle against the consuming weight of his own turmoil. He clenched his fists until his knuckles turned white, his heart pounding like a drumbeat in his chest.

Disappointment gnawed at him from within, a bitter reminder of his own perceived weakness in the face of his past. He had prided himself on his self-control, on his ability to keep his emotions in check even in the most trying of circumstances. Yet here he was, unraveling at the seams like a tattered tapestry, his facade of composure crumbling before his very eyes.

He bowed his head, his hands interlocking tightly as he sought solace in the cold embrace of the bathroom floor. The tiles were the exact opposite of Taesung's warmth, a tangible reminder of their separation. He felt like an old building in the suburbs, beautiful on the outside but crumbling within, his exterior masking the fragile vulnerability lurking just beneath the surface.

Yunseo returned to the table to find Soae singing to the entire group, using a spoon and an empty soju bottle as a makeshift microphone. Her hair, once tightly wrapped in a bun, now had strands framing her face, while her free hand gathered her skirt and waved it back and forth, as if she were trying to tempt a bull. Yunseo glanced over at the rest of the table and felt his mood slightly improve. Moonbin and Minseok were her backup dancers, Mikasa was recording the whole ordeal, Subin held up the phone with the music, Soyeon was laughing, and Taesung sitting still, picking apart one of the bungeoppangs that still laid untouched in front of Yunseo's empty seat, as if he were asking questions to a flower.

"Yunseo," Soae slurred as she held out the impaled bottle, "sing with me."

Yunseo looked around at the group as they cheered. He understood they must have been drinking while he was gone, but what he didn't understand was why he was doing the tango with Soae while Moonbin was dipping a flustered-looking Soyeon.

Moonbin's hands nestled perfectly around her waist, just below her ribcage. As he guided her through twists and turns, he couldn't help but notice how her curves felt firm and full against his hardened body, like a missing puzzle piece. He savored her response to each movement. The soft inhalations of breath as he drew her closer, the occasional grip of her fingers on his shirt when he changed direction abruptly, and her eyes... *Fuck*. Her gaze traced his features as if committing them to memory. It sent chills down his spine. It had been a long time since Moonbin had been with a woman, and now, the prospect was becoming increasingly addictive, especially with his hands firmly grasping her ample hips.

Yunseo's eyes remained fixed on Moonbin and Soyeon, enchanted by their graceful twirls that filled his heart with joy. They seamlessly and effortlessly complemented each other's steps and it created a captivating scene in the cramped restaurant, transcending physical boundaries.

Immersed in the intensity of their gazes, Yunseo grappled with overwhelming emotions, the lump in his throat growing heavier. Blinking back threatening rivers, he pressed on with his singing, harmonizing with Soae while stealing glances at Taesung.

Observing him, Yunseo noticed a vacant expression, a voided of emotion in stark contrast to Moonbin and Soyeon's warmth. Yunseo wished for the night to end and the comforting graces of his pillows.

As the song came to its conclusion and the server ushered the group into their seats, the rest of the customers applauded, delighted to see such a display of youth. Soae swayed as she grabbed for her seat, awaiting its slightly dull wooden corners, yet all she felt was air. It took a second and a pair of hands to realize that she had missed and was in the process of falling when Mikasa caught her.

"Thank you," Soae said as Mikasa guided them upright, her words dipping at the ends.

"Don't worry," said Mikasa as she placed Soae into her seat, earning a look from her visually impaired friend. "I'll always catch you."

Soae looked away as her hands slid from Mikasa's fingertips and cupped her cheeks, making them puff up like pastries. Mikasa wanted to bite them.

Subin checked his watch and realized how late it had gotten. He downed the rest of his drink and waved his hands at the group, trying to draw their attention.

"Guys," he exclaimed. "We should get out of here, it's getting pretty late."

Soae opened her mouth to argue, but Soyeon slapped a hand over it.

"Yes," she said, thinking of the ways she would have to get Soae to their apartment tonight. "I think that is a great idea."

"You're not leaving already, are you," Moonbin queried, his hands still remembering the feeling of her body trapped between them.

"I have to," she replied. "Whenever she is like this, I have to take care of her," she said as she lifted Soae, placing one of her hands firmly around her friend's waist. "Unless you want to see her dancing topless to Rihanna."

"Rihanna," laughed Mikasa.

Smiling, Soyeon began to gather their things.

"College was a fun ride."

Mikasa smiled at the prospect of experiencing those moments while the rest of the group rose and collected their things; Moonbin sneaked one last piece of meat before following the others.

Taesung was the first to stand and beeline it to Big Momma, who was greeting a young couple. Taesung glared at the couple and their interlaced hands. He longed for the same. Once finished, Big Momma greeted him.

"Already leaving? I felt like the show was just starting."

Taesung plastered a smile on his face and let out a sound that resembled a laugh.

"Yes, well, it's best to get the ladies home."

Big Momma tilted her head.

"And Yunseo? Are you taking him home too?"

Taesung grimaced and shut his eyes tightly, willing the prickling sensation behind his eyelids to cease their relentless assault. He knew the tears would inevitably come, perhaps he'll let them fall later when he was alone in the solace of his residence. Its stark, colorless interior would provide the perfect backdrop for his evening: a glass of scotch accompanied by the silence of his tears.

"No," he said, passing her his card. "Not tonight."

Big Momma took the card, and as she swiped the plastic object, she looked back over at the group that neared them. They seemed so alive and filled with joy. She thought the group was wonderful, even the Japanese girl. So why were her favorite people in the world so miserable?

"What happened," she finally asked, placing the card in his hand, "to my lovesick boys?"

Taesung shook his head and cast his eyes to the entrance, unable to face Big Momma.

"I ruined it, Momma," his voice barely audible as the group drew closer. "I ruined us."

Her heart sank, and she reached for his hand, but he stepped out of her reach.

"Please hand the bungeoppangs to Yunseo to take home. I'll come back to visit soon."

Taesung walked out as his parade of friends and acquaintances followed behind him, each one bowing and thanking Big Momma for the delicious food and the wonderful hospitality. Subin squeezed between the giant Moonbin and the fidgeting Yunseo to kiss the old woman on her cheek, one that she returned as well. The group had walked out of the restaurant, and Yunseo was following, giving a kiss to Momma and turning to leave when she stopped him, handing him a bag that their server was giving to her.

"Wait! Taesung wanted you to have these," she said as she handed him a takeout bag. By the smell, Yunseo knew what it was and passed it back to her.

"I don't want it."

"But Taesung wanted you to have it," she insisted as she pushed the bag back into his hand.

116

"I don't care what he wants," Yunseo growled as he picked up the bag and threw it into a trash can stationed next to them.

Big Momma brought her hands to her lips as she watched in horror.

"You two were so in love, Yunseo. So incredibly in love."

He clenched his hands into fists at the weak voice of his beloved Big Momma before giving her a quick hug goodbye. He rushed outside, feeling his heart beat faster. The night had grown colder, and the streets were beginning to fill with college kids and trash. He looked over at Soyeon and Soae, thrusting his hands underneath his armpits.

"Where is your car," Moonbin said, coming to stand next to the shivering women, Mikasa behind him.

"We don't have a car," Soae giggled. "Too much money."

Moonbin laughed and ruffled her hair, "I'm sure it is, little one."

Soyeon smiled at the tender way he treated the drunk Soae, speaking to her as if she were five years old and not the twenty-three-year-old woman that she was.

"I'm just gonna get a cab. We should be home in no time."

The two bodyguards nodded as they came to stand in front of them, each of them grabbing their respective woman's hands. They placed a kiss on their hands, and while Mikasa lingered, Moonbin lifted his eyes to Soyeon's, trying to capture their last moments together for the night.

"I'll see you tomorrow," his voice came out as smooth as silk. It struck something deep in Soyeon. So deep, she hooked her foot against the other, breathing in as much of the crisp Seoul air as possible.

"Tomorrow."

The promise hung between them as he watched the two women climb safely into a cab and drive off.

Turning towards the rest of the group, he felt his eyes grow heavy and thought it best to go home as well.

"I'm packing it in."

Minseok raised a brow.

"You? The man always left standing after our drinking marathons, is calling it a night," Minseok said mockingly. "I'm shocked!"

Moonbin rolled his eyes as he hugged his friends goodbye and waved at Subin and Yunseo. Walking over and fastening his flamed helmet, he revved the bike, scaring a few bystanders. Smirking, he rode home, thinking over and over about the feeling in his hands and the throbbing of his heart.

"And then there were five," said Subin, rubbing his hands together. "Are the rest of you tired?"

Taesung looked over at Yunseo as his friends remarked a boisterous "No". He wouldn't look at him. Yunseo wouldn't give him the satisfaction.

Taking the other two men's silence as agreements, Subin suggested going into Gwangjang Market, stating that he could go for some more beer and meat. The others agreed, and as they walked their way over to the market, Subin took note of their formation. Yunseo and himself walked in the front, Taesung and the other falling behind them. Mikasa was to his right, Minseok to his left, and for the first time since they had met, Subin could see the danger they imposed. The way they walked. The way their eyes scanned the crowd and held their hands against their sides, ready to strike any attacker that dared to show himself, all scared Subin. He started to question if working for and with such people was such a good idea after all.

The market was loud and colorful. Speakers from inside thundered with different types music: K-pop, trot, Khip-hop, etc., and the various choices of beer, dessert, and meals all started to invade their senses, luring them closer to the warm haven in front of them. The place had been packed and filled with foreigners, yet the lines were short and the prices cheap. The flags of different countries flapping overhead made Yunseo smile. His eyes traced the Thai flag and gazed at the others that he wanted to travel to. All those countries. All those possibilities. All those stories untold. Yunseo had to look forward again to avoid bumping into an ahjussi as his mind floated back from paradise.

Subin had rushed to a vendor selling so tteok so tteok and cans of Cass that was near the entrance. The man selling the so tteok was kind and smiled behind his mask as he lifted his arm to wipe the sweat off his forehead, offering a quick bow as he listened intently to Subin's order.

"Good evening, sir," said Subin, pointing to the pile of so tteok in front of him. "May I have five skewers and one beer?"

Nodding, the man placed the glazed mini sausage and rice cake skewers into a cardboard box, placing a can of beer on top.

"That would be five dollars and fifty cents, cash only please."

Subin handed the man the money and turned towards the group with the goods.

"Everyone take one, I wanna eat more things after this."

Smiling, they did as they were told and groaned at the smoky flavor that coated their tongues.

"This is delicious," Mikasa said as she went in for a second bite. "I don't think I've had this before."

"Really," said Yunseo, wiping his mouth with one of the napkins that the old man had managed to give them. "I thought you said that you've lived here for three years."

"I have, but as a bodyguard."

"So?"

Mikasa rolled her eyes.

"So," she said as she lifted her hoodie, causing Yunseo's eyes to bulge and Minseok and Taesung to bark out laughing. "You don't get abs like these eating like this."

Yunseo brought his hand over his belly as he laughed at the toned stomach of Mikasa and Subin stupidly poking at the cubes of muscle.

This was turning out to be such a multifaceted night, he thought to himself, throwing the empty wooden stick back into its takeout box. The group followed Subin to another vendor, requesting another can of Cass and one of their twisted doughnuts when Minseok's phone buzzed in his pocket. Looking down and smiling at the letter "A" that popped up on his phone, he pulled Taesung aside.

"Something came up. I gotta get home. You'll be fine with just Mikasa, right?"

"Is the sky blue," Taesung smirked.

"Technically, it's black right now."

"Just go, you idiot," said Taesung, rolling his eyes at his smart-mouthed friend. Minseok called out to the others about his departure and quickly made his way back to his motorcycle, excited at the surprise that awaited him.

By the fifth vendor and the fourth beer, Subin was toast. He swayed on his feet, and Mikasa was the one holding him up. *What a baby,* she thought. Yunseo, a little ways behind, was making his way to them when he was bombarded with the smell of bindaetteok. Like a child to the Pied Piper, Yunseo followed the smell to a young-looking woman, flattening the mung bean batter onto the hot and oily surface of a long stove. The browning corners and the golden center of the pancake made Yunseo's mouth water, and he wondered when was the last time he had had bindaetteok.

"I can buy you one if you like."

Yunseo didn't turn around.

"I don't want anything from you."

Taesung sighed heavily, growing tired of their childish back and forth.

"Is this how it's going to be? Me trying to get your attention and you neglecting me of it?"

Yunseo turned quickly at this, his hands gripping the fabric of his pockets.

"You wanna talk about neglect, Taesung?"

The ground beneath Taesung's feet quaked at his name left Yunseo's lips.

"You left me, okay? You left me to pick through the home we shared and the memories we created, alone and forgotten. You put me through hell, a hell that I am still paying for, and now you want my attention? You want my thoughts…my insight," Yunseo said as he walked over to Taesung, going toe to toe with the man, regardless of the six inches Taesung had on him. "Do you really, honestly, truly believe you deserve that from me? After all that you've done?"

Taesung stared at those brown eyes again. The emotion they held cut him inside, but what hurt more was the fact that they hadn't changed. They held the same sincerity and depth they did when they had first met all those years ago, when he was twenty and Yunseo was eighteen. If only he could see the warmth they held for him then. Maybe then he wouldn't feel like reuniting with Yunseo was a mistake. Maybe then he wouldn't feel like the monster his father was turning him into.

"No, Yunseo," Taesung said. "I don't."

Yunseo smiled at his victory and took a step back. Pulling out his phone, he ordered a cab. The night was over, and he was done.

"I'll work for you and your family, but this," he said as he waved a finger between the two, "is over. Your 'family' and friends can never know. Is that clear?"

"Yunseo, if you would just listen to me—"

"Is. That. Clear."

Taesung surrendered. He knew he couldn't win and would try to have Yunseo talk to him another day. Yunseo's cruelty had lost its shock on Taesung, and now... Now Taesung realized he was no better than his father; both had a tendency to take innocent things and warp them beyond recognition.

"Crystal."

"Good," Yunseo said, walking over to his intoxicated friend and curious-looking co-worker.

"Everything okay," Mikasa said, letting Yunseo pull Subin out of her arms and into his.

"Yeah, just needed to tell Taesung that Subin and I are leaving. You know, gotta rest before our flight on Monday."

"Right," Mikasa dragged, not believing what was being told to her. "That's not what it looked like."

"Well, it was," he snapped. Mikasa's eyes narrowed and he felt exposed under their gaze. "I'm sorry. I guess I'm just tired. I'll see you on Monday, yes?"

Yunseo lifted Subin's heavy body to stand and pulled one of his arms behind his neck. Yunseo made no eye contact as he passed Taesung, looking only ahead at the exit in front of him.

"That's him, isn't it," Mikasa said as she returned to her friend's side, her voice full of dejection. "That's the one you spoke of when we first met. The one who was taken from you."

Taesung said nothing as he turned and walked past Mikasa, leaving her to stand alone in the market, nothing but children's laughter and adults' drunken celebratory yells to keep her company.

✦ ⁺ ⸱✦⸱ ⁺ ⸱✦

Yunseo was going to leave Subin here. At least that was what Yunseo was contemplating. Maybe he could just take a picture of him in his intoxicated state and sending it into the group chat he shared with the others as confirmation of life. He mused over the thought but decided that he should just take Subin home with him.

Quickly seeing the cab, he shoved the now sleeping Subin in, not caring that he banged his head on the roof. The cab driver laughed at the sound and flashed the boys a kind smile; its been a while since a passenger made him laugh. Yunseo smiled bashfully as he struggled to get Subin's limbs in the car. Growing more embarrassed as each passing moment, he asked the kind cab driver for help. This pleased the cab driver and caused the man's smile to widen as he stepped out of the car and around to Yunseo. Placing his hand on Subin's shoulder and planting foot onto the floor, he pushed on the count of three and successfully managed to push Subin into the vehicle.

In a moment of heavy breathing, the driver and Yunseo high fived each other before Yunseo reminded himself that he should be bowing in thanks instead of high-fiving the poor man. Before he could finish assuming the position, the driver's hands were at his sides, pulling him up and flashing him another smile.

"It's quite alright, son. This has been the highlight of my day."

The drive to Yunseo's apartment after this had been pleasant. He found him smiling at the pleasant encounter while also wrestling with a drunk Subin who occasionally would try and lay his head on his lap. When they had arrived at his home, the kind man helped bring Subin into his building without even being asked. When Yunseo tried to pay the man, he refused, saying that the absurd experience was enough. Yunseo begged the man to let him tip him, which the man allowed and then bid the two pilots farewell as he walked out of the building. Yunseo laughed at the thought of the man's face when he realized that the five dollars he gave him were actually thirty-five dollars. Taesung had taught him how to manipulate money and give off the illusion of a sum being more or less than it actually was.

Feeling his mood turning sour from the memory, he dragged Subin into the elevator and pressed his floor button wanting nothing more than a hot shower and his warm bed. Soon the elevator doors opened and Yunseo dragged the drunk Subin into his apartment. He thrusted him inside and onto his couch leaving him cozying up with a pillow while Yunseo walked towards his bathroom and turned on his shower. As he undressed, he allowed his mind to float back to the events that transpired that night. Being invited out with Taesung's friends, going back to eat at the place that the two lovers favored among all others, talking about their past, and finally, the way he had reacted to Taesung's advances in the restroom. The man had a way of clouding his mind and making him see stars. He hated it. He hated him. He loathed him. He didn't want a damn thing to do with him. So why for the love of God, was he still able to be affected by him?

Why did he have to work for this man's family? Why did Yunseo have to like his new employer when he knew the woman posing as Taesung's mother wasn't really his mother? The woman was dead. Taesung told him she had died of cancer. He couldn't have lied about that, could he? Could everything that he has ever told him have been a lie? He wouldn't put it past him. This was the man who walked out on him leaving behind nothing but memories and broken promises. He was alone. How can someone who was your whole world also be the reason why you almost went extinct.

Yunseo slammed his hands onto the shower wall, letting the beating hot drops of water punish him for thinking about that man. Whether he liked it or not, Taesung was back in his life and there was nothing he could do. He wouldn't think of the way he ate his cookies. Or, how every time Taesung smirked, Yunseo's eyes would be glued to it. He shouldn't think of the way his heart still jumped at the sight of the man he used to love. He wrapped his shower up with a scowl and walked out with a towel around his head, not even bothering to dry off his body or hair. Feeling that the temperature had dropped, he moved to his closet and grabbed an extra pair of sheets to wrap Subin under. He had noticed him shivering out of the corner of his eye.

Subin, for being as perverted as he was, looked innocent as he slept. It was remarkable, really. To think that the man who constantly gave the impression of a rich and shameless young man, was now sleeping soundly on Yunseo's couch with his hands wrapped in his sheets and the material tucked under his chin. Yunseo might give him a hard time in his mind but Subin was a good man. Stupid, but a good man nonetheless. There seems to be a shortage of that.

Deciding that this was enough thinking to today, he retreated into his room to prepare for bed. Once he entered his room, he shut the door and fell on top of his sheets, not bothering to put on some clothes or get underneath. He had underestimated how much of his energy was taken out of him today. Feeling a chill go down his spine, he cursed loudly as he pulled himself upright, walking over to his pajama drawer. He rummaged around the drawer looking for his favorite pair of fluffy pants and socks, he didn't feel like wearing a shirt to bed. Once he found the pink fur, he quickly snatched it out, causing several pieces of clothing to fall onto the floor. Rolling his eyes in annoyance, he bent down to grab the clothes and threw them all back into the drawer.

He tried closing it, but it was stuck. That had been his last straw. He began slaming the drawer, trying to force it close, demanding it to close. He kept slamming, and slamming, and slamming as he felt something hot and wet slid down his face. He deserved some type of control. He managed to slam the drawer one last time and caught his hand, muffling his screams with his left. He peeled his injured hand back from the drawer and sank to the floor, weeping.

He had sat on the floor until his legs lost their feeling and the throbbing in his hand had momentarily subsided. Slowly, he lifted himself up from the floor, trembling with the immense effort it took to place one numb foot in front of the other. Somehow, he managed to lay himself in bed again, sobbing into his sheets as darkness kissed his eyes. He was exhausted from it all: the bathroom, the market, Taesung, the kind man, and now his drawer wouldn't close. He was done with the day and welcomed REM with open arms.

Purgatory greeted him the next morning. Yunseo had been waiting twenty-five minutes in the emergency room for his self-imposed injury. He had woken up that morning with excruciating pain in his right hand, and when he tried to stretch it, the pain only dug itself deeper. Slowly, he got up from his bed and went looking for Subin, only to be greeted by a folded blanket and a note from Subin thanking him for taking care of him in his intoxicated state. Since Subin had gone home, most likely under the misery of a massive headache, Yunseo had to drive himself over to the hospital. He couldn't risk having his sister ask him questions about his hand, so here he was, sitting in this white room with what felt like two hundred other people.

Yunseo refused to look at the others around him when he first walked in, yet now all he could do was watch. There was an older couple to his right and a mother and son to his left. The husband of the couple had his hand over his wife's chest, constantly asking her if she could breathe. His other hand was brushing her hair behind her ear, no matter the fact that not a single strand had fallen out of place. One of the wife's hands was clutched around her husband's, while the other was stroking his cheek, willing him as best as she could to calm down. The sight might have been heartbreaking to some, two elders with their white hair, calming one another as the other was obviously unwell, having to sit in an emergency room for a nurse who was never going to come when they needed it. However, Yunseo thought it was sweet, to stay by a person no matter what and to see them through things even in old age, especially in old age. While it served as a reminder of what he did not have, he was not bitter enough to wish ill will upon the couple.

Turning his head, he saw the mother and son. The mother looked a lot like his own: dark brown hair, matching colored eyes, and a moderately attractive face. Yunseo blinked a few times, casting the image of his own mother out of his mind. His eyes traveled to her hands and stared. *No ring.* Glancing at it longer than he should've, he moved to look at her child. The child looked nothing like him. He was leaner, his eyes wider than Yunseo's were when he was eight. He was missing two front teeth. Looking at the child's hand, displaying two little white cubes, Yunseo could guess what had happened. He felt his soul struggle to process the loving pair before him. The mother had a worried look on her face and kept petting her son's head, whispering how much she loved him and how everything was going to be alright. The boy, not understanding what he had, smiled up at his mother, asking if he could have candy later.

Yunseo shifted in his seat, his eyes looking forward as he drew his hand closer to his body. He had never had that—a mother who cared. Yunseo feared his mother the most. His father was skilled like his mother at throwing physical blows, but his mother was something entirely different. She could cripple your entire being with just a few words and a laugh. She entered your mind and manipulated it from the inside out until you questioned if you deserved anything good, anything harmless in the world. All of his mother's fights and words lived in his mind, but one particular night when he had overheard his parents fighting lingered the most, its memory more vibrant and louder than the others. It had been fresh after Haeran's escape, so there was no one else to stroke his head and feed him hidden treats to distract him from the angry voices down the hall.

It was in the early hours of the morning, and Yunseo had heard screaming from his parents' room. He opened his door and tip-toed his way down to their door, passing Haeran's room as quickly as possible. His parents' door had been opened slightly, just enough for him to see his mother at her vanity, waving her arms in a frantic manner. On his knees, he pressed his face softly against the small opening and listened.

"I don't understand why you can't just tell me where you were, Eunae! It's one a.m! You don't think I deserve to know where my wife has been!"

Eunae laughed at this and stood from her vanity.

"Your wife? When was the last time you made me your wife? A year ago? Two years ago? Eight! Maybe if you were a man, I wouldn't have to come home so late. Maybe if you were a man, your son wouldn't be *so* special!"

Yunseo could hear something in the room shatter and his father's guttural scream.

"Special? Special! What do you mean my son is special? That boy is nothing but trash. You should have swallowed him or at least done me the favor of aborting him."

"Trust me, I would have," cried Eunae, sitting back on her vanity, pinning her hair back and removing her smudged lipstick and mascara. "If your mother hadn't found my pregnancy test in the trashcan, we wouldn't be here. That bitch cost us our freedom."

"I just don't understand why you're being such a whore. If you wanted some dick, you could have asked me! I'm your husband!"

"Yes, Hoseok! Unfortunately, you are! And if I could go back and stopped myself from marrying you and having children, I would. If I could go back and tell you not to get into your friend's car and get into that car accident, I would. But now we are stuck together as a bread-winning wife and a handicapped husband of two mistakes, so unless you're going to divorce me, I highly advise you to shut the fuck up!"

Yunseo heard his father quiet for a moment before shutting his eyes as he heard a door from inside the room slam shut. He slowly opened his eyes again to see his mother looking at him through the mirror, her stare menacing yet her face remained soft. He prepared himself for his mother to approach him and give him a beating, but what she did instead was far crueler. She reached for one of her lipsticks and wrote in elegant writing Yunseo's secret. One that had him running to his room and incapable of sleeping for weeks.

Faggot.

CHAPTER NINE

Looking at her phone, Soyeon had questioned if this was a mistake. Standing outside her apartment complex, she had kicked a rock into the road in front of her with her brown boots, her stomach turning. The weather had been colder than she had expected, and she was too stubborn to go back upstairs to change. In this forty-degree weather, she had chosen to wear an off-shoulder emerald top and a pair of black sweats. Her handbag strap was constantly falling off her shoulder, and her phone had warmed against her hand. She opened her phone once again and looked at Moonbin's last message.

Moonkkoch: Good morning, Soyeon! I'll be there in ten minutes. You'll know I'm there when you hear the engine.

Soyeon almost greeted the floor with her forehead when she heard her phone ring, running over and abandoning her vibrating toothbrush.

NabiSoyeon: Good morning! Ok! I'll keep my ears open!

Fifteen minutes and a full-body shave later, here was Soyeon, on her tiptoes, awaiting the sound of Moonbin's arrival. She had left Soae soundlessly sleeping in her room, leaving her a note that she was going out and that if anything should happen, to call her. She had begun to wonder what might have happened to him. *Was he struck by lightning?* She had looked up to the sky and had seen its pretty blueness and milky white clouds. Nope, definitely not lightning. *Did he blow a tire? Did he have to go home to get another shirt because he had hulked out?*

Soyeon bent down to sit upon the building's steps. She had started to believe that she had been foolish, but it had been a long time since she had done this. Her mind wandered back to her college days. Soyeon had always been thicker than the average Korean woman. She had never been ashamed of it or apologized for wearing shirts without bras or shorts that showed off her tanned legs. However, she could hear what the others were saying about her.

Should she really be here looking like that?

Shouldn't she be at her treatment appointment for her skin?

Does she think she can get a husband with tree trunks for thighs?

Soyeon shook her head, running a hand through her hair. She hadn't cared about the gossip, but what had gotten to her, what had planted a seed of doubt in her well-tamed garden, was a group of boys in her hospitality class. They had been better than average looking and had made it a ritual to greet everyone in their class, but with Soyeon, they shrunk away, as if scared. It had been four weeks before the end of their course before Soyeon had brought it up to them.

"You're frightening, Soyeon."

"How," questioned the nineteen-year-old Soyeon, brushing her short hair behind her ear. "How am I scary to you three? I've never threatened any of you nor disrespected you. So, how?"

"You're too manly," remarked one of the boys.

Soyeon had been puzzled and held her binder tighter against her chest.

"Why?"

The boy had slid off the table he had been sitting on and walked over to where she was.

"You're dark, with red lipstick and thick eyeliner, wearing longer and brighter colored nails than the other girls," the boy had said, looking her up and down. "You behaved in such a self-assured manner that none of us dared to approach you. You seemed too independent."

That conversation had puzzled Soyeon for months until she had realized what he had meant. She hadn't been the meek and soft woman Korean men wanted. She was loud, bold, and had unapologetic qualities that Korean men had deemed important in men and dangerous in women. She had felt crossed and angry at the reality that had been presented to her; she had to play small to be desired.

Fuck that.

Why did she have to play weak for men's selfish and insecure need for validation? No—that's not how her life was going to go, and whoever didn't want her because of the way she was— good riddance.

Her brain had wanted to rant on when a flash of blue came into her eyeline. Roaring sounds had greeted her ears before the image of Moonbin, clad entirely in electric blue biker gear, graced her eyes. His body, amplified in size by the leather, exuded allure to Soyeon. Thick muscles straining against his jacket as the silver pendant around his neck swung with his movement as he expertly maneuvered his bike to a stop in front of her, tapping his kickstand with the tip of his boot. Once settled, Moonbin removed his gloves, revealing rings adorning his fingers, and lifted his helmet, exposing perfectly gelled hair and the absence of his glasses. His smile was dazzling, mirroring the glistening silver ring that laid upon the middle of his bottom lip.

"Sorry I'm late. The store had to search in the back for your size."

Like light to a moth, Soyeon glided toward him, a slow and deliberate approach that held him captivate. He observed her advance with a sense of delight, relishing the bewilderment evident in her gaze. Aware that she was taking in his unadorned face, he reveled in the moment. Moonbin usually kept his lip ring at home when at work and rarely rode without his glasses, but today, he wanted all of her attention on him. He desired to consume her thoughts entirely with his presence. Little did he realize how successful his plan had been executed.

Upon reaching him, Soyeon tightened her grip on the strap of her handbag, pulling it closer to her body.

He's beautiful.

Moonbin chuckled softly and leaned in closer, his fingers gently gripping her chin.

"Right back at ya," he murmured, his close breath fanning her loose hair.

Her eyes widened.

Shibal! I said that out loud.

"You're doing it again," Moonbin whispered, his amusement evident in his words as they danced upon her lips.

Inwardly chastising herself, Soyeon withdrew her chin from his grasp, diverting her gaze to the motorcycle parked beneath him.

"You're late."

Moonbin nodded in acknowledgment.

"I know, I know, but to be fair, guessing your size was very, very hard. I had to text Soae to help me."

"Soae? I left her asleep upstairs.

"I texted her earlier in the morning?"

Soyeon laughed, "About my size? Why did you need my size?"

He swung a leg over his bike and lifted his seat, revealing a pile of neatly folded yellow-adorned black leather, his smile brightened. There laid other items beside it: gloves, joint pads, and a matching helmet. Soyeon reached for the helmet, beholding at its feline elegance and the yellow stripes that adorned the upper and lower sides, wrapping completely around. She looked inside and saw that her initials had been sewn into it; a sense of warmth flooded through her and when she lifted her head, she met with Moonbin's slightly anxious gaze.

"Do you like it? Soae said that yellow was one of your favorite colors and when I saw it in the store, I knew it had to be yours."

Soyeon looked at the helmet again before responding.

"It's perfect, but why do I need all of this? I thought you were just going to ride around and show me the different parts of your bike."

Moonbin laughed and wiped away an invisible tear.

"That's rich. You thought I was just going to let you watch," Moonbin said as he pulled the rest of the gear out of the seat, slamming the cover down. "Sorry, darling. You aren't getting off that easy. Now you," he said as he placed the clothes into her hands, "need to get changed. And while you look so incredibly stunning, I wanna get us to the racetrack while the sun is still up."

Soyeon looked at the clothes and looked back at him.

"You want me to change? Now?"

He nodded, "As fast as you can. I wanna see how it fits. We need it to see if it's too big or small."

Soyeon was currently hopping up and down, willing her ass to get into the new black and yellow leather pants he had given her. She had made it past her thighs and was now attempting to pull the rest over her bottom. With a grunt, she pulled the leather up and found purchase when the material made its way over half her rear. Adjusting her grip, she pulled once more, and by the grace of God, the pants went up. Smiling, she buttoned the front and slid her arms into the jacket, zipping it over her laced bra. Buttoning the top of her jacket at her neck, she threw the rest of her old clothes onto her bed and rushed downstairs.

The breath had left his body. The sleek lines of the gear adorning her body outlined her curves. Each contour and muscle was accentuated by the snug fit of the attire, creating a striking silhouette against the backdrop of her building. The leather jacket hugged her breasts, carving out the outline of her bust, while the pants molded to her legs, emphasizing her powerful, delicate thighs. She held her helmet below one of her arms and with every movement, the biker gear seemed to amplify her femininity. She embodied sin, and Moonbin was more than eager to succumb.

"You look... You look," Moonbin covered his mouth, attempting to hide his perverted smile. "Sorry, there just aren't any words."

Blushing, Soyeon lifted her hand that carried the pads and gloves.

"Could you help me," she asked.

Not trusting himself to speak, he waved her over. He took her helmet and placed it behind him, then grabbed the materials, thinking it was the perfect time for a lesson.

"These," he said as he picked up a glove, "have to be secured at the wrist. The gloves add a layer of protection and control when your bike starts to hit potholes or becomes slippery due to rain."

Fastening the gloves, he reached for her leg, placing it into his knee. Soyeon held her breath as Moonbin massaged her calf while he slid the guards up to her knee. His thick fingers worked the knots in her leg, causing her to bite down on the noises that threatened to leap out from his actions. He did the same to the other leg, pulling the straps tight and knocking on the hard material to demonstrate its capability.

"This will keep your shins protected, and these fabric-like ones," he continued as he pulled one of her arms towards him. Soyeon shifted forward and positioned her eyes on a light post across the street, willing it to calm her beating heart. For a few moments, Soyeon felt nothing, and curious, she looked down, only to feel heat surge between her legs. He had her arms trapped between his hands and was drawling tiny circles on the inside of her elbows. She noticed that he had been able to place the elbow guard on her other arm and furrowed her brows. *How did he move so fast?*

"These are for keeping your elbows from being gashed but also allowing you to maintain flexibility," he explained.

"You're doing a good job of scaring me, Moonbin," Soyeon remarked.

Soyeon could have sworn that his teeth morphed into fangs.

"Good. Riding is supposed to be scary; that's where the thrill comes from."

"Now," he said, turning around and handing her helmet back to her. "This is where you get on the bike. First, put on your helmet like this."

She followed his demonstration, making sure to push her hair back before securing it over her head.

"Where is your phone?"

Soyeon pointed to her chest, and Moonbin's jaw tightened. *Of course it would be there*, he thought.

"If it feels secure, leave it there. Put your foot on that foot peg there and use my shoulders as leverage to pull yourself up. Once in the air, swing your leg and realize that you've just successfully mounted your first bike," he finished, turning around to fasten his own gloves.

Soyeon tamed her racing thoughts as she followed his instructions, finding ease in being led for once. She placed her foot on the silver step and gripped onto Moonbin's shoulders, feeling them relax and tense under her touch as she pulled herself up, swung her leg, and brought it back down. The bike wavered a bit under their combined weight, but eventually balanced itself out, causing Soyeon to unclench her jaw and release a breath she didn't know she was holding.

"See! Not so scary," he said, grabbing onto the handles of the bike and looking over his shoulder. "Put your arms around me."

"What," Soyeon asked.

Moonbin rolled his eyes, "Put your arms around me. It'll steady us, and you'll have something to hold."

Suspicious, Soyeon hugged his waist.

"Harder," he said, reaching for her arms and wrapping them tighter around him. "Like you don't want to let go."

Soyeon laid her head against his back and just let herself be consumed by the smell of new leather and wind. She didn't know if it was from the new helmet or the man beneath her, but she didn't care. She relaxed into him, and for a moment, the heartbeat she felt may not have been her own.

"Ready," he called out.

"Ready!"

"Attagirl. Just pinch me if you need me to stop."

The bike under her came to life, and she yelped, not expecting such rumbling between her legs. Squeezing her eyes and calming her racing heart, she felt Moonbin pull out from in front of her building and dash down the road, the roaring of the engine greeting those who tried to sleep away an otherwise mundane day.

Moonbin was right; the thrill was amazing. As he weaved between cars and zoomed past pedestrians, she couldn't help but laugh. She had never felt so alive. Her hair whipped in the wind as if possessed, her screams of delight swallowed by the wind rushing past her. Feeling bold, she threw her hands up, reaching for the stars hidden away from the sun. She had been on numerous flights to places all over the world, but this... doing something with complete and utter trust in oneself, was something Soyeon could happily get used to. The ride lasted twenty minutes, and when they pulled into the empty racetrack, she felt saddened that her magical ride had come to an end.

Moonbin pulled under a stationed roof and dismounted his bike, stopping Soyeon when she tried to do the same. Moonbin reached over to turn off the engine and removed his helmet.

"You're gonna ride my bike, so there is no need for you to get off."

Soyeon panicked and clawed at her visor, trying to look this seemingly deranged man in the eyes. Moonbin grabbed her helmet with both of his hands, flicking the visor with his thumbs.

"Hey! Hey! Hey! I'm right here," he said, his tone soft and comforting. "I'm always going to be right here."

Soyeon stared into his eyes, looking for any doubt, but she only found honesty and reassurance.

"You promise?"

Moonbin eased his head against Soyeon's, the reinforced fiberglass of the helmet biting into his soft flesh.

"Your life is in my hands, darling. Of course, I promise. I'm just going to walk you around the track a few times, alright? No riding today. Just you, me, and Angel."

"Angel?"

"It's the name of the bike."

"But, your bike's black."

Moonbin smiled and pulled away from Soyeon, letting his eyes shamelessly rake all over her.

"Beauty comes in all types of colors. Especially the dark ones."

Soyeon couldn't shake the way he emphasized the word 'dark' as they strolled around the track together. Even when he placed his hands on her thighs, showing her how she had to cling around the biker for control, his touch was still imprinted on her skin. The massages on her calves, the circles on her arms, the sensation of holding onto her waist—it took everything for her not to let her hand travel and play with her aching clit.

She checked in on Soae in her room when she first arrived and chuckled when she saw that Soae was back in the position she had left her: mouth wide open, legs tangled in her sheets, with her right arm hanging off the bed. Closing the door, she made her way to her bed, brushing her hair back as she settled into it, the setting sun casting a golden ray into her room. Letting herself drift, she gazed upon the pile of black and yellow neatly arranged in her hamper, wondering if her dreams would be filled with rushing winds and calloused hands.

◆ . ⁺ . ◆ . ⁺ . ◆

The next day had been colder than expected. The sky was cloudy and the breeze was brisk. Yunseo worried that there would be turbulence today due to the winds. As he got out of his car and made his way around the building and into the airstrip, he was first greeted with the sight of Soae holding her head and what seemed to be an iced Americano.

"You know that stuff tastes like mud water, right?"

Yunseo grinned as he stood in front of her.

She groaned at his ill-timed joke and rolled her eyes, but she grimaced at the sharp pain that came from it.

"Must you make a lame ass fucking joke at six a.m?"

Yunseo laughed loudly, never hearing Soae curse so brazenly in public before.

"Wow, someone is very, very cranky today."

"Yeah, well, tell me how you would feel after being forced to watch videos of yourself singing at a restaurant without remembering any of it. Mikasa wouldn't stop sending the videos. They were all from different angles, thank you very much."

Yunseo flashed a smile.

"If you are all messed up, how's Soyeon."

"Oh, she is just peachy."

Soae grunted as she flashed him a sarcastic smile.

He nodded at this, understanding that she was feeling a little irritable towards her friend's healthy appearance. Looking around the airstrip, he recognized some familiar faces. He saw the same bodyguards from when he first flew with the Park family as well as Minseok's and Taesung's bikes. Yunseo had to grit his teeth together to avoid clenching his injured hand into a fist. He had exceeded the sadness that Taesung's presence evoked and was just angry now. Angry at the stunt he pulled at the restaurant. Furious at the memories he obviously still remembered between them. Livid that his touch still ignited something deep in him, an ache that he hasn't felt in an extremely long time. He could still recall the muscles that flexed under his touch when Taesung pulled him down onto his knee. Smooth and soft skin that he could have sworn matched his goosebumps. It had been the first time they had touched each other since Taesung left. Since, he abandoned him.

Subin had brought his attention back to the present. His voice broke through his mind like a knife.

"Good morning, Yunseo. I see you have met our very own grouch for today. Seems like she won't be playing nice with others today."

Her face wrinkled up in annoyance and shot Subin a middle finger as she dragged herself to the inside of the airplane.

Subin shot her his signature smug smile as he passed her and grabbed Yunseo's suitcase from his hand.

"Come on, let's get you inside."

"Hey! I can take my own luggage inside the plane, thank you very much," Yunseo yelled as he raced after Subin.

"Not with that hand, you can't."

His rebuttal died in his throat when he realized Subin was right. After the nurse had taken him in and done X-rays on his hand, it showed that he had fractured his wrist and three of his fingers. The doctor told him no surgery was needed, but that he couldn't go back to work. Yunseo tried to convince his doctor that this was the wrong call, but his doctor was having none of it. He had said it was better to rest the hand for the two to three months it needed than to never use his hand again. His doctor tried to give him a cast, but he refused, discharging himself before anyone could stop him. Yunseo didn't want to call Myunghwa, knowing she would give him an earful. Instead, he took the five milligrams of Vicodin the doctor prescribed him and wrapped his hand with a reusable bandage from the pharmacy he bought when he went to pick up his Klonopin.

"Are you sure you want to be here today? I mean, are you going to be OK enough to even help me," inquired Subin as he lifted the suitcase onto the plane and passed it to an ill-tempered Soae, wearing quite the scowl.

"I'll manage. It's nothing major," Yunseo lied as Subin eyed him, not believing his friend.

"You aren't on any painkillers, right? You know you're not authorized to fly under them."

Yunseo narrowed his eyes.

"Subin, of course, I know. Don't worry so much, I'll be fine."

Weighing the option to further question his co-pilot, Subin let it be, disappearing into the aircraft. Yunseo followed carefully behind him, climbing the steps to the airplane until he lost his footing and was now falling face-first onto the metal stairs. He closed his eyes, wrapping his hand around his bandaged one, bracing for impact. However, the impact never came. Somehow, Yunseo found himself in the arms of a six-foot-two man whose skin made his own sting.

"Still clumsy I see," Taesung said as his breath fanned the nape of Yunseo's neck.

Taesung heard Yunseo's sharp inhale and smiled to himself, feeling elated that he still had an effect on him, even after their disastrous night at Gwangjang Market.

"You can get up now."

Yunseo pushed Taesung back and turned around to, hopefully, kill him with his other hand. Yunseo wasn't surprised to see Taesung in expensive sunglasses or smiling like a kid in a candy store. What did surprise him was how boyish Taesung looked. He wore an oversized sized hoodie and jeans with a plain pair of white shoes. Gone was the fancy attire and back was the playful, relaxed charm Yunseo all but fell in love with. He looked like he did when they first dated. He must have been staring too long when he didn't hear the words that formed from Taesung's lips.

"What?"

Taesung was no longer amused as he had just been, instead, his gaze was fixated on Yunseo's chest. Yunseo, noticing Taesung's attention, realized he was staring at his injured hand, which he now held close to his heart.

"I said, what happened to your hand?"

"That's none of your business."

"The safety and health of my employees is my business."

"Really? Then why don't you ask Soae why she's in such a bad mood if you care so much," Yunseo spat angrily, knowing that Taesung was only inserting himself in with his personal life.

"I'm not asking her about her troubles, I'm asking you about yours."

"Look, don't you have a motorcycle to race or something?"

Taesung glared at Yunseo as he gripped the rails on each side of Yunseo and straightened to his full height, effortlessly towering over him. He said nothing for several moments, which only added to Yunseo's anxiousness. Knowing he would not drop it until he told him, Yunseo took a step back, attempting to create some space between them. However, he failed miserably when Taesung took a step forward as well. Rolling his eyes in frustration, Yunseo surrendered.

"I got it pitched while trying to close a drawer, okay? Happy now?"

Taesung shook his head as he gently took Yunseo's hand and lifted it to his lips, pressing a gentle kiss against it.

"You must stop being so clumsy, Little Star."

Sparks had erupted when Taesung had used the forbidden nickname. It evoked memories long buried and Yunseo all but ripped his hand back, yelling in pain as he lost his footing.

"Yunseo," Taesung roared as he reached out, trying to grab him, but it was no use. Yunseo was now lying on the stairs and here was Taesung, cradling his injured body.

"Yunseo," he repeated, trying and failing to grab his attention. Yunseo was in so much pain that he felt tears welling up in his eyes and the world around him was getting darker and darker.

"Yunseo-ah! Do you hear me! Keep your eyes open! I'm gonna get you help!"

Taesung held Yunseo close as he lifted him up, securing his legs with one arm while the other hugged his body tightly against his chest. Yunseo rested his head where Taesung's heartbeat was, feeling its rhythm. Taesung rushed to the nearby guard, barking out orders that Yunseo could no longer hear.

The pain had taken too much out of him. He was slowly fading into nothingness and as he was swallowed by the darkness, he felt something cold and wet fall onto his face. He was gone before he could question it.

The beeps of the heart monitor were the first thing he heard. The assaulting smell of cleaner was the second. The metallic taste of blood was the third. The fourth was the feeling of hospital tape on his arms. And the fifth. The fifth had awakened sadness, anger, frustration, and the smallest bit of joy. The fifth thing was Taesung, sitting in one of those uncomfortable, ill-cushioned chairs, with his hand around Yunseo's. Taesung's head was buried into his elbow and his hoodie was now covered in days-old-stains. He looked like a husband who had been by his spouse's bed all night long, worried sick and going out of their minds.

Yunseo went to move, but white-hot pain shot through his body when he tried. It sunk itself into his chest and curled itself around his heart. It hurt like hell and Yunseo couldn't do anything, but whimper at the pain. Taesung's head shot up, eyes red and puffy. Like he had been crying all night. He ran and yelled for someone to get a doctor before returning to Yunseo's side and pressing their foreheads together.

"What are you—," Yunseo all but croaked as he felt a sharp pain begin to blossom in his throat.

"Shh, you've been out for two days. Just relax. I'll get you some water," whispered Taesung as he caressed Yunseo's cheek.

Taesung reached to the side and picked up the jug that was placed by the bed. He had requested that the water be changed periodically. He was happy that he did. He poured the liquid into a glass before carefully lifting Yunseo's head to slowly feed it into his mouth. Taesung saw the tormented expression on Yunseo's face when he tried to work up the strength to swallow. It crushed his heart. He was so furious that he couldn't do anything to take away his pain. That he, someone with status and money, couldn't even keep the person he loved safe.

Am I really that useless? What was the fucking point of having all this money and not being able to protect the ones you love?

By the time Yunseo was done drinking from the glass, the doctor had come in. The doctor was quiet and serious. Like he had some bad news to share. Taesung must have thought the same, judging from his returning grip to Yunseo's hand.

"Is there anything wrong with him," the question forced its way out of Taesung's mouth.

"Well, that depends. Mr. Jeong has a fractured wrist as well as two fingers," the doctor said, flipping open a file in his hand. "However, it's noted here that he had previously visited a hospital

140

and was informed about his injuries. The combination of Vicodin and Klonopin may have contributed to his fall, potentially increasing his risk of feeling dizzy and drowsy."

The heat that was coming from Taesung could have rivaled the heat from the sun. Yunseo saw his jaw lock and his lips set into a tight line. His eyes had hardened and he had begun to grip the blanket that covered Yunseo. He was pissed and Yunseo was not excited for what came next.

"So, you're saying that he already knew about this injury and still decided to come into work, even though those two meds could cause him to extreme side effects? Is that what you are saying, doctor?"

"Yes, Mr. Park. That is exactly what I am saying."

Taesung's corner of his lip curved up as he released a chuckle. He was so angry it was all beginning to become a bit humorous.

"Why didn't the hospital give him a cast? Why did they waste their time telling him of his injury if they weren't going to treat him? Why did they let him leave!"

The doctor picked up on the hostility in Taesung's voice and straightened up as best as he could.

"Mr. Jeong discharged himself before they could."

Anger was now replaced with boiling magma as Taesung's body tensed at the announcement of Yunseo's foolishness. He shot a glare Yunseo's way before turning back to the doctor, rising from his chair, pacing in front of Yunseo's bed.

"What now, then?"

"He has to stay another day to make sure his vitals are stable, but after that, he can go home. Which brings me to my next question. Who are we discharging him to?"

Taesung stopped and breathed in heavily, trying to calm himself.

"Me."

The doctor looked at him puzzled.

"Are you his family?"

"I am his lover," Taesung snarled as he settled himself back into his chair and picked up Yunseo's hand again.

"Will that be a problem," Taesung challenged.

"N—no, sir. I was making sure I was asking the correct questions for Mr. Jeong's safety," the doctor replied, feeling scared from the wrath he could see radiating off the man in front of him.

"Well, congrats. You did your job," Taesung said in dismissal as he turned his head back to Yunseo, holding his hand close to his mouth. The doctor bowed and made his way out of the room. Yunseo was now on a high alert. He took in the needles in his arms and the stiffness of his right hand. He looked down and there it was. A disturbingly bright green cast that covered his entire forearm.

"I know what you are thinking. Why lime green," Taesung declared as he straightened up in his chair, never dropping Yunseo's hand. "I remembered how much you hated the color and thought it was a fitting punishment."

"Why—" Yunseo gasped, the energy to speak escaping him, "are you here?"

Taesung's nostrils flared and he raked a hand through his hair. His shoulders were tense and Yunseo couldn't believe that Taesung's jaw could get any sharper. He kept his view on Yunseo's cast, not trusting himself to answer without scaring or hurting Yunseo's feelings. He didn't want to do that anymore.

"Because, regardless of how much you hated me, I still cared about you."

Yunseo turned the other way, not wanting to cry in front of the man.

"Liar."

He caught the sound of Taesung swearing under his breath as he made his way out of his chair and towards the door. Yunseo braced himself, expecting the door to slam shut behind Taesung, but instead, there was only silence—a tense anticipation punctuated by Taesung's dry and rigid voice.

"Why are you taking Klonopin?"

"Jesus," Yunseo replied, voice thick with emotion. "You just won't stop."

"Just answer me, God damn it."

"No!"

"Answer me, Jeong Yunseo! Before I drag in that doctor to tell me why himself," Taesung's voice rose, echoing off the walls of the sterile hospital room.

Yunseo lips trembled as he threw his free hand over his eyes. His anger had dissipated, leaving behind a hollow ache of exhaustion and defeat.

"They're for my general anxiety, Taesung," Yunseo confessed, his words barely a whisper. "My psychiatrist prescribed them to me because of you."

Taesung leaned his head against the door, agony clawing at him with sharp talons.

"How long," he pleaded, his voice tinged with desperation.

Yunseo offered no response.

"For how long, Yunseo," Taesung pressed, his voice trembling with emotion.

Yunseo remained silent, his refusal to speak feeling like a betrayal. It wasn't fair to him; his secrets were already laid bare, and now Taesung wanted more? Anger surged within him, a simmering resentment threatening to boil over.

He could rot in hell.

Taesung turned to walk away. He could estimate when the pills started, having never seen Yunseo take them before. Something stopped him from leaving, his heart yearning to speak one last time.

"If you think me a liar, fine. I'm a liar. I'm the one who carried and drove you here. I'm the one who held your hand until the nurses had to physically rip me away from you, screaming and kicking the entire time. If caring for you and having my heart ripped open from my chest after seeing you hurt makes me a liar, then I'm a liar. I'm the biggest, most foolish liar there is."

The door shut, leaving a confused and throbbing Yunseo ignoring the streaks going down his face. *Why won't he just go away,* he thought as he pulled the pillow closer to his face, just like he had done nights before.

Yunseo laid there, his mind a whirlwind of conflicting emotions. He couldn't deny the truth in Taesung's words, even if he wanted to. Memories flooded his mind—moments when Taesung's care had been undeniable. When his concern had shown through his tough exterior. But alongside those memories were the

143

scars of betrayal, the wounds of past hurts that still throbbed with red hot poison.

As he laid there in the dim light of the room, Yunseo felt the weight of his own emotions pressing down on him like a suffocating blanket. He wanted to believe that Taesung's words were sincere, that there was still some shred of honesty left between them. But how could he trust someone who had hurt him so deeply?

The tears continued to flow, unchecked and unstoppable. Yunseo buried his face in the pillow, seeking solace in its softness, wishing for a reprieve from the tumultuous storm that had raged inside him. But deep down, he knew that the pain would linger, that the scars would remain long after the tears had dried. So, as he laid there, lost in his own thoughts, he wondered if he would ever find the strength to forgive, to let go of the past and embrace the possibility of a brighter future.

CHAPTER TEN

There was tension between the two. Taesung had taken care of all the paperwork and expenses while Yunseo had said nothing the moment he woke up. He felt uneasy and unsettled, particularly because Taesung wheeled him out of the hospital and helped him into the front seat of a very luxurious-looking car, but mostly from the way Taesung had casually let everyone believe that they were together. That they belonged to each other. *What was he thinking?* Yunseo felt his body tense up as Taesung opened the car door and slid into the driver's seat. Yunseo watched as Taesung flexed his hands over the wheel, knuckles turning white. He wasn't brave enough to look in his direction; it would only further intensify the agonizing, knife-twisting feeling in his gut. Soon, he heard him roar the car to life and pull out of the parking lot.

They drove in absolute silence. Neither of them had shown signs of wanting to speak to one another. Yunseo soon got tired of looking out of his window and turned to pull out his phone. He was surprised to find that his phone was dead. Finding a charger plugged in underneath the dashboard, he gulped the saliva that seemed to have gathered and turned towards Taesung.

"Can I use your charger?"

He waited for a response: one with words. Yet, he was met with furrowed brows, widened eyes, and a dark sneer.

"You're joking, yes? You earnestly just asked me to pass you my charger when you have not spoken to me all morning," Taesung said, not believing that he had heard such a request from those rosy lips.

"Yes," Yunseo replied, feeling as if he had just asked the stupidest thing in the world.

"Yunseo," he enunciated as he turned on a sharp left turn; causing Yunseo to become more on edge than he was before. "We haven't spoken, genuinely spoken, to each other in over five years. Now, here you sit, in my car, asking me if I can lend you my charging cable?"

Yunseo fumbled with his hands as he pulled on the loose strings of his sweater. Taesung had ordered his luggage to be taken to the hospital after the doctors told him that he needed to stay overnight. After the argument, Taesung had done the same routine over the last two days: sit in his chair, ask about Yunseo's condition, watch him eat, and leave. It drove him crazy that all he did was monitor him. He wouldn't speak to him. Wouldn't touch him. *Did I want him to touch me?* He often pondered this whenever Taesung would close his room's door. He would replay the actions between them in his head. It had been so long that his body had sung for another person. He often found himself looking at Taesung's hands when he wasn't paying attention. He was distracting in the most devilish way. His clothes were always out lining his body and he smelled only like the richest of spices. Yunseo would often feel an ache after inhaling his cologne though he knew it wasn't hunger that was plaguing him.

He was broken out of his train of thought when a familiar sign caught his attention. The sign had his emotions shift from ones of nervousness to ones of fury.

"Why are we heading to Seocho?"

Taesung couldn't help the shit-eating grin that consumed his face.

"We're not. We are going to my residence in Gangnam. I'm just making a quick stop over in Seocho."

Yunseo felt his blood boil as he widened his eyes at Taesung and bared his teeth.

"No, we are not," Yunseo forced out through clenched teeth, trying to resist his desire to strangle this man in front of him to death. "We are going to turn around and head back to the hospital so I can call my sister."

"Haeran? She might not like me very much."

"Oh, I wonder why? Look what you did to her little brother."

Taesung closed his eyes remorsefully and slowly stopping onto the side of the highway. He turned his body completely towards Yunseo, not letting a single facial expression out of his sight.

"I understand that you are pissed at me—"

"Pissed? You fucking bas—"

"But," he sneered, his upper lip curling into his mouth, "you have obviously shown that you are incapable of taking care of yourself, so I am taking you to my apartment where I can watch over you."

Yunseo cursed the day this man was born. Has all the fancy champagne and all you can fucking eat caviar rotted his brain? He was not going to his home.

"No, I am not," he remarked as he reached for the cable, but Taesung grabbed it and threw it out of the window before he could touch it. Yunseo groaned at Taesung's childishness and tried to open his car door but no matter how hard he pushed against the door it wouldn't budge. Without thinking, he threw his shoulder into it and pain had sunk its teeth into him once more. His scream was sharp and filled with frustration. He looked at Taesung with tears forming at the corners of his eyes.

"Why are you doing this to me," Yunseo pleaded as he laid his head down onto the headrest and closed his eyes, too angry and consumed by pain to look at the man. "You were gone and I had finally decided to move on with my life. So, why Taesung? Why are you tormenting me again? Haven't you done it enough?"

Yunseo couldn't see Taesung's softening face or defeated body language. Taesung felt like he was going to be sick. His stomach clenched at the suffering and sorrow soaked voice that came from the boy he once saw filled with life and delight. He was a monster. He fucked up and wasn't manly enough to come back to him sooner. He had failed Yunseo in ways that he couldn't comprehend and he would likely always be repentful for what he has done to Yunseo. However, he needed to have him around. He needed to see him. Needed to touch and feel him. He was being selfish and cowardly.

He turned back to the steering wheel and shifted the gear to drive.

"You will have your own room and the freedom to roam around. I will come to check up on you daily, but if you genuinely don't want to see me, I will leave you be. I will never touch you without your consent or force anything upon you. I just want you safe."

Yunseo sighed in defeat and kept his vision focused by the black painting that were his eyelids. The car returned onto the highway with a sort of renewed purpose. As if the belt of the engine was proof of the Taesung's stern promise. Yunseo relaxed as the pain subsided and allowed himself to sleep. He saw no point in looking for an escape he knew would never come.

◆ . ⁺ . ◆ . ⁺ . ◆

"Hey, get up," a voice said as Yunseo felt a weight suddenly appear on his shoulder, rubbing him up and down. He mumbled for it to go away as he waved off the imaginary force.

"Do I seriously have to carry you inside, Little Star?"

Upon recognizing the speaker, he jolted awake, bumping his head on the ceiling as he sat up abruptly. Taesung, witnessing it all, burst into laughter, clutching a THANK YOU shopping bag. Yunseo rolled his eyes at Taesung's amusement but couldn't help a faint smile.

"Where are we," he inquired as he finished rubbing his head and reached for his suitcase in the back seats. A suitcase that Taesung had already ordered to be taken upstairs into his apartment.

Taesung cleared his throat in an attempt to hide his mirth.

"My hotel in Gangnam. Your suitcase is already upstairs, we just need to exit the car and take the elevator up."

"Your hotel? You live in your hotel?"

"Yes, in the penthouse."

"Why am I not surprised," Yunseo said, shaking his head as he exited the vehicle.

The car was parked in the basement of the hotel and there was an elevator that lined the wall in front of him. Taesung emerged from the car with a tray of beverages and that mystery bag from earlier. He made his way to the elevator and looked over his shoulder, confused.

"Aren't you coming?"

Tired of hearing his voice, Yunseo took his time walking over to his side and pressed the 'UP' button.

"I don't really have a choice."

"No, you don't."

The elevator came and both entered quickly while Taesung instructed Yunseo to press the penthouse button. Not like it was hard to miss. The elevator was similar to the one in Thailand, but with a cool tone palette with a silver elevator plate. All of the buttons had been in unoriginal black lettering yet the penthouse button was the only one in white. It stood out against the rest and it made Yunseo's already bitter mood sour. Naturally, *Boys Over Flowers* over here would have the only button that would signify the importance he has in the hotel. He wasn't nearly this flashy when they were together. Then again, he was a completely different person then. It almost didn't feel real. The money, the private jet, the hotels, the fake family. What exactly happened during the time Taesung left him?

The elevator doors opened and the sight took Yunseo's breath away. The ceiling was unnaturally high with pristine windows. The penthouse was a mixture of blacks, grays, and whites. The lighting bounced off perfectly from the freshly polished black marble on the floor. The penthouse was like a black palace and Yunseo had to take it all in in parts.

Satisfied with Yunseo's reaction, Taesung nudged him out of the closing elevator doors and made his way into the kitchen.

"Are you going to stand there all day? If you are, please don't drool on the flooring."

This broke Yunseo's frozen stance. He released a rumble of protest as he followed. The kitchen was just as magnificent as the rest of the penthouse. All the appliances were black as well as the countertops but the backsplash had been white. Not a single crumb in sight. Everything was polished and untouched. As if no one had lived there and it was only for display.

Taesung placed the drinks and bag on the island before opening one of the cabinets. Even the plates were made of expensive black ceramic; how much more irritating can this man's wealth get? He waited for Taesung to be done before taking his seat on the island. He watched as Taesung opened the bag and pulled out the best thing to ever be created: the breakfast sandwich. Yunseo felt his mouth water at the possible taste of sausage, egg, and cheese. Taesung saw the hunger on his face and smiled as he pulled one of the coffee cups out of its cell and placed it in front of him.

"Hot chocolate. I remember you hated coffee."

"It's just too strong," Yunseo replied as he took a sip and was consumed by the delicious taste of dark chocolate, whipped cream, and the slight hint of hazelnut. Yunseo was helpless when his body closed his eyes and released a moan. He froze and snapped his eyes open, greeted by Taesung's darkening gaze. They held something in them that had Yunseo straightening up in his chair. Taesung glared at the cup as if to shame it for pulling such a sound from Yunseo's lips and pushed the plate filled with food toward him.

"What's this," Yunseo said as he picked up a rounded shaped cookie filled with what seemed to be cream in the center.

"It's called a macaron," Taesung explained he placed two large boxes filled on the island. Taesung had brought them while Yunseo was asleep. He may have gone overboard. "They are a sweet meringue-based confection made of egg whites, granulated sugar, and almond flour."

"These ones," Taesung said as he pointed to the five macarons that sat perfectly on Yunseo's plate. "Are differently flavored. The red one is cherry, the yellow one is lemon, the light pink one is strawberry, the white one with cacao powder is tiramisu, and the blue one is almond."

Yunseo picked up the blue macaron, inspecting its structure.

"Why is it blue? Aren't almonds brown?"

Taesung pulled back and crossed his arms, momentarily distracting Yunseo, and spoke in a frank tone.

"I just buy the cookies. If you want to ask the bakery why they dyed it blue, I can take you to the owner."

"Can you get a meeting with the owner?"

"Have you not realized how much money I have, yet?"

"No, I haven't. We are definitely not in a fucking gigantic penthouse that's rent is worth ten times more than my yearly salary,"

Yunseo sarcastically remarked as he took a bite of the macaron and tried to hold back another moan that threatened to spill out.

"You're funny."

"And, you're a piece of shit."

Taesung smiled faintly and nodded as he sunk his teeth into the paradise that was a cheesy sausage, egg, and buttered croissant. The bakery was the best one he had ever been to in Seocho. As he chewed and watched Yunseo devour his meal, he decided that he definitely should take him to the bakery after he was better. Knowing his soft spot for sweets, he believed it was a great idea. He waited until Yunseo was finished before having him follow him down the hallway, showing him the guest bedroom that he would be sleeping in for the remainder of his visit. Taesung opened his mouth to tell Yunseo where he could find the extra blankets, but a sudden message made him groan in annoyance.

"It seems like I have to go. Sleep and we'll discuss the terms of your stay when I will see you tonight. Sweet dreams."

"You can't keep me here for two months," Yunseo shouted as Taesung rushed toward the elevator.

Groaning, Taesung looked back over his shoulder, using that grin he knew used to make Yunseo's toes curl.

"You are not a prisoner. This isn't *Beauty and the Beast*."

"You're a beast."

"And you have always been beautiful."

"Taeung!"

Smiling, Taesung pressed the elevator button.

"You can go out or have the driver take you places. All I ask is communication and for you not to come home late. Like it or not, the hospital released you to me and it is my responsibility to take care of you as your employer."

The door dinged and Taesung entered, feeling confident he had won their little spat.

"Mrs. Park is my employer."

Taesung's smile could have split his face in half, "And, whose plane do you think you're flying in, sweetheart."

The doors closed, signaling Taesung's victory, leaving Yunseo stunned in the belly of his tormentor's black palace.

Cabrera

CHAPTER ELEVEN

A chill licked its way down Yunseo's spine, prompting him to burrow deeper into the comforting embrace of his plush comforter. His eyelids fluttered open, finding himself greeted by the embrace of nightfall, its velvety cloak shrouding Gangnam in a mesmerizing tapestry of darkness, casting the city into an enchanting tableau of darkness illuminated by a myriad of flickering lights. Gangnam, in the veil of night, resembled a sprawling field teeming with millions of luminous fireflies, each radiating a distinct hue—some azure, some blush pink, and others ablaze with fiery oranges and reds. They pulsed with vitality, a symphony of light amidst the urban sprawl.

Beneath this celestial display, the city thrummed with activity. The cars below appeared as diminutive ants scurrying along the illuminated veins of the streets, while the people, mere specks in the grand tapestry of the night, moved with purposeful yet almost imperceptible motions. Gangnam Boulevard, a monumental thoroughfare resembling a ten-lane runway, stretched out like a colossal nest, perpetually abuzz with life, its pulse synchronized with the city's ceaseless heartbeat.

Yunseo stood transfixed by the scene before him, captivated by the mesmerizing beauty of the city at rest. The simplicity of the night's splendor held him rapt, its radiant allure drawing him in deeper with each passing moment. Mesmerized, he gazed into the face of this nocturnal masterpiece, feeling its ethereal glow reflect back at him, as if beckoning him to become one with its luminous embrace. But as the moments slipped by, Yunseo reluctantly tore his gaze away from the captivating scene outside, realizing that it was time to venture beyond the confines of his luxurious yet ink-stained prison. With a resigned sigh, he reached out to close the window, severing the connection with the mesmerizing nocturnal vista outside. As he fumbled his way through the darkness of his room, the feeble glow of his phone's flashlight casting eerie shadows across the walls, Yunseo couldn't help but marvel at the dichotomy of beauty and isolation that surrounded him.

When he found the switch for the lights and turned it on, the whole apartment came alive with a hum. Rubbing his blinded eyes, he made his way to the kitchen and saw the boxes of macarons from earlier. They were huge and most likely held twenty pieces. Yunseo walked over and traced his hands over the bakery's label. Swirls and lines going in different directions pressed in a golden emblem. Opening the box, the lightest smell of sugar welcomed him with a caress. He took it in, absorbing it, as he looked at just how many were really in the box. He lifted up the card that had been placed in the right-hand corner and read the many flavors he had yet to try. On the card, it had the ones he tried earlier that day, but many other colorful ones as well. Yunseo's eyebrows shot up at the macarons he had yet to try and felt a tinge of excitement at the opportunity to taste them all.

Biting into a light purple macaron, Yunseo moaned with delight, savoring the light floral taste of lavender, complemented by a hint of honey in the buttercream. His peaceful solitude was swiftly interrupted by an immense growl from his stomach and a need for something more substantial. Closing the box, he sneakily indulged in another treat while searching Taesung's kitchen for dinner. Among the finds in the pantry and opening several glossy cabinets, Yunseo discovered a treasure trove of his favorite snacks, sparking confusion and gratitude. In front of him, he found onigiri, packaged sausages, chips, puffed bread, sour candies, drinks, and many other treats. Taesung had all of Yunseo's favorites. Wondering if Taesung had been enjoying his favorites in his absence, Yunseo examined the recently purchased snacks and felt a small spark of appreciation for the thoughtful gesture.

Deciding on Budak noodles, tuna onigiri, tiny sausages, and cheese, Yunseo continued his culinary adventure. As he prepared his meal, he turned to open Taesung's fridge, moving a few cans of Hanok Village Ale, and stumbled upon Binggrae, his beloved banana milk. He was over the moon to find it was the strawberry flavor. Grabbing some bottles, he began to prepare his feast. He poured hot water into his ramen bowl and poured in the sauce packet. After a few seconds of whisking, he emptied out the water and topped it off with the sausages and cheese. While it warmed up a bit more, he finished his onigiri and began to drink a bit of his milk. The ding of the microwave signaled Yunseo that the noodles were done and he didn't even make it to his seat before he descended onto the noodles like a falcon. It was delicious and he couldn't think of a better meal to have late at night in Korea. Feeling satisfied, Yunseo couldn't help but think about Taesung running around buying all this stuff, just for him.

Is this all for me?

Yunseo was lost in his thoughts, a simmering anger began to rise within him like a slow-burning flame. With each passing moment, his fingers flexed and tightened as resentment coiled around his stomach and gratitude wrapping around his heart. This was an injustice to him. To have his mind and heart betray each other and leave him reeling. He deepened his breath and calmed his pounding head and simmering skin, drinking the rest of the broth that was at the bottom of his plastic bowl. He thought it best just to be thankful for the gesture and softened his rigid body.

He explored Taesung's freezer, finding it filled with an impressive array of ice creams, chocolate mochi, and what seemed like a crepe cake. Overwhelmed by Taesung's eagerness to please, Yunseo settled on a Screw Bar, making himself comfortable on the sofa, sighing with satisfaction.

The sofa was soft and comfortable, it was as if he had sat on a cloud. He tried to open the ice cream with his teeth, but the damn thing just kept slipping. He remembered the trick his sister taught him when he was younger and slammed the ice cream on his thigh, popping his frozen treat out of its wrapper. He discarded the wrapper onto the coffee table and began to enjoy the delightfully strong strawberry and apple flavor. The frozen treat was tangy and sweet, almost to the point where Yunseo wanted to stop and grab a glass of water. It reminded him of his days in primary school when his sister would sneak them into a convenience store and buy the ice cream. He would eat it with her as they walked back home. Their parents never let them have snacks or sweets. They often ranted about how it would make them fat and that they didn't need to add more things to the list of reasons why their children were so useless.

Yunseo still remembered his sister's cries when she would lock herself in the bathroom and force fingers down her throat. He would be on the other side of the door banging and begging her to open it. Soon the school had made calls to the house. Omma placed Haeran into therapy for her eating disorder, afraid that people might look at her differently.

Their unspoken conversations carried volumes, laden with the weight of Haeran's unyielding resolve to challenge the toxic norms entrenched in the fashion industry. Yunseo, attuned to his sister's silent struggles, understood the driving force behind her journey into the realm of fashion, into the corridors of power as a fashion editor. Each anecdote she shared, each glimpse into the insidious workings of the industry, served as a poignant reminder of the injustices she fervently fought against.

He witnessed the shadow of anguish that clouded Haeran's eyes whenever she recounted the callous directives of past supervisors, who callously demanded models to shrink their already fragile frames, heedless of the toll it exacted on their health and well-being. The specter of his sister's sorrow loomed large whenever news arrived of yet another friend or colleague subjected to the industry's ruthless standards—rejected for refusing to conform to unrealistic beauty ideals, pressured into undergoing invasive surgeries to meet arbitrary criteria.

The echoes of Haeran's misery reverberated through Yunseo's consciousness, reverent whispers that spoke of a soul deeply wounded by the industry's callous disregard for human dignity. He bore witness to her tears, shed in silent protest against the tragic loss of young lives sacrificed on the altar of unattainable perfection. And in those moments of shared sorrow, Yunseo glimpsed the indomitable spirit that fueled his sister's tireless crusade—an unwavering empathy, a fierce determination to shield others from the same scars that marred her own soul.

For Yunseo, their shared pursuit of knowledge, the countless hours spent poring over fashion brands and industry trends, was worth it. It was a testament to their bond, a testament to the unspoken pact between siblings to stand united against the injustices that threatened to erode the fabric of their shared humanity. And in that silent solidarity, Yunseo found solace, knowing that their collective efforts were not in vain and that she was out in the world forging a path towards a future where beauty was not measured by the harsh standards of an unforgiving industry, but by the boundless depths of empathy and compassion that dwelled within each soul. With her help, of course.

Yunseo finished his ice cream and delicately placed the flushed-colored stick on the coffee table. Deciding to explore further, he wandered around the living room until he stumbled upon an altar nestled in a secluded corner, hidden from the view of the elevator. Puzzled, Yunseo approached the altar, its small and intimate presence drawing him in.

As he drew closer, Yunseo observed three tiers on a weathered tabletop, each adorned with a unique object. At the top rested a bronze statue of a mid-sized man, his serene countenance exuding an aura of tranquility as he meditated with closed eyes. Yunseo marveled at the intricacies of the statue—the large ears, the jewel positioned between the eyes, and the elaborate headdress and robes that draped over the figure, revealing his chest while veiling the rest of his body save for his hands. It was a depiction unlike any Yunseo had encountered before, captivating him with its enigmatic allure.

Continuing his exploration, Yunseo's gaze fell upon two identical bowls, each containing intriguing objects. One bowl held what appeared to be rosary beads, though upon closer inspection, Yunseo noticed they were crafted from a rich, dark wood and adorned with a mustard-colored thread. Though he refrained from touching them, their simple yet captivating design transported him to a state of awe that he could only describe as sacred.

In contrast, the other bowl contained a powdery substance with a single stick protruding from it. The stick, tall and slender, was coated with a mysterious substance, its vivid red hue seducing Yunseo's attention before his gaze was drawn to the large candles flanking the table. White and pristine, they stood tall beside fresh lilies, their stems still attached.

Finally, on the last tier, Yunseo's eyes picked out the tiny jade elephant figurines, their trunks held high in a gesture of joy. Mesmerized, Yunseo found himself yearning to unravel its significance, to understand why it had found its place in the cold and dark residence. With a sense of curiosity tinged with reverence, he reached out to touch one of the elephants, eager to feel its weight and texture. His desire was interrupted when the ringing of the elevator signaled Taesung's return. He walked in through the doors, tired and holding his blazer in one hand. Yunseo quickly moved from his spot and stood behind the couch, thankful that Taesung had been massaging his eyes. He looked as if he had been through the ringer and couldn't be happier to be home. Taesung looked up and was slightly alarmed to see Yunseo standing, comfortably. He looked at the couch and saw a discarded ice cream wrapper on the coffee table. *Ice cream?* Realizing where he must have gotten it from, he moved to open the trash can and was slightly disappointed to see that Yunseo had ruined his surprise.

"You know," Taesung started, his voice rough and raspy, as if he had been speaking for hours. "The food was supposed to be a surprise."

Smiling slightly at Taesung's obvious disappointment, Yunseo reached forward and grabbed his trash, heading over to the bin beside Taesung.

"Oops, my bad."

"You're an ass," Taesung fired back as he reached into the freezer and pulled out a chocolate ice cream cone. "Were you at least pleased with the selection?"

Yunseo thought about being sarcastic and responding with a rude comment, except he could see how hard Taesung's eyes were fighting to stay open and decided against it.

"It was startling, at first, to see that you had remembered all my favorites and bought all the ice cream in South Korea, however, yes. I fully enjoyed my meal. Thank you."

Taesung bit into his ice cream and chewed.

"Why is it surprising I would remember?"

"Because it has been five years?"

"So?"

"So," Yunseo huffed as he looked up at Taesung, "it's been five years and you could have been having sex with god knows who and had forgotten."

Yunseo saw the puzzled look on Taesung's face disappear as anger consumed its place. Taesung stared hard at Yunseo, unnerving him, as he balled up the wrapper of his ice cream and threw it into the trash. The two were now chest to chest. Yunseo was painfully aware of that damning cologne Taesung wore as well as the slight hint of chocolate that came from his mouth. His eyes were glued to it. Those lips have kissed his body more times than he could count. His skin was familiar with being imprinted with his teeth and strained with saliva, being marked like territory. Sometimes, very late at night, he would recount the first time they had sex. How gentle he was. How he coached him through the process and held him when he apologized for not being able to push through the pain. Taesung did nothing that day but kiss the tears away and whisper comforting words into his ears.

"I haven't," Taesung stated firmly, looking down at Yunseo, not wanting to believe he would think so low of him.

"Haven't what," Yunseo replied, confused by why they were so close and even more confused as to why he hadn't moved away yet.

"I haven't had sex with anyone after you."

Yunseo's heart tightened as he forced his face to hide his shock.

"You're lying. There is no way that someone like you would stay celibate after five years."

The corner of Taesung's lip lifted.

"Someone like me? What do you mean someone like me?"

Yunseo frowned at the words he had mistakenly said and threaded his fingers through his hair.

"Someone who knows enough tricks to get what they want."

Taesung's grin turned feral.

"The only pants I have ever truly wanted to get into were yours. It's hard to restrain myself every time I see you. Even now, with your arm banged up and in a cast, all I can think is how much I want to bend you over this island," he said as he pressed his hand firmly on it, demonstrating how strong it was. "And fuck you into oblivion."

"You said you wouldn't touch me without my consent," Yunseo said breathlessly, feeling the air around them heat up with each passing moment. "Are you going back on your word?"

Taesung's grin was turning more animalistic with every breath Yunseo tried to suck in. His eyes wouldn't stop moving across Yunseo's face. His eyes, nose, mouth. It was all distracting. It felt so goddamn good to be this close to him. His hands were itching to bend him over and rip his jeans off his milky skin. To see if that skin would still change in color with each spank he gave and if Yunseo still remembered how to count them. His sounds would echo loud enough to let everyone in the hotel know how good he was feeling and who was responsible for it. He prayed that Buddha would bless his selfish desires and open an opportunity for him to fulfill them.

"No," Taesung said as he backed away, making his way out of the kitchen. "You were just in my way. I'm heading to bed. Goodnight, Little Star."

Yunseo rushed after Taesung as he descended down the hall and grabbed his elbow, spinning him around.

"Kim Taesung! Stop calling me Little Star! It's not funny anymore!"

Taesung suppressed a shudder at his name falling from Yunseo's lips. His *true* name.

"Why," he said as he approached Yunseo, his tone softening. "Does it bother you? I want to understand. That name belongs to me. To *us*."

Yunseo took a deep breath, meeting Taesung's gaze.

"There is no 'us'. There is no point in you calling me that anymore."

Vexed, he turned to go back into the kitchen, attempting to build distance between the two men. But Taesung reached out, gently placing a hand on Yunseo's shoulder, his other hand resting casually beside his head.

"You're lying," he breathed.

"What?"

"When I held you back in the restaurant in Seoul, you couldn't stop your whimpering. You tried so, so hard to stop it that you cut your lip," Taesung let go of his shoulder, tracing the wound with his thumb. "You keep denying you feel anything for me, but your body betrays you."

"Let go," Yunseo said as calmly as he could, gently pushing against Taesung's hand. Taesung paused, his expression softening even more as he withdrew his thumb from Yunseo's mouth. Instead, he lightly brushed his fingertips against Yunseo's lips, savoring the warmth there. Taesung reminisced about how Yunseo's tongue used to caress him. He leaned in closer, smelling a hint of sweetness likely from the ice cream Yunseo had just eaten. As he savored the moment, Taesung reflected on the intimacy they once shared, a gentle smile playing on his lips.

"You loved that name. You loved it when I crammed inside of you, making you come over and over until you begged me to stop, crying out that you needed to walk the next day. You loved it when I sucked your cock, swallowing every bit of your essence that I could pull out of you. You especially loved it when I would make you ride me slowly, guiding your hips as I whispered praises into your ears," Taesung said as his thumb slipped into Yunseo's mouth. He thought Yunseo would bite him due to the slip but was shocked when his tongue licked his finger instead. Taesung ran his thumb along the smooth muscle, watching as Yunseo's saliva pooled and dripped onto the floor, resembling the fucked-out expression he had worn many years ago.

"And now you hate it," Taesung stated, sadness edging his words. "My love, if I recall, that was your favorite prayer that would fall from my lips."

Yunseo's world was spinning. His sight was growing hazy, and Taesung's words were taking effect. His legs were having trouble keeping him upright, and his cock fought against the restraint of his pants, begging to be freed. The pre-cum was starting to slid down the underside of his rising dick, making him moan when Taesung noticed the growing appendage. He wanted Taesung. Secretly, he always knew that he did, but he had to fight. He had to win.

"Taesu—" Yunseo moaned as he pulled his tongue out, rubbing it between his index finger and thumb.

"I missed you. I missed this pretty mouth of yours. I missed the way it would try and take all of me. I missed the way it would lick my balls as you rubbed my cock faster and faster, repaying me for the happy endings I kept giving you, night... after night... after night," Taesung trailed off, his voice filled with desire. He gently released Yunseo;s tongue and brushed his lips against his neck, groaning at the taste and sucking on the skin, his teeth grazing the red spots occasionally. And as he did so, he felt Yunseo's cock on his thigh, making him relieved to know that he wasn't delusional for believing that Yunseo still wanted him too. The last thing he wanted was to force Yunseo into anything. He would rather die than do so.

"Please," Yunseo whimpered. Why was he loving this? He should be hating him— hating him for the actions he was committing, hating him for the licks he was blowing on, causing goosebumps to form across his skin. Hating him for the way Yunseo was thinking about sleeping with him, craving the taste of his cock down his throat.

"Please, what? Use your words, Little Star."

Taesung was on cloud nine. He was losing control, and he was sure that God himself could not remove him from Yunseo.

"We can't—"

"We can—"

"I can't! Not with you, Taesung. Not again."

Taesung paused, registering Yunseo's reasoning. Instead of pressing further, he leaned in close, placing a gentle kiss on the spot where he had just bitten. He felt Yunseo's body relax slightly under his touch, a sign of consent. One Taesung was glad to receive.

"I'm sorry," Taesung assured, pulling back to meet Yunseo's eyes. "I won't do anything you're uncomfortable with. And I promise, I won't use that name again unless you tell me to."

Yunseo's expression softened, relief flooding in his eyes.

"I won't," he said sincerely, the tension between them dissipating. "But thank you."

Taesung stared at him, his gaze pleading, "God, I hope you're wrong."

He kept his head down as he walked the rest of the way to his room and grabbed the door's handle.

"Goodnight, Yunseo."

As Taesung retreated to his room, Yunseo watched him go, feeling a mixture of emotions. Relief that they hadn't gone further, sadness that they didn't, and longing for what could have transpired. Yunseo held himself as he entered his room and climbed underneath the now-cold covers, watching the twinkling night sky, wondering if there was anyone out there observing them.

Sabotaging them.

Rooting for them.

Taesung leaned against the door as he closed it, calming down the tornado of need and remorse stirring around in his heart. After a few moments, he gradually went into the bathroom, unbuttoning his shirt as the promise of hot water beating down his back guiding him there. As he entered the shower, it greeted him with water so cold it almost made him jump out of his skin before hot water started licking at his body. As though apologizing for soaking him in ice instead of fire. He stood under the water, letting it beat itself into his hair and chest before guiding his hand down his stomach and wrapping it around his cock. Slowly going up and down while images of Yunseo flashed in his mind.

The memory of Yunseo gripping the sheets as he arched his body off the bed and cried Taesung's name flashed into his mind. He braced an arm on the wall as a flash of pleasure ran its course through his body. He rubbed faster when he imagined taking Yunseo over to his kitchen's island, having him so fucked out of his mind that he would begin to drool, incapable of closing his mouth from all the sounds pouring out of it. Taesung sunk his teeth into his bottom lip as he neared his peak. The memory of Yunseo spreading himself wide was what tipped him over and had him coming with a shout. He groaned as he took a few moments to calm down, letting the now-cold water wake him out of his lustful haze.

The shower had been quick and the slumber had been quicker, but what Taesung had forgotten was that he had a new roommate staying with him and his roommate had heard his shout from down the hall. Thus, leaving a red face Yunseo wondering why Taesung was shouting shortly after confessing how badly he wanted to fuck Yunseo. The mere thought had him running and locking the door to his room, not wanting to know or *see* the reason for his shouting.

✦ . ⁺ . ✦ . ⁺ . ✦

In the dimly lit lobby of the movie theater, the air was filled with a faint aroma of popcorn and anticipation. Soae, holding a large bucket of buttered popcorn and two cans of orange soda, was waiting for Mikasa to come back from the bathroom. The former shifted from one foot to the other, worried that they would miss the beginning of the movie if she didn't hurry. Soae couldn't help but smile when she saw Mikasa make her way from behind a group of girls coming out of the bathroom, an apologetic smile on her lips.

"Sorry! Those girls hogged the sinks while they fixed their hair," she said as she took the food and beverages from the blonde. "How late are we?"

Soae rolled her eyes as she looped her arm around Mikasa's waist and dragged her to their movie room.

"We have two minutes before the white screens are graced with Sophie and Howl's beautiful presence so let's hustle, woman!"

Mikasa laughed as the smaller woman steered them through the crowd of people. Mikasa was glad she had seized the opportunity of their canceled flight to ask her out.

Mikasa had heard from others that Yunseo suffered a nasty fall and that Taesung took him to the hospital. Her heart sank, and she ran to privacy to call Taesung. She coaxed him through his babbling and prayed with him in Thai, trying to convince him that everything would be okay. Her heart bled as she listened to his cries and fought with him to let her ride over there.

He declined, stating that this was his burden to bear and that he just wanted it to be Yunseo and him. Fortunately, the nurse came out moments later and escorted him to Yunseo's hospital room. Mrs. Park believed it best to cancel the flight and resume after Yunseo felt better. Not having anything else to do on this free day, Mikasa decided it was the perfect chance to ask out Soae. Thankfully, she hadn't changed her mind about Mikasa.

Soae had recommended that they watch a limited re-showing of *Howl's Moving Castle*. Being one of Mikasa's favorite Studio Ghibli films, she immediately said yes. They selected the seven-thirty p.m. viewing, and here they were, trying to find their seats in the dark theater. After finding seats numbered thirteen and fourteen, they shuffled towards the corner where the seats were positioned. Mikasa was glad to see that the seats were secluded from the others and rather private.

The women settled in and watched as the promotions of the upcoming movies ended and the screen blossomed into the wonderful colors and imagery of Hayao Miyazaki. Soae's eyes danced back and forth, consuming the fine details of Sophie's town. She gasped at the treatment of Sophie and cheered when Howl saved her from the nasty policemen. She swooned when he called Sophie his girl and cried when she turned into an old woman. And unknown to her, Mikasa watched her reaction to it all.

Mikasa followed every blink, tear, laugh, and bending of her brows. Mikasa could watch the film at any time from her room, but she could never record nor access so easily the reactions of her dear Soae. She reached over and grasped her hand, wanting to feel that this woman—this beautiful, kind, sweet woman—was really with her. Really chose to honor her time and energy with Mikasa to watch a movie that came out years ago.

"What," Soae said, smiling at Mikasa. "Am I hogging all the popcorn? I have a tendency to do that during movies."

Mikasa shook her head, her thumb brushing over her knuckles.

"You're so beautiful."

Soae smiled shyly and brushed her hair with her free hand. She looked at Mikasa's hand and felt her heart fill itself with adoration. Mikasa had the same lovely tan as Soyeon, yet her skin was not as flawless. Mikasa had faint scars of different sizes on the skin below her hands. Soae turned their hands and found some lines at her wrist, ones that caused panic to course through her and had her lift her head to Mikasa, the film in front of her long forgotten.

"Mikasa," she uttered softly. "When were these?"

Mikasa's smile faded, and she squeezed Soae's hand tighter.

"A long, long time ago," Mikasa whispered back, leaning forward and petting her head. "It was a time before I came to Korea. Before I met Taesung and the others. Before I met you."

Soae's heart broke as she looked back down, her fingers tracing the ripples carefully.

"Will you tell me how they happened?"

Mikasa looked at her and thought hard. Was she ready to tell someone other than Taesung how these happened? What made her want to submit to eternal slumber? Of the things that still lurked in her dreams, keeping her from a restful night's sleep? Could she truly trust Soae with her ugly truths? With her fragmented self that she had spent so long taping together?

"Yes," Mikasa said as she brought their foreheads together, looking into her eyes. "Not today, but one day."

Soae stared at her eyes before looking at her mouth.

"I've..." Soae stopped, feeling ridiculous. "I've never done this before."

Mikasa smiled.

"What? Seen scars?"

Soae smacked Mikasa's arm as the redhead snickered.

"No," Soae exclaimed, receiving shushes from the audience around them. "I've never been with a woman."

Mikasa's face calmed into a small grin and just looked at Soae as she fidgeted with her fingers.

"I've liked girls and have wanted to be more with girls, but I... It's just that... well—God I don't know what I'm saying!"

Soae felt her hair be moved from her face and hands cup the back of her head. Mikasa carefully brought her lips upon Soae's, gently moving them around. Soae gasped at the gentleness of it all, Mikasa used it as an excuse to dip her tongue into her mouth, running it along her teeth, savoring the whine that it pulled out of Soae. Mikasa slowly let go of Soae, placing their forehead back together, and stroked her cheeks with her thumbs.

"I don't care. Whether I'm your first or your last, I just want to be here with you."

"But, I don't know how to please you."

Mikasa rubbed their noses together.

"You please me just by breathing."

Soae slumped against Mikasa as she kept kissing her. Everything fading except the familiar sounds of a certain orchestral song filling the air all around them, making their heads spin as if they were on a merry-go-round.

CHAPTER TWELVE

Yunseo was in the kitchen when he spotted Taesung's note.

My sister wanted me to leave you her KakaoTalk since she is currently visiting the city and heard about what happened to you. Her ID is SweetTooth214. You should add my ID as well. It is Taesung1084. See you at nine p.m.

Yunseo shook his head at Minseo's username and chuckled as he pressed it into his phone. He was reluctant to add Taesung, wondering why he would need his number if he saw him every day. He punched the username into his phone and went back to looking for something to eat. He settled on making French toast with some Japanese bread he found in one of the cabinets and set out to gather all the ingredients he needed. Finding what he needed, he began to make the mixture. His first round had been unsuccessful; the slices of bread were undercooked and he had already used two large pieces of bread. He didn't want to waste any more bread and pulled the plug on breakfast. He poured chocolate syrup and scooped out a ball of vanilla ice cream, believing that it may save the ruined dish, when his phone buzzed next to him. He smiled as he read the message that graced it.

SweetTooth214: Hey Yunseo! How's your arm? Is it bad? Does it hurt? Has Taesung been a good host? I'll kill him if he hasn't!

YunseoOnFire: No, he's been fine. It's a little weird for me to be in my employer's family member's home, but I have no complaints.

SweetTooth214: The two of you used to be close friends in college, correct? I'm sure it's not that weird?

YunseoOnFire: It's been five years. It's a little different than how we just are.

SweetTooth214: How were you guys before?

Yunseo felt his thumbs cramp as he thought about his response. He couldn't really tell Taesung's sister that they used to chase each other around, missing classes and covered in love bites. Not that he would, of course.

Who tells someone that?

YunseoOnFire: We used to be more familiar with each other. Things have changed so much since we were last together.

SweetTooth214: I understand. Things will be like before soon. I'm sure.

I surely hope not, Yunseo thought as he waited for Minseo to send her next message.

SweetTooth214: Come have breakfast with me. There's a new cafe that just opened and I have no one else to go with.

YunseoOnFire: Are you sure that will be ok? Your brother told me not to leave the apartment unless I had his permission.

SweetTooth214: Permission? ㅋㅋ ㅋㅋ ㅋㅋ Is he insane? No, I'm picking you up in 20 minutes, so be ready. See you soon!

He laughed at her bossy nature and thought it resembled her brother's perfectly. He looked at the clock and realized he better get ready. He cleaned up his mess and ran to the shower. He had done more exploring last night and found that one of the doors in his room lead to a bathroom. The shower had followed the same design as the rest of the apartment but was somehow grander. Instead of black granite, the sinks were made of marble. The shower was enormous. It could easily fit four people. The best part was the lighting. Everything was lined up and glowing with a soft yellow-ish hue. This bathroom was even better than the one in Thailand.

He stopped gawking and stripped naked. The tiles in the shower were warm, a stark contrast to the cold tile he was just standing on. He wondered if Prince Charming had heated floors installed in his showers. *Was that even possible?* Yunseo tried not to think too much as he played around with the setting and turned a knob that had water cascading from the ceiling. It was as though they were able to capture Mother Nature's magic and install it into his own little world. It was amazing, Yunseo's curiosity—and disbelief—might have been what caused him to be undressed when Minseo texted him she had arrived. He had been too busy playing in wonder that he let time slip and now was running to pull a shirt over his head; it was hell trying to do it, even harder trying to not get it wet. It was impossible.

He managed to make it to the door with it halfway on when Minseo came in, purse in hand and a bright smile on her face. She looked beautiful as ever, wearing a simple dark pink sweater and jeans. Her hair was pinned up and she wore light makeup. She was stunning. How she wasn't married yet, Yunseo would forever wonder.

Minseo gave Yunseo a full body once over and laughed.

"Do you need help?"

Yunseo looked down at himself and groaned. Feet bare, jeans unbuttoned, and a shirt with only one arm through its hole. It would be an embarrassing state to be in for anyone, however, to be in this state in front of a wealthy, well-dressed woman—Catastrophic.

"If I say yes, will you act as if nothing happened?"

Minseo's laughter could have put a child's to shame. It was light and airy, yet hearty and true. The type of laugh that only came out if it was earned.

"Nope, but I'll buy you hotteok for your embarrassment," she said as she placed her bag on the counter.

She first helped with his shirt, careful to avoid touching his chest. She fixed his hair before moving on to his pants; the mere act had Yunseo looking up in shame as she zipped and buttoned him in.

"Make those two hotteoks," she remarked as she looked back up at Yunseo and patted his shoulder. "Bring your shoes. I'll help put them on."

"Minseo, you've done enou—"

"Just bring them, Yunseo. I'm starving and would like my companion to walk in with me *fully* clothed," Minseo leaned closer and grabbed his shoulders. "It is not shameful to accept help when provided with it."

He smiled at her appreciatively and nodded. He turned and grabbed a pair of shoes, returning with a jacket hung around his as well.

Minseo guided Yunseo to the couch as she leaned down and helped place the shoes one by one on his feet.

"Good call on the jacket. It's not freezing but it is very windy. At least the leaves are changing."

"I haven't seen them yet. They were still green last time I checked."

She patted his knees when she was done and grabbed her purse as she walked towards the elevator.

"Well, we will just have to take a walk through the park after we eat."

The cafe was small. Seemed to be owned by a small group of friends and was decorated to appeal to those who liked aesthetical things. Minseo was never one for aesthetics. Though she loved fashion and colors, she thought that looking, appreciating, and loving things that were perfect to the human eye was boring. She didn't want that for herself. She didn't want to be loved only for the perfection people perceived her to be. Young, beautiful, thin, wealthy and powerful. All things in the book that should make her overjoyed yet the causes of her past hardships. Too beautiful for people to be friends with. Too young to be taken seriously. Too rich to understand how different others' lives are. She often struggled with these things until Taesung came into her life. She had been sixteen and tired of the whispering she knew others were doing. She didn't feel comfortable talking to her mom, her funny and bubbly Omma. She couldn't bear breaking her mother's spirit with her reality. Taesung had just been introduced to the family and she still didn't know what kind of person he was.

One day, as she sat alone in her room, tears streaming down her cheeks, memories flooded back to a day not long ago. She remembered the gentle knock on her door, followed by his familiar voice calling her name. In that moment, she felt a glimmer of hope amidst her despair. The door creaked open, and there Taesung stood, holding a plate of brownies and a glass of milk. She was taken aback, too stunned to speak as he entered the room without a word. His presence alone brought a sense of comfort, yet she couldn't understand why he was there.

For the next hour, they sat together in silence as she poured her heart out, sharing her darkest fears and deepest insecurities. He listened attentively, offering nothing but a reassuring squeeze to her hand. His kindness and understanding enveloped her like a warm embrace, easing the pain in her heart. When her tears finally subsided, he gently nudged the plate of forgotten brownies toward her and suggested they watch an American movie together. In that moment, she felt peace wash over her, grateful for his unwavering support.

Later that night, as they sat side by side, she mustered the courage to ask him to share his own struggles and hardships. He hesitated at first and eventually declined, instead promising to be there for her whenever she needed him. As she drifted off to sleep, she realized that in that moment, she finally understood for the first time what it truly meant to have an older brother by her side. And she knew that no matter what challenges laid ahead, he would always be just a brownie and glass of milk away.

"So, what's it like being a pilot?"

Yunseo nearly choked on his hot chocolate when Minseo asked him the question. Her mouth was currently covered in chocolate mousse from the donut she had been eating. Minseo had attempted small talk on the way over, but her hunger got the best of her, rendering her speechless until the waiter arrived to take their order. It had been the first thing she had said since devouring her first treat whole. When the waiter came, Yunseo hesitated for a moment, unsure of what to order. Eventually, he decided on a few chocolate pastries, donuts, and a hot chocolate. He was pleasantly surprised to see that Minseo shared her brother's fondness for chocolate. However, he couldn't help but feel disapproval when she ordered an Americano.

"I guess it's exhilarating, but terrifying."

Minseo tilted her head as if to say she didn't understand.

"One minute you could be laughing and guessing the shapes of the clouds passing by, then the next you must steer the plane through heavy winds and fierce rain. It all can get overwhelming, yet it's the one place where you can be above your problems. At least for me."

Minseo nodded her head and popped a piece of her donut in her mouth.

"Did you ever want to do anything else?"

Yunseo smiled at her curiosity in him and bit into his apple fritter.

"Honestly? No. I didn't have any idea what I wanted to do, just that I didn't want to stay still all my life. It wasn't until I got into the Air Force and flew airplanes at Seoul Air Base, that I decided that being a pilot was the job for me. The brotherhood it creates and the danger we all shared," he smiled, remembering Gohyun and his goofy smile. "It made me feel alive after a lifetime of stillness."

She was silent as she drank from her coffee, feeling the weight of his words.

"Too much," he asked sheepishly, insecure that he may have been too passionate.

She released her straw with a pop and ate the last bit of donut.

"Not at all. You just reminded me of Taesung. He speaks that passionately only when he is talking about cars or motorcycles. Omma almost had a heart attack when he opened his customizing business."

"He owns a motorcycle business?"

"Not exactly. He customizes motorcycles and sells them to the highest bidder. He has auto shops in Thailand, Korea, and pretty much everywhere else. Though, he said Thailand is the best place for his headquarters. Said the sons of businessmen were keeping his pockets fuller more than anywhere else."

"Is that where he met Mikasa and the others?"

"The M&Ms," Minseo questioned as she picked up her next donut. "I don't really know. One day he popped up with them and it felt like they were always there. Like they were the missing pieces to our puzzle."

Yunseo nodded and smiled at her as she sipped on her drink. Yunseo needed this. Needed a friend to laugh and eat with. He had the others, but he hadn't gotten the chance to have alone time with them and after losing contact with Gohyun after the military, he was just happy to have that again. His happiness soon turned into dread as he heard a little voice poke at him from the back of his mind.

Ask her. You know you want to. Ask her.

"I have to ask you something."

He whined as his hands began to shake. Seeing how nervous he was, she grabbed his hand and gripped it tight.

"Go on, Yunseo. You can ask me anything," said Minseo as she bent down to his eye level and gave him a reassuring smile.

Yunseo closed his eyes, not wanting to see her face when he asked the damning question.

Ask her. Ask her! ASK H—

"Are you Taesung's real family?"

Yunseo didn't dare open his eyes. The room felt as if all the air had been sucked out of it and the only thing that was left was her reply. His heart pounded like a janggu drum, reverberating throughout his chest. His once steady breath now came out in shallow ones, unable to satiate his desperate need for air. He felt the hot grip of tension clutching at his throat, making it hard to swallow. He knew his hands were trembling, yet they were trapped in an iron grip. He didn't understand why she was still holding on to him.

She is going to slap me, throw her coffee in my face, kick and scratch at me, or at least humiliate me. She's going to kill me. I deserve it. I always deserved it.

The blood thundered in his ears, drowning out Minseo's calls. Immobilized in his turmoil, it resembled a nightmarish sleep paralysis episode—trapped, unable to move. He strained to open his eyes, to flex his fingers—anything. Yet, the more he struggled, the tighter the grip became. Tears streamed down his face, intensifying his overwhelming sense of helplessness. He craved answers, fiercely demanded the truth, resentful that he had to seek it from his ex-lover's sister. He yearned to break free from Taesung's web of lies and secrets. Yunseo vowed to unearth the truth, even if it cost him everything. Eventually, he regained some semblance of control, opening his eyes to find Minseo cradling him, whispering comforting words into his ears, soothing his troubled soul.

"I'm here, Yunseo. I am not angry with you," Minseo said soothingly, her voice steady and clear. "I'm not going to hurt you. I need you to breathe. Please breathe with me."

He stared at her and looked at her arms wrapped around him. *Is this how I am going to die,* he thought. *Smothered to death under the arms of the woman his lover calls sister?* Of all the ways he has contemplated his demise, this was not the vision he saw.

He registered her arms tightening; it felt like his thoughts spoke truth. He *was* going to die in this set of arms. The spots in his vision become less of ones of heavenly light and colorful spring and more of darkening winter and freshly fallen soot. Minseo felt his body tremble more and softened her grip, her lips falling to the ear of her friend.

"I am sorry that this has frightened you so. Speak to me."

What?

"Please," she cried. "Just breathe."

Like the first rays of dawn, her voice broke through the deafening noise of Yunseo's prison. He responded to her embrace with a trembling one of his own, tightly clinging onto her as if she were a lifeline in the midst of the anarchy. He failed to keep his cries inside his throat; Minseo only kept her arms encircled around him, determined to provide a sense of security. She pulled back, grabbing ahold of his face and tried her best to make eye contact with his swollen and bloodshot ones.

"Follow me, okay? Inhale. Exhale," Minseo took Yunseo's hand and placed it on her chest, demonstrating the rise and fall of her breathe. "Inhale. Exhale. One at a time."

Yunseo focused on her chest, matching it with his own. After a few failed attempts, Yunseo was finally able to get control of his breathing again and stop crying long enough to properly look at Minseo.

She looked raptured. Her forehead mirrored the one of the concerned mother back in the emergency room and her eyes, stern with determination. Yunseo wished she would have not helped him. He wished she had hated him. It would be easier. He knew how to deal with molten hot emotion, not one that made you understand why the songbird sings and why the skies clear after a storm.

"I'm sorry, but I can't hold it in anymore. Your brother and I... we were more than friends when we knew each other. Much more. He was my first love, Minseo," he said, taking in a shaky breath. "So, call your mother and tell her to fire me for my disrespectful behavior. Wish me dead if you truly hate me, but please. Tell me what's going on here. Tell me the truth. I deserve the truth," Yunseo croaked as he bent his head.

Minseo's head was spinning. She had her guesses as to why the two men were so tense when within the same room, but never this. It was frightening her. How much she still didn't know about her brother. Yet, looking at Yunseo now, a stark contrast to the fun-loving and laughing man that was just before her not five minutes ago, she wanted nothing but to reassure Yunseo of her unwavering concern and care for him. She only hoped that he didn't notice the cracks of her own as she did it.

She breathed heavily as she picked up their belongings and ordered a bag of pastries to go.

"Let's get out of here. We will discuss everything once we get somewhere more private."

Yunseo looked down at the table and couldn't help but wonder if this was Minseo's true reaction, regardless of the kindness she had just shown him. Gently, Minseo helped Yunseo to stand and interlocked their arms, trying to stop the obvious tremble being showcased in his legs. As they headed towards the cafe's front door, Minseo continued to offer words of encouragement.

"You're safe. Just keep breathing. You're doing great."

Yunseo noticed Minseo's indifference to all the whispering and staring that were directed their way, inspiring Yunseo to emulate even a morsel of her behavior. Yunseo started by staring straight ahead and, once outside, feeling the gentle sun on his skin. The sunlight felt gentle yet powerful, like an ethereal caress from the heavens. It helped calm him down and his legs gradually regained their strength. Minseo noticed the subtle changes in Yunseo's behavior and praised him on his progress, fostering a sense of accomplishment in her friend's battle against his panic attack.

As the attack receded, he felt a renewed determination to find his voice.

"Are we heading back to the hotel," Yunseo whispered, his voice still shaking but full of resolve.

"No. You asked a question and deserve an answer," Minseo replied, adjusting her grip to hold Yunseo closer. She maintained her proximity, ready to provide immediate assistance if needed.

Yunseo said nothing as they rounded a corner, heading toward a nameless building with a staircase that scaled its side to the roof. As they neared the mouth of the stairs, Yunseo tightened his grip around Minseo's elbow.

"Don't be scared of the way this building looks. I promise you that what's waiting on top is well worth it."

Remembering how gently Minseo took care of him back in the cafe, he nodded stiffly, still afraid of the run-down building. Minseo held his hand as they scaled the stairs and entered the gate of the most beautiful garden he had ever seen. The gates were pearly white with golden accents, which led to an entire rooftop filled with tables, benches, plants, and flowers. The ground was covered in gravel and the crunch underneath his boots helped his senses come back to life. The air was filled with sickly sweet flowery scents and the plants had attracted a number of different butterflies that surrounded Yunseo as if they knew what he had just been through, trying to remind him that everything was going to be okay.

Minseo led them to a table that was placed next to a bed of flowers and overlooked the city. The flowers planted beside the table were like a celebration of the country's rich floral heritage, showcasing a diverse array of native blooms that weaved a tapestry of colors and textures, captivating all who sat beside it. Many of the flowers he hadn't seen since he was a child: mugunghwa, lilies, hydrangeas, and gentians. He couldn't stop staring at the large box of flowers as he sat down. Minseo smiled broadly at the wonderment plastered on Yunseo's face. That was the exact face she had when she came here years ago. With *him*. Her smile faltered, but she refocused her mind on Yunseo's question from earlier.

"To answer your question from earlier," Minseo began, causing Yunseo to turn his attention to her voice. "I'm Taesung's half-sister."

"Half-sister?"

Minseo nodded her head as she leaned back into her chair.

"I was sixteen when Taesung arrived at our house. It was shortly after the accident," Minseo breathed out heavily, tilting her head up to the sky, recounting the days after his arrival. "It was hard for my mother and I to get used to him, to him being part of our family as well as the plan our Appa had for him. He left after a few months to go to Thailand for graduate school. He was different when he was over there. Taesung has always been a good person, but something changed. He turned to…substances for relief. We all knew he was struggling with something when he first arrived, he just wouldn't talk about it."

Yunseo remained silent, not daring to interrupt the flow of answers that he has been yearning to hear since his union with Taesung.

"Omma loved him. I know it's a trend for stepmothers to hate their spouse's other children, but Omma," Minseo smiled, feeling prideful of her mother. "She saw how hurt he was. How much pain he was in and wanted to love him. I guess that's just a mother's instinct. After he finished grad school and started his business, he soon started calling my mother Omma and we were a family. He was my brother and I was his sister. We never found a reason to introduce one another to people differently."

Minseo looked over and raised her eyebrow at him.

"I guess it was a matter of time before someone figured it out."

Yunseo was quiet for a long time, not knowing how to respond. He was surprised to hear that Minseo and Taesung were actually blood siblings and had become so close in such a short amount of time. He felt admiration for Mrs. Park for embracing Taesung with open arms and an open heart. It was admirable and something not many could do. His mind began filing the information, filling in the blanks before raising his head back up, flustered at something she had said.

"You said that Taesung was having a tough time. Why was he having a tough time? Why did he turn to substances? Why didn't he return home to Korea?"

Minseo chewed on her lip, surprised at the list of questions that fell from Yunseo's lips.

178

"I didn't know then, but my guess, it's because of you. I mean, what other reason did he have to stay away other than our father?"

Yunseo was filled with more questions than ever before. More than when Taesung had left. More than when Taesung had reappeared. More than when Taesung held his hand in the hospital.

"Do the M&Ms know," Yunseo asked weakly, not having the strength to speak any louder. "About your family?"

"They do."

Yunseo nodded as he reached for the bag and grabbed a breakfast sandwich that was buried at the bottom.

"Before Taesung, I had another brother," Minseo said as she played with her bracelet that had been hidden under her coat sleeve. It was a singular gold bangle with the words 'To my Lily,' on it. "Sungmin was my mother and father's first child. Taesung looked so much like him that it scared me when I first met him. He was a wreck, always chasing the next epic high. My father blamed him for his death. My mother blamed herself and I blamed my father, but it was all useless. *He* was the one who decided to base jump off Daepo Jusangjeolli. *He* was the one to ignore his friend when he told him the wingsuit was faulty and *he* was the one who crashed into the rocks below. My father called him a disgrace and a dishonor to our family, but all I did was cry, remembering the places he took me and the nickname he gave to me," Minseo stopped, briefly wiping the tears that slid down her face. "This was our favorite place. This was where he would tell me about the plants here and the lilies that sat in the middle of our tiny table. He said that their purity reminded him of me. It's the most painful memory I have of him."

Yunseo leaned over and held onto one of her hands.

"Why is it painful?"

Minseo reached for a napkin and wiped her nose, closing her eyes at its softness.

"All the beautiful ones are."

"But, why didn't you or your brother meet Taesung before then? Why did you meet your brother only when you lost the other?"

"I asked myself that for years," Minseo admitted, dabbing her nose again and accepting the double chocolate chip cookie

Yunseo offered. "But why Taesung appeared then, that's Taesung's story to tell. It wouldn't be right telling you."

Yunseo felt his curiosity grow as the day turned into night. The clouds slowed, stars began to steal the attention the sun once commanded, and the air had become sharper, like a knife scraping your throat. It was painful, yet Yunseo took delight in the pain. He took deep breaths of it when he could, balancing the act of responding to Minseo's conversion and the bites he would take from his food. His throat was raw, his fingers numb, yet he didn't mind. He knew a bit of the truth, and that was enough as he listened quietly to the music coming up from the city below.

"There is something I am curious about," Minseo declared.

Yunseo turned to look at her.

"What?"

"Why wait all this time to ask me about my brother? You obviously had your suspicions, so why hold it all in."

Yunseo pulled on his ear.

"It wasn't my place before. I didn't know you well enough to have the confidence to ask such an intrusive question. I mean you saw what happened. Imagine if I asked sooner."

Minseo hummed as she sunk her teeth into her egg tart.

"I think you should talk to him."

He shook his head.

"It doesn't matter anymore. It was a long time ago. He is just my employer, now."

She looked at him from the corner of her eye.

"Yunseo?"

"Hmm"

"Today alone, you have told me that you used to know my brother and I, in return, have told you that he was my long lost brother, who showed up once my other brother died. We told each other this even though we were strangers three months ago. And do you know why we did this?"

"Because if I didn't ask you, I would have combusted into a million pieces?"

Minseo's hearty laugh echoed into the night sky and, for a moment, the stars seemed to twinkle in response.

"Because we decided to trust one another. We took a leap of faith and told the truth. So as someone who has told you the truth, I will tell you another; you two still care for each other. Maybe, it's time for the two of you to stop running and tell each other the truth. You know, seize the opportunity."

Yunseo's heart jumped at those words. Those same damn words he kept trying to avoid since Dr. Im had recited them in his car a few days ago.

Seize the opportunity.

Minseo stood up, pulling her sweater closer to herself, realizing just how cold the air had gotten.

"You should take that bag of treats. It's a good conversion starter if you offer one to him."

Yunseo glared at her and she threw her hands up in surrender.

"Just saying. It's getting late anyhow. We should get you back to the apartment."

Yunseo checked his phone and was surprised at how late it had gotten. After all the talking and eating, he hadn't realized how late it was.

"Come on. Before Taesung kills me," Minseo said as she pulled Yunseo out of his seat; making him lunge for the bag of pastries and start their descent down the stairs.

The penthouse was a dark and soundless void. Time had no meaning and there was no point in giving it any importance either. At least that was how Taesung felt as he sat in the dark, with a glass of scotch, waiting for Yunseo to come home. He had messaged Minseo earlier during the day to see how everything was going but hadn't received a message back. It was very late and not knowing where an injured Yunseo was in a city he had never been to had Taesung on the edge.

As the hours passed by, his patience began to wane. He was fidgeting restlessly in the dark, taking deep and thoughtful sips from his glass, distracting himself from wanting to get up and call Moonbin and Mikasa to scavenge the city. The room was enveloped in shadows, only severing his growing annoyance and frustration. He polished off his glass before pouring himself another, remarking in the back of his head how ridiculous he was being. He looked over at the clock above his TV and stared at the time displayed. Eleven fifty. He crossed his arms tightly across his chest, and tapped his foot rhythmically on the floor, giving sound to his growing agitation. With each passing moment, his annoyance seemed to intensify, as if the darkness itself conspired to magnify Taesung feelings of exasperation.

With a growl, he checked the clock for what felt like the hundredth time and the sight had only made his jaw clench impossibly tighter. It had been no more than five minutes since the last time he had checked. He was tempted to contact Yunseo and demand why he had not notified him of how late he would be returning, yet a part of him hesitated, not wanting to appear overly possessive or overbearing. He was just worried and scared that something happened to Yunseo on his outing with his sister. As he picked up his glass and stared at its contents, he wished for the cosmos to end his suffering and have Yunseo come through the elevator doors safe and sound. Until then, he would continue to sit on this chair, waiting for his return, displaying the perfect picture of annoyance and impatience.

Fortunately, it seemed that the cosmos heard him because the elevator doors opened, and in walked in a cold and bright pink Yunseo, carrying a mysterious bag. Taesung watched as Yunseo cast a look of confusion at the lights being off and turned them on using the remote beside the elevator. The lights sprung to life, causing Yunseo to throw a hand over his eyes, shielding them from the fluorescents, making Taesung's deep annoyance slightly melt away as he inwardly smiled at him.

"You're late," Taesung stated, putting down his glass.

Yunseo removed his hand and blinked several times before settling on Taesung's fuming form. It was impossible to not notice how furious he was, but what caught his attention was the attire he was wearing. He had on a simple gray tank top with black sweatpants. His hair was unruly, wild, and covered most of his forehead. His face had a glow and freshness to it, clearly just washed and moisturized. Yunseo let out a breath he didn't know he was holding and placed the bag of food on top of the counter.

"I brought you some pastries from the cafe Minseo and I went to."

Taesung only looked at the bag.

"That's not an answer. Do you know how worried I was? I almost lost my mind and was tempted to go out into the city to find you myself."

Yunseo threw his jacket on the island, squaring his shoulders at the weight of Taesung s authoritative tone.

"I was fine," he retorted, his voice edged. "I was with your sister. I didn't think it was a big deal if I came home late."

"Not a big deal? Everything that concerns you is a big deal to me. I was imagining all sorts of terrible scenarios! I thought you were hurt, or worse!"

Taesung couldn't stop the pounding in his chest, all the worrying and anger bubbling up in his chest and coming up his throat, consuming his thoughts. The fear of losing him gnawed at his soul and made him nauseous. He couldn't lose him again.

"You could've called! Texted! Told Minseo to shoot me a picture of you flipping me off! Something," Taesung yelled. "There was no reason you couldn't have communicated with me!"

"What about you," Yunseo retorted, his voice raised and tinged with defiance. "Since you're mister communi–fucking–cation, tell me the truth about why you left me all those years ago."

Taesung blanched at the request, he was unable to control the tremor in his voice.

"What are you talking about? What did Minseo tell you?"

"Uh-nh, you don't get to blame this on your sister. At least she told me something about you. Since we have reunited, you have refused to acknowledge how we parted. How we used to be. How—," Yunseo cracked, his body trembling with the adrenaline coursing through his body. "How you destroyed me."

Taesung walked around the island and reached to grasp Yunseo's hands, but Yunseo backed away from him. Dropping his arms in defeat, he planted his feet to stop him from moving closer.

"I never meant to hurt you."

"That's not good enough," Yunseo responded with a melancholic tone, his anger tempered by the underlying sadness that still gripped him from all those years ago. "Do you know how it feels to be worthless and unwanted? To have someone you loved and gave all your firsts to suddenly be ripped away from you? I cared about you, Taesung," Yunseo sobbed. "No, that is not good enough to describe how in love I was with you. You were my sun. My day started and ended with you."

Yunseo buried his face in his hands as the words hung heavily in the air, the tension palpable. Yunseo felt weak and small, exposed and raw, and his vulnerability...his trauma laid bare in the argument. He was trapped in a conversation that he wanted to have for years and all he wanted was the world to swallow him whole, never to be seen again.

The utter silence that filled the room made Yunseo wonder if he was still there or if he had left him again. The fear of being abandoned pushed him to look.

There stood Taesung, staring at him with tears running down his beautiful face. The face Yunseo remembered holding numerous times.

He opened his mouth and attempted to speak, but the words were dying in his throat. He closed his mouth and tried again.

"I wanted to tell you—" he swallowed. "I have wanted to tell you the truth since I had first found your profile in the piles of candidates for our family's flight crew. At first, I believed that it was a coincidence. That the world wasn't as cruel as they said it was. But, when I saw you," Taesung paused, feeling his throat closing on itself, his erratic breathing becoming too much to control. "It took everything, *everything* for me not to run and bow at your feet."

Yunseo watched as Taesung fingered through his hair.

"You say that I was your sun? You were the moon and the stars to me. Every time I looked into those eyes of yours, I would see my past, present, and future. I could hear the prayers that I yelled into the night to be answered echo back to me. I could feel the longing embraces I wished for granted. I could smell our room filled with our passionate love, and I could taste the way our bodies eclipsed together. Your days started and ended with me? Yunseo, you were the reason why my darkness felt so bright. You were the reason why I needed to exist. The sun blinds and burns where the moon shines and cools. You cooled the parts of me that were burning, and in turn, I burned you."

Yunseo felt as if the frame of his world was shattering, and a giant piece of wall crumbled from his cerebrum into his stomach.

"Why didn't you come back to me? Why act so indifferent when we first met? Why act like I was a simple friend, a nobody from the past, when all you wanted was to talk to me?"

Taesung braced himself backward against the granite of his island, finally daring to make eye contact with Yunseo. The pain and sorrow in his eyes stole Yunseo's breath away and his own eyes welled up with tears.

"Because I am pathetic? Because I am a waste of a human? Because I'm an insecure fuck who couldn't face the damage that I had caused you. I was terrified of you," his voice cracked. "I wanted to tell you the truth when I am strong enough. When I was worth your time and forgiveness, yet I wasn't smart enough to realize your need for the truth was more important than my need for your fucking understanding."

Yunseo inched closer and closer to Taesung until they were face to face. Yunseo was tired of this. Tired of the pain, the confusion, the wondering. Minseo was right, they needed to stop running.

"Just tell me the truth, Taesung. I'm done not knowing what happened. I deserve to know. Now."

Taesung held his gaze and nodded. In need of strength, he opened one of his hands and waited for Yunseo to give him permission to grab his. Yunseo stared at Taesung's invitation and gave Taesung a look that he knew meant yes. Intertwining their hands, Taesung led them to his bedroom and sat them on his bed. He left the door open in case Yunseo changed his mind and wanted to leave.

"Before we do this, please understand that I never expected this to happen and I am incredibly sorry for all the trauma that I have caused."

Yunseo nodded slowly, fearful of what Taesung would tell him.

"What did my sister tell you, exactly?"

Yunseo shrugged as he recounted the events from earlier.

"She only said that the two of you are half-siblings and that Mrs. Park is your stepmother. She said that the truth was your story to tell."

Taesung smiled weakly, grateful for his sister's respect.

"Do you remember Omma," Taesung began.

"Mrs. Park?"

Taesung smiled softly and shook his head.

"My real Omma."

Creases formed on Yunseo's forehead and he searched his mind for an answer. He tried to remember all their conversations from years ago before recounting the picture Taesung had shown Yunseo one night after dinner. It was a woman, no more than twenty-five years old, smiling into the camera, holding a chunky Taesung as a baby. She was so young, hair long and black as coal, and her eyes held the same twinkle that Yunseo had fallen in love with all those years ago.

"Haneul," Yunseo whispered. "You said that she died of cancer in your junior year of college. I remember when my parents died, you were exceedingly understanding and comforting. It was one of the first moments I knew I loved you."

"*Loved?*"

Yunseo said nothing.

"Right," Taesung murmured as he stood and grabbed a picture frame from beside his bed.

He took it apart before passing the photo to Yunseo.

Yunseo took the mysterious photo and only saw Taesung, Minseo, and their step-mother. He looked back up at Taesung, perplexed.

"Unfold its sides."

Looking down and unfolding the photo, he was now introduced to a balding, overweight man in a suit. The man had his hand clasped on Taesung's shoulder. While the others were smiling, the man supported a deep scowl of disappointment. Yunseo didn't know why, but he felt very uncomfortable looking at the man in the photo.

"That's my father," Taesung stated, taking the photo from him. Yunseo looked up at him alarmed and Taesung stiffened his laugh. "I know. I definitely got my looks from my mother. He wasn't a parent in my life when I was growing up. One day, when i was five years old, checks from an anonymous person started to flood in. I asked my mother who the checks were coming from, but she wouldn't tell me. It wasn't until I had entered college and she started losing hair, that she sat me down and told me who my father was. Park Kwangsoo, owner, founder, and Chairman of NSCo, your most dependable and responsible security company in South Korea." Taesung laughed sarcastically. "Yeah, that ugly bastard right there is my father."

"They supposedly met in a club in Hongdae and had a one-night stand," Yunseo raised his eyebrow. "In my mother's defense, she was drunk and her reasoning was impaired. Once she found out she was pregnant with me, she contacted him and got indifference in return. Father of the year. After that, my mother raised me on her own as a single mother, but I believe he kept tabs on us throughout the years because one day, strangely, my mother's medical expenses were paid for as well as my schooling," Taesung spewed; Yunseo felt the venom in each word grow more potent as they spilled from his lips.

"We never had much money and, at times, we would struggle, however my mother made sure I had everything I needed and kept me fed. I had started to make some money as an apprentice at a local custom shop when letters demanding my mother to set up a meeting between my father and I began to arrive. Shortly after my mother had been admitted to the hospital, he began withholding his money to blackmail my mother into making me accept him. I had to protect her from him. I bought an apartment closer to her hospital and decided to go to school near the hospital as well. I took up double shifts at work and threw out the money and the threats he kept sending."

"After a while, everything was fine. My mother was getting chemo, I was going to class, and we were hidden from his watchful eye," Taesung rolled his eyes. "Or so I thought."

Yunseo felt his hands clam up, noting Taesung's tone.

"What do you mean?"

Taesung lifted his head as he cast a pained look toward Yunseo.

"That night before our anniversary, I was kidnapped."

Cabrera

CHAPTER THIRTEEN

"What do you mean you were kidnapped," Yunseo screamed in terror.

Taesung's body trembled and his knees weakened. He didn't want to do this. Looking up to the ceiling and asking Buddha for strength, he continued.

"I had been walking home with Lino and a bag filled with decorations. I had planned to decorate the entire apartment so that when you came back from your sister's, you would be surprised."

Yunseo's heart refrained from staying still.

"I was turning the corner when a van pulled up and stuffed me and Lino inside. Lino had been barking while three men kicked and beat me until I was unconscious, suffocating me with a cloth soaked in chloroform."

Yunseo gasped.

Taesung shot him a look of reassurance.

"When I woke up, I was alone in a board meeting room with my father sitting across from me. I still remember how satisfied he was to see me beaten up and bloody. He remarked how good it felt to see me be put in my place. I would have punched him if they had not tied up my hands."

Yunseo grimaced at the image of a blood-caked Taesung and pushed it to the back of his head.

"Why did he kidnap you?"

Taesung breathed heavily.

"After sleeping with my mother, he went back to his normal life where he met Ahin, my stepmother. They got married and had a son named Sungmin. Sungmin was destined to follow in Kwangsoo's footsteps and one day take over the company. Except, he was an adrenaline junkie. He would sneak out of his home and consistently get in trouble with the police. One day, he illegally jumped from Daepo Jusangjeolli and couldn't pull open his wingsuit."

Taesung looked out of his window, images of Sungmin's mangled body plastering themselves behind his eyes.

"The accident was fucked and Sungmin died on the way to the hospital."

The urge to comfort Taesung surged through Yunseo, but nothing would present itself. So, he settled on sitting closer and touching his chest, feeling his brisk heart under his palm. Taesung looked down at Yunseo's hand and put his own on top, savoring the feeling of their skin.

"What does this have to do with you and me?"

Taesung swallowed hard, wishing he could push their laced hands through his chest.

Maybe then it would calm its frantic drumming.

"Kwangsoo needed a new heir for his empire. With my mother dead, he saw an opportunity and seized it. He stated that since I was the firstborn, it was my duty. The bastard stuck me in Ahin and Minseo's house without telling them what was going on and shipped me off two months later to Thailand to study business. It was one of the worst times of my life."

Yunseo was puzzled.

"One of them? What could be worse than being stripped of everything you've ever known."

"Losing you," Taesung whispered as he brought his attention back to Yunseo's face.

"Losing you felt like I was losing the air I breathe," Taesung shakenly admitted. "I was lost, scared, and regretful. I turned to drugs and alcohol, but nothing helped dull the ache that was birthed the day I was taken from you. I thought my life was over. I even thought about taking it too."

Yunseo said nothing. He was too afraid. Too afraid to tell Taesung he thought the same.

Taesung brought his face closer to Yunseo's and pressed their foreheads together.

"One day, after an intense night of drinking, I was stranded," Taesung sighed. "A monk saw me and gestured to me to follow him. With nothing to lose, I did. We walked for miles and miles until we reached his temple. There, he asked me to shower, have something to eat, and then pray with him afterward. This was at a time when I didn't know as much Thai as I do now. The man simply wrote something down and gave it to me to translate after our prayer."

Taesung released Yunseo's hand, noting Yunseo's quiver as he did. He walked over to his dresser and pulled out an old folded-up piece of paper, passing it to him. Yunseo unfolded it and found, in fading ink, the words ศรัทธาไปไกลกว่าอุปสรรคของภาษา written on the page.

"What does it say?"

"Faith goes beyond language barriers."

Taesung leaned against the drawer, the wood groaning underneath his weight.

"I stayed at that temple for three months, then officially converted to Buddhism a month after leaving. My father didn't care; for him, it was just another thing he could ignore or use to promote his heir. But for me…" Taesung paused, memories flooding back, the mixture of joy and pain from the day he declared himself a Buddhist lingering in his tissues. He remembered the warm smile from the man who took him in, the cheering that came from the M&Ms, and Ahin happily waving at him with tears streaking down her face. However, the one person he wished to be there was unable to attend. The sound of the buzzer his teacher used on his head was his only comfort.

"That day was mine and mine alone. It gave me hope for the future."

There was silence for what felt like an eternity. The emotions that filled the air were almost too potent to exist. The anger that Yunseo felt at Taesung abandonment and the pity he was experiencing for him were creating a lump inside his throat and water to collect in his eyes. The thought of a disarrayed Taesung walking the streets of Bangkok, drunk and alone, was an image that would haunt him forever. Yunseo folded the note back up and walked over to Taesung.

"Here," he whispered, handing the note back. Taesung opened his hand and Yunseo pressed the note inside, but before he could pull his hand back, Taesung closed his hand around it. Yunseo gasped, wrapping his other hand around Taesung's and pulling to be freed. This made Taesung pull him in closer and against his body.

With a groan, Taesung shakenly opened his mouth, "I dreamt of you every night when I was in that temple."

Taesung slid his head to Yunseo's right temple.

"Your scent," he breathed.

"Your eyes," he kissed Yunseo's eyes one by one before kissing the small mole below the left one.

"That beautiful nose," he kissed Yunseo's nose before hovering over his lips.

"And these lips. Every night and day, I would pray to anyone who would listen to let me kiss you again. One last time."

Yunseo was frozen to where he stood and the heat coming from Taesung was too inviting to ignore.

"Taesung," Yunseo pleaded. He couldn't kiss him. Not after everything that he was told. He needed time to think. To process. He couldn't just jump back in like the last five years didn't happen. That his suffering never happened. "I need time to wrap my head around everything you've told me. I am devastated for everything that that man has done to you, but that doesn't take away all the tears and breakdowns I have had because of you. I—I just need…maybe a week or—"

"He wants me to marry now, Yunseo," Taesung said as he caressed Yunseo's sides. "He wants to make us proper chaebols. Because he's new, he needs me to prove ourselves. He wants me to sire another member to the Park family so he can groom him and mold him into something better than me… something more like him. All to run his godforsaken company."

As Taesung leaned in, brushing their noses together, Yunseo felt a surge of warmth enveloping them.

"I never thought about being a father before. But if there was anyone I wanted to have children with, it would be you, Yunseo. I would want to wake up every day, clean up soiled diapers, and have the darkest eyebags with you, Yunseo, because at least we would be sleeping in each other's arms, worry-free about the kind of person our children would become."

"Taesung," Yunseo whispered, his mind reeling with the weight of it all. "This...this is too much."

"It is. It is and I'm sorry," his voice was heavy with regret. He tenderly pressed a kiss to Yunseo's temple, slowly releasing his grip on Yunseo, allowing space for gravity to sink in. "You hearing what happened is more than enough for me. It's enough for me forever if that's all I'm allowed."

Moving to the bedroom door, Yunseo permitted himself to look at Taesung. He looked tired. Depraved from sleep and in need of a hot meal. Yunseo was going to remark on such a comment but was distracted by the red ink that was visible on his skin.

"What is that?"

Taesung, bewildered by his sudden question, glanced around the room for Yunseo's sudden curiosity.

"What is what?"

Yunseo pointed to Taesung's arms.

"That red ink. Do you have tattoos?"

He smiled sadly at the realization that Yunseo had discovered his tattoos. It was only a matter of time. *I mean, I am wearing a sleeveless shirt,* he thought.

"Would you like to see them?"

Yunseo shook his head as he eyed the red-marked skin. He needed to leave. He needed distance.

"Another time. Sleep well, Taesung," Yunseo's words hung in the air, soft yet heavy. He turned and left, disappearing into the darkness.

Left alone, Taesung stood in silence, his heart heavy with a longing that threatened to crush him. He breathed heavily, the weight of Yunseo's absence pressing down on him like a weighted blanket.

"Without you," Taesung whispered into the empty room, his voice too strong in the stillness of the night. "Impossible."

As the hours passed, sleep remained elusive for both men. The night stretched on, filled with the haunting echoes of broken dreams and shattered hopes. The once quiet and empty void of

Taesung's apartment now seemed to reverberate with the ringing of their shared pain.

The sobbing of broken men sounded down through the halls, a symphony of anguish that seemed to permeate every corner of their shared space. And amid the cacophony, the steady ticking of the clock in the living room served as a relentless reminder of the passage of time, each tick a harsh punctuation mark in the time they lost.

In the darkness, they were both consumed by the overwhelming sense of loss, their souls intertwined in a dance of sorrow and yearning. And as the night wore on, it felt as though they were suspended in time, trapped in a liminal space where hope and despair merged into one. Yunseo in the what-ifs of their relationships and Taesung's recount the day of his kidnapping.

✦ . + . ✦ . + . ✦

When he walked home with Lino that night, the loving and loyal dog happily trotting alongside him, he was the happiest he had ever been. The bag of decorations swung gently from his hand, a silent promise of the surprise he had meticulously planned for Yunseo.

As they turned the corner, a van screeched to a halt beside them, shattering the peaceful evening. Before Taesung could react, masked men leaped out, overpowering him and Lino with brute force. Lino's frantic barks filled the air as the assailants mercilessly assaulted Taesung, their blows raining down on him until darkness engulfed him, suffocating him with the sickly-sweet smell of chloroform.

When consciousness reluctantly returned, Taesung found himself in a sterile board room, the harsh glare of fluorescent lights illuminating the scene before him. Across the table sat his father, a sinister smirk twisting his lips as he gloated over Taesung's battered form. Bound and unable to defend himself, Taesung seethed with potent rage, fists clenching in futile defiance. Kwangsoo looked the same as in the picture he had shown Yunseo earlier, only filthier. He disgusted Taesung to no end.

"My son! You're looking well! Have you been getting the letters I've been sending," Kwangsoo's voice was like nails on a chalkboard, ugly and irritating.

"Why can't you take the hint, old man," Taesung said, earning him a slap across the face from one of the henchmen standing next to him.

"Old man," Kwangsoo laughed. "I'm only fifty-six years old. I hardly look it too."

Taesung bit his tongue, trying not to laugh and earn himself another smack.

"Now, my dear son," Kwangsoo said, getting up and rounding the table. "I assume you've been watching the news. Have you heard about that kid who died jumping off Daepo Jusangjeolli?"

Taesung didn't respond.

Kwangsoo reached forward and squeezed his jaw, manually moving his head up and down.

"Great! I thought you might have. Well, that idiot was your half-brother, Sungmin. The idiot ignored his friend's warnings and used a faulty wingsuit. A disgrace," he said, releasing Taesung's jaw. "Can't believe he was going to control NSCo after my death. Thankfully, I have a spare."

Taesung stared at him, bewildered.

"A spare?"

"Oh come on, Taesung. You didn't think all those attempts to contact you were because I wanted to spend time with you," Kwangsoo bellowed with laughter. "Fuck no. I need you to take over your brother's place."

Taesung's blood turned to ice, and his burst lips were forgotten as he screamed.

"No fucking way! I'm not your fucking puppet! I don't even know—"

Kwangsoo smacked Taesung's face this time and ripped his head up when his son didn't have the energy to lift his head.

"Let me introduce myself then. I'm Park Kwangsoo, Chairman of NSCo, and I own you. Your entire life belongs to me, and if you try to run, if you try to fight, I will find everyone you love and kill them in front of you as I record it all."

Taesung was delirious; he couldn't stop his head from swaying side to side. He was helpless.

"You're bluffing."

Kwangsoo smiled.

"Bring the dog."

As the henchmen brought the angry and barking Lino into the room, Kwangsoo kicked it, sending it flying across the room.

"I see why you have this dog. Perfect size for soccer."

Taesung screamed with all his might as his father kicked Lino again and again. He looked at the men as they poured kerosene over him and shot daggers at them as they brought the jug over to the whimpering white dog cowering on the floor, pouring it all over him.

His father pulled a white lighter out of his pocket and flicked it on, its flame burning bright.

"You or the dog," he smiled. "Choose quickly, I would like to go back to sleep."

Taesung tried to yell out, 'Take me instead', but his lungs failed him, unable to speak through the nasty cough that tore from his throat.

"The dog then."

Kwangsoo dropped the lighter, and the room was engulfed by the smell of burning flesh and the earth-shattering screams of his and Yunseo's beloved Lino.

The memory of his father's callous satisfaction still burned in Taesung's mind, a reminder of the cruelty that lurked beneath the veneer of familial obligation. The scars, physical, mental, and emotional, served as constant reminders of the price he had paid for defying his father's twisted expectations.

But it was the memory of Lino's agonized cries that haunted Taesung the most. The smell of kerosene, thick and suffocating, filled his nostrils as his father set the beloved dog ablaze before his eyes. Taesung recoiled from the vivid recollection, the raw anguish of that moment clawing at his heart even now.

In that moment of misery, Taesung had felt the weight of his own cowardice, the bitter taste of failure lingering on his tongue. He had vowed never to forget the pain and loss that had shattered his world that day, carrying the burden of that memory with him as he forged ahead into an uncertain future.

CHAPTER FOURTEEN

Subin had absolutely no idea why he was here, in front of a gigantic building, watching Taesung carry what he assumed was Yunseo's luggage out of its entrance and into his car. He was even more confused when he saw Yunseo's pained expression as he thumped the bottom of his shirt, one that looked two sizes too big for him and had a piss-green neon cast on his arm. Subin thought it made him look like a highlighter.

They had said their goodbyes and Subin noted how both of their bodies had been ridged and frozen in place. Like they didn't want to say goodbye. Yunseo was the first to move, making his way into Subin's front seat.

"We can go," Yunseo said, settling himself into the leather.

Subin flicked his eyes over the stoned face of Taesung to the broken one of his friend and tilted his head.

"What about him?"

Yunseo pulled his feet up and buried his face into his legs. Well, as much as a person with a cast could.

"Let's just go. He won't go inside until I leave."

Subin didn't understand what was going on much less what this had to do with their employer, but noticing the tremor in Yunseo's voice, he turned the keys, pushed down on the gas, and high-tailed out of the parking lot into the freeway.

When they arrived at Subin's apartment and walked into his kitchen, the first thing Yunseo said was something Subin would never forget.

"I thought it would be bigger."

Subin whirled around and threw his hand over his heart in typical dramatic shock.

"It's big!"

Yunseo smirked and hauled his bag onto the counter.

"Who told you that it was?"

His lips quivered and he leaned forward.

"Are we still talking about my apartment?"

Yunseo bellowed out a laugh and pushed Subin away. Subin grinned at the joy entering his friend's face and felt a wave of triumph shoot through his body. Mentally high-fiving himself, he told Yunseo to place his bag in the second door to the left while he ordered pizza and Korean fried chicken. When he finished ordering, he looked up to see Yunseo in a new shirt holding something in his hand.

"What is that," Subin pointed.

Yunseo looked down and smiled bitterly, "Macarons."

He bursted into tears so suddenly that Subin didn't have time to catch the box before it fell. The macarons had spilled out and rolled in all different directions. Subin noted that it was like watching fireworks explode. He reached for Yunseo and rocked him back and forth while he closed his eyes in return, feeling the urge to cry sneak its way under his eyes. He picked and dragged a sobbing Yunseo onto his conch and wrapped him in a blanket Subin had forgotten to put away the day before. Yunseo held onto it as he drenched it in tears. Bright blue now turning into a deep indigo.

Subin had waited until Yunseo's tear dots were dried to exhaustion to ask him what had made him so distraught.

"Yunseo, what happened?"

He shook his head and tried to suck in as much air as he could.

"Yunseo," Subin said firmly. "You called me to pick you up from Gangnam, entered my car with our boss on your heels, kept silent the whole way here, and now you won't tell me what's wrong?"

Yunseo's voice trembled as he fought to find the words to describe the unthinkable.

"I... I just can't..." his voice caught. He took a shaky breath, trying to regain his composure. "You won't believe me."

Subin's gaze softened and placed his hand on Yunseo's knee, "Try me."

Taking a shaken breath, Yunseo explained his long and tortuous past with Taesung. From their early days at the bookstore to the apartment they both shared and to the nights before their world was shattered. His words were punctuated by sobs that threatened to overwhelm his speech. Each syllable was a struggle, the weight of his current situation too much to bear.

"I thought—I thought he didn't want me," he continued, his voice cracking. "I believed that he grew sick of me, and now—"

The tears streaming down his cheeks were making it difficult to see clearly. He wiped them away with the back of his hand, taking another deep breath to steady himself.

"Now, I don't know what to think," he implored, his voice small and meek. "He was taken from me... stolen from me. Though I can't help, but be angry with him, regardless of what happened to him. Does—does that..."

His voice trailed off. He gripped the back of his neck and squeezed, trying to calm his trembling body as he regained any semblance of self-control.

"Does that make me a terrible person," he managed to say, his voice barely above a whisper. "It hurts, Subin. It all hurts so much."

Another gut-wrenching sob made its way out of his throat, causing him to bow into his hands, overwhelmed by the rawness of his current situation.

Subin swallowed the developing lump in his throat. Even though he was confused and wanted to cry with Yunseo, he needed to be strong for him.

"If you're a terrible person then I don't know what I am. I must have a presidential suite in hell."

Yunseo lifted his head and rolled his eyes at Subin, smiling weakly. Always trying to weasel in a joke. He sat back and took deep breaths.

"I'm scared, Subin. I don't know how to feel anymore," he managed to say, his voice a mixture of sadness and helplessness. "I feel so lost, and... confused," he slammed his hand down and balled it up into a fist, squeezing as hard as he could, feeling his nails print crescent moons into his palm. "I don't even know why I'm telling you all of this."

Subin reached over and uncurled the painful-looking fist and soothed the dents with the pad of his fingers.

"You are telling me this because we're friends," Subin deadpanned, not letting Yunseo retreat from this moment. "Hell, we might be best friends after everything you have told me," he joked, trying to bring light into Yunseo's twisted situation.

He nodded softly at Subin's words and allowed him to cradle him. It had been a long time since he had a friend that he could be vulnerable with. As a man, he was taught to be strong and never, ever reveal his emotions to another man. Having a man, a man who was bigger and stronger than him, allowing him to cry and share his burden with them platonically, was something he was grateful to finally have.

Amid their comfort, the food arrived and Subin helped Yunseo to the table. The meal was filled with comfortable silence and occasional bursts from Subin; ones that made Yunseo laugh. As this ended, Yunseo offered to wash the dishes to which Subin strongly objected and ordered him to stay in his seat.

"You're an ass, you know that," Yunseo said softly, his voice a blend of genuine enjoyment and an unspoken appreciation.

Subin threw a smile over his shoulder.

"I'm the asshole who is letting you stay until your wrist gets better. I'm sure there are worse assholes out there."

"I doubt it."

Snorting, Subin finished washing the dishes and braced himself against the sink.

"What do you want to do now?"

Yunseo touched his puffy eyes and winced.

"I'd better go to sleep. Any more crying and my eyes will burst out of my face."

Subin smiled at Yunseo's change of attitude.

"Go then. I'll put everything away."

Mirroring Subin's happiness, he got up and hugged him good night, whispering his gratitude. Letting go, he made his way down the hall. Subin waited for the door to close before letting the impact of Yunseo's story weigh on his shoulders. Heavy-hearted, he recounted everything Yunseo told him and slumped back down in his seat.

Tears welled up in his eyes as the thought of Yunseo being alone all those years, feeling unlovable and worthless, streamed into his mind. It was soul-crashing and the image of Yunseo crying himself into panic attacks reminded him of himself and it was as if a dam had burst, releasing a flood of sorrow that he kept hidden.

Each tear that fell carried with it a mix of relief and shared grief. For too long, Subin believed he was the only one unworthy of someone's love and strangely felt connected with Yunseo through their shared insecurity. Yunseo had been the only person Subin had met to vocalize their low self-esteem.

Subin never let anyone see his struggle, always trying to be a pillar of strength. The one who held it all together for everyone else. Masking his pain and struggles behind a façade of composure was something he had mastered when he was just thirteen years old.

But now, in this moment of solitude, he allowed himself to surrender to the tide of emotions that had been built within from the start of Yunseo's story. The tears that came were not a sign of weakness, but a sign of relief. He pinched his skin trying to stop it in fear of Yunseo hearing his cries but couldn't. His body shook as he muffled his sobs with his hands, one clamped down on the other, wanting to rather choke than have Yunseo walk in and see him in his unguarded state.

Soon several moments passed by and he knew this had to stop. Taking a shaky breath, he clenched his fists and willed himself to regain control. The sobs had wracked through his body, leaving him drained and exhausted. Now, with determined resolve, he focused on slowing down his breath and reigning in the overwhelming emotions.

He closed his eyes and took deep, steady breaths, savoring the feeling of the cool air filling his lungs. Exhaling slowly, he wiped away the remaining tears and straightened his posture, as if the physical act could somehow translate into emotional composure. He decided it was time to head to bed as well. He packed up the rest of the food and placed it in the fridge. After grabbing a pint of Baskin Robin's mint chocolate ice cream, all he wanted was an episode of *Nevertheless*, ice cream, and a shit ton of sleep.

◆ . ⁺ . ◆ . ⁺ . ◆

"Where are you taking me, Moonbin," Soyeon screamed, her braid starting to unravel in the wind as the man against her chest turned a sharp corner. Moonbin chuckled at her reaction, enjoying the way she squeezed around him.

"I told you! You have to wait and see."

Rolling her eyes, she laid her cheek against his back, listening to the music he had synced to her helmet.

It had been a month since Mrs. Park decided to halt all private flights. Myunghwa was not happy about this, and when she suggested hiring another pilot, Ahin firmly stated that she would not fly with anyone outside the original four. Soyeon had never seen Mrs. Park so angry. The usually wonderful and kind woman now stood in front of Myunghwa, defending one of Soyeon's dearest friends and co-workers. Soyeon was deeply touched by Mrs. Park's loyalty and thanked her, to which she responded that they were her family now—and that she preferred they start calling her Ahin from now on. Soyeon was shocked, not expecting such a gesture from her employer, but she agreed nonetheless, not wanting to waste the moment of familiarity. A few weeks after Moonbin and Soyeon's lesson, he convinced her to let him take her somewhere. With Soae constantly occupied with Mikasa, Soyeon found herself with more and more free time. So, she said yes.

The sun dipped below the Seoul skyline, casting a warm orange glow over the bustling city streets as Moonbin met Soyeon at her complex once again. From Incheon to Seoul, he promised her a surprise that would change her life. Soyeon clung to that anticipation as Moonbin turned another corner, and the sound of buzzing gradually surrounded them. At first, she didn't notice it, but then the buzzing intensified, pulsating in her chest, then her hands, until it was right in front of her.

Over the horizon, Soyeon was greeted by the dazzling sight of a million headlights from motorcycles and cars of all kinds. A surge of anticipation and excitement washed over her as the glow of vibrant lights shimmered against the dark skyline, drawing her in with their mesmerizing allure. Closer now, the lights grew brighter, casting a radiant glow that illuminated the landscape, revealing the racetrack as a ribbon of asphalt twisting beneath the canopy of lights. Tall floodlights cast dynamic patterns across the surface.

The air hummed with the engines of vehicles speeding around bends, while neon signs flashed, adding to the exhilaration. As Moonbin drove closer, they were greeted by people revving their engines and cheering. It was as if he was king of the realm. Vibrant colors painted the scene as cars approached, their headlights slicing through the darkness like shooting stars.

Moonbin parked his motorcycle near the track and hopped off, adjusting his glasses.

"Surprise," he yelled, throwing his hands out and walking in circles.

Soyeon hopped off and removed her helmet, her hair flying everywhere, causing Moonbin's heart to skip a beat. She looked stunning. Her eyes widened with wonder as she took in the numerous men, women, and teenagers gathered around cars and motorcycles. It was a scene she never knew existed until now.

"What is this place," she asked.

Moonbin smiled and dropped his hands.

"We call it Homeland. This," he said, gesturing with his finger, "is where I come to pray."

"What are we doing here?"

"Well," he took her hand, leading her to the track before them. "I promised I was going to show you how to ride. I thought this was the perfect place to demonstrate what can happen if you master the art of it."

Soyeon stared at his face in disbelief when she saw a familiar shadow. She veered closer, leaning against the cement border of the track, her hair falling around her face, and when she saw the brown curls and handsome face, she knew.

"Minseok!"

She turned back to Moonbin, and he looked proudly at her, as if to say, *That's my brother! That's my hyung!*

Moonbin squeezed her hand, nodding.

"Yup. Our lovable old man is about to race."

"But… how… when—"

Moonbin brought their laced hands up and placed his finger on her lips, momentarily getting distracted by how soft and moist they felt.

"No more questions, just look at the way he rides the bike. Look at the way he respects it and lets it guide him, not the other way around."

Bringing her attention back to Minseok, she saw him positioned at the starting line, waving at her before taking off at the sound of a gun. Soyeon watched as Minseok became a deity in motion, commanding the sleek machine with a mastery that mirrored a god astride a mighty dragon. With every twist of the throttle, he unleashed the beast's power, propelling them forward with a ferocity that echoed the thunderous roar of a dragon's voice. His grip on the handlebars was firm yet fluid, guiding the motorcycle with divine precision as if he wielded reins of flames.

Soyeon screamed as Minseok's opponent tried to sabotage him, attempting to cut in front of him and shove him into the wall, but Minseok was able to swerve around them, throwing them a middle finger as he did so.

"Why did he try to do that to Minseok?"

"That's how we do things here, Soyeon. We only have three rules. Go hard, go fast, and don't lose."

This made Soyeon scream louder when Minseok won the race, watching as others jumped the barrier and crowded around him. Moonbin helped her jump over and protected her as they made their way through the crowd and hugged Minseok in congratulations.

"How did you do that," she said, trying to be heard over the chanting of his name.

Minseok's grin was captivating, drawing Soyeon in with its charm and warmth.

"Practice. I heard Moonbin is teaching you," he said, taking in her appearance, his eyes brimming with elation. "You'll be a demon on the road."

Soyeon shook her head.

"I'm just a flight attendant. I'm only learning because Moonbin is teaching me."

Minseok laughed and pulled her in closer, eyeing Moonbin.

"I know my brother, Soyeon. He wouldn't be teaching you if he didn't think you had potential."

Soyeon clasped her hands and hugged him tightly, not believing that this was happening to her.

Moonbin pulled Soyeon out of Minseok's embrace, giving the man a quick one of his own before taking them back over to the sidelines. When Soyeon gave him a funny look, he laughed.

"We have to get ready for the next race, darling. Don't wanna be roadkill, right?"

The night went on just like this. Moonbin's hand around hers, giving it occasional squeezes and kisses, and Minseok, throwing her finger hearts after each win. Soyeon was starting to think that trusting these men wasn't such bad idea after all. That at the end of the day, there are still a few good apples lurking around the patch. Even the ones that were covered in leather.

CHAPTER FIFTEEN

"Excuse me, but you're five minutes late for your seven a.m. meeting," the assistant reminded Taesung as he gazed out of the sleek sedan window, observing its graceful navigation through the bustling streets of Gangnam.

Taesung reflected on the morning, filled with regret and turmoil. He had spent the previous day in prayer, seeking guidance from Buddha to ease the pain piercing his heart and tearing his thoughts apart. His home was a sanctuary of prayer and tears, a silent testament to the inner turmoil he battled.

With a sense of purpose fueled by his phone's screen, Taesung realized it was time to end the game his father had ensnared him in. Dressed sharply in all black, he felt the weight of determination as the car surged through the streets, a solitary vessel carrying him toward a confrontation that felt more like a funeral.

"Very well. Ensure we arrive within the next five minutes," Taesung replied, turning his gaze back to the passing scenery outside.

Through tinted windows, Taesung found himself absorbed in the pulsating heartbeat of Gangnam, where towering skyscrapers pierced the sky, each one a testament to the district's modernity and prosperity. Neon signs adorned every corner, their glow painting the streets below with a tapestry of vibrant hues, while bustling crowds moved with purpose amidst the endless stream of activity. From the chic boutiques lining the boulevards to the elegant cafes tucked away in hidden alleyways, every facet of Gangnam exuded an irresistible allure that captivated both locals and visitors alike.

As the car approached NSCo's imposing building, Taesung's anticipation grew, his body vibrating with adrenaline.

Entering the board meeting, Taesung found the room tense, his fellow board members frozen in their seats, some impeccably dressed while others appeared disheveled, their faces flushed with red handprints. His gaze moving, it soon settled on the source of the chaos: his father.

Park Kwangsoo remained unchanged in appearance, yet time had etched its mark upon him with precision. His once jet-black hair now bore the hue of silver. His teeth had dulled into a shade reminiscent of aged parchment. His suit clung to his frame as if in protest against the passage of years, its buttons straining against the size of his gluttonous belly. But it was his eyes that pulled Taesung's attention. They were sunken, depths consumed and voided of any flicker of humanity save for that single, burning ember.

Rage

Smirking, Taesung took his seat, his hands resting calmly on the mahogany desk as he surveyed the men around him, understanding what had taken place before his arrival.

"Ah, here comes my worthless son. Enlighten me, what excuse do you have this time!"

Kwangsoo swept a stack of papers into the air, the sheets cascading like fallen snow onto Taesung's lap. No need for him to glance at them; he already knew what they contained.

"Father, we've exhausted every effort to salvage the company's reputation," Taesung began, his voice measured. "Despite our best attempts to identify the source of leaked illegal dealings and firearm trades, our efforts have been in vain. Shareholders have withdrawn, clients have canceled contracts—it was inevitable."

"I don't care about your failures! Why didn't any of you use your resources," Kwangsoo bellowed, his fist crashing onto the polished surface. "My photos and those of our dealers have been circulating on the internet, yet none of you have acted! Do you want to lose your jobs?"

Taesung glanced at the trembling men beside him, fear evident in their eyes as they recoiled from the threat of his father's wrath. Quietly gathering the scattered papers, Taesung rounded the table, positioning himself next to his father.

"Actually, we're all losing our jobs," Taesung announced calmly.

Kwangsoo's eyes widened in disbelief, his shoulders squaring off against his son's stature.

"What are you talking about?"

"We're filing for bankruptcy, Appa. It's a decision we've all agreed upon in your absence, considering it's the best course for the company and its employees."

Kwangsoo's fist shot into the air, aiming for his son's face, but Taesung intercepted it with his palm. Attempting another strike, Kwangsoo found his other fist caught as well, leaving him stumbling back into his chair, humiliated.

"How dare you," he shouted, scanning the room. "How dare you make this decision without my knowledge! This is my company, mine! I hold the majority of shares. I made you all who you are. I own you!"

Taesung's laughter filled the room, chilling in its wickedness. Kwangsoo watched in shock as his son's laughter grew louder, more sinister with each passing moment.

"What's so amusing? Have you lost your mind," Kwangsoo demanded.

Taesung wiped away tears of laughter, his demeanor shifting from amusement to a menacing sneer.

"You haven't checked your reports, have you?"

Confusion washed over Kwangsoo as Taesung revealed the truth—a truth that shattered his world. Taesung now held the majority of shares, a fact he had concealed, waiting for the opportune moment to reveal and humiliate his father.

"What do you mean? Speak clearly boy!"

It was as if thunder had struck, gone was the laughing boy and here was a terrifying man, sneering in his father's face, eyes darker and crueler than his.

"You don't own the majority of the shares anymore, I do. I bought them a little while ago and have been waiting to tell you. To embarrass you," he shifted, coming close to Kwangsoo's ear. "To ruin you."

Kwangsoo pushed Taesung back, eyes beaming back and forth.

"Is this true," the men only watched him, fear in their eyes. "Speak!"

"Yes," exclaimed a man, the gentleman small and thin, pushing back his brown colored glasses and straightening his tie. "Mr. Park owns sixty-five percent of the shares, the board owns twenty percent, and you... you now own fifteen percent, sir."

Kwangsoo was enraged, his world was crumbling around him. He wouldn't accept this defeat, wouldn't allow everything he'd built to slip away.

"I won't let you destroy everything I've worked for," Kwangsoo declared, turning back to his son.

Taesung clinked his tongue and rounded the wooden slab again, making his way back to his seat.

"We shall see. All those in favor of keeping Chairman Park Kwangsoo on board, raise your hand."

Kwangsoo watched in horror as no one in the room raised their hand.

Taesung chuckled, "All those who oppose."

Every single man's hand went up and just like that, he had lost everything.

"You're fired, effective immediately," Taesung declared, sealing his father's fate.

The events that ensued happened in a flash. Kwangsoo leaped onto the table and made his way over to his son, a murderous gleam in his eyes. Taesung was able to dodge the man and strike him down his back, his elbow digging into his spine. The men stood and called for security, knowing that the brawl would only get worse. Kwangsoo was able to land a hit on his face, blackening one of his eyes and cutting his cheek. He didn't feel the pain though. Not when he was watching his father get dragged out of the company he so violently fought to keep. Not when his abuser had just lost everything. Not when he had won.

"You sound different today," Dr. Im said as she pressed the phone closer to her ear. "Calmer. Almost like you're numb."

Yunseo stared into his mug.

"Maybe because I am. Feels like I'm running on empty."

Dr. Im rolled her eyes, moving her notebook closer to her and starting her, bruising the inner part of her middle finger against her pen.

"You've missed our past appointments the last month," Dr. Im's eyes narrowed. "Have you been taking your Klonopin?"

His blood flared.

"Please don't tell me you are suggesting my disinterest in feeling is because you think I've been misusing my medicine again," Yunseo was antagonized. "Do you even have a genuine degree?"

Dr. Im wrote faster.

"Nice, being rude and defensive. Totally by the book signs of a stable and healthy client."

Feeling stupid, Yunseo's face dropped to his hands.

"What do you want me to say, hm? I've been taking my pills, answering your questions and I still feel like shit. When will it get better, Doctor," he raged. "When do I get better!"

She leaned back into her chair and listened to his labored breath. It was clear that he was upset and didn't want to discuss what was going on, but she was a pusher. It's what she gets paid to do.

"Did something happen with Taesung?"

Yunseo felt his stomach drop and his blood run cold.

"What does he have to do with this?"

"The last time we talked, you were verbally upset about meeting him and now you're telling me that you are numb. Sounds like quite a coincidence."

"Isn't it a good thing I am not mad at him anymore," Yunseo fired back.

Dr. Im breathed deeply, holding onto her composure.

"No. At least then you were actively communicating how you were feeling," she stopped writing. "You and I both know something is bothering you, so you have two options: a) stop wasting your time and hang up *or* b) tell me what has made you so infuriated that you refuse to acknowledge it."

Yunseo fumed at the straightforwardness of Dr. Im. He wanted to hang up and refuse to ever speak to her again. While thinking of excuses to make to Haeran, he heard Dr. Im's softened voice creep into his ear.

"Yunseo, I have been your psychiatrist for two years. Let me do my job and help you."

Rubbing the rim of his mug, he reluctantly held the phone closer to his ear, feeling his defiance dissolve.

"I stayed with Taesung for a few days. It was… chaotic to say the least."

She paled at the news, her pen cracking across her pages with renewed purpose.

"That bad?"

Yunseo chewed on a cuticle as he recounted the way Taesung skin felt against his own. A tugging in his stomach had him shifting in his seat.

"It wasn't so bad. It was… you know… therapeutic? I guess?"

She was intrigued.

"Go on."

"I mean. It wasn't anything crazy," Yunseo said, downing the rest of his hot chocolate.

"We talked."

"Talked?"

"Yeah… At first, we argued. About the past. About what happened and he told me things that I didn't know about. Things that were out of his control."

"Out of his control," Dr. Im questioned.

She was skeptical of what Taesung might have told Yunseo to have him suddenly hating him less after all these years and sessions.

"What did he say?"

"He said that after his mom died his father wanted to see him. Taesung had refused, but his father took him away and cut off communications, alienating him from those he knew. His father wanted Taesung to be made in his image, not his mother's," Yunseo said as he cherry-picked what to say.

He couldn't tell his psychiatrist that his ex-boyfriend was stolen in the night and kept hostage for five years and was being forced into a marriage with a woman he didn't love and have a child he didn't want, could he? No, he couldn't.

Dr. Im pulled up her search engine and began to type Taesung"s name.

"Taesung's father," she questioned as she was welcomed by the sight of the gallery of photos of his father. "Is he short and bald?"

Yunseo stiffened at her perfectly detailed description.

"How did you know that?"

Dr. Im smirked at Yunseo's surprised tone.

"I looked him up."

"Are you allowed to do that?"

"Not relevant," she said. "Yunseo, I'm having a hard time understanding. He explained his side of the situation to you and now you've forgiven him? Or are you more furious that he didn't fight his father to stay? What are you feeling? Try and explain it to me."

Yunseo hated this. Hated that he had to answer questions he didn't know the answer to. He fought the urge to retreat into himself and disappear. He didn't know how to feel.

He looked around the room seeking some form of distraction, as if the boring details of Subin's dining table could shield him from this conversation. But the psychiatrist's voice, patient and soothing, guided him back to the topic at hand.

"I don't know how to feel about it, Dr. Im," Yunseo admitted. "I'm angry and sad, and lost, and broken, all at the *same fucking time*, and I feel like I'm drowning. I can't help, but blame him for the abandonment issues, anxiety, and depression I went and currently go through, but the thought of him going through even a fraction of what I went through, it's enough to cripple me."

He bit his lip, trying to keep the urge to cry at bay. Not that he had anymore tears to give.

She let his confession hang in the air. She needed Yunseo to realize how much of a breakthrough this was, to declare his complicated emotions while still feel the need to dissect them and label them in a box was brave. He needed to know that.

"You love him," she revealed softly. "You love him regardless of everything he put you through and you hate yourself for it."

Yunseo released a laugh and Dr. Im listened carefully as it transformed into Yunseo trying to steady his trembling breath. He didn't want to believe her. He wanted to fight her, insult her again, tell her she wasn't doing her job right, but in the end, he knew. He knew she was right. No matter how much he watched his chin to stop shaking and his eyes watering, he knew.

I never stopped loving Taesung.

"Yes," he conveyed in a low voice, feeling a load come off his chest. "I do. After everything, I still love him. Does that make me a bad person?"

"No," she expressed quietly. "It makes you human."

The phone call only lasted twenty minutes before Dr. Im scheduled him for his next appointment. Yunseo felt exhaustion take over his body. He slumped over the table and decided he would lie there until Subin strolled out of his room, rubbing a towel on his head.

"Get dressed. We're going out."

Baffled, Yunseo perked up in his seat.

"Why?"

Subin grinned at Yunseo's dumbfoundedness.

"Because I heard your screeching tone and I think it would be healthy for you to get out of the house."

Yunseo felt embarrassed.

"How much did you hear?"

"Nothing I didn't already know," Subin said. "We don't have to talk. We can just go out and have fun."

Yunseo narrowed his eyes.

"What do you have in mind?"

Subin stopped drying his hair and flashed Yunseo a grin.

"Camping."

And that was how Yunseo found himself sitting in dirt watching Subin set up their tent. Yunseo was impressed how fast Subin was able to gather all the supplies they needed. He had lamps, a canteen, camping beds, meats, desserts, etc. It was insane. He had asked Subin how he found a campsite in Incheon, to which he responded, "I'm filled with surprises, Yunseo. I'm just that interesting."

Yunseo had no idea what that meant.

"I'm done," Subin shouted, clapping his hands and brushing invisible dust off his shoulders. "Come help me with the food."

Yunseo gave him a thumbs up before helping him with dinner. It was nothing crazy: Korean rice cake skewers, Coke-a-Cola, leftover fried chicken, and rice. It was an impressive spread. Yunseo had set the portable gas stove and grilled the skewers and chicken when Subin pressed a beer bottle against his neck. Screaming and almost burning himself, he glared at Subin.

"What the hell, Subin. I'm cooking here. Which, by the way, isn't easy when you're doing it one-handed."

He rolled his eyes as he took the tongs from Yunseo and replaced them with a beer.

"If you can't multitask then move over. Go over by the firepit and look at the scenery while I do all the work."

Yunseo, cursing at Subin's absurdity, walked over and sat in one of the two chairs beside the fire pit. The view in front of him was indescribable. The sun was setting over the water as the sky was layered with pastel colors. Sunsets were always Yunseo's favorite. To some people, the sunrise represented a start to a new day, its colors washing away any remnants of the night before. Yunseo on the other hand, felt as if sunsets were like the world was giving him permission to reset and let him know that it saw his best. The swirling colors were like his own personal firework show, alive and bursting with life. It only made the heat from the fire lit next to him that much warmer.

Subin had brought over the food and carried over two new beers. The meal had been quick and the beers had been quicker. Yunseo had been on his second beer, Subin on his third, when he opened his mouth.

"I'm still in love with Taesung."

Subin took a thoughtful drink from his bottle before replying.

"Are you okay with that?"

Yunseo looked back at him stunned.

"Are you not angry at me?"

He furrowed his eyebrows.

"Why in the hell would I be angry with you? After everything you've been through, the last thing you need is my judgement instead of my compassion."

Yunseo stared at Subin, confused. He never thought of that. All he's ever known was judgment ever since he was a child.

Yunseo remembered the yelling coming from his mother's mouth. He remembered feeling less than and unworthy. He would ask himself things like: *How did I get here? How did I become the monster of the family? In reality, am I the one who is wrong? Everything I have thought, done, said; were they all wrong due to my way of thinking. Due to... me?* All those questions replayed more and more in his head after his parents' death.

✦ . + . ✦ . + . ✦

In the gentle hum of the fabric store, time seemed suspended for Yunseo and Haeran as they reveled in another weekend spent together. Haeran, engrossed in selecting fabrics for her latest project, moved gracefully among the colorful bolts while Yunseo watched her with admiration, occasionally capturing snapshots of her work to share with Taesung. He pondered whether to ask her to craft something special for Lino once again. But their peaceful moment was shattered when Yunseo's phone abruptly interrupted the serene atmosphere, its insistent ringing cutting through the air like a sharp blade. An unfamiliar number flashed on the screen, igniting a spark of apprehension within him as he hesitantly answered, half-expecting the call to be from the new co-worker his boss had hired that week.

"Yunseo," his mother's voice thundered through the phone, crackling with static, and rattling his very mind. Haeran's quick instincts kicked in, sensing trouble, she ushered them both into the sanctuary of an empty bathroom at the rear of the store, the door slamming shut behind them as she snatched the phone from Yunseo's trembling hand.

"How did you find his number? What do you want," Haeran demanded, her voice slicing through the tension with a sharp edge of defiance.

A mirthless laugh echoed through the phone, dripping with malice and a twisted sense of triumph.

"You thought we wouldn't find you, you sneaky brats," Eunae sneered, relishing in the power she held over her children like a vengeful deity. "We got a letter from Yunseo's school, asking to confirm the change of his address. We're on our way to Seoul right now."

Haeran's eyes darted up from the phone to meet Yunseo's wide, terrified gaze. Frozen in place, memories of past beatings and worthlessness flooded his mind, staining the fragile fabric of the new life he had painstakingly woven for himself.

"Come here, and I'll have you arrested," Haeran threatened.

"And our daughter has forgotten her manners," Hoseok's voice, like a cold hand gripping their hearts, interjected with chilling finality. "I'll beat that defiance out of you. By the time I'm done with you, you'll be begging for remission."

"Appa, I—" Yunseo's attempted to speak, yet he was swiftly silenced, drowned out by the cacophony of his parents' rage.

"And you! Just wait until I get my hands on that little boyfriend of yours," Hoseok's words were a venomous hiss, promising unspeakable horrors to come.

Yunseo's heart raced, dread settling over him like a suffocating blanket. And amidst the torrent of threats and hatred, one word reverberated in his mind: *Hide.*

I must hide him. I must save Taesung.

"We know about that boy of yours," Eunae's voice dripped with poisonous satisfaction. "We'll make him wish he never loved a worthless waste of space like you. You deserve nothing but death. You serve no purpose. Explain to me, what purpose do you serve others who matter?"

With a heavy heart and trembling limbs, Yunseo slid down the cold tile wall of the bathroom, his sister's arms encircling him in a desperate embrace, offering solace amidst the storm of their parents' cruelty.

But even as he sought refuge in his sister's comforting presence, Eunae's voice continued its relentless assault, each word a dagger plunged deep into his wounded soul.

"I should have aborted you two. I should have carved you out of me and thrown you into the river," Eunae's words were a twisted symphony of hatred, echoing the horrors of their shared past. "No one will love you, care for you, or need you."

A thunderous pounding on the bathroom door shattered the fragile semblance of safety, the sound echoing the merciless blows Yunseo had endured for years. And in that moment, amidst the chaos and despair, Haeran's defiant cry pierced the darkness like a beacon of hope.

"You're wrong," she screamed through tears, her voice trembling with raw emotion. "I love him! I love him more than I fear you, and he loves me! No matter what you do, we have something you'll never have."

"What is that, child," Eunae spat, her voice dripping with contempt.

"Each other. We have each other," Haeran's words hung in the air like a whispered prayer, a fragile lifeline amidst the tempest of their parents' hatred.

But even as hope flickered in the darkness, fate intervened with bone-chilling finality. A deafening crash screams of terror, and then... silence.

As the door behind them swung open and the shopkeeper approached with a mix of concern and confusion etched upon his face, the siblings exchanged a silent glance, the weight of their newfound reality settling upon them like a suffocating shroud.

Dead.

Their parents were dead, and they had heard it all.

Haeran collapsed into her brother's arms, her sobs echoing through the crowded confines of the bathroom, while Yunseo sat iced, a numbness spreading through his veins like icy tendrils, longing for the comforting embrace of Taesung, his beacon of light amidst this darkness.

✦ . ⁺ . ✦ . ⁺ . ✦

"Subin"

"Hmm"

"Do you think..." he looked away, ashamed of what he was going to say. He waited for Subin to ask him a question yet heard nothing. He looked over and saw that he was just waiting. No jokes. No sexual innuendos. Nothing. Just a blank face and silence.

Releasing his breath, he pressed on, "Do you ever think life would be better if we weren't here?"

Silence.

He waited, and, *waited... and wai—*

"Yes."

Surprised, he leaned towards his direction, but didn't see Subin. This person before him was someone else entirely. There was an aura to him unfamiliar to Yunseo. It gave him goosebumps. Taking a swig, Subin cleared his throat before looking over to him.

"When I was younger, I lived in the United States. I had a father who was arrested, and my mother and older sister had to pick up the slack. I believe that at first, it all came from a place of love, but—" Subin tightened his hold on his icy beer. "When the welts are taking a month to heal and the fear of going home becomes you spending an extra ten minutes of every day teetering on the edge of the Golden Gate Bridge because you believe that death...nothingness, must be better than this..." Subin snapped closed his eyes shut, the whites of his knuckles rivaling the brightness of the fire.

Yunseo could only survey this Subin. After some time, Subin opened his eyes again with a shuddering breath.

"I may not know exactly how you may be feeling at this moment, but what I will say is that taking that leap is not worth it. All it does is take up space and hurt the people you love."

The noise from the cicadas was their music as silence laid its hands upon the duo.

Yunseo responded after a while.

"You're Korean American? No wonder you're so shameless."

The sound of Subin's roaring laughter and Yunseo's pained groans from Subin elbowing his ribs were the only things heard as the baby blue sky faded into a gorgeous nightfall.

CHAPTER SIXTEEN

As the morning sunbathed the Han River in its radiant glow, Mikasa and Soae walked hand in hand to the spot they had chosen for their picnic, the tranquil view of the water perfectly mirroring their mood. The gentle breeze carried the delightful sounds of children's laughter and the tempting scent of breakfast sandwiches, enveloping them in a serene atmosphere.

As they settled down, Soae couldn't help but admire Mikasa's thoughtful gesture as she twisted open the lemonade bottle and handed it to her with a soft smile.

"I'm so glad we decided to come here so early. It's so peaceful," she remarked.

Mikasa nodded her eyes gleaming with excitement as she opened her own beverage.

"Me too. I remember when I first came here. It felt like an oasis in the middle of the city, completely separate from Seoul's bustling atmosphere."

Soae reached into the basket they had brought, retrieving slices of fruit, while Mikasa went to her bike, returning with a bouquet of red roses tied in beautiful wrapping.

Soae's eyes lit up with delight as she accepted the roses, planting a kiss on Mikasa's cheek. The roses adorned the space between them as they enjoyed their meal, their conversation flowing effortlessly, filled with shared laughter and stolen glances. They discussed everything from favorite books to childhood dreams, each revelation bringing them closer together.

Soae couldn't help but tease Mikasa about her favorite song choice.

"Lonely Boy? By TXT? That's your favorite song," she exclaimed with a laugh.

Mikasa rolled her eyes, popping a grape into her mouth.

"Why are you judging me right now? It's a good song! And Yeonjun is hot."

Soae stopped laughing, a mischievous grin spreading across her face.

"Aren't you a lesbian, Mikasa?"

Mikasa allowed a playful smile to grace her lips as she spun around, propping herself up on her elbows.

"Yes, but that doesn't mean I can't appreciate perfection when I see it."

Soae leaned in closer to Mikasa, feeling suddenly daring.

"And now? What do you see now?"

Mikasa took her time to look at Soae, her gaze filled with admiration. It had been two months since their canceled trip to Tokyo, and during this time together, Mikasa never ceased to be captivated by Soae's beauty. She traced the curve of her nose and the soft jawline that gave her a youthful appearance. Mikasa admired the way the glitter on Soae's eyelids sparkled, but her favorite feature was the mole at the bottom-center of Soae's left eye. She reached out to touch it, using it as an excuse to bring her face closer.

"A being crafted by the universe itself," Mikasa whispered.

"That's cheesy," Soae replied, feeling the heat of Mikasa's lips, longing for their touch.

"It's working, right," Mikasa teased.

Soae hummed in agreement as Mikasa gently parted her lips, their tongues dancing in a tender embrace. Soae placed her hands on either side of Mikasa's face, savoring the intimacy of the moment. They kissed leisurely, cherishing each other until Soae accidentally opened her eyes and caught a few people looking at them, whispering and pointing.

Startled, Soae pulled away, Mikasa whining at her sudden retreat and already pulling her back in.

"Mikasa," Soae said. "We're being watched."

Mikasa dropped her hand, turning around to look at the group. The onlookers jolted when seeing Mikasa straighten up and throw them the middle finger, turning and licking Soae square on the lips in front of them.

"Mikasa," Soae yelled, slapping her hands over the older's lips. Mikasa pulled her hands away from her mouth and placed kisses all over them, rubbing her face against them.

"Let them look. Let them envy and fantasize about being in our place," Mikasa declared, biting one of Soae's knuckles, stealing her breath. She looked up with a mischievous grin. "You're mine in this moment. I'm yours in this moment. Let us have this moment. Let them witness the beginning of something great. Something special."

Speechless and touched, Soae nodded, resting her head on Mikasa's lap and playing with the yellow grass. She twirled the plant as she looked up at Mikasa, who was already gazing down at her like a flawless angel.

"Is this the part where you ask me to be your girlfriend," Soae teased.

Mikasa chuckled and nodded her head, stroking Soae's forehead.

"Soon, Soae, soon. I want to learn every little thing about you before I do."

"Why," Soae asked, her heart pounding.

"Because," Mikasa said, her voice filled with adoration. "When I do, I'm convinced that it will be my last time asking that question. I want to be sure that when I ask, I can recall everything about you from memory. That your memories and thoughts are locked in my brain as my own. Because when I do, I'll know then that I am irrevocably and incandescently in love with you."

Soae found herself unable to think, her heart pounding so fiercely it felt as though it might leap from her chest.

"Are you close to it?"

Mikasa looked out into the river, placing her hands behind her.

"Almost there, little one. Almost."

Yunseo stood beside his car, nerves churning within him like a tempestuous sea. After two months, this was the first day Yunseo was cleared to fly. It had been a week since he had stopped taking the Vicodin, and the grueling pain of his hand had ended. He had gone back to his apartment two weeks ago, feeling grateful for Subin's honest words and selfless hospitality. He had continued his therapy sessions throughout his recovery. The sessions were tough, stressful, and liberating. Admitting out loud that he still loved Taesung was still jarring, but it was freeing to know that he wasn't stupid, wasn't a fool for loving a man who he had believed stopped loving him.

Sometimes, after the sessions, when he had finished recording their conversations and lessons learned in his journal, he would sit on the floor and stare at the memory box he couldn't bring himself to throw out. Inside were photos, ticket stubs, candy wrappers, and letters. Taesung had this habit of leaving letters in Yunseo's books when he first stayed over at Yunseo's apartment. It was endearing and touching until Haeran found a partially spicy letter in his copy of *The Song of Achilles*. From then on, Yunseo decided it was best to sleep over at Taesung's apartment.

But now, as he walked onto the tarmac with the wheels of his suitcase rolling behind him, he tried to guess the reactions of the M&M and others. He looked around and was surprised to see a lack of guards and guns, only spotting one or two employees from the airport fueling the plane. He thought of asking where the others were until he felt the arms of Soyeon and Soae around him.

"Oppa," Soyeon said. "When Myunghwa told us that you were coming back to work, I almost didn't believe her."

"Yeah," agreed Soae. "We've been texting you over and over for the past two months, but you hadn't texted back. We had to get our updates from Subin."

Yunseo smiled apologetically. He pulled back but held them close.

"I know, I'm sorry. A lot of things have happened during the months I've been gone."

"I'll say, Soae is basically dating the redhead biker girl."

Soae pinched Soyeon, earning a hearty laugh from Yunseo.

"You're one to talk! What about you and Mr. Glasses."

Soyeon shushed her friend as she looked over her shoulder, watching three motorcycles draw closer.

"Can we please talk about this later," she said, rushing the trio into the airplane. "Subin is already inside, setting up for the takeoff."

Stepping onto the airplane, he was greeted by Minseo, who embraced him fondly.

"I'm so happy to see that you're all healed now. I hope that the conversation with my brother went well," Minseo whispered, leaning back and pinching his rosy cheeks.

Yunseo laughed like a child as Minseo did this.

"Of course not," Yunseo said, folding her hands into his own. "I don't know what's worse; knowing the truth or having to face him after knowing it.

"I guess we'll see, won't we," she said as the roaring of the motorcycles came to a stop beside the plane. "I'll let you get ready."

Yunseo turned to walk away before, he stopped, realizing someone was missing.

He glanced around, noticing the absence of Ahin.

"No Mrs. Park?"

"No, she and Minseok are staying behind for some errand," Minseo said, waving her hand. "Those two are always up to something."

He smiled, remembering the pair's soft curls and auburn hair.

"Can I ask you another question?"

"You can ask me all the questions, Oppa."

Yunseo smiled graciously, a little taken by the endearment reserved for brothers and the closest of male friends.

"Why are we flying at night?"

Minseo looked outside her window, watching as the stars said hello back.

"Because it's peaceful," she said. "At least that's what I like to think the reason is."

Yunseo questioned this as he entered the cockpit, finding Subin with his uniform jacket off, picking at his nails, bored out of his mind.

"Thank god," he said, turning around, relief evident in his voice. "Now I can finally fly a plane again."

Yunseo sighed heavily, smirking as he took his spot next to him.

"Yeah, whatever asshole. Just don't get in my way."

"I would never!"

Yunseo ignored him as he pulled his things out of his bag. He felt a familiar bottle of pills and looked at Subin, realizing he was already being watched.

"My old pills," Yunseo said, holding up the bottle.

"Do you want me to flush them," asked Subin, his hand already open and waiting.

Yunseo wrapped his fingers around the orange bottle, shaking his head.

"No... no. I need to be the one to do it."

Getting up, he walked over to the curtains and pulled them back, greeted a rather tired and handsome specimen.

"Taesung."

He blinked, not ready to see his love.

"Yunseo."

"Taesung," Yunseo said tentatively.

"Yunseo," he replied, bowing quietly, walking over to a seat, not sparing his sister a single look while doing so.

Feeling like a deer caught in headlights, he opened the bathroom door and slammed it close behind him. He poured the pills into the water of the toilet and flushed it, vanquishing the last of who he was. He slipped the bottle back into his pocket, exiting the bathroom. During the extra ten minutes they had before takeoff, Moonbin and Mikasa came in and greeted Yunseo, saying how happy they were to see him back and healthy. Swiftly afterward, each one made their way to the flight attendants, Mikasa kissing Soae's temple, causing her to giggle while Moonbin openly and lustfully stared at Soyeon, smiling in a way that reminded Yunseo of Taesung when they would play with each other in the dark.

Yunseo looked over at Taesung but found that the tall man had his head buried in his arms, headphones snuggly hugging his ears.

Frowning, he turned and sat back next to Subin, cursing under his breath.

"This is about to be a long flight isn't it," Subin asked, moving the airplane to where the men on the tarmac were directing them.

Yunseo grimaced, taking off his hat and placing it on top of his bag. He rolled his neck and cracked his knuckles, as if ready for a fight.

"You have no idea."

The flight stretched on for what felt like an eternity, lasting a mere two and a half hours. Yet, in that confined space, time seemed to crawl at an agonizingly slow pace for Yunseo. It provided ample opportunity to observe the interactions around him: the flirtatious banter between the bodyguards and his friends, Subin's relentless chatter, and Minseo's indulgence in mukbang videos. But amidst the cacophony of voices and distractions, there was one notable absence—Taesung's voice.

Yunseo strained his ears, longing to hear even a whisper from Taesung. He began counting the minutes, hoping for some sign of his presence, but each passing moment only deepened his unease. Beads of sweat formed on his forehead, trickling down his face, forcing him to constantly swipe them away. The worry gnawed at him incessantly; Taesung was never one to remain silent. He had always been the most outgoing person Yunseo had ever met, second only to Subin. For Taesung to be quiet now was deeply unsettling, filling Yunseo with a sense of foreboding.

Perhaps that's why he found himself standing alone in the chilly weather, clutching Taesung's long-sleeved shirt tightly, his eyes fixed on the horizon without blinking, even as the wind tousled his hair and stung his eyes. Meanwhile, the others were being hurried away by Subin, who valiantly attempted to shield Yunseo and Taesung from the prying questions of Soae and Soyeon, with Moonbin chuckling at his futile efforts to move him. Mikasa and Minseo offered supportive smiles, silently hoping that their loved ones would find solace and relief from their inner turmoil.

As the group finally receded into the distance, their voices fading into the background, Yunseo seized the opportunity to break the silence.

"What is wrong with you?"

Taesung didn't turn.

"You need to be more specific," Taesung said dryly.

Yunseo spun him around, taking in his appearance in detail. The face of his ex-lover carried a myriad of emotions and physical signs of fatigue. His eyes, once bright with vitality, appeared dull and weary, with dark circles underneath indicating sleepless nights or stress. His gaze, lacking its former intensity, appeared distant and unfocused. As if he was lost in thought or weariness. Lines and wrinkles, once subtle, were more pronounced, etched into his skin by the weight of whatever was pressuring him. His complexion, once tan and rich, was now pale and shallow.

Yunseo was unsettled.

"You look—look..."

"Sexy," Taesung joked, a small spark of his former self entering his pupils.

Yunseo grabbed his arms and shook his head.

"Taesung," he said in that voice. The one that told Taesung that he wouldn't be able to charm his way out of this. Not with him. Not with his Little Star.

Taesung looked at him and brought his body closer, Yunseo allowing him.

"I'm tired, Yunseo. So, so tired."

They stayed like that for a while until they pulled away, Yunseo cupping his face.

"Tell me what was going on."

Reaching up and rubbing one of his hands, he guided Yunseo to one of his waiting sedans. Taesung said something in Japanese to the driver and off they went. Taesung had interlaced their hands, something that still took Yunseo's breath away, making him feel lightheaded.

Arriving at the grand entrance of a hotel, Yunseo found himself enveloped in a world of luxury and sophistication just like in Thailand. Towering above them, the hotel's sleek glass reflected the vibrant lights of Tokyo's bustling streets, creating an aura of elegance that was impossible to ignore.

Stepping out of the taxi, Yunseo couldn't help but feel a sense of awe at the sheer opulence of their surroundings. A cascading waterfall greeted them at the entrance, its crystal-clear waters sparkling in the soft glow of strategically placed spotlights.

The sound of the water mingled with the gentle hum of city life, created a harmonious symphony that set the tone for their arrival.

Taesung offered Yunseo his arm as they made their way into the lobby, their footsteps echoing against the marble floors. The lobby itself was a masterpiece of modern design, with soaring ceilings adorned with intricate crystal chandeliers that cast a warm, inviting light over the space. Plush velvet sofas and armchairs beckoned guests to relax and unwind, while impeccably dressed staff bustled about, attending to every need with sincerity.

Approaching the check-in desk, Taesung and Yunseo were greeted by a concierge who welcomed them with a warm smile and a bow. The check-in process was swift and seamless, only handing him a key card in a sleek black envelope embossed with the hotel's emblem and a silver letter P.

"Let me guess," Yunseo said as they made their way to the elevators. "You own this too."

Taesung turned to him, his eyes looking more and more like before, easing Yunseo greatly.

As the elevator doors opened on their designated level, they were greeted by a corridor adorned with exquisite artwork and lush floral arrangements, a testament to the hotel's commitment to refinery.

Reaching Taesung's room, Taesung slid the key card into the slot and pushed open the door, revealing the suite. Floor-to-ceiling windows offered panoramic views of the glittering city below, while sumptuous furnishings and tasteful decor created an atmosphere of indulgence and comfort.

Yunseo shot Taesung an awed glance as they stepped into the room. He caught sight of the room's well-sized marble bathroom to the plush king-sized bed adorned with crisp linens; every detail had been meticulously curated to ensure guests' stay was nothing short of extraordinary.

Taesung moved to one of the nightstands and threw the key onto the desk. He placed his elbows on his knees, cradling his head in his hands. Yunseo nervously stepped closer and sat beside him, hands folded in his lap.

Taesung turned to Yunseo, his voice barely above a whisper.

"I liquidated my father's company. I took him for all he had and destroyed the thing he loved most."

Yunseo's mouth fell open, his pupils dilating. His stillness caused Taesung to look over at him and release a breath, humored by his Little Star's reaction.

"I won, Yunseo. I finally won his game."

His admission washed over him like icy water. Yunseo reached out to take his hand, his touch soothing Taesung's demeanor.

"Why do you look so miserable then? If you won, why do you look like you lost everything?"

Tears welled in Taesung's eyes as he looked into Yunseo's confused gaze, his walls crumbling with speed.

"Because the thing I want doesn't want me."

Yunseo stilled.

"What do you want, Taesung?"

Taesung shook his head, walking away from Yunseo.

"You know what I want."

Yunseo rose from the bed, his hands picking at his uniform.

"I need you to say it, Taesung."

Taesung stood with his back to Yunseo until he suddenly marched toward him. Kneeling, he bowed his head, sending a surge of panic through Yunseo.

"I want to be with you again. I want to be happy again. I want to have dinners with my family with you, watching you laugh at Minseo and my friends' banter. I want to get a pet and watch it grow old with you," Taesung said, lifting his head, tears streaming down his face. "I want to have children with you and show them what true love and family is."

Yunseo watched as Taesung wrapped himself around his legs, holding him tight as he pleaded into them.

"I just want to be myself again, Yunseo. The person I was before all of this. I don't even remember the man I was before all of this."

Yunseo reached down and brushed his hair back, lifting his face and feeling his tears dampening his skin through his clothes.

"I do. He was smart and charming, able to enchant me out of my clothes and into bed. He was able to make me see stars with the slightest touch and make me feel loved with the smallest look. He was my dream answered, and the way he held me and nurtured me was the reason why I believed love existed in the first place. After my family's crash, he proved to me night after night how wrong they were and how much love I deserved. That man," Yunseo stopped, tasting tears on his tongue. "That man saved me, Taesung."

"Then I broke you," Taesung whispered, forcibly wiping his tears, angry at what he had done.

"Maybe," Yunseo said as he lifted his head again. "But it wasn't all your fault, Taesung. I don't think any of this was."

Taesung slowly stood as Yunseo's hand slid to his neck, feeling his pulse quicken under his touch.

"You should leave," Taesung said, enjoying the other man's touch a little too much.

"Why," Yunseo said, intoxicated by their proximity.

"Yunseo, if you don't, I'll lose my mind," Taesung confessed, gently removing Yunseo's hand from his neck. "I want to be fully present when I am with you, but right now," he sighed, "my thoughts are a jumbled mess, and I don't want that for myself."

Yunseo's heart clenched at Taesung's words, the pain of their situation weighing heavily on him. He knew it was best to give Taesung space, to allow him time to sort through his emotions.

I won't want to leave you.

With a heavy sigh, Yunseo reluctantly stepped back, releasing Taesung from his touch. He looked into Taesung's eyes one last time, seeing turmoil and longing reflected in them.

"I'll go," Yunseo said softly, his voice barely above a whisper. "But if you can't talk to me, talk to the M&Ms or Minseo. Promise me."

Taesung nodded silently, his expression a mix of gratitude and sorrow. As Yunseo turned to leave, he felt a pang of sadness in his chest, wishing things could be different.

As Yunseo walked away from the room, he couldn't shake the cloud of emptiness that had settled over him. He longed for the days when their love had been uncomplicated, when they could simply be together without the weight of their past looming over them.

But for now, all he could do was give Taesung the space he needed. He opened his phone and called Subin, listening to the rings. Subin answered the call after the second ring.

"What happened? Did you guys hook up?"

Unexpectedly, Yunseo burst out laughing, his bellowing echoing down the hall.

"What room are we in?"

Yunseo heard Subin release an exaggerated sigh.

"That's a no."

"Subin—"

"It's room 613. I expect details," with that, he hung up.

Yunseo entered the elevator and pressed the sixth button, hoping that Subin would give him the courtesy of letting him get some sleep.

CHAPTER SEVENTEEN

Despite Yunseo's hopes for some rest, Subin's relentless curiosity deprived him of any hope for sleep. Throughout the flight, Subin bombarded him with questions about Taesung and what had transpired between them. Regardless Yunseo's attempts to dodge the interrogation, Subin's persistence wore him down, leaving him barely able to keep his eyes open as they flew back to South Korea.

Flying back to South Korea from Tokyo during daytime, allowed the cityscape below to bloom in the most spectacular way. The sun casted the landscape with a warm glow, causing long shadows to dance across the streets and buildings. From above, Tokyo looked like a bustling ant colony, tiny figures moving in the rhythm of daily life. Yunseo marveled at the sight—the skyscrapers stood tall and proud, their windows reflecting the sunlight in a dazzling display of colors. From this vantage point, the city felt alive with energy and possibility, a vibrant metropolis brimming with life.

As they landed in Seoul, Yunseo felt a sense of relief wash over him. Taesung's quiet acknowledgment was bittersweet, a silent confirmation of their conversation last night and the truths they shared. Despite the weight of their spoken words, Taesung remained distant, never addressing the elephant in the room again.

Through the exhaustion weighed heavy on his shoulders, Yunseo found solace in the breathtaking view. As they flew closer to Seoul, he couldn't shake the feeling of gratitude for having experienced such a remarkable city.

As he stepped out of the aircraft and watched Taesung mounted his bike and ride off, he asked Minseo beside him, what was the point of going to Japan if they were only there less than twenty-four hours.

"I wanted taiyaki and castella," she said, lifting her bags, showing him the goods. "I wouldn't let Taesung hire a chef to cook it for me so he took me to Japan so I could buy it myself."

Yunseo looked at her, shocked that their mind worked that way.

"You know how that sounds, right?"

Minseo shrugged.

"I got what I wanted so I'm happy. What about you," she questioned. "Did you get what you wanted?"

Yunseo mused over the question as he sat on the floor, two nights after his return, staring at Taesung and his memory box. He had worked up the courage to go through it all day and finally was going to open it. Lifting the lid, he looked at everything fondly before picking up a Polaroid. It had been the first one they had taken when they first moved into their apartment. The same one Yunseo had stood alone in, staring at the white walls that used to echo back their laughter at Lino's outrageous barking.

The polaroid was worn with age and the edges were soft. The once-vibrant colors had mellowed into a gentle reminiscence of a bygone era. The image was of Lino being sandwiched between Taesung and Yunseo faces. Their eyes were closed, the deep creases at the corner of their eyes showing how happy they were at that moment. Holding the photograph, Yunseo was flooded with nostalgia. As he traced the faded hues of the Polaroid, solace landed her hand on his soul and pushed him to release the anger he felt and accept that Taesung had no control over what happened with his father. Accept that Taesung was hurting like he was. Accept that he wasn't unlovable, invaluable, unworthy of being loved or held or even kissed.

Taesung had not left him. Taesung had not chosen to hurt him, to cause him issues that he still dealt with today. This was not a matter of blame anymore. This wasn't a matter of betrayal or abandonment. This was a matter of Taesung being taken away from him. Yunseo placed the photo down and looked at his phone: five-thirty. Looking back to the box, he opened KakaoTalk. Smiling softly, he pressed the call button.

"Hello," came Taesung's voice, tinged with surprise and curiosity.

"Hey," Yunseo replied, his voice steadier than he expected. "I was thinking... Would you maybe want to go out for dinner?"

The weight of the past hung in the air as Yunseo waited for a response. Yunseo held his breath as he heard a soft exhale, almost as if Taesung had been holding his breath as well.

"Dinner?"

Yunseo nodded instinctively, though Taesung couldn't see him.

"Yeah. I thought it might be nice to talk about...everything."

Another beat of silence passed, and then with a soft voice, warmed with gratitude, he broke the silence.

"I'd like nothing more."

Yunseo's heart skipped a beat, heat spreading over his face.

"Great! Meet me at Auntie's Barbeque. Eight o'clock."

He didn't hesitate.

"Sounds perfect. I'll meet you there."

Yunseo was hanging up the phone when he heard Taesung whisper something faintly. It almost sounded like Thai.

The wind felt like razors on his face. Yunseo was currently outside of Auntie's Barbeque waiting for Taesung to arrive. Pulling his wool scarf over his mouth, he cursed at himself for leaving his facemask. He was dressed casually, opting for a cream sweater and washed jeans. He was regretting not putting on more layers.

Tired of the cold, Yunseo decided to enter the restaurant and wait for Taesung inside. As he placed his hand on the handle, he felt a hand gently tug on his elbow.

"Hey," Taesung panted. "I'm so sorry for being late. I was rushing over here, but then I accidentally drove into a pothole. Then, I had to call Moonbin to come, pick me up, and drive me here while Mikasa took my car back to the garage."

Stunned by Taesung's panic, Yunseo couldn't stop the foolish smile that came over him. Taesung was speechless and stared at Yunseo, perplexed as to why Yunseo was smiling so wide. Taesung was distracted by the smile lines under his eyes. It was his favorite thing about Yunseo. He never thought he would see it again.

He opened the door and held it for Taesung.

"Come on," Yunseo beamed. "Let's talk over some bibim-guksu."

Feeling shocked and a little uneasy, Taesung stumbled, trying to grab the door from Yunseo and hold it open for him in return. This only added to Yunseo's elated mood.

Once inside, and receiving a big hug from Big Momma, they sat and ordered their meals. Yunseo watched as Taesung squirmed in his seat nervously, no doubt wondering why he was there and why Yunseo wanted to talk to him. Yunseo couldn't stop his good mood. Yet, knowing Taesung was probably shitting bricks, Yunseo took pity on him.

"Nervous," Yunseo playfully questioned.

Taesung jumped slightly at Yunseo's confident tone. He had never seen him so assured. So playful. It made him anxious.

"Of course I am," Taesung admitted. "After I sent you away in Tokyo, I cursed myself for it. I chased after you, but you were long gone by then. I believed I had messed up the opportunity to reconcile with you. Not that I deserve to. I wouldn't have been surprised if you never wanted to speak to me after that."

Yunseo looked at him thoughtfully as he took the bowls of noodles from the waiter's tray and pushed one toward him.

"What if I did," Yunseo tested. "What if I never wanted anything to do with you again?"

Putting down his chopsticks, he bowed his head.

"Then I would leave and never come back," Taesung lifted his head, his expression hard and determined. "I would swear to never darken your doorstep again."

"So serious," Yunseo jested. "Relax, Taesung. I'm not here to banish you. I'm here to talk," he stopped, fixing his wording. "More like talk to you about how I feel about everything after hearing your side of the story."

Taesung tilted his head, confused, but waited for Yunseo to continue, his meal forgotten. Deciding he had tortured Taesung enough, he placed his own chopsticks down.

"I have been discussing everything with my psychiatrist," he stopped when he saw Taesung's panicked face. "Don't worry! I haven't told them about everything! Just the necessary... details."

"Details," Taesung scratched his eyebrow. "What kind of details?"

It was Yunseo's turn to squirm in his seat.

"That it wasn't your fault that we broke up. That it was out of control what happened to us. That it wasn't your fault that you left me..." he cleared his throat, trying to regain control over his wobbly tone. "You being taken away from me caused me to have issues and fears surrounding abandonment. Surrounding self-worth. Surrounding whether or not I was worth being loved," Taesung opened his mouth to the object but was silenced by a wave of Yunseo's hand. "Please, let me finish."

Reluctant, Taesung pressed his lips tightly together and folded his hands together, if for nothing else but to hide the pain Yunseo's words were causing him. Yunseo lowered his hand.

"My suffering was not your fault. Though I do at times catch myself being loathing you, I can't stop myself from imagining how lonely you were. How different it was to be taken away from everything you've ever known and be thrusted into your father's twisted world. To be held prisoner," his eyes burned, but he fought to finish the truth he had been neglecting these past couple of months. "And, more than anything, it's unbearable and agonizing to see you and lie to myself."

Not caring to wipe away the tears that dripped from his face, he leaned forward and took note of Taesung's face. It was laced with anticipation, worry, and...hope? The air was heavy and thick, only amplifying the raging beat and thunder Taesung was feeling in his chest. Yunseo smiled, feeling grateful to see Taesung hadn't lost his transparency. He had always been an open book.

"I love you," Yunseo confessed. "Even after everything that has happened, I still love you."

Taesung's blood ran cold. His eyes widen, a mixture of shock and disbelief washing over him.

"What—what did you just say?"

Yunseo nodded, his gaze unwavering.

"I love you, Taesung. I've tried to move on, God knows I've tried. But I can't. Being with you and knowing the truth about what happened, I just can't do it anymore. I can't ignore the hole in my heart. A hole that has been there since you left. Since you were stolen from me."

Tears glistened in Taesung's eyes, his lips trembling as he struggled to find words.

"I never stopped loving you," he reached over and grasped Yunseo's hands, softly running his thumb over his knuckles. "I fought every day trying to come back to you. Being without you was hell. I cried every night hoping, dreaming, praying that something, someone would take pity on me and let me see you one more time."

Taesung pressed a kiss onto Yunseo's hands before burning his face in them.

"Thank you. Thank you for loving such a terribly flawed man like me."

Yunseo shook his head as he wiped away Taesung's tears.

"It wasn't your fault, Taesung. None of this was your fault."

Taesung only cried into his hands as Yunseo brought their foreheads together. Neither cared if people were looking, judging, or whispering about them. After years of being apart, they couldn't give a shit if people condemned them for loving each other in public. They weren't going to hide, not now. Not ever.

Silence settled between them, heavy with the weight of unspoken truths and lingering regrets. And then, as Taesung pulled back from Yunseo's hands, a smile broke across his face, a radiant expression of joy and relief.

"You have no idea how much I've longed to hear you say that again," Taesung whispered, his voice filled with a mixture of tenderness and elation.

Yunseo's own lips curved into a smile, the barriers that had kept them apart for so long suddenly crumbling before them.

"*You* don't know how long I've wanted to say it again."

Taesung pressed their foreheads back together, slightly rubbing their noses.

"Nothing can take me away from you, now. You're stuck with me."

Yunseo tightened his hold on Taesung's hands, interlocking their fingers.

"That's the idea."

As they held each other, a sense of warmth and familiarity enveloped them, as if the years of separation had been erased in an instant. Their hardships and misfortunes crumpled away, leaving only the two of them, locked in a moment that held the promise of a new beginning.

Taesung pulled back, wiping his tears away with their interlocked hands. It was silly, but he didn't care. The fact that he was in this moment, holding Yunseo's hand, was enough for him to rocket into the atmosphere.

"So, what do we do now," his voice was soft but resolute.

Yunseo's gaze held steady, a newfound determination burning in his eyes.

"We take things one step at a time. Rebuild what we had and not let anyone get in the way this time."

Taesung's smile grew wider, a mixture of gratitude and happiness radiating from every pore.

"I'm in. But I have just one question. Well—three actually," mischief dripping from his words.

"What are your questions," Yunseo said, already feeling heat spread through his body and down to his center.

"One," Taesung said as he let go of Yunseo's hand and held a finger up. "Can I tell my family?"

Laughing, Yunseo nodded happily.

"Only if you tell Minseo first. I have a feeling she would kill me if you didn't."

Chuckling, Taesung agreed.

"You and I both."

Yunseo smiled, "Second question?"

"Can I call you Little Star again?"

The words washed over him, a gentle grin tugging at the corners of his lips. The old endearment stirred a feelings of love and fondness, evoking a rush of joy tinged with a hint of wistfulness.

"I was always your Little Star, Taesung. What's your third?"

Taesung signaled to come closer. As Yunseo leaned in, he snaked a hand onto the back of his neck and pressed his mouth to his ear.

"Can I touch you?"

Yunseo felt his knees buckle as his eyes fluttered shut. He gripped the edge of the table, trying to keep from falling back into his chair. Licking his lips, he thought it was now or never to be daring.

"Only if you're willing to give me everything you got."

Yunseo regretted that immediately.

CHAPTER EIGHTEEN

Taesung had Yunseo hot and breathless. Pinned to the wall with his arms above his head, he was helpless to Taesung's dominating mouth as he made his way down his throat. He licked slow and burning strips as he spoke soft words against his skin.

"How do you taste so good," Taesung said as he nibbled on Yunseo's neck. "You taste just like before. It's driving me insane."

Taesung continued his descent down Yunseo's neck and onto his chest. He kissed him through the fabric of his sweater as he let his hands wander. When he had reached his nipples, he tilted his head back to watch as Yunseo squirmed and struggled against his grip. With eyes shut tight and a reddened face, Yunseo was completely under Taesung's control.

"Aw, look at you. You were all red," Taesung stated in a teasing tone. "I wonder if the rest of you is this red."

Letting go of Yunseo's suspended arms, he lifted him and walked them from the entrance of the apartment to the black island in the kitchen. The same island where Yunseo had enjoyed macarons and wonderfully cheap convenience store food. Now, he would be the one eaten.

Moaning at the cold surface of the island, Yunseo held onto Taesung's back and buried his face into his neck.

"Taesung, it's cold. Take me somewhere warm."

Taesung grinned as he laid all of his weight onto him and leveled his head next to his ear.

"Don't worry, Little Star," Taesung growled as he flattened his groin against Yunseo's. "I'll make you feel as if you're burning."

Taesung lifted himself onto his elbows and began to thrust their clothed groins together. He watched as Yunseo's eyes screwed themselves tight and grabbed onto his forearms, breathing heavily with his head thrown back. The sight alone made him want to skip foreplay and thrust deeply in him. He wanted Yunseo drooling with ecstasy. He wanted to swallow him whole.

Yunseo's moans filled the hot air with passion and submission. He had forgotten how it used to feel like. Letting someone feast upon him as he slowly drifted up and up towards sickly sweet pleasure. Feeling safe and at peace as the one he loved had his way with him. Though he had remembered how well Taesung knew his way around the bedroom, what Yunseo missed most was how he made him feel. With every stroke of Taesung's hands, he had the ability to, even if momentarily, make Yunseo forget all his troubles. With every kiss on his neck, he released a cry of satisfaction instead of one of torment. Taesung's cock was not what Yunseo only wanted. He wanted to connect his soul with Taesung's again. He wanted Taesung to be his again.

Taesung rubbed a little harder as he pulled off Yunseo's sweater and kissed down his naked chest, leaving marks of his existence. He had missed how responsive Yunseo was to his tongue. He knew the marks he was doing would only pale in comparison to how red Yunseo's skin was. Be it impatience or arousal, Taesung couldn't take it anymore. He reached down between them and unbuckled Yunseo's pants.

"Taesung! Wait," Yunseo said, snapping out of the deliciously hot daze. "I'm dirty! I need to clean myself."

Taesung chuckled as he ripped off Yunseo's pants, taking his underwear with it, and pumped Yunseo's cock slowly.

"Nothing about you is dirty to me. Not one thing."

Yunseo wanted to object but the swipe of Taesung's tongue silenced the rest of his protest as he fell back onto the hard surface, arm coming over his eyes as he grabbed onto Taesung's hair. Taesung groaned at the taste of Yunseo and sucked harder, as if the flavor would bless him with the gift of permanently imprinting itself onto his tongue. He shifted his mouth from the shaft to the balls. Yunseo tugged at Taesung's hair, causing Taesung's cock to twitch in return. Not wanting to let go, he grabbed hold of Yunseo's thighs so he wouldn't be able to inch away. Yunseo couldn't stop the heaving of his chest as Taesung licked and sucked his way down to his hole. He felt like there was no air left. He could only breathe in Taesung. Could only feel Taesung.

The flattening of Taesung's tongue against him had him moaning his name and grabbing the edges of the island.

"Please Taesung," Yunseo groaned as his tongue dug deeper. "Just take me already."

Taesung stopped and raised back onto the balls of his feet.

"Already begging, jagiya? I have barely begun."

Yunseo could only crack his eyes open and welcome the most erotic image he has ever seen. Taesung stood before him, mouth wet with saliva and pupils blown out, breathing heavily. He had a hunger in his eyes that he had never seen before. Yes, when they had sex before it had been passionate and rewarding, but this was entirely new. The hunger in Taesung's eyes looked as if it could never be extinguished. Taesung could eat and devour Yunseo for thousands of years and never tire. Never complain. Never be satisfied with only the insertion and release they would share. He would never be satisfied until their souls were fused into one, a promise to never share one another with others.

"Please," Yunseo tried once more. "Take me."

Taesung smiled a self-satisfied wolfish grin and leaned in close to Yunseo's face, bringing his mouth meters away from Yunseo's.

"Call me hyung. Call me hyung and I will give you what you need. Do it and I am yours to do with."

Yunseo's eyes flicked from Taesung's mouth to his eyes. He was acutely aware of Taesung's cock throbbing against him and it took everything inside him not to whimper at the sensation.

"Hyung, please make love to me."

Taesung crashed their lips together as he scooped Yunseo's by the thighs and carried them into his bedroom. Yunseo held tightly to his neck as he suddenly swarmed with the scent of Taesung everywhere. Taesung's woody and spicy aroma sunk its claws deep into him and ground him. It felt as if the very smell of his partner was trying to claim him.

Carefully placing Yunseo onto his bed, Taesung pulled himself away and stared at the perfection in front of him. He was reddened, breathless, and his. He was his again to love, to treasure, and he would not let anyone take him away from him again. Five years of aching, needing, begging, and Buddha had finally taken pity on him. Granting the one thing he wished for on the day of his *buat nak*. A second chance.

Yunseo raised himself onto his elbows in time to see Taesung unbuttoning his shirt. Taesung was deliberately going as slow as he could, savoring the impending reaction Yunseo would have to his new body. As he threw his shirt to the floor and pulled his pants off, leaving him only in his black boxer briefs, he heard Yunseo suck in a breath. Looking back up from the floor he saw Yunseo on his knees, calling him closer with his hands. Taesung swallowed a lump of nerves that suddenly appeared in his throat and granted Yunseo's request. Yunseo stood up on his knees and laid his hands upon Taesung's chest, exploring in wonderment at how drastically the man he loved had changed from the last time he had seen him.

"You are beautiful," Yunseo whispered as he pressed a kiss onto the middle of Taesung's chest, causing the twenty-six-year-old to groan so deeply, he was sure he did not sound human.

Standing up, Yunseo circled him as he furthered his exploration. He slid his hands from Taesung's chest to the back of his arms, but stopped when he was greeted with the sight of the mysterious red ink again.

"Your tattoos."

Taesung clenched his hands and steadied his feet, "Yes?"

"Their... their..."

Yunseo couldn't find the words. It was impossible. Yunseo didn't believe the words even existed.

Understanding why Yunseo was speechless, Taesung picked up where he couldn't continue.

"They're for the ones I've lost. This one," Taesung pointed to the back of his neck, "is my mother's name, Haneul."

Yunseo traced his finger on the Korean lettering, awed by the beautifully spelled tattoo.

"These two," Taesung continued, reaching and guiding Yunseo's hand to the space at the back of his arms right above his elbow, "are for you."

The tattoos in question were simple. On the back of Taesung's forearms were two stars next to one another. The tattoos mirrored each other and, funny enough, the stars were modeled after the stars in Peter Pan. The ones that he used to guide Wendy and her brothers to Neverland. Yunseo's eyes welled up with tears because he had never thought that a simple declaration of escapism would lead to this.

Taesung had once asked why Yunseo's name tag had stars and he had only responded with, "Peter Pan was the only movie my parents allowed me to watch from America when I was a little boy. Seeing Peter Pan help children escape from their parents was something I wished for, prayed for as a child. Obviously, he never came. But, the stars of Neverland never left me."

Now here was Yunseo, staring at his stars on the body of the man he loved.

"How... when..."

Taesung turned around and held a teary-eyed Yunseo close to his chest.

"The night after declaring myself as a Buddhist, I decided to immortalize you on my skin. My father took away my ability to touch you, but he couldn't take away my ability to remember you."

Yunseo cried harder after hearing this and slid to the floor with Taesung as his mind, body, and soul soaked up what Taesung had done. Five years of believing he was unlovable and here was Taesung showing him how much he couldn't bear to be without him. Taesung wiped Yunseo's tears away in hopes of calming him down, stopping when Yunseo's voice broke from his throat in a wet and almost non-existent whisper.

"That's three."

"What?"

"You said you had four tattoos, you have only shown me three."

Taesung stared at Yunseo before stretching his neck to the side, baring his tattoo to the eyes of his star.

Yunseo stared at the tattoo with confusion.

"What does 222 mean?"

Bringing his gaze back to Yunseo, Taesung lifted one of his hands and cupped Yunseo's face.

"It was the time I was taken from you. July 11, 2016, at 2:22 a.m. This number reminds me of the best and worst day of my life," Taesung said as he rubbed away a new freshly fallen tear. "It reminds me of the best moments I had with you."

Yunseo couldn't hold himself back anymore. He launched himself onto Taesung's lips and kissed him like he was going to disappear. Taesung returned the gesture with the twist of his tongue and guided them from the floor onto his bed again. Pushing Yunseo back onto the bed, he pushed them to the top of the bed. Their kiss was a clash of teeth and tongues, desperation and hunger bleeding out of them. Taesung pinned Yunseo's arms to the sides of his head, capturing his fingers with his own. Yunseo licked his lip as he felt Taesung press himself against Yunseo's dick, flesh rubbing on flesh, the evidence of their arousal being smeared onto each other's thighs.

Yunseo moaned as Taesung sucked on his tongue, feeling him smirk at his sound.

"You sound so helpless, Little Star. Do you want me to help you?"

Yunseo nodded, unable to talk as he bit down on his bottom lip.

"Words, pretty boy," he said, kissing his jawline. "*Words.*"

This man is gonna kill me.

"Please Taesung," Yunseo whined, feeling Taesung's tongue lick below his ear. "Help me."

Taesung reached into his drawer, pulling out lube and condoms. The sight of Taesung holding such objects had Yunseo excited beyond belief. Coming back to Yunseo, Taesung instructed him to get on his hands and knees to prepare him for himself. Eager, Yunseo obeyed him.

The prep was sensual and painless. Taesung, regardless of his own desire, waited patiently for Yunseo to become comfortable with the stretch of his fingers and would stop if the pleasure became too much for him. Soon, Yunseo was ready and prepared for him. After rolling on a condom, he positioned himself behind Yunseo.

"Are you sure you want to do this," Taesung said as held himself to Yunseo's hole.

"Hyung," Yunseo gasped out. "Do it already."

Smiling, Taesung pushed himself inside Yunseo, earning a yelp of pleasure from the man below him. He trembled as he guided Yunseo's body to the hilt of his cock. Breathing heavily, he pushed Yunseo down and slowly began to move in and out, not wanting to hurt him. However, that did not last long before Yunseo reached around and pinched Taesung's nibble in annoyance.

"Don't be foolish. You know what I want."

Smirking, Taesung gave him what he wanted.

Soon the room was filled with sounds of skin slapping and the high pitched moans of Yunseo and the deep groans of Taesung. Sweat stuck to them like honey and the pillow Yunseo held against his face was soaked with saliva and tears. Taesung moved his hands from Yunseo's waist onto his back, deepening his arch. Yunseo moaned harder at the change of position and grabbed hold onto Taesung's ass, not wanting him to stop. Taesung was fucked. He never wanted this to stop. He swore to last as long as he could, to give Yunseo his life essence as long as humanly possible.

Wanting to see his star's face, he flipped him over and was welcomed with a face full of tears and climatic pleasure. Taesung felt that he could come right there and then. Taesung cradled his face, whispering sweet nothings onto Yunseo's lips.

"I love you. I loved you when I was lost and I love you as I am found," Taesung said, driving himself inhumanly faster into Yunseo. "You found me, and I am yours. I am yours as the sun belongs to the moon and the moon to the stars."

Oh god, Yunseo thought. *I'm gonna come.*

Taesung dove into Yunseo's mouth as he felt him tighten around him, eyebrows furrowing as he tried to delay his own release. Claiming his tongue, he eyed Yunseo's blissed face and declared honestly.

"You're mine, Little Star."

Fuck, Fuck, Fuck, Fu—

Yunseo cried Taesung's name as he came. He felt his body become numb as his eyes roll back. His breath was rugged and his mouth stayed open until Taesung licked it closed and propped himself onto his knees, pulling out of Yunseo and throwing the soiled plastic into the trash. Returning to the bed, he pulled

Yunseo's exhausted body close to his, lazily tracing circles on his shoulder.

After regaining his breath, Yunseo looked at Taesung's face over his shoulder with a frown.

"You didn't finish."

"It's okay, Yunseo-ah. I got what I needed."

Yunseo lifted himself, straddling Taesung's lap, wrapping his hands around his cock, rubbing it up and down.

"You might not need it, Taesung, but I do. I've been thinking about your cock down my throat since Tóyko. You wouldn't deny me that, would you?"

Taesung growled and wrapped one of his hands around Yunseo's hands, rubbing it faster.

"I wouldn't think about it, my love," Taesung said. "Take what is yours. Show me what I've been missing."

Yunseo bent forward, sticking out his tongue and brushing it against the tip of him. Taesung moaned his name as he sucked the tip of his cock before sliding his tongue up and down his shaft, massaging his balls with his free hand. He kept licking up and down until he had reached his balls, smushing his face against them, licking and sucking the flesh. Taesung dug his hands into Yunseo's hair, pulling at his locks, trying to last as long as he could.

"That's it, baby. Keep licking me like that, just like that."

Yunseo pulled himself back up to the tip, lowering his mouth to take him as deep as he could, hollowing his cheeks and humming around it.

Jesus Christ, I'm gonna come down this little throat of his.

Yunseo savored Taesung's moans and grunts as he kept sucking and moving his hands over his cock and balls until he felt them grow taut and his moans grew higher pitched.

"Oh fuck! I'm gonna! I'm gonna! I'm g—"

Taesung slammed Yunseo's head until his cock was deep in his throat, Yunseo choking around him. He tilted his head back, making eyes contact with Taesung, watching him empty himself deep in his throat. Taesung's heavy breaths and screwed shut eyes made Yunseo want to do it again. Wanting to keep making Taesung come over and over again, milking for everything he was worth.

Calming down, Taesung let go Yunseo's head, helping him take his cock out of his throat. Yunseo's face was exactly what Taesung had remembered. He smiled as he watched Yunseo wipe the corners of his mouth and lick his fingers clean.

"Satisfied, Little Star?"

Yunseo chuckled, giving his dick one last kiss and laid back down next to his lover, wrapping himself around him.

"Not even close."

The way Yunseo had been looking at Taesung made him understand that Yunseo wanted more, but he watched as Yunseo fought to keep his eyes open. Taesung leaned forward and kissed his eyes, gripping his waist.

"Maybe next time, jagiya. Let's go to sleep now."

Yunseo wanted to argue, but the combination of Taesung's comforting touch and physical exhaustion wrapped itself around Yunseo's consciousness and lullabied him into the most comforting sleep he had had in years.

CHAPTER NINETEEN

Thundering rain and flashing of bright, white light woke Taesung from his peaceful slumber. His breathing was heavy and his sight was still blurred from his sleep. Blinking rapidly, he was greeted with the fluffy black hair and rosy-skinned face of his partner. He lifted his hand and softly stroked the stray hairs that stuck to Yunseo's face back into place. The joy in Taesung's heart was indescribable. Here he lied, sexually and romantically satisfied, with the one person who truly loved him. Okay, that was a lie. He knew that Ahin, Minseo, and his friends loved him, but the one he wanted. The one he craved. Jeong Yunseo. The man who entered his life like a shining ball of light.

The thunder became louder, and Yunseo whined at the sudden noise and snuggled closer to Taesung's body. A wide smile blossomed on his face as he tucked Yunseo's head under his chin. He felt elated by the unconscious action. He felt safe with him again, just like before. Maybe more.

The ringing of Taesung's phone cracked the perfect moment like a baseball to a window. It snapped him out of his joyful daze and caused Yunseo to groan in annoyance. Taesung tried his best to ignore it, but the more it rang and the more disturbed Yunseo's once tranquil state got, the less patience Taesung was able to preserve. After the fifth ring, Taesung grabbed his phone and smashed the pick-up button.

"Whoever this is, you better have a good goddamn reason to disturb me," Taesung said as he stroked Yunseo's head.

"Is that any way to speak to your father?"

His breathing had stopped. Suddenly, he could smell it. The smell of kerosene. The same one his father drenched him in before doing the same to Lino. He felt like a coward for not being able to save him, looking away as Kwangsoo set the dog on fire. His screams haunted him as he walked the streets of Thailand all those years ago.

"Can't talk, boy? Where is that attitude you had back in the board room!"

Taesung couldn't find his voice. He felt his blood pumping in his ears as he tried. Petrified that Kwangsoo's voice would wake up Yunseo, he detached from him and walked toward the room's door. He couldn't see anything but flashes of pieces of his room. His legs wobbled as he neared closer to the door and cursed as he threw his body against it, trying desperately to demand his body to stand tall. To not be weak and fearing boy afraid of his father. Clutching his phone closer to his ear, he squeezed himself out of the room and into the hallway. He allowed his other hand to guide him down the dark and cruel hallway of his apartment and onto his couch. Rubbing up and down his legs, he willed himself to respond.

"What do you want?"

His voice was weak and his hands trembled. The clacking of his earrings against the screen of his phone was the only noise in the night.

"You took everything from me," Kwangsoo said as he relished the effect he had on his son. "You froze my accounts, liquidated my company, and you expect me to just let you go? I don't think so. I've kept tabs on you, son. Where you've been going. Who you've been talking to."

Taesung's breathing was dangerously uneven. Feeling his skin prickle at his father's words, his mind raced with a hundred possibilities.

Did he know about Minseo's desire to bake? Did he know about the flights Mom and I have been taking to Thailand? Did he know about my plan to get the family away from him? Did he—did he know about Yunseo?

"Who you've been fucking."

Panic strained Taesung's voice into a loud whisper, afraid to scream and awaken Yunseo.

"What do you want!"

Kwangsoo clicked his tongue.

"I want my fucking company back, you little shit. Did you think that I would just roll over and play dead as you humiliated me? Letting all the chaebols watch as they laugh and drink at my demise? Not only that, my whore of a wife and your cunt sister have refused to speak to me in the last few months. My cards have been declining. None of my friends are answering my calls and you are relishing it, aren't you. You fucking mistake! Have you forgotten you are nothing but a replacement!"

Not needing Taesung to respond, his father continued.

"You are nothing, Taesung, but a mistake I wished your mother would have swallowed. If I could have forced her to have an abortion, I would have done it or ripped you out myself! You want to be a man, Taesung? You want me to have nothing? Fine, but I'll make sure you have nothing too. I took back what was mine, Taesung. What will always be mine," Kwangsoo said as he fixed his tone into one of chilling indifference.

Taesung froze.

"What did you do?"

His only response was Kwangsoo's disgusting, cackling laughter.

"Go check your elevator."

Taesung rushed to his elevator, anxiously waiting for his father's surprise. The worst circumstances raced across his mind. *He has killed them. He has killed them and now he is sending him their bodies. Would it be their hearts first? Their fingers? Their ears?*

Taesung smashed the buttons of the elevator door harder. He would break this door down if he had to.

The elevator doors soon opened and the sight inside made Taesung vomit. Inside the beautifully decorated elevator was a brand new monitor, displaying a bloodied and tied up Ahin and Minseo, unconscious and void of life. Taesung's insides twisted as his head began to throb. He vomited and vomited until he was covered in his filth. He was dying. This is what it felt like to die. This was his fault. Taesung tried to get up and smash the monitor against the elevator's walls, but his limbs were useless. His body was useless. *He* was useless.

His phone buzzed and he realized that his father had hung up. The only thing that illuminated the once peaceful night was a single message.

Unknown: Meet me at the Incheon Airport. Bring anyone and I will kill them.

Standing on trembling legs, Taesung stumbled into one of his spare rooms and searched for a pair of clothes. He threw open anything he could get his hands on until he found a random pair of pants and a white T-shirt. Leaving the soiled clothing on the floor, Taesung made quick work of locating his phone before running into the elevator and smashing the basement button. He demolished the monitor into pieces as he hyperventilated. This was all his fault. Why did he have to push his father? Why did he have to support Ahin when she had voiced her disdain towards Kwangsoo. Why did he fail yet again to keep someone he loved safe?

He raced through the parking lot once the doors opened and thrusted his keys into the ignition. Revving his engine, Taesung ripped through the lot and onto the crowded streets of Korea. Cars were bumper to bumper to each other as their drivers yelled out slurs and profanities. Most of them towards Taesung as he zoomed passed them all. The rain pounded on his back without mercy. It reminded him of his father's beatings. The feeling of his father's fists and the image of his bleeding gums flooded his head. He felt fear penetrate his heart and his stomach stir at the possibility of being subjected to his father's abuse again. Then he saw Ahin's face. The woman who took him in with open arms and never blamed him for his father's shortcomings. The woman who constantly flew from Korea to Thailand just to bring him his favorite treats. The woman who allowed him to be part of his sister's life and never treated him like an outsider.

He imagined that woman lifeless and motionless somewhere with his beloved sister alongside her. He rode faster. They needed him and he would rather die than let his father hurt them anymore than he already had. He wouldn't let anyone else suffer because of him. Even if he has to die in order to ensure it.

When arriving at Incheon Airport, his surroundings were normal. The front of the airport was alive and bursting. Hugs from rejoicing families and their tears of being reunited combated the rapidly beating heart caged inside Taesung's body. Not seeing his father, he rode further. He had reached the end of the road before catching the mysterious black vehicle parked next to an unusual wall flashing their lights at him. He only started as the car breathed and gestured to him to follow. He cried his last prayer as he followed the vehicle.

The ink colored vehicle rode until it had Taesung isolated. Taesung's once bright surroundings were now replaced with the cold colored walls of the back of Incheon Airport. He had never seen this side of the airport. Even at night, the airport had always had this sense of safety and warmth. Yet, now it looped over him like a silent and cold promise. Almost like it knew what was going to happen. It sent shivers down Taesung's spine.

The car stopped a few feet away from Taesung as a man stepped out of the driver's seat. The man was large and covered head to toe in leather. This must be his executioner. Fitting, he would be dressed in leather. It was easier to wipe off the blood that way.

"Get off your bike."

Taesung only stared at the him. He noted that the man was much older than him and had a gun strapped against his thigh. *Why wasn't it hidden,* Taesung thought. *Was the man forever ready for a flight? Ready to do what was necessary. To kill?*

"Where is Kwangsoo?"

The man laughed.

"You don't get to ask the questions here, boy."

Enraged, Taesung got off his bike and, foolishly, approached the man as he screamed.

"Where is he? Where are my mother and sister! Tell me or I swear—"

Crack!

Taesung landed on the ground as the leather-covered man only watched him with measured precision. The man was now pointing the silver gun Taesung had seen earlier towards him.

"You will either come quietly or I will deliver you to your family in pieces."

Spitting out blood, Taesung flashed the man a disgusting red smile, causing blood to gush out of his split lip.

"Will you at least save some pieces for my father to choke on?"

The man struck him again with the back of his gun. Taesung felt his eyebrow split before he was repeatedly kicked in the stomach. He tried to laugh. To say something snarky but, he could only cry out into the rain. And while the rain camouflaged his tears, it couldn't camouflage his screams nor could the thunder mask the torment in his voice.

"You know," the man said, "not even your mother screamed this much." The man laughed. He pulled Taesung to his knees, lifting his face.

"Your sister is the screamer."

Taesung tried to open his mouth, but the man swiftly brought his knee up and clashed it with Taesung's chin. As the man's haunting laughter carried into the night, Taesung grasped at the ground for anything he could find. A weapon, a forgotten needle, even a pen. Something to save him.

"Enough, Du-ho," a voice called out from inside the forgotten car. "Get him in the car before you fucking kill him."

"Oh, shut up! You know the boss won't mind seeing his son a little broken," the man said as he backed away from Taesung.

He looked like a broken toy, worthless and forgotten.

As he heard the footsteps of his tormentor fade away, Taesung grabbed onto the man's foot.

"Please, just take me to them. You can kill me then."

The man lowered himself to be eye level with the poor boy and grabbed onto his face, sneering at the pathetic display.

"Are you begging, boy? How sissy of you."

Taesung surrendered to the man's insults and disgusting words as the only thing he could think of was his family. They needed him. He would let this man beat him to his heart's content if it meant he could save his family.

The man groaned as he saw that Taesung was no longer fighting him anymore. Bored, he shoved his face back, causing Taesung to fall to the floor.

"You're no fun."

Taesung raised himself onto his elbows in time to see the man walk back from the car with a white bottle and a dirty rag. Eyes widening, Taesung began to shake his head fiercely as the man got closer.

"Please, don't. I'll come willingly. Please, don't burn me!"

The man drenched the cloth as he tilted his head.

"Burn you," the man questioned. "You *really* are fucked up."

And with that, he reached out and held the back of Taesung's head as he slammed him into the chloroform-soaked rag over his mouth. He screamed into the white rag, and before the chloroform had won its victim, he felt the man lean down and whisper ever so quietly into his ear.

"Burning you is child's play. Your father has bigger plans than that."

✦ . ⁺ . ✦ . ⁺ . ✦

When Taesung had awoken, he was welcomed by the screams of Ahin.

"Kwangsoo! Please! Let him go! Take me! For the love of God, don't hurt my son!"

Feeling sluggish, Taesung felt his body piece back together with his vision. He had blinked just in time to catch the fast, hard slap that landed on his mother's face, effectively, slicing her lip open.

"Did I give you permission to speak?"

Taesung's body reacted before he could process what he was seeing. About thirty feet away from him was his bloody, broken, and beaten family. Ahin sat with her hands and feet tied to a rusty and jagged looking metal chair. Her clothes, a white blouse stretched out from someone pulling on it and stained crimson jeans, rips lining sides and exposing her knees. His sister, Minseo, did not have the same luxury as their mother. Minseo mirrored their mother's bondage, yet she was in a once pale pink—now gray—tank top with ashy black sweatpants. Her once auburn hair was now caked in dry blood and matted against her head. Taesung couldn't get a good look at his sister's face, her head was bent down in the most unnatural way, making him dizzy.

Taesung screamed. He screamed and screamed, but it wasn't until his tongue brushed against a rough material that he realized what was happening. He was gagged, bonded in the same way as his family, with a body stripped of most clothing except his pants. Exposed and at the mercy of his father. How disgusting.

Kwangsoo turned from Ahin and slowly made his way to his son. He somehow looked older than he had a month ago. More stray gray hairs in his beard and eyebrows, with a permanent wrinkle imprinted onto his forehead. His pot belly, grown in size, highlighted the lack of care he had for himself. The man whom his real mother had once described as handsome at the time was now a shallow shell of his former glory.

He smiled as he looked down on Taesung's tied up body. The ceiling lights highlighted his father's yellow-stained teeth. He bent down, greeting his son with a poisonous smile.

"Hello, my dear son. Enjoying the view?"

Taesung clenched his hands, causing Kwangsoo's eyes to flicker over to them.

"I guess not."

Sighing, Kwangsoo circled his son, clasping his hands down onto his shoulders.

"It took a lot of effort to get everyone here."

Kwangsoo grabbed Taesung's jaw and squeezed, making him growl in pain.

"The least you could do is take it all in."

Forcing his head side to side like a puppet, Taesung was subjected to the horror of his surroundings. They were in an abandoned warehouse of some sort. The pristine ceiling gave off the impression of a well-kept area, yet the cracks in the foundation said otherwise. Some were shallow and only surface level. Others ran deep and were rooted in place. Almost as if the entire room was built around cracks like a bandage on a wound, only there to hide the damage happening from within.

The doors were guarded with his father's henchmen and each seemed to carry pistols of their own. Looking across from him, he looked closer at his family. Acrylic nails ripped off and feet rubbed raw. The lights above their heads gave off the impression that they were in some sort of show. One drenched in the crimson of spilled anguish, streaked with suffering that clung like a shadow. It made Taesung shiver as he guided his eyes above himself, where his very own spotlight was waiting for him, eager to show him what was to come.

Kwangsoo stepped into Taesung's line of sight, the firm grip of his jaw only growing stronger. The white light above Kwangsoo made him look like a demon masquerading as an angel. Taesung wanted to spit at the artificial halo.

"Now," he hummed, releasing Taesung's jaw, slowly stroking along the angry imprint of his hand. "Why don't we speak comfortably, yes?"

Snapping his fingers, he moved forward and gestured for something in the dark. Suddenly, the man appeared. The man that had beaten him senseless what felt only moments before. He looked the same, yet he carried something that confused Taesung. It was a silver briefcase with a pair of handcuffs attached to its handle.

Are we in a fucking spy movie?

Taesung felt his gag release and the corners of his mouth began to scream. The rough texture of the towel only helped the chemical seep into his skin. Rubbing his corners together, he looked at his father.

"Chloroform? Again? No new tricks, Appa?"

Kwangsoo settled into a chair, waving one of the guards to bring the case over. With his legs crossed and the silver suitcase secured across his lap, he flashed Taesung a grotesque grin.

"I could get the kerosene if you like?"

Taesung's sarcasm ended as quickly as it began.

Kwangsoo smiled at his son's entrapped form. Beaten and bruised, he thought he looked good. He looked right. Kwangsoo reveled the fact that he had the power again. Looking over his son, he recounted the things he was not at his age: broken, pathetic, and weak. He was not ever allowed to just *be*, thanks to his father. He was whipped to shape day in and day out, never stopping for yakgwa or hotteok from the vendors outside his poorly structured school. No. He had to be the success of the family.

Blamed for his mother's death at childbirth, he knew two things: he had no other choice other than to succeed, and that his father would kill him if he didn't.

This bastard of a child would not destroy what he has worked so long to create.

"You know," Kwangsoo began, "I didn't want to do this. I didn't want to be the bad guy. But," he gestured to the room while one hand clutched his heart, "when you took everything, I felt so forgotten. So disposable. So...so—"

"Powerless?"

"Yes," he said. "I felt powerless. Powerless to save my company. Powerless to protect my assets. Powerless to see my family."

"You deserved everything I did to you."

His father's fury felt the same. He always led his slap with his palm first, fingers second. Minseok said that it was the best way to effectively transmit all of your energy into the gesture. Taesung hated how right he was.

"Don't interrupt me, boy! *You* respect me! *You* obey me! You are nothing, you hear me! Nothing!"

Taesung could do nothing as he watched the drool of blood leak from his lips onto the discolored floor, adding life to the otherwise dead and forgotten building.

Kwangsoo rose from his seat, energized. He paced from right to left as he mumbled.

"You know, this is exactly why I wanted to get rid of your mother sooner. I could have raised you in a way that you wouldn't have turned out to be such a failure."

Taesung swung his head, the motion causing his chair to rattle.

"What did you say?"

"You being a failure? Oh, come on now. You know this already—"

"No," Taesung's voice rang out. "What did you mean about 'wanting to get rid of my mother sooner'?"

Kwangsoo stopped his pacing and looked at Taesung. He stared at him for what felt like an eternity before he understood what laid before him.

Kwangsoo walked closer to Taesung, so close Taesung could smell the tobacco that coated his tongue. Letting his eyes close, he pressed his lips to his son's cheek.

"Your mother never had breast cancer, my son. The doctors I paid said that. It was the 'chemo' that killed her."

CHAPTER TWENTY

Yunseo knew something was wrong when he first awakened. It wasn't the empty, cold bed or the continuous thundering and blinding rain. It was the smell. The smell of something rotten raised Yunseo from the bed like a mummy and guided him out into the hallway.

The scene in front of him was unimaginable. The floors, once sparkling, were covered in sickly green and milky beige. There were chucks and…blood?

He called Taesung's name, praying that Taesung just had an upset stomach and that he was off into one of the many bathrooms he harbored taking a shower. No one answered. He called out again, yet like before, no answer. Feeling unsettled, he searched the apartment. It wasn't until he found a pile of vomit-covered clothes that he felt panic set in. Yunseo ran back to Taesung's room, his body begging to empty its own stomach.

He barely made it into the bathroom, leaving a trail of vomit behind him. He emptied himself into the sink as he ran water over his fingers. Once finished, he wiped his mouth and ran to Taesung's bed, throwing the covers and searching for anything that may tell him where he might have gone.

It wasn't until his phone cased its light onto the ceiling, did he remembered he could call him. He called and called and called. No answer ever came to ease his nerves.

Frustrated, he threw his phone and pulled at his hair, rocking himself back and forth.

Where is he?

His thoughts were silenced by the ringing and thrashing of his phone. He crawled towards it and, with trembling hands, cried into it.

"Hello! Can someone please help me!"

"Yunseo," Mikasa yelled. "Where are you! Are you safe!"

"W—What? Where is Taesung? He's missing!"

"Yunseo, I need you to tell where you are."

Yunseo clawed his throat, his breath escaping its enclosure.

The world was fading into spots. The bed, walls and floor were consumed by darkness and Yunseo's only friend was his shaking, trembling body. He was gonna die. Karma, God, Buddha, whoever was laying their claim on to his flush and blood, preparing him to welcome death with a stilled body. At least he was loved one last time before being thrown away again.

"Yunseo? Yunseo! Hey!"

Mikasa screamed and screamed but it all fell onto deaf ears, her only feedback was the drop of Yunseo's phone as his head crashed onto the cold, beautiful floors of the once lust filled apartment.

She cried as she dialed Moonbin's phone number and ran to her motorcycle. *Two rings,* she thought. *It should only take two rings.*

Moonbin came in a deep and raspy tone.

"Hello?"

"It's happening, Moonbin. He's back. Minseok just called me. They're," Mikasa's voice quivered. "They're gone, Oppa."

"What are you talking about? Who is gone?"

"It's him," she said, mounting her bike. "Kwangsoo has taken them."

Moonbin sprung onto his feet, feeling his blood run cold.

"Please tell me this is a fucked up joke. I'm begging you, Mikasa."

Mikasa felt tears enter her mouth as she pressed the phone closer to her ear, not wanting the sentence that was about to come out to be true.

"I can't reach them, Oppa. I called the residence, and when Minseok answered, he was screaming and yelling that Kwangsoo had taken them."

"And Taesung! Where is he!"

"Oppa," Mikasa whispered as she heard Moonbin's heart break into two.

Moonbin felt his soul being ripped out of him. He raced across his bedroom, corner to corner looking for clothes to put on. He was going to Seocho. He had to see it. Had to see that their worst nightmares were *truly* confirmed.

"Where are you, Mikasa? I'll come find you. Tell me where you are."

Mikasa cried harder at Moonbin's nurturing tone. Moonbin had always been loud and a trickster, but to hear him sound so soft, so light. It was enough for her to stay broken forever.

"I'll be fine. Go find Yunseo. I'll meet you at the safehouse in an hour, I've got to get Soae and the other. Minseok will be waiting for you at Seocho."

"But, Mikasa—"

"I've sent you his location and phone number. Please Moonbin," Mikasa said. "Just find Yunseo and bring him the house."

Moonbin groaned. He hated having to choose one from the other.

"Fine, but be there no later than an hour or I'll come looking for you."

Hanging up he drove down the streets of Seoul, pleading all the way that Mikasa was wrong and that Minseok was still alive.

Unknown to him, Mikasa was wishing for the same. Praying that once she reached the safehouse, her family would all be there, Ahin with a plate full of cookies and Minseo with her, displaying one of her loving smiles.

✦ . ⁺ . ✦ . ⁺ . ✦

Yunseo felt his body going up and down. He felt as if he was a doll in the hands of a child. Was this death? Was God making fun of him, shaking him like a worthless piece of plastic. Hasn't he had his fun? Hasn't God shaken and torn and thrown and destroyed him enough. What more could this monster want?

Yunseo felt his body against a hard, slippery surface. Was he on the floor of heaven? He tried to push away from the surface only to be pushed back down.

"Don't move. You'll make us fall."

Yunseo's eyes snapped open and raised his head to look at a man's helmet. The helmet was black with electric neon blue flames on the side. It frightened him.

"Taesung?"

The man shook his head and guided Yunseo's head onto his shoulder as he raced down the roads.

"It's Moonbin. You're safe now. Just hold on until we get to the safehouse."

Safe? Yunseo would never be safe as long as he had desire and love in his heart. Life had a funny way of haunting him with the niceties of its compassion, showing him what he would never possess.

He took in the position he was in. He was soaked and wore an oversized sweater of deep purple and white pants. His feet were bare, and his body was backwards to the scenery passing him by. Not that he could see it anyway, everything came at him like flashes of a camera, and he couldn't do anything, but clutch Moonbin closer while a shiver tore through his body like a firecracker erupting into the sky.

If Moonbin felt him, Yunseo did not know nor did he care. If they crashed, Yunseo would welcome death like an old friend. It was all he had the willpower left to do.

The winds quickened their assault on Yunseo's ears and the frosty Korean air bit at his feet.

Great, I'm gonna lose limbs before I die.

Yunseo assumed he must have still been out of it because he did not feel the motorcycle stopping nor the lifting of his body from Moonbin's motorcycle.

Yunseo willed himself to cease his hiding and be brave enough to look up.

The safe house stood in stark contrast to its surroundings, a solitary figure amidst the desolate landscape. It resembled a giant cement block, its exterior voided of any distinguishing features save for a single metal door, its surface reflecting Yunseo's helpless form and Moonbin's determination. No windows broke its monolithic appearance, shrouding the interior in perpetual darkness.

As Moonbin led Yunseo inside, they were greeted by the eerie silence of an empty room. The air hung heavy with the scent of dust and mildew, a testament of time unused. The lack of furniture was immediately apparent; the room barren save for a few makeshift crates scattered haphazardly across the floor. These crates served as makeshift seating, their rough edges and splintering wood offering little comfort.

Against one wall stood a massive gun arsenal, a stark reminder of the dangers lurking outside. Rows of weapons lined the wall, gleaming ominously in the dim light. Rifles, handguns, and ammunition sat in neat rows, their presence a chilling reminder of the new kind of violence that permeated Yunseo's world.

Despite the spartan accommodations, Moonbin's eyes flickered with relief as he surveyed their surroundings. This may not have been the most luxurious safehouse, but it was their best chance at evading Kwangsoo's reach. It offered something far more precious... *Safety*, however fleeting. With a silent prayer on his lips, he lowered Yunseo onto one of the crates, grabbing a dusty blanket from one of the corners of the room.

"What is this place?"

"It's a safehouse," Moonbin said, pulling the tethered cloth tightly around the smaller male.

"Taesung had it built two years ago for this day."

Yunseo stared at Moonbin as he finished wrapping, watching him move towards the firearms, picking up a pistol and checking its functions.

"What is happening," Yunseo cried. "Where is Taesung?"

Moonbin stuffed the gun into his pants as he grabbed another. Walking back over to Yunseo, he grabbed one of his hands and pressed the handle of the gun into his palm.

"I'm guessing Taesung told you about his father," asked Moonbin.

Yunseo casted his gaze to the floor, not sure he should reveal their relationship. Moonbin pulled his chin up, giving Yunseo his best smile.

"Hyung has never been good at keeping secrets, Yunseo."

Yunseo returned his smile with a meek one of his own, relief making its crescendo through his body. Moonbin stroked his chin before putting his hand on top of the gun in Yunseo's hand.

"I received a call from Mikasa saying that Kwangsoo may have taken the others. I didn't believe it until—didn't *want* to believe it until—seeing Taesung's apartment and the lack of his motorcycle..." Moonbin pulled a face, anger simmering under the surface. "I need to go to Minseok and see what happened."

Yunseo stood up as Moonbin let go and made his way out of the cement block and to his bike.

"You're not leaving me here, are you?"

Moonbin swung his leg over the seat and pulled his helmet over his head.

"Mikasa will be here soon," he lifted his hand, pointing a finger at the gun Yunseo still held in his hand.

"If anyone but her tries to come inside the house, shoot them."

"You're crazy!"

Moonbin kicked back Angel's stand and turned the bike, looking over his shoulder.

"Stay inside until I'm back!"

"Moonb—"

But he was gone, pushing a hundred and twenty miles per hour, trying his best not to let the dread seep its way deeper into his gut.

The home was nothing short of destroyed.

The gates hung off their hinges and bits of wood were shattered all over the lawn. The statues, once beautiful and alluring, were broken in half, their heads on the ground below them. The open and comforting home was now covered in shards of glass and its blue and neutral colors were now covered in differentiating hues of red and black. The wooden floors now reflected the patterns of a Dalmatian while covered in pages of what Moonbin assumed were Ahin's precious books and the windows that allowed the warmth of humanity in, were now nothing but empty frames. The only thing in its wake were punctured holes carved in by gunpowder. Even the furniture was marked with big black Xs, torn in half as if to see them bleed out. Though he could not see it, he knew that the kitchen was nothing more than a memory. The magical sanctuary was now a shrine of brokenness, envy, and anger.

"Hyung," Moonbin called out, walking around the remains of the once glorious home. "Hyung!"

"In here," a voice grunted from the second floor, Moonbin was already running after it.

Moonbin dashed down the sullied hallway, falling to his knees once he reached his friend.

Minseok's face was covered in roguish colored cuts and his jaw supported a bruise of black coloring. His hand was holding onto his left eye, a jagged tear in the skin that oozed blood in thick rivulets down his face, staining his skin crimson. The edges of the wound were ragged and torn, revealing glimpses of the underlying tissue beneath. It appeared as though a blade had sliced through it with brutal force, leaving behind a gruesome gash that pulsed with pain and irritation. Swelling and bruising had already begun to form around the wound, distorting the man's features and adding to the overall grotesque nature of the injury. Despite the agony etched across his face, he clenched his jaw in silent determination, his eyes flashing with a mix of fury and agony as he struggled to endure the searing pain.

His forearms were exposed and covered in the same colors and cuts as his face yet these seemed to be shallower. The sight unnerved Moonbin, his stomach growled and clawed as his throat constricted.

Moonbin inched closer, taking in the deep gashes and feathers leaking out of the bed behind Minseok, ribbons of green and white swaying at the bed's sides. The baby blue walls were ravaged, the insolation ripped out of its once peacefully dark habitat and the floorboards were rooted upwards. Every single thing ever possessed by the room's owner was tattered to pieces. Moonbin looked from the pieces with sorrow and disheartenment.

Reaching out and gathering his wounded brother, he placed him on the ruined bed, his friend wincing the whole way through. Moonbin placed a hand on his shoulder as he balled up some of the torn sheets and placed them underneath Minseok's back.

"What happened?"

Minseok's eyes scanned Moonbin's face as he didn't answer, the grip on his shoulder tightening slightly.

"Minseok, I need you to talk to me."

Minseok opened his mouth to speak. A voice, deep and shattered, emerged.

"Kwangsoo took them."

Moonbin nodded, eyebrows furrowing.

"I can see that, but why now? Why a month after Taesung liquidated the company?"

"I'm unsure. I was holding Ahin when his guards barged in and began to tear at the home."

Moonbin dropped his hand from Minseok's shoulder as the wheels in his head began to turn.

"What do you mean you were holding her?"

"I," Minseok started, "We... Moonbin, you have to understand we did not plan for this to happen."

Minseok watched as Moonbin's chest heaved up and down. He was infuriated. His hands were opening and closing, his body was utterly still. It was as if his body internally was buzzing and one word, one tone inflection, one breath offbeat, would cause him to go off the rails into an oblivion filled rage.

"What did you mean 'I was holding Ahin'?"

"Moonbin," Minseok started, trying to sit up but the pain of his eye forced him onto the bed again. "We wanted to tell you."

Moonbin approached Minseok with the promise of violence in his wake. He was eye to eye with him, staring at Minseok's raptured skin with fearlessness.

"Have you been fucking Ahin?"

It was only after Minseok's short nod that he was plastered onto the floor, holding his eyes with both hands and Moonbin grabbing him by the collar, screaming.

"Are you fucking insane! Kwangsoo will kill her! Kill you!"

"Moonbin please," Minseok choked out, the back of his head throbbing from the blow he received from the floor. A fresh coat of scarlet painted his teeth.

"Listen to me. Let me explain."

"How long have you lied to me," he spat. "How long!"

Minseok held onto Moonbin's hands and smashed their foreheads together, coating their hands in his blood.

265

"It's been eighteen months, Moonbin. We have been in love for eighteen months, six hours, twenty-five minutes, six seconds and I am not sorry for it! Kill me if you want."

Letting go of his hands, Minseok held his arms in the air and leaned his head back. The position whispered *crucify me.*

"You'd be doing me a favor."

Gritting his teeth, Moonbin dropped Minseok's aching body onto the floor, stammering back and dropping himself onto the bed, trying to find solace in the pain Minseok created by gripping his hair.

Minseok stayed lying on the floor, arms spread wide at his sides. He turned his head to avoid looking at Moonbin's troubled form, already feeling his heart breaking.

"Minseok, how could you have lied to me? I was your best friend. Your brother," Moonbin uttered, his voice strained with betrayal.

Minseok licked his lips, tasting his blood, and raised his hand to cover his eye.

"I did it for her, Moonbin. It was all for her, and I would do it again," his voice was weak and small. "We talked all the time about telling you, all of you. But it was always too dangerous. With Kwangsoo and Taesung executing their plans, it never felt right. Never safe to share our secret."

Moonbin's vision blurred. His mind was on fire. His nerve endings felt like they were dying. He was sure that if it weren't for Minseok's voice, he would have been elsewhere in his mind, tearing apart the past bit by bit.

"Hyung," Moonbin said, coming to stand and pulling Minseok up from the floor. "Just tell me we can save them. Tell me we can get our family back."

Minseok placed his hand on the nape of Moonbin's neck.

"I promise you we will. We will."

"Good," Moonbin said, pushing Minseok's hand off his neck, shivering at the slippery flesh. "Let's patch up your eye and drive over to the safehouse. The others should be there by now."

Nodding, Minseok chased after him as he marched down the hall, chanting a singular thought in his head.

God, please let me be right.

Rain was still falling when Moonbin guided the two outside the house and towards his bike, ripping it open and pulling out some gauze and disinfectant. Minseok didn't speak as Moonbin cleaned him up, his eyes fixed on the cold and motionless expression of his companion. Minseok hissed at the rubbing alcohol, the tissue shriveling at the liquid. Moonbin threw the bloody cotton onto the ground and began to wrap Minseok's head, tying it off at the back.

"Where's your bike," Moonbin inquired.

Minseok stepped away, his fingers grazing the white wrapping.

"It's at the back of the home, near the greenhouse."

Moonbin nodded, walking to the backyard, planning to retrieve the beast. As he turned the corner, there in the large fertile backyard, were four neatly lined up bodies. Each one wearing black, housing a hole in their forehead. All patiently waiting to wake up again. They had been wiped clean of any blood or sweat. All that was left for them was the impending decay that was inching its way toward them, anxiously wanting to finish what their partner, death, had accomplished.

He heard footsteps behind him.

"Ages and gender?"

"Four males, all under fifty."

"Ethnicity?"

"Korean."

"Time of death?"

Minseok stepped beside him, answering with an anger-ridden voice, "Forty minutes ago."

"Where are their guns?"

"Hidden in their jackets. The numbers were scratched off. I killed them when they were stuffing Ahin and Minseo into the back of their car. Unfortunately, I only got four out of the twelve that were here."

Moonbin cursed and grabbed onto his hips, his head bending forward. He wiped his nose and turned around, walking—no, running back to his Angel.

"Let's get the fuck out of here."

Cabrera

CHAPTER TWENTY-ONE

Yunseo stood frozen in front of the door, his heart pounding against his ribs like a frantic bird trying to escape its cage. In the cement room, he watched the rattling of the door handle in front of him. Yunseo's breath caught in his throat as his eyes widened in terror. He could feel the hairs on the back of his neck stand on end as adrenaline surged through his veins.

He clutched around the gun's handle, the cold metal trembling in his grip. The weight of the weapon offered little comfort as he raised it shakily, aiming it at the door.

The seconds stretched into eternity as Yunseo stood there, his senses heightened and his mind unfocused. He strained to hear any sign of movement outside the door, his heart hammering in his chest at the impending doom.

Suddenly, the door ripped open, welcoming him with the sight of red and blonde hair at the doorway.

"Mikasa," Yunseo said, lowering his gun and dropping it on the crate behind him. "Soae!"

Soae helped Mikasa into the room, her hands holding onto her bleeding ones, Subin and Soyeon following behind them. Soyeon's face was frozen in shock, Soae was crying, and a beaten Subin slammed the door behind them, leaning against it as he wrapped his hand around his right arm, keeping pressure against the cut it harbored. Blood seemed to slide down an opening from one of Subin's eyebrows, but he paid it no mind when he caught Yunseo's horrified eyes and ran towards him, overcome with relief.

"You're alive! You're alive," he wailed. Yunseo held onto him tighter, and Subin gripped him harder. "They were chasing after us. We crashed and barely made it out. We thought we were going to die."

Looking over his shoulder, he watched as Soae guided Mikasa to a crate, Mikasa instructing her to grab one of the bottles of water in the crate below her and pour it over her hands. Mikasa had a black eye and a bruise on the corner of her lip. Scratches lined her neck as she turned her head and her body was moist with sweat.

"Hey Yunseo," she whispered, looking up at him, seeing him examine her hands. "I can't feel them," she said as Soae rubbed the blood and grime off. "But I've been through worse."

Pulling away from Yunseo, Subin's attention was drawn to the arsenal on the wall.

"What is going on," he said, eyeing the various sizes of weapons and ammunition.

He turned to Yunseo again, looking at the gun behind him.

"Yunseo, tell me what is going on."

"Taesung's father is after us," Minseok said as he walked in, making a beeline for Mikasa's hands. He tore off pieces of his shirt and wrapped them around her injured hands before turning to the group.

The group's eyes were fixated on Minseok's face, their eyes drawn to the once pristine bandage now tinged with a cherry hue.

"What happened to your eye," Soae asked, terror curling around her words.

Minseok hesitated, his gaze briefly darting away before he offered a faint smile.

"Knife fight," he admitted. "I won."

"And the other guy?"

"Didn't make it," Minseok stated matter-of-factly, turning his attention to Mikasa. "How did this happen?"

Mikasa winced as the fabric pressed against her wounds, a sharp hiss escaping her lips.

"I was on my way over to Soae's place. When I got there, Kwangsoo's men were dragging them into their van, Subin fighting against one of them," Mikasa said, looking over at Soae and taking in her bruised cheek. "They were beaten up pretty bad."

"Where's your bike?"

Sorrow filled her eyes.

"Gone."

Minseok said nothing.

"Did she steal a car to get you all?"

Subin spoke first.

"She hotwired a car while they—," he broke off, feeling the ice settle back into his veins. "While I distracted them."

"Distracted," Minseok questioned as the corner of his lip lifted. "Needed to protect them?"

Subin only stared.

"Mikasa needed time. I was of no other use."

Minseok nodded, respecting Subin's integrity. He watched Moonbin walk in and rush to Soyeon's side, asking her if she was okay. Soyeon said nothing in return, pushing him away from her.

This is all my fault, Minseok thought.

Sleeping with his friend's and employer's mother; he was a pathetic man. He remembered feeling wrong and telling Ahin that they needed to come clean. That they betrayed everyone long enough, but Ahin had repeated that what they were doing was nothing wrong. That their love was not a crime and that she would not be made to feel guilty for finding love for the first time in her life since her family had forced her to marry Kwangsoo. She called Minseok her blessing. Her knight in shiny armor.

How did her knight fall so far?

They're scared, Minseok thought. Broken and terrified, all because he loved a woman he shouldn't have.

He braced himself against one of the walls of the room and spoke in the softest tone he could muster.

"I need you all to forgive me. Forgive me for the selfishness Ahin and I have caused you. We didn't want this. We only—" he slid his eyes across the room, pinpointing Moonbin's. "We only wanted to be happy."

Moonbin looked at him. He was still seething with rage beneath the surface of his chilled skin, but he understood. No matter how betrayed he felt, he knew that what Ahin and Minseok did was the right decision. A decision he would have chosen a thousand times if it had been Soyeon.

"*Onii-chan*," Mikasa whispered behind him. "Just tell us what happened."

Exhaling deeply, he nodded to her, wanting to be freed of the guilt he had been carrying for the last year and a half.

"It was after she had returned from France. The rest of you were in Jeju with Minseo and she had gotten home from her flight early that morning. She looked grieved. I've heard her broken hums ringing out in the home before, but that day…"

Minseok broke off, remembering how she looked. Her skin glowed as the liquid-like silver dress captured her curves and highlighted her breasts. He had found her in the kitchen, perched next to the sink, tearfully eating a box of sugar cookies, watching the way her lips wrapped around the little treat, enrapturing him.

"I asked her if something was wrong and if I could help her with anything. She softly shook her head and told me to send away the other guards. Soon enough, I followed her to her room after hearing a loud fall. I found her, shocked and looking at the floor. She had dropped her hairbrush. I went down to pick it up and when I looked up, she had a look I didn't recognize. She softly touched my lips and asked if I found her beautiful. I was stunned and didn't know what to say. Time had passed and she let go of my face, turning back to look at the mirrors on her mantel. As I placed the brush onto the mantel, I made eye contact with her phone. It was a picture of Kwangsoo with another woman. A younger woman. He had been with her on their anniversary."

Moonbin felt his heart fall at the idea that Ahin, the closest thing to a mother he had, being disrespected so publicly.

"That still doesn't answer how the two of you ended up together," Mikasa said.

"She asked me to spend the night," Minseok said, rubbing his temples. "I know it was wrong, but I couldn't resist. She all but begged and I caved. From then on, we have been inseparable."

Yunseo spoke, his voice rough and dry.

"Is that why Taesung and the others were kidnapped? Because you guys fucked?"

Minseok raised his head and Yunseo could have sworn he had seen a flash of regret in his eyes.

"No, but it is a part of it. After Taesung began his plan to liquidate Kwangsoo's company, Ahin grew restless and wanted to run away. She had spoken to Taesung about wanting to move and they were crafting a plan to have all of us escape South Korea and live in Thailand."

Minseok lowered his head, feeling nausea creep its way into his throat.

"We must have had a rat."

The room quieted and the only noises were the pounding and howling of the rain outside. The air was thick and the tension was its only rival. Mikasa stepped back from Minseok, letting go of his arm. She looked upon the ceiling and murmured a prayer.

"We need to find them," Mikasa sighed. "How do we find them?"

Minseok said nothing as he slowly raised his head and looked at Yunseo's direction. He could see just how scared Yunseo really was. He was shivering and staring at the guns to his left. They were older, worn with time. His eyes moved from the barrels of the guns to their magazines and, finally, their triggers. Minseok doubted that the pilot had ever fired a gun, let alone killed someone. His gaze stayed a little longer on the objects before he snapped his eyes back to Minseok's. They had stared at one another before Yunseo's eyes widened.

"Me," Yunseo said. His voice booming throughout the room, the safehouse groaning in response. "You need me?"

Minseok nodded firmly.

"Yes, we need you."

"Why," Soae urged. "This has nothing to do with us. We were only supposed to be your flight crew. Nothing more."

Minseok's answer was hard and slow. Measured to perfection.

"Because they're in love."

Yunseo's head whirled at Subin. He raised his hands in surrender.

"I didn't say anything!"

Minseok scoffed at Subin's nervous outburst before facing Yunseo, causing him to look at him with caution.

"No one had to tell me. I know what longing looks like."

Everyone was staring at him now. He didn't know what to do. He wanted to run again. Yunseo eyed the room's door with lust, yet Moonbin had stepped in his line of sight, blocking the exit.

"There were bodies."

Everyone looked back, shocked to have heard Soyeon's voice. She looked empty. She clung onto her shoulders, creating an X across her chest. It looked as if she was trying to signal anything evil coming towards her to stay away, to see her defense and run. It was fruitless. Evil had come and lurked around her every thought, marking its scent on her ruined clothes.

"While Mikasa was burning her hands trying to hot-wire the car, one of Kwangsoo's men ran towards us. Subin already had two men on him, so I guess there was an opening for an attack," Soyeon's eyes traced the blank wall before her. "He came at us so fast and so hard that at one point I believed that I imagined him. The adrenaline vibrating in my body had me envisioning things. I knew he was real when he scratched and grabbed at Mikasa's throat."

Soyeon traced stars onto the wall's canvas, its coolness biting at her finger. She ignored it, moving her finger like a conductor commanding his orchestra.

"Soae and I could do nothing but scream in the backseat as he yelled to us the vile and disgusting things he would do to us. All the places he would *touch*. At the places he would cut and burn. We—," her voice broke, allowing a sob to come out as she dropped her finger and grabbed onto her shoulders harder. "We didn't know what to do. It was only over when Mikasa grabbed a hold of his gun and fired three shots into his chest. So much blood... everywhere."

Moonbin went to grab one of the water bottles Soae had not used and flashed back over to Soyeon's side, grabbing hold of her waist, and guiding her to sit on the floor. He placed his hand on the nape of her neck as he lifted the bottle to her lips. Soyeon wanted to push his hand. She wanted to be as strong as Mikasa when she killed that man and the two others who were pulverizing Subin. But, as the water from the plastic slid down her throat, coating it with its cold hand, she did nothing. Being nursed like a helpless child was exactly what she deserved.

"You should have never been in that position in the first place," Minseok said, his hand ghosting over his eye. "You're safe now; we're trained to do to protect and fight. It's what we are good at."

"*Were*," Mikasa said. "We were good at it. Now we have lost the most important people in our lives."

"How could I be of help," Yunseo said, looking at everyone. "I'm just a pilot."

"No," Minseok said. "You're the key to Taesung's torture. If Kwangsoo grabs you, then he can lead us to where he is keeping the others."

Yunseo shook his head.

"How does *he* know about us? How do *you* know, Minseok? Tell me how!"

Minseok had reached around and pulled out a rather elegant looking phone. Its case was blue with a 3D white bear in the middle. Yunseo recognized it as Minseo's phone.

"I hacked Minseo's phone. She writes down everything that happens during her days. Including the day she went to that bakery in Gangnam with you. I also found that Kwangsoo had a bug installed in Minseo's phone that reported everything she did."

Hands began to shake, and Yunseo's breath started to quicken. Knives felt like they were carving themselves down his throat and into his lungs. He rocked his heels back and forth, dismissing the hand on his back. Subin brought his body closer to his chest and hushed him back to Earth.

"How can I save Taesung?"

Mikasa dragged herself from her seat and picked up one of the guns hanging off the wall.

"I have a plan."

Dragging the gun across the cement floor, she ignored the blazing pain blossoming in her palms, focusing on carving her plan to life.

Taesung's body was falling apart. His skin was covered from head to toe in slashes and blood trickled down his body like a river luring back its disciples.

Du-ho was wiping off the blood of his knife on his rugged clothes. The thought of infection entered Taesung's mind and he knew if the blood loss didn't take him, disease would.

"Are you done screaming?"

His father's smile was the only thing other than the lights above his family that shined in this hell.

Taesung raised his head and leaned against restrained arms.

"Why are they here?"

Kwangsoo looked over at his wife and daughter. Ahin's screams had awakened Minseo, and the entire warehouse was engulfed in screams and pleas. Kwangsoo ignored them as he continued to command Du-ho. He couldn't lie that their fear didn't please him.

"Why do you think?"

Taesung grimaced at his father.

"Because you're a sick, psychotic bast—Ah!"

The tip of a small knife entered his shoulder as his father's face memorized the pain transpiring across his face.

"You know, being this close, you look like your mother."

The knife being pulled out of his shoulder hurt more than when it went in. Tears streamed down his face and the rope around his wrists tightened as he swayed.

"Why? Why did you do it," Taesung lifted his head. "We were nothing to you. We never threatened you for money. I didn't even know who you were. You had everything, so why us!"

For the first time, Kwangsoo looked at Taesung. His smile dropped, his eyes tightened and held a sternness he had yet to see from his father.

"Because you belonged to me."

Kwangsoo spun, gesturing around the room.

"You all belong to me. When I found my possessions weren't acting accordingly, I had to do something."

Taesung couldn't take this anymore.

"What are you talking about? We've done nothing!"

"Ah," he interrupted. "But, you have. Some of you have even fallen in love."

Taesung felt the blood in his veins stop, his eyes erratically flicking from right to left.

"What…what are you talking about?"

Sneering, Kwangsoo opened the silver case he still carried and began to throw what seemed like papers from inside of it as he paced around him.

Papers?

No

Taesung's blood began to soak the items back to life.

Photos.

At his feet were pictures of Yunseo and himself. Some photos were of Yunseo entering the plane the first time he flew Ahin and Minseo, some were of Yunseo and his friends drinking with Taesung and the others from their time in Itaewon, some were of the day Yunseo and Minseo spent together, but the main ones. The ones that the blood seemed to highlight above all else were of Yunseo and Taesung kissing at Auntie's BBQ.

"Here," Kwangsoo said as he tossed copies over to Ahin and Minseo. "Take a look at these as well."

Ahin watched as the photos fell onto her lap and around her toes. She stared at the picture of Yunseo and Taesung as if it were treasure.

How could I have not known?

All this time they have been right in front of her and she was too blind to see. She couldn't help but wish she could have known this under different circumstances.

She grew more horrified at the fact Kwangsoo had been able to follow them for so long and saw their most intimate moments without the M&Ms noticing. Her eyes widened as she recognized the timing of these photos.

"Appa," Minseo said. "That boy is my friend. He has nothing to do with this."

Kwangsoo walked to his daughter and struck her across the face.

"You dare lie to me! That is your brother's lover!"

Kwangsoo turned his head.

"Isn't he?"

Taesung continued to stare at the pictures at his feet.

"Isn't he!"

"Yes!"

The confession echoed throughout the sullied building, shocking Kwangsoo. He didn't expect his son to admit his affair so easily. *How disgusting.*

"I love him! I love him with every fiber of my being and everything I have done. Every breath, every sound, every thought, has belonged to him. He is the star in my sky when you took away my sun. My mother was everything to me and he saved me. So, you can kill me and rob me of my dignity, but know that if I die tonight, my soul is his. My last breath will be his. And when my eyes close, my last thought will be his. I never belonged to you, and I never will."

Kwangsoo scoffed. This boy is worse than he thought.

"My boy, you are not the only one at the stand. Recall, I said *some of you*. Not just you."

Kwangsoo threw one more picture in Taesung's direction. He made out a slender form in front of his stepmother, its hands in her auburn hair and her neck. She had her arms around the form as she kissed its neck. His eyes shot up in bewilderment.

"Look closer."

"No," wailed Ahin, squirming against her restraints. "Have mercy, Kwangsoo!"

Ignoring Ahin, Taesung leaned as close as the rope would let him and began to make out the other figure in the picture. It was a tall man with light brown hair and sun-kissed skin. The bridge of his nose was long and there were two moles on the lower ride side of his face. Just like…

"Minseok," Taesung whispered. "Ahin, you've been with Minseok?"

Ahin's shoulders slumped as her truth laid bare in a pooling of blood. She bent her head in shame, unable to look her children in the eyes.

"I was going to tell you once we settled in Thailand."

"Omma," Minseo gasped.

"Ah, yes," Kwangsoo said. "Thailand. Thank you for reminding me to send your realtor a gift."

Taesung shifted his gaze to his father.

"My realtor? Why my realtor?"

Kwangsoo smiled boyishly.

"Son, I can make a spy out of anyone with the right price. It's your fault that you and my whore of a wife had planned so far ahead of time."

"You motherfu—Ah!"

Du-oh pulled Taesung upright and slashed his back. His body was humming at the new wave of agony that pierced his vision, his sight darkening slightly.

Blood pooled even more.

"Well, now that everyone has been caught up, I believe it is time for me to clean up your mess."

Ahin craned her neck to look up at Kwangsoo. He wasn't a very tall man, but the chair gave her a disadvantage.

"What are you talking about?"

Kwangsoo placed his hand on the back of Ahin's seat and breathed her in deeply. It had been a long time since he and his wife were this close to one another. He had believed she had lost her witt after having two kids, but if that sorry excuse of a bodyguard could have some use for her, he guessed she was still fuckable after all.

"I have destroyed your home, your lover, and your plan to leave me. All that is left is the boy."

Minseo screamed, "No!"

Taesung followed his sister's distress.

"You can't have him!"

Kwangsoo groaned at his children's childish outburst.

"I already do."

Snapping his fingers, two men came in dragging something of notable size behind them. The men took their time dragging whatever it was before throwing it into Taesung's blood.

To Taesung's horror, during Ahin and Minseo's screeching, there laid a battered and dirtied Yunseo. Blood had encrusted out of his ear and his cheek was an ugly purple.

"Hello jagiya," Yunseo croaked out. "Did you miss me?"

CHAPTER TWENTY-TWO

His face would forever haunt Yunseo. Yunseo looked upon Taesung's swinging body and only felt boiling, seething rage at the man who stood next to him. How could anyone do this to their own child?

Taesung's body was a bloody mess. Anywhere that there was exposed skin, he was leaking from it. The only place he had no cuts was his face, which would have seemed odd if Yunseo had not remembered how deeply Taesung's father prioritized appearances above all else.

From below, Yunseo could see Kwangsoo's yellow teeth and fading hair. His neck, his chin, and his hands were so fat, that they could have been confused for being inflamed. The man was grotesque to look at. Yunseo wondered again how a man this disgusting could have helped in the creation of the most beautiful creature he had ever seen.

The floor was cold and the air was damp. Yunseo couldn't see very well and the laughter and snickers of the men around them were of no help. The men's violence rivaled his parents, though his parents would have been victorious if this was an actual battle.

"So, this is the cocksucker that stole my son's heart."

Kwangsoo stooped down and yanked Yunseo's hair, forcing his back off the ground and against his body.

"How disappointing. He's so—so plain. You could have at least offered plastic surgery. His eyelids are too small."

Through Yunseo's swollen eyes, he saw Taesung struggle against his rope and the red marks around his wrists began to bleed.

"Leave him alone! I'm the one you want!"

His voice was foreign to Yunseo. It was too weak. Too broken. Too scared to be the voice that used to sing him lullabies and laugh so loudly that Yunseo's ears would ring for days. It frightened Yunseo how unrecognizable his lover's voice was, but his father's capability scared him more.

How can a parent do this? In life, children do not ask to be born but are blamed for being children, for being naive and lacking in sense that has yet to be given to them. When children speak, they are out of turn. When they are quiet, they are depressed. When they cry out for help, they are incapable. When will children no longer be the broken and forgotten toys of their parents' pasts and become people of their own making?

Would they even be free? Are those who have endured strong enough to survive the rest that is yet to come? Can they put back together the parts of themselves that their family has stolen? Can scars be just that without throbbing back to life? Can habits long killed come back from the dead? Are the children of the broken strong enough to heal fractures that never belong to them?

Will we survive this mess of a life we didn't ask for, Taesung? If it were different, would we be happier? Would I have still met you?

"Appa," Minseo said. "Just let us go. No one has to suffer anymore."

"You see," he said, standing and twisting Yunseo's head along with him. Yunseo yelped at the pain and cried as he was dragged to her side of the room. She still looked beautiful, he thought. Though blurry and turning blue, she still looked like the embodiment of kindness. Of hope.

"That's just it, sweetheart. Suffering is the only way children learn."

Kwangsoo threw Yunseo into Minseo's chair with so much force that the chair fell alongside Yunseo.

"Shoot him."

A loud bang was heard from the outside of the warehouse. Alarmed, Kwangsoo looked around. The swaying lights overhead did no favors to hide his aging face.

"Don't just stand there, you idiots. Move!"

The guards scrambled a bit before making their way outside. There was no one left except those Kwangsoo tormented and the man holding Taesung's damaged body.

"Who did you bring," he fisted the front of Yunseo's shirt, shaking him.

"Who's here!"

Yunseo smiled a little as he lifted his head and grabbed Kwangsoo's wrists, "Your maker."

Yunseo was thrown to the ground, and he heard a click.

"Time to end this."

"No!"

Taesung's rocked his body into a distracted Du-oh and thrust his head back. Du-oh let go of the rope as he grasped his shattered nose.

He ran as fast and as hard as he could, knocking Kwangsoo to the ground, and choking him with only the strength he had left. There was a wild look in his eye as his father kicked his legs. The iron grip he had on his father was the only thing his blood-soaked vision could concentrate on. Taesung heard a scream from above him and looked up to see Ahin screaming and banging her back against her seat.

Why was she screaming? He was winning. Why would she be screaming if he was winning?

Then he felt it.

They say when death first greets you, it's cold and dark. But it seemed to be the opposite. Every warm memory in his life wrapped him up in a cannon and carried him up toward a new high he had never been before. It wasn't evil nor was it scary. Death was not monstrous or unforgiving, it was fair and welcoming. Like an old friend that has been waiting for your return. It was relieving to be welcomed in such a maternal way.

Kwangsoo rolled his son's body off him as he stood. The gun in his hand was still pouring smoke from its mouth. His breath was heavy, and his body was vibrating. He looked upon Taesung's body, his eyes darting from left to right, and felt something pull at his chest. How odd?

Yunseo's scream broke through Kwangsoo's mind as he crawled to his body and cradled his head onto his lap.

"Taesung! Taesung! Please," he begged. "Please don't leave me here! Please don't leave me here!"

Taesung lifted his hand and cupped Yunseo's puffed-up face. *He looks like a chipmunk.* A smile blossomed and his heart swelled with contentment.

"My Little Star," Taesung whispered. "No matter where you are, what form I take, I will always belong to you. You were the best gift the world could have given me."

Yunseo shook his head and faced Kwangsoo. He had seconds to think of a plan, yet before he could, his body was moving.

Leaving Taesung's side, he grabbed onto Kwangsoo's gun and wrestled for it. He had managed to wiggle it out of Kwangsoo's hands and kick it somewhere before Du-oh had managed to put him in a chokehold.

"Let me go! Let me go!"

He kicked and buckled, but no grace was given to him.

"Don't worry, Yunseo. You'll reunite with my faggot son soon enough."

Kwangsoo turned, wanting to see the horror on his wife's face, only to be welcomed with a hole in his chest.

The force had knocked Kwangsoo onto the ground and the room stilled as the trembling of Minseo's hand seized. Kwangsoo's head crashed against the cracked floor, and he felt something warm pour out of his body. He stared at the ceiling and couldn't help but scoff a little.

His sons, gone. His wife, useless. Yet, his daughter, his precious little daughter... How ironic that her sweetness became the very weapon that pierced his heart.

Minseo watched as the life from her father's eyes drained and his gurgling stopped. Everything was quiet before the room exploded with men in black gear and rifles stormed into the warehouse. Six men circled Du-oh and Yunseo in perfect coordination and their muffled voices only added to Du-oh's terror.

"Get on the ground," one called out.

"Put down the civilian, or I'll blow your head off," another man in black yelled.

"You have 'til the count of three!"

Du-oh hands began to sweat, and he scanned his brain for escape planes. There were none. He only had two choices. To die like his boss or take one more life before meeting his demise.

"Three."

The countdown echoed in the tense silence, each digit marking another moment of impending doom. With a steady hand, he fastened his grip around Yunseo's head, tilting it to the side, the angle straining the muscles in his neck.

"Two."

His other hand found its place across Yunseo's shoulders, its iron grip a silent promise of death.

"One."

The final countdown ended abruptly, shattered by the deafening bellow of gunfire. Du-oh fell to the pavement, a life extinguished in an instant, leaving behind a haunting silence and a black hole on his forehead.

As the men dispersed, one of them stepped forward, concern etched into his features as he reached out to Yunseo.

"Are you alright," his voice was laced with genuine worry, but Yunseo's mind was elsewhere, consumed by fear and desperation.

Pushing the man away, Yunseo rushed after the paramedics who were already attending to Taesung's motionless body.

"Is he alive," his voice trembled with uncertainty, the weight of the moment pressing down upon him. "Is he dead?"

Outside, Yunseo watched in grief as the paramedics loaded Taesung onto the stretcher and into the waiting ambulance. They drove away without a word, leaving Yunseo to grapple with the uncertainty of Taesung's fate, his heart heavy with dread.

The sight of blanketed Ahin and Minseo being guided out of the building was one he rushed towards.

"Yunseo," Ahin yelled as he crashed into them. They all wrapped their arms around one another, Ahin stroking the heads of her loved ones as hot tears fell against each other's faces.

"I'm so sorry, Mrs. Park. We meant to tell you. We had onl—"

"Stop," she commanded. "None of this is our fault and I am not angry about you and Taesung's love. I consider myself lucky to have two sons again."

Yunseo fastened his arms tighter around Ahin's waist and cried all his worries into her chest.

"Call her Ahin from now on. After all, we're family now," Minseo announced as she buried her face into Yunseo's shoulder.

Family?

Yes, that was the unmistakable warmth flooding his senses as he watched the vibrant hues of Mikasa's hair, along with the others, rush towards them. It was a warmth that resonated deep within him, a reminder of the bonds forged not by blood, but by choice.

It was the most genuine and enduring warmth imaginable—the love of a chosen family. At that moment, he couldn't help but marvel at the sheer luck and blessing of being enveloped in such a miraculous embrace. *Perhaps*, he mused, *the fickle hands of fate had a different plan for me after all.*

Maybe, just maybe, the gods were not indifferent to his plight but had orchestrated this beautiful tapestry of companionship and love as a testament to the power of connection and resilience in the face of adversity.

The familiar beating of the monitor brought Yunseo comfort. Its beats were a confirmation, a certain promise that the man he loved. The man with an IV drip, tubes down his throat and nose, with eyes kissed shut, was still alive. Still fighting and living, if only artificially.

Machines of which Yunseo did not know the names for surrounded him like sheep to their shepherd. Taesung was a strong man who had his youth, yet death claimed him without hesitation. He comes for all who are at his border.

The cries that echoed within the confines of the hospital room seemed to have no end. It had been three long weeks since the incident, yet the lingering scent of suffering clung to them like a stubborn shadow. Despite their efforts to bathe, eat, and groom themselves, the oppressive weight of torment still clung to their clothes. Each of them carried their own burdens – the tang of blood, the sting of betrayal, the crushing of guilt. And though they tried to mask it with routine, the anguish remained palpable.

Every moment of visiting hours were seized eagerly, and they hung onto the doctors' every word, desperate for any sign of improvement. The physician's updates on Taesung's condition seemed to fall on deaf ears, overshadowed by the rhythmic beeping of the monitor that served as a grim reminder of the fragility of life.

Yunseo and his friends had abandoned their jobs, taking refuge in one of the hotels owned by Ahin's family. But even in their temporary sanctuary, they found no respite from the relentless news coverage of Kwangsoo's demise. The screens in the hospital constantly broadcasted the tragedy that had shattered their lives, captivating the attention of the entire world. While some well-meaning individuals attempted to offer their support by visiting the hospital, their presence only served to exacerbate the already overwhelming sense of suffocation.

As Yunseo navigated the stifling atmosphere, he couldn't help but wonder if Taesung, lying in his hospital bed, felt the same weight pressing down upon him. The relentless scrutiny of the media, the intrusion of concerned strangers—it was all too much, it threatened to crush them under its weight. And yet, amidst the chaos, they clung to hope, desperately seeking a glimmer of light in the darkness that engulfed them all.

"I'll go for refreshments," a voice said.

Yunseo didn't bother to look. He knew it was Moonbin.

"Why don't you come with me?"

Yunseo turned, still holding Taesung's unmoving hand.

"I want to stay."

"When was the last time you had eaten?"

Shaking his head, Moonbin walked towards the door of the room, announcing as he passed the doorway.

"I'll bring you a sandwich."

It was one of the rare times when it was just Taesung and Yunseo. It was two o'clock and Ahin, Minseo, Mikasa, and Minseok were at church while the others decided to get Taesung some new flowers. Yunseo cast a look at the dying tulips next to Taesung's bed. Tulips were often gifted on special occasions and to important people. Taesung was the most important person.

Yunseo leaned in closer and pressed his lips against Taesung's hand. A long scar that went across his hands fit perfectly in the seam of his lips. Taesung's body was covered in varying scars with varying sizes. Some were still bandaged, and others were healing nicely. Ahin made sure he had the best doctors and plastic surgeons helping put him back together. They had managed to have most of his scars look like mere paper cuts, but others were a bit more lifted and prominent.

He was still so beautiful to Yunseo. The scars, tubes, and bandages only survived his beauty, highlighting the strength he had to endure his father's torment.

Pulling back, he reached out and stroked his hair.

"I miss you. I miss your smile. I miss your laugh. I miss your hands against my skin. I miss how the slightest touch of your lips on mine sends my body into overdrive. I miss everything about you, but most of all, I miss your eyes."

He guided his hand down the side of his face and ran his thumb across Taesung's beautiful eyelashes. How he missed how they fluttered.

"Can you open them for me, jagiya? Will you bless me with their promised love and hopeful future? Will you be my sun again?"

His body began to shake and he bent his head down onto Taesung's stomach. He allowed his tears to soak the crisp white blanket that smelled of cleaning products. The sounds of the room soothed Yunseo into a stage of consciousness and subconsciousness. He was almost to sleep's edge when he jumped at the sound of something dropping.

Turning his head, he saw Moonbin at the doorway of the room, hands still hovering in mid-air with a look of astonishment. Yunseo was going to ask what was wrong, but he felt it. A slight grip pressed into the palm of his hand. He looked down and saw that his hand was still in Taesung's. Dragging his eyes up, he was welcomed with the warmth of Taesung's chocolate brown eyes.

His eyes were unmoving and focused. It seemed like his one purpose was to look upon Yunseo and only Yunseo. He only blinked when he was crushed by Yunseo's weight and Moonbin's shouts for medical attention. Yunseo's arms snaked around his neck as hot, wet tears slid down his face and onto Taesung's skin. It reminded Taesung of the time he would hold a broken Yunseo, only now it was Yunseo holding a broken Taesung. He wanted to hug him back, but he was unable to move. When he tried to open his mouth, the plastic down his throat reminded him he couldn't. His eyes grew distraught when Yunseo was gently pulled back by Moonbin and doctors and nurses descended upon him.

"Mr. Park," one doctor said. "Mr. Park, can you hear me?"

Taesung looked at him. How could he respond to this idiot when his throat was currently occupied with other things?

"The ventilator," Moonbin shouted. "He can't talk with a tube down his fucking throat."

Taesung would have laughed if he could.

The doctor rushed to instruct the nurse to pull out the tube and with some discomfort, it popped out without much struggle. His throat felt raw and sore but was eased by the cup of water given to him by one of the nurses.

"Test out your voice before answering my question."

The first sound was inaudible. The second gained strength and by the third, his voice was a low and raspy whisper.

"Is this heaven?"

Smiling, the doctor brushed her salt and peppered hair out of her face as she took a seat on the edge of the bed.

"No, fortunately not. It's just really white in here."

Taesung's lip curved up and for that Yunseo was extremely grateful.

"What was the last thing you remember, Taesung?"

His face strained as he attempted to clear the fog in his mind. Everything was fuzzy and had a hue of gray. He walked among the memories with caution as the feeling of liquid coated his feet. Looking down, he saw blood and heard the sound of a gun.

His pupils dilated as the memory of the event came rushing back.

The gun. The blood. Ahin's scream. And... and...

"Where is my family," Taesung frantically said as he tried to stand, but molten hot pain bloomed from his side, causing him to wrap his hand around his torso.

Yunseo grabbed his arm and placed him on his back again.

288

"They're fine, Taesung-ah. Healed and on their way over here right now."

Struggling to pry his eyes open once more, he managed to speak through gritted teeth.

"And Kwangsoo? Is he still out there?"

"That's precisely what we need to discuss with you."

Taesung's gaze tracked Moonbin's taut figure as he settled at the edge of his bed.

"He's gone, Taesung."

Taesung's eyebrows shot up in disbelief, his chin quivering at the revelation.

"What?"

"Park Kwangsoo is dead, Taesung. Your father is gone."

A dam had cracked and tears dripped from Taesung's eyes. His breath had quickened as a fathom smile captured his lips. His body was unclenched and his mind released a deep and tortured sob. Fear creeped out of its throne of flames and thorns and was cast out of his mind as safety and freedom replaced it instead.

He was free. Free of pain. Free of hateful words and cruel torment. Free of guilt and suffering. Kwangsoo was gone and Taesung had won. He was the last man standing.

Words of Thai origin fell from his lips as he thanked and praised Buddha for his help. The pain in his throat was forgotten and he yelled with all his might.

"How!"

Moonbin and Yunseo looked at the medical professionals moving around them like ants.

"Can we please be alone for a moment?"

"Of course," the gray-haired doctor said as she followed the nurses out the door. "We will be back later to further check Taesung's condition."

Once the door was closed, Moonbin took a deep breath in, straightening his spine.

"It was Minseo, Taesung. It seems that when you were shouting and Yunseo rushed at your father—"

"He what!"

"Minseo managed to grab the gun and shoot your father. He was dead upon the arrival of the NIS."

Taesung looked away from Moonbin and looked at Yunseo, not understanding.

"Sweettooth? She killed our father?"

Yunseo nodded.

"She was very brave. If she hadn't, Kwangsoo would have killed me."

Taesung beckoned him over with a slight wave of his hand. It still hurt to move but he needed him close. He needed to feel the breath enter and exit from his lungs.

Moonbin got up from the bed as Yunseo attempted to lie above the covers.

"Climb inside. I need to feel your skin on mine. I need to know that you're real and I'm not just dreaming."

Yunseo held his eyes with his own as he pulled the covers back and carefully slid his body next to Taesung's bandaged one. Groaning, Taesung wrapped an arm around Yunseo and landed his chin on his head.

"Thank you."

Taesung's eyes glossed over as he lifted his head and pressed his lips against Yunseo's lips. The kiss was chapped and filled with love. Filled with gratitude. Filled with relief.

Moonbin stared at the two, grateful that they had each other.

As they pulled back and Moonbin flashed him a smile, Taesung's hospital room door opened and he was greeted with the wet cries of his loved ones. He was surprised to see Subin's scarred eyebrow and Soae and Soyeon's tearful eyes.

What had he missed?

As he was ambushed by his family's kisses and hugs, Minseok stood at the doorway supporting a bandage over his left eye, hesitant to enter his dongsaeng's room. Minseok followed everyone's movements and scanned Taesung's face when Ahin hugged and kissed him.

"I'm so sorry, my son," Ahin whispered into his ear. "I never meant to lie. I was just scared."

Taesung heard his heart crumble and tightened his other arm around stepmother.

"Omma, it's okay. I forgive you."

Turning his gaze over to his hyung, he softened his eyes. If he had the energy to run over to him, to apologize for what seemed to be the loss of his eye, he would. If he could trade his eyes for his own, he would.

"What happened to your eye?"

Minseok shook his head.

"Nothing. Nothing compared to what happened to you. Nothing that was allowed to happen."

Taesung dropped his head. He didn't want to hear this. He lifted his hand out, beckoning him forth.

"Come over here, you dumb ass."

Minseok did nothing but go onto his knees and bow deeply. The room froze at the action, everyone watching for Taesung's reaction with bated breath.

Taesung looked upon his hyung with despair and called for him again.

"Get up from the floor, Minseok."

"I failed you and betrayed you. I am not worth being by your side. Please know that I am sorry for what I have caused."

He peered up from the dirty floor and Taesung could see just how large the area around his eye was damaged.

"I couldn't live with myself if you had died."

Taesung's lips trembled. How could this man think so little of him? How could he think that he wanted the man he looked up to, the man he cherished, to bow in front of him so publicly? Does he not know that he loves him? Does he not know how grateful he is to see him alive?

"Hyung," Taesung said. The word broke Minseok's form and cracked his stiff bow. "Come here and hug me. You owe me that."

Minseok raised himself onto his legs and ran forward, engulfing Taesung in a bone-crushing embrace.

"I owe you so much more than that, Taesung."

Taesung shook his head, pulling Minseok's arms off him, and interlaced the man's hands with his mother's.

"If there was anyone I would pick for you two, it would be each other."

Minseok released a relieving smile and Ahin leaned forward, pressing a kiss to Taesung's cheek.

Taesung patted their hands before turning to look at his sister. She was different. She had cut her hair, having it fall sharply to her chin. It was a stark change for him, but what caught his attention was her eyes. They seemed hollow and underneath them were purple circles.

"Are those because of me," Taesung lifted his hand and touched under her eyes.

Minseo shook her head gently before reaching out for his hand and placing it on her face. She smiled as tears rolled down her face and kissed the center of his palm.

"How do you feel, Oppa?"

"I know what happened with Kwangsoo."

Minseo's smile dropped and tightened her grip on his wrist.

"Oppa, I—"

Taesung stroked her face, hushing her.

"It's okay, Minseo. I'm proud of you. Thank you for doing what I couldn't."

The room hummed with disagreement and Minseo bursted in shock.

"Oppa, you are the reason why we are still alive! You came running to save Omma and I and then you threw yourself at Kwangsoo—"

Kwangsoo? His eyebrows shot up. She has never referred to their father by his first name.

"—to save Yunseo. Not to mention, after Sungmin died," her voice wavered. "You were my support, my guide, and, most importantly, my friend. I did what I did because you showed me that even in the darkest times, we can rise above and do the unthinkable."

"And what is that?"

Minseo stroked his hand before lowering it down onto the bed.

"Survive."

Taesung squeezed her hand before turning to Mikasa, eyeing her glove covered hands.

"So, what did I miss?"

✦ . ⁺ . ✦ . ⁺ . ✦

The hours of the next morning arrived, and Yunseo counted the number of times Taesung would inhale and exhale. If Taesung took too long to exhale, Yunseo would place his finger underneath his nose and feel for his breath. He felt it every time. He had been doing this for the past week and in a few hours, they would be discharged from the hospital and would be able to go home.

They had told Taesung about Seocho and how the house he loved so much was gone. They told him about why Mikasa had been wearing gloves. They told him about Subin, Soae, and Soyeon's bravery and commitment to saving him and his family, which he thanked them for and would never forget. They told him about how the media were all over this, but they had paid a few journalists and newscasters off, effectively steering the population away from the truth.

"Are they believing it?"

Ahin nodded her head as she poured water into Taesung's plastic cup.

"They are. Some of the onlookers are trying to spread rumors and dig deeper, but we released a statement saying we would sue for defamation, so many of them have stopped."

"Are we sure that will be enough? I mean, there will be records of this. Of what really happened."

"And we will bury it, my son. If your father—," Ahin stopped, feeling disgusted. "If Kwangsoo has taught me anything, it is that money can cover up anything."

Taesung opened his mouth to refuse, but Moonbin beat him to it.

"Look, I know you're worried about this, hyung. I know you're worrying about our safety, but our job—my job—is to protect you."

Moonbin leaned forward and clasped Taesung's shoulder.

"Let me do that. Let *us* do that."

Taesung stayed up all week long, poring over news articles and videos, searching for even the slightest hint of the truth. It amazed Yunseo to see Taesung still so physically weak, eating only to ensure his family's secret remained safe.

Yunseo tapped against Taesung chest, trying to wake him up.

"It's time to get up, jagiya."

Taesung twisted, drawing Yunseo's body close to him. He smiled and tightened his arms around him, hearing him groan as his deep voice penetrated Yunseo's ears.

"Do I have to get up?"

Yunseo drew circles on his back and whispered so he wouldn't wake up Ahin and Minseo sleeping on the couch to his right and the others on his left.

"You must. It's time to go home."

Taesung raised his head, and his face joined the arsenal of expressions Yunseo would never forget.

"That place is no longer my home."

Yunseo lifted his hands and rubbed away the wrinkles on his forehead.

"Where is home then?"

"Thailand," Taesung said as he raised himself slowly, leaning his back against the board of the bed. Yunseo watched as the muscles in his forearms flexed and he felt guilt for his rising desire in front of their unconscious family.

"Thailand is where my business is. Where I have felt my truest self and have built a company of people who care for me and my family. The only thing I was missing was you and now that Kwangsoo is dead, my sister and mother have no reason to stay anymore. *I* don't have a reason to stay anymore."

Yunseo paused, letting his words settle onto his skin. He stomped the creeping panic and breathed his way through. He closed his eyes and counted to ten each time he would inhale and exhale. On his third exhale, he opened his eyes.

"When are we leaving?"

Taesung whipped his head and widened his eyes.

"What?"

Yunseo smiled at his lover's confusion. He raised himself onto his forearms and leaned his head on Taesung's shoulder.

"I almost lost you. Permanently this time. Five years was more than enough time without you and I never, ever want to be without you again," Yunseo raised Taesung's hand and interlaced their fingers. "You are stuck with me forever. Where you go, I go."

Taesung's lips found Yunseo and they moved with grace only he could possess. Taesung ate his lips like a man dying for water and outlined them with the tip of his tongue. Soft moans bellowed out of Yunseo and Taesung bit his lip to keep him quiet. He sucked on the wound before gently tugging the lip into his mouth, savoring the pink flesh. He could do this forever.

Yunseo broke the kiss and placed his index finger on Taesung's lips.

"One condition."

Taesung licked a long stripe from the base to the tip before nibbling at Yunseo's skin.

"Anything."

"Soae, Subin, and Soyeon have to come with us."

"Done."

Giggling, Yunseo removed his finger and rubbed his nose against his.

"When should we move?"

"As soon as possible," shouted Minseo as she jumped out of her fake slumber, awakening the entire room.

They chuckled and Yunseo spoke.

"We didn't know you were listening."

Minseo rolled her eyes and walked to their bedside.

"Doesn't matter. I want to go there as soon as we can."

They laughed as Ahin lifted her head and rubbed her eyes open. *Why were they so loud this morning?*

"What is going on?"

Minseo spun around and hugged her mother out of her chair.

"Taesung and Yunseo agreed to move all of us to Thailand and I'm getting a motorcycle!"

Ahin turned her head quickly and glared at her son.

"You are getting her a motorcycle!"

Taesung held up his index finger.

"Never said that. But we are moving to Thailand. We hope to do it by the end of this month."

"This month," Soae shrieked as she ran to Taesung's side. "I need more time than that to stock up on my favorite beauty products."

Minseo interlaced their arms and nodded in agreement.

"Don't worry. I'll help you."

The laughter that erupted in the room only grew as the others were informed and agreements were made. Yunseo became afraid when seeing Subi's expression shift into one of dispute.

"Will I still be able to be a pilot?"

Taesung nodded.

"I have powerful friends in the Suvarnabhumi Airport. One phone call from me and the job is yours."

He looked at Soae, then Soyeon, then Yunseo.

"The job will be all of yours and you all can continue to work together.

"No strings attached," Subin asked.

"You helped save my life and are a dear friend of my lover, which makes you family. This is the least I can do."

Taesung held his hand out.

"What do you say?"

Subin looked at his friends before dipping his chin and shaking Taesung's hand.

"Deal."

Where the Stars Remember Us

Pronunciation of Characters' Names

1. Jeong Yunseo: Jung Yoon-suh
2. Ahn Soyeon: Ahn Soh-yun
3. Seo Soae: Suh Soh-ay
4. Lee Subin: Lee Soo-been
5. Park Taesung: Park Tay-soong
6. Suzuki Mikasa: Soo-zoo-kee Mee-kah-sah
7. Choi Minseok: Choy Min-suhk
8. Kang Moonbin: Kahng Moon-bin
9. Park Ahin: Park Ah-heen
10. Park Minseo: Park Min-suh
11. Park Kwangsoo: Park Kwang-soo
12. Park Sungmin: Park Suhng-min
13. Jeong Eunae: Jung Eun-ay
14. Jeong Hoseok: Jung Ho-suk
15. Jeong Haeran: Jung Hey-ran
16. Kim Haneul: Kim Han-ool
17. Kim Myunghwa: Kim Myu-ng-hwah
18. Park Gohyun
19. Du-oh
20. Dr. Im

Pronunciation of Places

1. Seoul: Suh-ol
2. Incheon: En-chun
3. Seocho: Suh-cho
4. Gangnam: Kang-nahm
5. Yongsan Garrison: Yong-sahn Garrison
6. Gyeonggi Province: G-young-gi Province
7. Jeju Island: Jay-joo Island
8. Daepo Jusangjeolli: Day-po Joo-sahng-juh-lee
9. Bangkok, Thailand
10. Tokyo Japan
11. Shibuya, Japan

Glossary
Titles/Nicknames/Slang

---

1. Appa: father
2. Omma: mother
3. Noona: older sister
4. Oppa: term meaning older brother from younger women.
5. Hyung: term younger men to older men
6. Dongsaeng: younger sibling (male or female)
7. Sunbaenim: superior
8. Sajangnim: boss
9. Ahjussi: a polite and respectful term for middle-aged or older men.
10. Ahjumma: a polite and respectful term for middle-aged or older women.
11. Jagiya: honey, darling, sweetheart
12. Geonbae: cheers
13. Aigoo: oh dear, oh my, and/or oh no
14. Onii-chan: older brother (Japanese)

Food

1. Soju: a clear and colorless Korean distilled alcoholic beverage, traditionally made from rice
2. Hotteok: flour dough pancake filled with sugar syrup and cinnamon inside
3. Bingsu: Korean shaved ice dessert
4. Samgyeopsal: pork belly
5. Yangnyeom Galbi: Korean BBQ short ribs
6. Chadolbaegi: shaved beef brisket
7. Tteokbokki: spicy rice cakes
8. Mul Naengmyeon: regular Korean cold noodles
9. Bibim Naengmyeom: Korean spicy cold noodles
10. Bungeoppang: fish-shaped pastry stuffed with sweetened red bean paste
11. So Tteok So Tteok: sausage and rice cake skewers
12. Bindaetteok: mung bean pancake
13. Bibim-guksu: Korean spicy cold noodles with the addition of vegetables on top.

ACKNOWLEDGMENTS

I would like to thank my writing professor from Penn State University, Jimmy J. Pack, for being my editor and mentor during the year I wrote this book. Whether it be in the classroom or in your office, you made me a better writer despite our differences of opinion. I would like to thank my best friend, Diya, for giving Taesung his name and for being Moonbin and Mikasa's number one fan.

I would like to thank my sisters, Tracey and Stacey, for being there the whole time. Through the pandemic, the nightmares, and the dreams. There is so much of our story in this book.

Finally, I would like to thank my readers. Thank you for giving this newbie a chance. I hope this book has redefined the definition of family for you and always remember, life is but a dream.

So make it one you can be proud of.

ABOUT THE AUTHOR

Oshelynn M. Cabrera is a Puerto Rican writer born in Philadelphia, Pennsylvania. With a degree in Psychology and Writing from Penn State University, she draws on both emotional insight and literary craft to tell stories that center identity, resilience, and underrepresented voices. Her work has been recognized with the Thomas R. and Eileen Watson Award for Achievement in the Arts and Humanities and The Exemplary Leader Award, honors that reflect both her creative vision and her commitment to community impact.

A passionate storyteller and editor, Oshelynn believes in the power of literature to spark dialogue and drive change—one novel at a time.

Follow her journey and upcoming projects on Instagram: @oshelynn.m.cabrera.

Cabrera